THE
SECRET
SISTER

A breathtaking family saga set in WW2 Wales
and sixties Sicily

JAN BAYNHAM

Choc Lit
A JOFFE BOOKS COMPANY

Choc Lit
A Joffe Books company
www.choc-lit.com

This edition first published in Great Britain in 2023

© Jan Baynham

Cover art by Jarmila Takač

ISBN: 978-1-78189-548-1

For Alan, with love.

PROLOGUE

November 1942, Rural Mid-Wales

Carlo Rosso lay back on his bunk, drew on his cigarette and blew out circles of smoke as he exhaled. The noise of fellow prisoners talking echoed in the air, which smelled of damp and mould. He looked around the curved, metal walls of the building, and with his free hand pulled the coarse blanket around him. *So, this is where I'm going to spend the last years of the war.* Miles away from his mother and from Sicily — the country he loved so much. Thoughts of home made him uneasy as he realised, once again, that he might never be able to go back there. He felt for the crucifix that hung around his neck as an image of his accuser entered his head.

Sitting up, Carlo stubbed out his cigarette in the tin ashtray on the small table next to his bed. He found his pen and paper as the image of Lucia Rosso's smiling face came into his head, making his eyes mist with tears. He had to hope his mother's indomitable strength of character had protected her and she was safe.

> *Cara Mamma,*
>   *You must be wondering and worrying about me as I have worried about you. I hope you are safe and this letter*

1

finds you. I arrived at a prisoner-of-war camp five days ago. All I see through cracked, dirty windows are green fields that go on for ever. It is so cold and wet here. We are housed in big, round, metal buildings, which are freezing and draughty. Everywhere is grey. The camp is in the middle of nowhere — just farms and a small village a few kilometres up the road. Because they're struggling for workers here, we have been told we can choose to work. Some prisoners resent us and call us "cooperatori", but at least I'll be doing something. I don't see myself as a farm worker, so I've chosen to work on a building site. A bit different from my work as an artist back home, eh?

I hope this won't take too long to get to you so you can stop worrying. Please write back to let me know how you are. Remember not to seal the envelope so it can be read and checked. A price we have to pay.

Mamma, it will be over soon. I'm sure of it.

Con tanto amore, il tuo amato figlio, Carlo

CHAPTER ONE

Sara
April 1943, Rural Mid-Wales

Sara Lewis clutched her son's tiny hand a little tighter with every step she took nearer to the school. It was Aled's first day — a day she'd been dreading for so long. She'd put it off for as long as she could but, now that he'd turned five, she had no choice but to bring him here. The solid stone Victorian building, the beating heart of the small village where she lived, loomed before her. Tears pricked along her eyelids when she let go of Aled's hand and she watched him confidently cross the playground and enter the building through the boys' entrance. She looked around. She was the only mother there. A shrill voice mocking her filled every space in her head.

'Don't go molly-coddling the boy,' her mother-in-law had said. 'Anyone'd think no one else's child had ever started school before. His da would say you're turning him into a sissy . . . if he was here.'

But he isn't, is he? Thank God! Living with her husband's mother, Gwyneth, on Graig Farm was becoming more unbearable by the day. It had been bad enough when Fred

3

was home and Aled was a baby — she'd never been safe from her husband's bullying. But now that he was away training to fight for his country and Gwyneth was running the farm in his absence, it was just as insufferable. Sara worked hard, even though she was given all the worst jobs to do, but her mother-in-law continually undermined her. At least she idolised her grandson and didn't take things out on him.

She couldn't face going straight back home. The sun creeped upwards, and the earlier streaks of coral and amber were diluted now, leaving a pale sky that promised a fine spring day. She walked along the main street of Dolwen until she came to a large grey-stone building — the offices of Owens' Building and Timber Merchants, owned by her sister, Menna, and her brother-in-law, Gwilym. An impressive, double-fronted house stood at the side of the building and she went around to its back door.

'Hello?' she called as she entered the passageway.

Menna beamed when she saw her and gave her a big *cwtch*. 'Sara. There's lovely. What are you doing here at this time? I presumed you'd be working your socks off for the old dragon.' She stood back and a look of pity crossed her face. 'Aww, *cariad*. Don't cry. Whatever's wrong? What's she done this time? Here.' Menna handed Sara a handkerchief and waited for her to compose herself.

Sara sucked in a deep breath and dabbed away the tears. 'Oh, nothing. The usual. She's getting to me at the moment. Nag, nag, nag. Nothing's ever right. Didn't approve of me taking Aled to school on his first day, did she?'

Menna looked at the ceiling and tutted. 'Ooh, I forgot. How was it? I told Geraint to look out for him. I remember taking him for the first time. Felt like I was losing my right arm. Stupid, isn't it? And me being a teacher before I got married, too. Aled will be fine.'

Sara nodded. 'I know you're right, but he's my boy and I want to do what's best for him.'

The sisters moved into the huge, open kitchen, and Menna went about making cups of tea before they both sat down at the table. Sara reflected on how different their lives were, and it couldn't have been more stark. Here was her sister, a qualified teacher, married to a successful local businessman and running the builders' yard and sawmill single-handedly while he was away in the RAF. Then there was her. Pregnant at sixteen by a man much older than her and disowned by her mam and dad.

'I keep telling myself I should be grateful she took me in. At least I've got a roof over my head. But I can't take any more, Menna. And now Aled's in school all day, I know she'll be watching every move I make. I work bloody hard on the farm and all that woman does is give her orders.' Sara felt her voice rise.

Menna stretched her arm across the table to take her hand. 'Calm down. You shouldn't have to give in all the time if things are as bad as you say. You need time away from there, *cariad*.'

'No chance of that, is there?'

'Use that sharp brain of yours!'

Sara knew that her temper was about to get the better of her. 'You haven't been listening to our father by any chance? How his precious reputation was sullied by his wayward daughter getting herself in the family way at sixteen by the local bad 'un. That was always his expression, wasn't it? "That girl's got a sharp brain" . . . until he found out.'

Menna stood up and grabbed her sister's shoulder. 'Sara, stop it. What happened with our mam and dad was unforgiveable. But them moving away to the other side of Credenford has affected me, too, you know? I hardly ever see them now. Geraint misses out on not having his grandparents in the village anymore. I didn't mean to sound like Father. All I was thinking was that I could do with some help in the office. With the demand for the wood increasing, we can't keep up with the orders at the sawmill. Why don't you come and work here? It would be money for you and Aled, and it'd get you out of the old dragon's hair . . . or should I say *lair*?'

Despite her mood, Sara couldn't help but smile at that.

'And Gwyneth Lewis could pick Aled up from school and have him all to herself.' Menna finished with a point Sara could use to persuade Gwyneth to agree.

It was just then that the grandfather clock in the hallway struck half past the hour. Sara quickly finished her tea and rushed to the door. 'Oh my Lord. She'll be pacing the floor. Thanks, Menna. I'll consider it. You're my lifesaver. What would I do without you?'

* * *

'You took your time. My boy went in no trouble, like I said he would?' Gwyneth was in the barn next to the farmyard when Sara caught up with her.

Straight away, Sara began sweeping the floor of the barn to make room for the supplies of animal feed due to arrive later. Bryn, who worked more hours on the farm now Fred had joined up, had gone into Pen Craig to collect the order. A farm labourer and too old to sign up, he'd worked on Graig Farm for years but was glad of the extra work. Sara marvelled at the way he put up with the demands of Gwyneth most of the time, yet he was not afraid to tell her when she overstepped the mark. Determined to remain civil to her mother-in-law, she concentrated on the idea of seeing Aled again after he'd finished school. 'Yes. He went in with the others — didn't even look back. Menna told me Geraint will look out for him.'

Gwyneth's mouth formed a hard, straight line. 'Oh, that's all right then, if snooty Madam Owens says he'll be fine. When did you see her?'

Sara pretended not to hear and carried on sweeping towards the other end of the barn, putting distance between herself and her mother-in-law. It wasn't worth getting into an argument. It never was.

A few minutes later, Sara heard a bicycle bell outside. She knew from the time it would be Probert the Post's youngest, Selwyn. Gwyneth went out to meet him.

'Two letters for you. Maybe from your son. One for you and one for the other Mrs Lewis.'

Sara smiled as she heard her mother-in-law's terse reply. 'Thank you, Selwyn. I'd be obliged if you keep your opinions to yourself.'

Sara joined them in the yard, and Gwyneth handed her the envelope inscribed with Fred's spidery handwriting. 'Thank you,' Sara called after the post boy, who was now cycling away from the farm as fast as he could.

Sara retreated to the farmhouse to read her letter. Her hand shook as she slid her nail along the sealed edge of the envelope and unfolded the paper inside. Surely he wasn't due more leave already? Her heart thumped as she remembered the events of the last time her husband was home six weeks ago — how he'd forced himself on her after his return from the Draig Coch Arms, how she'd stifled the sobs as he'd slapped and punched her when she'd resisted. His mother in the next bedroom must have heard his angry shouting, yet the next morning Gwyneth had fawned over her only son as if nothing was wrong.

> *Sara,*
>
> *I have three days' leave and will be arriving on the four o'clock train on Friday at Pen Craig station. Last one until I'm posted. I'm looking forward to seeing the boy. Mam says he's looking more like me every day, lucky bugger. At least it proves he's mine. Make sure you're ready for me if you know what I mean. None of that bloody nonsense of a show you put on last time. Remember if it hadn't been for my mam, you'd have been out on your ear.*
>
> *Fred*

Sara screwed up the letter and threw it on the floor. *How dare he?* She'd moved Aled into her room after the last time, hoping that would keep her safe from Fred's drunken advances. She knew she had wifely duties, but not when her husband was violent and took pleasure in hurting her. She felt sick thinking about what he'd done.

'Good news, then?' Gwyneth called from the scullery. 'Aled will be so excited to see his da again. Let's make sure he gets a good welcome this time, shall we?'

Ignoring the comment, Sara left the living room and joined her. It was true — Aled did worship his father and was always playing soldiers around the farm. He loved listening to his grandmother's stories of when Fred was a little boy. 'Yes, Aled will be pleased,' she said quietly. *But I'm not.*

Wanting to keep on the right side of her mother-in-law, Sara kept busy, finishing all the jobs Gwyneth had asked her to do around the farm, as well as baking some Welsh cakes as a treat for Aled on his first day.

When it was time to head back to the school, she found Gwyneth in the henhouse collecting eggs. 'I won't be long. Popping down to pick up Aled. I'll let you tell him his dada's coming home on leave when we get back, shall I?'

Her mother-in-law's face softened for the first time that day. 'Thank you. I can't wait to see what he says.'

Sara wandered down the hill into the village. The afternoon sun was still high and the leaves on the trees lining the road formed circles of dappled shade. She loved this time of year and marvelled at the green of the countryside spreading out before her. Living at the farm was stifling, but the walk allowed time for reflection. She loved Aled dearly, but this wasn't what she'd dreamed her life would be like. Babies were for later. She should have finished school, qualified like Menna had. Much as she'd never forgive her parents for disowning her, maybe they'd been right about some things. Why, oh why had she got mixed up with Fred Lewis and his crowd? Flattery, it was. She'd believed him when he'd told her she was beautiful, pleased someone of his age was interested in her. What she hadn't realised then was that behind the charming facade was a bully who turned into a different person once he had some drink inside him. But she'd made her bed, now she'd have to lie in it. Wasn't that what her mam had shouted at her when her parents had found out she was expecting? Perhaps the coming weekend would be all right.

She'd make a special effort to be a good wife — although her chest filled with a heavy weight at the thought of it.

Sara arrived outside the stone wall surrounding the school-yard as the children were beginning to come out. She spotted a tiny copper-haired figure walking alongside his much bigger cousin, Geraint. She reflected on how her fair-haired nephew looked more like her than her own son. 'Aled, over here!' she called.

He beamed and ran to her.

'Did you have a good time?' She hugged him.

'Yes. I played with Geraint and his friends at breaktime. Dinner was horrible. *Ugggh*! We had frogspawn for pudding.'

'*Ych y fi.*' Sara laughed. 'Sounds like tapioca. Anyway, I've made your favourite for you this afternoon.'

* * *

Gwyneth was waiting in the kitchen when they arrived at the farm. Sara was surprised to see the table laid with a plate of her Welsh cakes next to three mugs.

'Let's have some tea and hear all about your day, *bach*.' Gwyneth put her arm around Aled's shoulders before she began pouring out the tea from the large, brown, earthenware teapot.

'I had frogspawn for pudding, Nana.'

Gwyneth raised her eyebrows in mock shock and went along with the joke. 'Never! I hope not. We'll have to check they don't turn into tadpoles inside your tummy.' She reached across and tickled Aled's stomach. He screamed with laughter, and Sara grudgingly realised the woman who was so harsh with her was full of love for her little boy.

Then Gwyneth stood up and retrieved the letter that was propped up on the Welsh dresser dominating the kitchen. 'Guess what came today? A letter from your dada! He's coming home to see us.'

Aled's face lit up and he clapped his hands. 'Dada's coming home?'

'On Friday. We've got to collect him from the station in Pen Craig.'

The little boy squealed. 'Mammy, Dada's coming home to us!'

Sara forced a smile. *Four days!* She took a deep breath as the constant lead weight shifted and completely filled her chest.

CHAPTER TWO

The platform was crowded when Sara arrived with Gwyneth and Aled to pick up her husband. The week had gone well. Aled loved school, to the point Sara already felt she didn't need to accompany him to the gates each day. He skipped out of the farmyard each morning, turning into a tiny speck as he travelled down the lane into the village.

Even more surprisingly, since their letters from Fred had arrived, the two women had got on better. Gwyneth's mood was much improved as she waited to be reunited with her son.

'How much longer, Mammy?' Aled asked, tugging at her hand.

Sara looked at her watch, smiling at the little boy's excitement. 'Five minutes. If you keep looking along the track and concentrate, you'll soon see a black shape in the far distance get bigger and bigger. It will be Dada's train getting closer.'

The sky overhead was laden with pewter-grey clouds threatening a downpour and, although outwardly Sara was trying to match the excitement of her young son and mother-in-law, inside, her mood mirrored the dismal weather. Surely she should be grateful her husband *could* come home on leave? There were many in the village who had already received the dreaded telegrams.

11

Aled clutched her hand more tightly and jumped up and down. 'The black dot's bigger. How much time now?'

Gwyneth looked across at him and smiled. 'I expect Dada's getting excited now, too.'

The steam train hissed to a halt and doors banged open. The crowd of waiting people spread along the platform, searching for whoever they were there to meet. Sara spotted Fred alighting the end carriage. She was surprised to feel her stomach flip and, for a split second, she saw the man she'd fallen for six years before, with his chiselled jaw and the copper hair he'd passed on to his son — although, now the curls had been replaced by the regulation short-back-and-sides haircut of a soldier. A cheeky grin spread across his face when he saw his welcoming party. *Why can't he always be like this?*

'Dada!' yelled Aled. The little boy let go of Sara's hand and rushed to his father. *The six weeks his father's been away must have seemed like an eternity to Aled, bless him.*

Fred put down his kitbag and scooped his son up into his arms, snuggling his face into his neck as he walked over to them. 'Sara, Mam! It's great to be home. What a welcome from this little 'un, eh?' He put Aled down then embraced Sara and his mother. 'He's so tall now.'

They arrived in Dolwen after a short bus journey and they trekked up to the farm. It wasn't far, but Aled insisted on being lifted onto his father's shoulders to balance on top of his kitbag. It was a slow journey with lots of stops for Fred. In the end, Sara insisted Aled walked alongside his father until they reached the old farmhouse.

'Sit down, *bach*. You must be weary after that long journey.' Gwyneth fussed around. 'There's *cawl* bubbling away on the range. Made your favourite. Not much lamb in it, mind. Mike the Meat had hardly anything left when I went down yesterday.'

'Thanks, Mam. Anything will be better than the muck they dish up in the mess. Smells good, anyhow.'

Snuggled tightly on Fred's knee, Aled showed him the collection of tin soldiers he'd found in an old Huntley and Palmers biscuit tin.

'I said it was okay for him to play with them, *bach*. It is, isn't it?' Gwyneth stirred the *cawl*. 'He spotted them at the back of the dresser when I was clearing out some stuff of your father's.'

Sara felt like she was a bystander, unneeded. She watched a mother delighted to welcome home her son, and a son adoring an absent father, eager to get every minute of his attention. Where did she fit in? Apart from the initial greeting, Fred had hardly seemed to notice her. Looking at them in that moment, she saw a perfect family scene. What happened behind closed doors was something she would have to deal with later. But perhaps everyone's husband was like Fred? It wasn't something she'd ever know.

Determined to show she was enjoying the day, she decided to try and get involved in the conversation. 'Tell Dada about school, Aled.'

'I'm learning my letters and my sums. We have frog-spawn for pudding, you know?'

Sara and her mother-in-law laughed. 'Tapioca. He remembers more about what he has for school dinners than what he's learned,' Gwyneth said. 'And you walk to school and back on your own now, don't you?' Aled nodded at Gwyneth's remark.

'So I hear. All that nonsense of your mam taking you and holding your hand. Big boys don't do that, do they?' Fred looked up pointedly at Sara.

'No, Dada.'

Is there anything that woman hasn't relayed to him? Sara was glad she hadn't told her about Menna's job offer yet. Fred wouldn't approve. He couldn't stand her sister — called her hoity-toity. He was always jealous and possessive of Sara, and she could imagine he'd get even worse when he was posted overseas, hundreds of miles away. No, she'd keep that news to herself until his leave was over. Menna would have to wait for her answer.

Sara stood up and laid the table. Instead of the dingy oil-cloth they normally used, Gwyneth had picked out the white damask-linen cloth only used for high days and holidays. The best china had been taken down from the oak dresser, and the canteen of silver cutlery was open for Sara to pick out the knives and soup spoons.

'Blimey, Mam. Expecting royalty, are we?' Fred stood up from the settee and hugged his mother. Sara felt a pang of envy. The love between them was clear. She thought of her own mother and how that gesture would never happen between them again. Her parents would never forgive her for what had happened, although she was sure they would love Aled — if only they'd agree to meet him.

'Can I sit the same side as Dada?' Aled asked.

'Of course you can, *bach*. We've got to make the most of it now he's here.' Gwyneth moved a chair to Fred's side of the table while the little boy beamed.

* * *

'Time for bed, *cariad*,' said Sara.

'I've put him back in his own room tonight. It's not right him being in with you now Fred's home, is it?' Gwyneth didn't make eye contact with Sara as she took Aled's hand to go upstairs.

'Too right, Mam. I'll take him.' Fred picked Aled up. 'Ready to walk up the wooden hill to the land of nod, my little soldier?'

As she watched them go, apprehension travelled along Sara's veins. She tried hard to remember how things had been when she'd first fallen for Fred, how he'd made her feel, how her heart had raced when they were together. It could be like that again, couldn't it?

Later, after Fred had turned off the bedroom light, he took down the makeshift blackout blind so the room was bathed in silver moonlight.

'Come here.' He patted the mattress. 'Let me look at you. God, I've missed you. I'm so sorry about last time, *cariad*.'

Sara sat beside him, her heart beating fast. He pulled her towards him and they fell back onto the soft bed. Could she dare to believe he was reverting back to the Fred she'd fallen in love with? He did seem different from the last time he'd been home.

Fred sought out her lips and kissed her gently. She'd missed the intimacy, the feeling of being wanted and loved. She owed it to Fred to try again, didn't she? She responded eagerly, finding that she wanted Fred to make love to her.

Afterwards, they laid in each other's arms, enjoying the moment, before Fred sat up and lit a cigarette. 'I've been dreaming about that for weeks, *cariad*. More like your old self, you were. Not like last time.'

Sara's heart sank. *Why does he have to spoil things?*

* * *

Sara was surprised at how much she was enjoying having Fred home — at last, she felt she was experiencing what she'd always imagined married life would be like. A warm feeling washed over her as she reflected over the last three days. They'd taken Aled out to the seaside by train on the Saturday — even Gwyneth had wished them well and made a picnic for them. She realised she'd be sorry to see her husband leave . . . and yet, as she watched Aled and Fred playing together, there was a niggle of doubt deep inside her that she kept having to suppress. *Stop it, Sara. Those days are over.*

'Mammy, come and look at our battle.' Aled's eyes sparkled as Sara walked over to let him show her how he and his father had set out the toy soldiers on the floor.

Fred got up and put his arm around her. 'I'm going to miss all this when I leave tomorrow. It's been good spending time with you and the boy.'

The niggle lay dormant for the rest of the day and Sara found she was actually looking forward to spending their last evening together once Aled was in bed.

But Fred had other ideas. He and Sara were sitting together in the living room watching Aled play.

'I thought I'd meet up with the boys tonight at the Draig Coch Arms, *cariad*, seeing as I don't know when I'll be home next.'

Sara's heart raced. She knew there was no point in objecting.

'Do you good to see them before you go, *bach*.' Gwyneth didn't look up from reading her magazine. Her comment didn't go unnoticed by Sara.

Sara looked at her mother-in-law with disdain. *Has she forgotten what happens when her son goes out drinking?*

After taking Aled to bed as he'd promised him, Fred went out to the pub, leaving Sara with Gwyneth for company. They listened to the Sunday-night variety show on the wireless, and Sara forced herself to laugh at the jokes and sketches. She was relieved when Gwyneth retired for bed early.

Her apprehension grew over the hours and at eleven o'clock, the back door was flung open with a clatter and Fred tottered into the kitchen, clearly the worse for wear.

'You don't know when you've had enough, do you?' Sara sighed.

'Shut up and get up those stairs, woman.'

'If you think I'm going to share a bed with you in that state, you've got another thing coming.'

Suddenly, he lunged towards her and hit her across her face with such force she fell against the dresser, banging the side of her head with a loud thud. She howled in agony.

'You little bitch. You'll do as I say. You promised to *obey* me, remember? Now get upstairs.' His words were slurred. He lunged again and dragged her into the hallway.

She screamed. 'No!'

He grabbed her hair and threw her against the banister.

It was then that Gwyneth appeared at the top of the landing holding Aled, who was wide-eyed and crying.

'Mammy, what's wrong? Why has Dada got a red face?' Sobbing, Aled pulled away from his grandmother.

'Aled, stay here!' Gwyneth tried to grab him. 'What's wrong with you two? Poor little soul is terrified by the racket you've made.'

Aled ran down the stairs to clutch hold of his mother, and Sara held him tight. She watched as Gwyneth turned and went back into her bedroom, slamming the door.

'Don't be frightened, *cariad*. Mammy'll sleep in with you tonight.'

With disgust, Sara looked down at her husband, now slumped in a heap on the flagstone floor in a drunken stupor. As she carried Aled up to his room, hot, angry tears streamed down her cheeks. How could she have been such a fool to think Fred would ever change?

CHAPTER THREE

Aled no longer followed Fred around the house the next morning. Instead, he didn't move from his mother's side. It was obvious how terrified he was of his father now. Despite cajoling from Fred and Gwyneth, the little boy had lost his sparkle. The bruise on Sara's cheek, where Fred had hit her, was changing from red to a deep bluish purple. A large lump bulged on the side of her head where she'd been thrown against the dresser. Gwyneth didn't mention it, but sent frequent accusing glares in her daughter-in-law's direction.

Sara overheard her talking to Fred in the hallway. Her mother-in-law's clipped words resonated in her ears. 'You're going to get in trouble using your fists like that, *bach*. A drop of drink inside you and you turn into your da. The only difference is I put up with it. Didn't make it right though, did it?'

'I know, Mam. I shouldn't have done it. I just saw red. She was spoiling for a fight as soon as I came in through the door. Can't a man have a drink with his friends? You have no idea what us boys are going to be facing out there.'

At last! His own mam can see he's wrong.

'Come here, *bach*.'

It went quiet and Sara guessed Gwyneth was comforting her son. But what she heard next made her blood boil.

18

'She'll come round. Don't you worry. She'll have to. There's nowhere else for her to go, is there? Next time, you'll have to turn on the charm. If only you hadn't gone out with them Morgan boys . . .'

Feeling numb, Sara knew there was no point in arguing so she slumped back on the settee and closed her eyes. She was still cuddling Aled, who was dropping off after his broken sleep the night before. There was no way he'd be fit for school today.

Someone gently shook her shoulder and she opened her eyes. It was Fred with a cup and saucer in his hand. 'Fancy a cup of tea, *cariad*? I'm sorry about last night. I don't know what came over me.'

Sara shook her head and looked away. All she had to do was stay where she was with Aled. He wouldn't hit her again with their son on her lap. She knew now she would never willingly share a bed with her husband again — his mother could throw her out for all she cared. What had happened the night before had convinced her nothing was left of the Fred she'd fallen in love with. He'd gone. Judging by the act he'd put on when he'd arrived home three days ago, she was starting to wonder if there ever had been a loving Fred — that tender Fred, who had wooed her with such determination. Had it all been a facade?

Sara didn't even move to see Fred off. His mother accompanied him to the station alone. Aled had politely waved goodbye, but the excitement and adoration that had accompanied his father's arrival had disappeared.

Now frowning and with his eyes full of tears, he whispered, 'Are you all right, Mammy? Does your head still hurt?'

'Yes, I'm fine, *cariad*. Mammy fell against the dresser, that's all.'

Sara looked at her beautiful son, wondering if he would end up a bully like his father. She shuddered at the prospect, determined that he wouldn't. After what she'd overheard earlier about Fred's father being handy with his fists, too, she was still afraid for her boy. *Did Gwyneth look at Fred this way when he was only five?*

19

When Gwyneth arrived back a few hours later, Sara heard her come in through the scullery. 'He got off all right,' she called.

Sara didn't answer. Perhaps now Gwyneth had seen proof of her son's violence, she'd be more sympathetic. Instinct told Sara she'd have to pick her moment carefully to talk about the job offer from Menna. Maybe her mother-in-law would enjoy having more time by herself with Aled? In any case, she wasn't going anywhere until her head and face had healed and the bruise had disappeared.

* * *

It was now nearly two weeks since Fred had gone back to barracks and Gwyneth hadn't mentioned the row again. Although she was still over-critical, Sara sensed they were getting on better. Sara sometimes wondered whether Gwyneth saw her younger self in her daughter-in-law, perhaps understanding her humiliation and fear at the hands of the man she'd married.

While they were preparing the evening meal together after Aled had returned from school one evening, Sara took a deep breath. She'd been going over and over it in her mind and had decided now was finally the right time.

'Gwyneth, now we don't seem to have so much work on the farm, how would you feel if I worked for Menna in the office? You said yourself, it's getting harder to make ends meet the longer this war goes on. I feel I should be contributing more financially.' Sara paused, watching Gwyneth's expression. 'I'd be home by six. You'd have special Nana time with Aled every day. What do you think?'

The older woman's mouth immediately formed a straight line and she stopped what she was doing. 'Become a working mother! What's the world coming to? Once there's a ring on your finger, your place is in the home, my lady. I suppose it's that posh sister of yours with all her airs and graces putting in her two penn'orth, is it?'

Sara bit her lip. She might have guessed her mother-in-law would not approve, but she knew she had to stand her ground. 'Lots of women work nowadays. Several of the girls I was at school with have joined the Land Army. Everyone is doing their bit.'

They continued preparing the meal in silence. Gwyneth placed the corned beef hash on the range and started to wash up.

'Here,' said Sara. 'You go and sit down with Aled. I'll do these.'

'I know what you're doing — so you can stop buttering me up. I'll tell you what I think about you going to work when I'm good and ready.' She paused. 'Anyway, Land Army work's different. They's helping the war effort. What would you be doing for King and Country sitting behind a ruddy desk?'

'Menna says they can't keep up with all the orders for wood at the sawmill. So, I *would* be helping the war effort. You have to admit there's not enough for both me and you to do now Bryn is working more hours doing all the heavy work Fred did.'

Gwyneth didn't answer, but Sara could see she'd given her mother-in-law something to consider. From living at the farm with her since her shotgun wedding nearly six years before, she'd learned that if she gave Gwyneth time to think things over, and even convince her it was her idea in the first place, she'd eventually come round. Sara would bide her time while she could, but knew she didn't have long. Menna needed her answer before the end of the week or else she'd advertise the position in the post-office window. Sara just had to hope her bruise had completely gone by then, too.

* * *

Sara took down the blackout blind from her window. Living in rural Wales meant they weren't enduring the nightly bombings of the big cities, but they still had to abide by the government's rules of a complete blackout each night to keep the villages and towns safe. Only the month before, a stray bomb had been dropped by mistake near Pont Newydd. A huge crater had been formed in the Radnorshire countryside. Luckily, it was far away from any houses or farms and no one had been hurt.

Sara looked out onto the farmyard beneath her bedroom. Bryn was already hard at work. Perhaps the *phut-phut* of the old tractor had disturbed Aled, because now he appeared at her bedroom door, rubbing his eyes. He rushed into her arms.

'You're awake nice and early, *cariad*. Come here for a *cwtch*. It's a special day for Mammy today. Nana's going to be here to look after you while Mammy works in Auntie Menna's office. Nana'll give you your tea.'

The little boy looked up at her and nodded. 'She told me we'll have fun.'

Sara smiled. Her tactic of waiting until her mother-in-law had come round to the idea had worked. She remembered the evening when Gwyneth had sprung the surprise after days of complete silence on the subject.

While she was clearing away the tea things, Sara had heard her mother-in-law talking to Aled. 'Nana's going to be looking after you now. Your mammy's going to work in an office.'

At the time, Sara couldn't believe what she'd heard. Gwyneth hadn't uttered a word to her. She'd gone back to sit with her son, remaining calm on the outside but with her insides somersaulting. She'd been so excited to tell Menna.

And now the day had finally arrived. She was going to become a working woman.

CHAPTER FOUR

Sara had never had a proper job before, and, as she cycled down to the village that morning, she remembered the summer of 1937. She'd just passed her School Certificate with flying colours and was to return to the grammar school in nearby Pen Craig to start her Highers with the intention of following her sister and going to college. At that time, she hadn't had a care in the world.

After all the studying her disciplinarian father had made her do, she took advantage of her newly acquired freedom and went out with her friends at every opportunity. Dancing was what she loved most, and when Fred Lewis sought her out to show her his impressive jitterbug moves, she was smitten. It didn't take her long to fall for his charms. Knowing her father wouldn't approve, they began meeting regularly in secret. Apart from Menna, who was home from college all summer, she made sure no one else knew. 'Be careful. Don't do anything stupid and get yourself in the family way,' her older sister had often warned her.

If only I'd listened!

But, as always, Sara had believed she'd known best and had convinced herself she and Fred would always stop things just in time. Then Fred had started telling her that if she'd truly loved him, she'd want to show him with more than kisses. He'd persuaded her to go all the way, assuring her he'd be careful.

Now, her thoughts took her back to when she'd been at Pen Craig Grammar and the day she'd told her mother she thought she was expecting. Sara had left it as long as she could before telling anyone, continuing to go to school as if nothing was wrong. She'd packed the knowledge she had Fred's baby growing inside her neatly away in a compartment of her mind, but an unseasonal, sweltering day for the end of September had forced her to unpack that compartment when she'd fainted in the school library. She was taken home in the deputy head's car and then had to face her mam. The look on her mother's face when she'd finally admitted the truth would stay with her for as long as she lived. Coming close to her face, her mother hadn't raised her voice. Instead, she'd poked her daughter in the chest repeatedly, whispering, 'You — are — no — daughter — of — mine!'

As Owens' Building and Timber Merchants came into view, Sara tried to bring her thoughts back to the present. Butterflies fluttered in her stomach as she wondered if she'd even be able to do the job — she'd had no training, after all. But she couldn't let her sister down.

She dismounted her bicycle and wheeled it around to the back door where Menna had told her to park it. Once inside the building, she knocked on the office door and entered a small, cramped space with three wooden tables, each with a single chair, along one wall, and a row of grey, metal filing cabinets opposite.

Standing by one of the tables was a woman in khaki uniform. A warm smile spread across her face when she saw Sara, and she stopped what she was doing to offer an outstretched hand. 'Hello. You must be Sara. I'm Nell. Menna asked me to come in a bit early to welcome you.' She nodded over to the empty far desk. 'Peggy's the other one working here. She'll be here soon.' With her red hair fashionably rolled around the sides and the back of her head, she flashed a wide grin that lit up her perfectly made-up face. *How do you manage that?* wondered Sara.

'Hello, Nell. Thank you. It's good to meet you.' Judging by her accent, Sara assumed Nell must be the new Land Army girl Menna had told her about, who'd arrived a few weeks ago from Manchester.

'That's your desk in the middle, chuck. Make yourself at home,' said Nell. 'A bit of a crush, but I'll be out most of the day checking on my girls.'

Taking off her coat, Sara hung it on one of the hooks on the back of the door. She sat down at her desk where there was a pad of paper, pens and a filing tray. Already feeling as if she was there under false pretences, her pulse raced when she realised she didn't have a clue what to do next.

As if sensing Sara's panic, Nell gave her another reassuring smile. 'Don't worry, chuck. Menna will go through everything with you. She's been called up to the sawmill. Today of all days! One of the cutters has split and everything up there's at a standstill. She shouldn't be long.' The sound of faint footsteps from the outer office announced another arrival. 'And here's your partner in crime. What time do you call this, Leggy Peggy?'

The office door crashed open, and a tall, slim girl Sara vaguely recognised rushed in. 'Sorry! I overslept. A late night last night.' She noticed Sara. 'You must be Menna's little sister. I remember you being in the form below me at the grammar.'

'Hello! Yes, I remember you.'

'First things first. I've brought a flask of tea, so can you get the cups out of the cupboard there?' Peggy indicated the pale-blue-painted cupboard that had seen better days tucked into the far corner. 'Nell can't be going anywhere without her first brew, as she calls them!'

While they sat drinking their tea, Peggy told Sara the details of the job. 'It's not bad. Menna pays well as long as you work hard. It'll be a lot better when we get a new office. More space than this. And the best news is . . .' She looked around and lowered her voice as if she might be overheard. 'I've heard on the grapevine a team of handsome Italian prisoners of war are going to be doing the building. Most of the local boys have signed up, see.'

'Now you're talking, chuck. We could do with some decent males to look at. There're only old ones left around here.'

Sara smiled. It was like going back in time to when she and her friends were in school and all they talked about was boys. She'd left all that giggling behind since she'd been living at Graig Farm — grown up before her time. Thinking about that reminded her of one person who would not be happy at the news of prisoners of war working on the site. Gwyneth Lewis had expressed her view on "the enemy" being housed so close to the village often enough. 'Same side as the ruddy Boche. Why should we have them here?' she'd often say. Sara knew she wasn't the only one in the village who thought like that.

She looked up at the heavy oak wall clock. *Half past nine.* On the farm, she'd have done an hour's work in the henhouse and barn by now, yet here she was sipping tea and talking about handsome Italians. And she'd hardly thought of her mother-in-law . . . or her lovely Aled either. And definitely not Fred.

CHAPTER FIVE

Sara had been working at the builders' office for six weeks and things were going well. Menna had been pleased with how quickly her sister had picked up the office jobs and had already raised her wages. Gwyneth didn't say much but Sara knew she'd also been pleased when she saw the money coming in.

There'd hardly been a cross word between her and her mother-in-law in all that time, apart from the odd grumble when she'd failed to get home before six o'clock, which hadn't happened often. The main thing was Aled was happy to spend time with his grandmother. Some nights, he hardly looked up from what he was doing when she rushed in, eager to hear about his day. It was the price to pay for becoming a working mother, she told herself.

But one morning, it all changed.

The door banged open and Nell rushed into the office, her face ashen. 'Sara. You'd better get home. It's all over the village. The telegram . . .'

'What's all over the village?' Sara's heart pounded as it dawned on her what her friend was trying to tell her. 'Fred? Oh God, I've got to get to Gwyneth. This will break her!'

She didn't say another word, just grabbed her coat from the back of the office door and left.

* * *

Gwyneth sat motionless at the kitchen table. Drained of any colour, she stared at the unopened buff-coloured telegram in front of her.

'I came as quickly as I could.'

'It's addressed to you. Next of kin, you are.' Gwyneth's voice was monotone as she slid the telegram across to Sara.

The hairs on Sara's arms stood up as her skin prickled into goosebumps. *Please God. Let him be injured, not dead. It will give his mother and Aled hope, at least.* She unfolded the telegram.

MRS S. LEWIS, GRAIG FARM, DOLWEN, RADNORSHIRE.
I REGRET TO INFORM YOU THAT YOUR HUSBAND, PRIVATE FREDERICK GWYNFOR LEWIS (ARMY NUMBER: 884679 OF THE EIGHTH ARMY), HAS SUSTAINED FATAL INJURIES WHILE UNDERTAKING ARTILLERY TRAINING.

Hot tears blurred her vision, and she grabbed the edge of the table to steady herself before taking a deep breath. 'Gwyneth, I'm so sorry you were here on your own when it came.' Sara drew up a chair beside her mother-in-law and held her. As if her action had given Gwyneth permission to react to the news, the older woman's shoulders shook and she let out a guttural howl before convulsing into violent sobs. Sara continued to hold her until they subsided. Then Gwyneth pulled away and they sat in silence for what seemed like an eternity. Together but separate with their thoughts.

Gwyneth spoke first. 'I want to tell Aled, right? I told him his dada was coming home on leave, didn't I? It's only right I'm the one to tell him his dada—' she took a deep breath — 'is never coming home.' Silent tears trickled down her cheeks.

Could Sara deny her mother-in-law that right? Gwyneth and Aled had grown close since she'd started work at the office. Maybe she'd handle it better than Sara herself could? But how could anyone explain to a five-year-old that his dada was dead? Despite the shock, she had a sudden thought. 'Of course. But I must get him from school in case he's already heard. When she told me, Nell said it was all round the village and the telegram hadn't even been opened then.'

She cycled as fast as she could down to the school, hoping she would be in time.

* * *

'Why can't I stay for playtime? Why did Mr Thomas say I had to go home? It isn't home time yet!'

Sara managed to curtail Aled's questions without breaking her promise to Gwyneth. She parked the bike at the side of the back door.

When they got inside, Gwyneth was waiting for them in the living room. 'Come and sit next to Nana, *bach*.' She patted the settee.

Sara sat beside them, her heartbeat thumping in her ears. No five-year-old should have to hear what Gwyneth was about to tell him.

'I've got some sad news,' she began.

'Is that why your eyes are red? Have you been crying?' The little boy looked at Sara. 'Yours are red too, Mammy.'

'Shh, *cariad*. Listen to Nana.'

'Aled, we heard today your daddy isn't going to come back to us.' Gwyneth wiped away a tear. 'He was very brave getting ready to go and fight the Germans, but there was a horrible accident when he was learning how to use the guns. He's gone to heaven.'

'Is he dead?'

Gwyneth nodded.

Aled persisted with his questions. How big was the gun that killed him? Did the bullet go right through his chest? How would he get to heaven? What was heaven like?

'Shh, *cariad*.' Sara looked anxiously at her mother-in-law.

Breaking down in tears, Gwyneth fled the room, leaving Sara to hold her son in her arms.

* * *

Strong and formidable Gwyneth Lewis had taken to her bed as soon as she'd told her grandson about the contents of the dreaded telegram. Her sobs resounded through the walls every night. Sara had been left in charge, not only organizing Bryn to run the farm, but also arranging the funeral — what hymns to sing, what to offer the men after the church service, where the women would congregate in the farmhouse. She'd never even been to a funeral before, let alone organized one.

Exhaling the pent-up breath in her chest, Sara wondered how she was going to break the news of Menna's visit that morning. She hadn't expected that! Surely it was too soon? Menna had been very apologetic but adamant. A week at the most. They were so rushed off their feet with orders that it was all the time she could spare her sister to be away from her desk. How would Gwyneth deal with what she had to say? Normally, there would be a tirade of verbal abuse, but now the older woman was in such a state, Sara had no idea what the reaction would be.

Wringing her hands, Sara paced the flagstone-floored kitchen. *How can I tackle this?* She took another deep breath. *Let's get it over with.*

Making a fresh cup of tea, Sara readied herself to take it upstairs to her mother-in-law. With each tiptoed step, her pulse raced a little faster. She steadied her hand, trying her best not to spill tea into the saucer. How she handled the conversation with Gwyneth would make all the difference between returning to the freedom of a job she'd begun to enjoy, or staying in the farmhouse drudgery of her life.

She knocked on the bedroom door. 'Gwyneth, can I come in?'

No answer. She lifted the cast-iron latch and entered. Her mother-in-law was propped up on two bolster pillows. Her iron-grey hair was lank and uncombed, her eyes red-rimmed and puffy. Sara placed the tea down on the bedside table, noticing an earlier one had not been drunk.

'I thought you'd like a fresh cup. You must try to drink, you know?'

Gwyneth turned her head away.

Sara drew back the thin curtains and opened the window a fraction to let some fresh air into the musty room. 'Why don't you get washed and dressed and come downstairs? Aled will be home soon.'

Gwyneth shook her head. She had aged since the news of her only son's death. Like Sara, Gwyneth had been a teenager when she'd had Fred, but the middle-aged woman lying in the bed before her looked like an old lady. Gwyneth's eyes filled with tears. 'You'll have to run things here now. My life is over. No point in living.'

Sara patted her arm. It was going to be much harder than she'd even anticipated. How could she tell her what Menna had said? *Perhaps it will be better if I do what she wants.* 'Don't say that. What about Aled? Isn't your lovely grandson worth living for?'

Gwyneth lay back, closing her eyes again.

'Gwyneth, you know I'm happy looking after you until after the funeral, don't you? You've had the worst news. I can't imagine what it would be like if it were Aled.' Sara kept her voice steady and watched for her mother-in-law's reaction.

Gwyneth's eyes snapped open. 'What do you mean "until after the funeral"? I'm not going to spring back into life in five days, am I, you stupid woman?' Her shoulders shook, and the sobbing turning into a wail. 'It's all on you now. High time you pulled your weight around here.' Gwyneth's voice rose to a screech.

Sara clenched her fists until the knuckles were white, her nails digging into her palms. Silently, she counted to ten, willing herself not to rise to the bait. Was she being cruel? If Fred had not tried to force himself on her again on his last leave, would she also be grieving his loss? Instead, she was relieved she'd never have to defend herself against his bullying again. But she also felt guilt. He was the father of her child, after all. Aled had worshipped him before that awful night. *Perhaps Gwyneth is right. We should all have more time to grieve.* But Sara knew in her heart she was doing the right thing — for everyone.

'Look, I know it's hard. It's hard for everyone, but I *have* to go back to the office. It's only a couple of hours after school, and Bryn says he'll increase his time to help you more around the farm. You've said yourself the extra money's come in handy these last few weeks. And Aled will have his nana all to himself again . . .' Sara took a deep breath. She knew that if she lost either her thread or her temper, she'd never get her mother-in-law to agree. 'When I do go back, I'll make sure I get away at six every night. And it's not until after the funeral. Until then, we need to keep Aled occupied. Take his mind off what's happened to his dada. It's harder when he's at home. He's fine away from the farm. That's why school's best for him. And about the funeral — I don't want him here when Pritchard's bring Fred into the parlour.'

The floorboard on the landing creaked, and the two women looked in the direction of the door.

'Oh no! Aled must be home already.' Sara grimaced. 'I hope he didn't hear about bringing Fred into the house . . .'

She came out of the room just as Aled rushed to his bedroom. She followed and scooped him up from where he'd flung himself on the bed, holding him tightly in her arms. 'There, there, *cariad*. Mammy's got you. Don't cry.'

'Why's Nana shouting? You told me you hit your head on the dresser,' he said. 'Why was Dada so angry?' The little boy was shaking.

Sara made her voice quiet, hoping to calm him. 'Sometimes grown-ups get cross with each other. Nana's cross today. You quarrel with Geraint sometimes, don't you?'

'The noise Nana makes is the same as the one you made. Has she hit her head too, Mammy? You're kind. You wouldn't hurt her, would you?'

Sara pulled Aled to her, kissing the top of his head. 'No, *cariad*. I wouldn't hurt Nana. She's upset because Dada's gone to heaven.'

Aled pulled away and searched his mother's face. 'So, if Dada *is* dead, how can he be coming to the parlour? The posh room's always locked. Why will Dada go in the parlour? Nobody goes in there.'

Sara's skin prickled. *How do I explain all this to a five-year-old?* Instead, she stayed silent and let Aled talk, allowing him to put into words all the confusion that was clearly whirling inside his little head.

'Perhaps Dada hasn't died after all. Are you lying?' Sara shook her head, and Aled continued talking. 'Sometimes there are flowers in Pritchard's window and big, shiny, black cars parked outside on the corner. Will Dada come here in one of the cars, sitting by the driver with a smart flat hat? Dada's a brave soldier. He's going to fight the Germans, isn't he? Perhaps the telegram's wrong! Billy Morris said his mammy had a telegram, too.'

Aled was clearly calmer now, but, as he wiped his eyes with the back of his hand, it was obvious he had more questions. 'Why does Nana cry every night? You put your hands over my ears to shut out the noise, don't you, Mammy? But I can still hear her. And why doesn't Nana want to look after me anymore?'

'I don't want it to upset you, that's all.' Sara *cwtched* him tighter. 'Nana will get better, I promise.'

Sara's heart filled with emotion for her little boy. Perhaps she was wrong to promise that Gwyneth would get better. How could a mother ever really get over the death of her child? And how could a little boy ever really accept that he would never see his dada again?

CHAPTER SIX

'Why can't I stop at home?' asked Aled.

'Funerals are not for children, *cariad.* You'll be a lot better off with your friends.' Sara hugged him. 'People will still be here when you come home and you can see everyone then.'

In the end, Aled had reluctantly agreed to go to school.

Left alone, Sara unlocked the door into the parlour. The curtains were shut, following the tradition, so she lit the wall gas lamps and turned towards the open coffin, which was supported on a metal bier in the centre of the room. She couldn't stop herself from gasping once again. Not having seen a dead body before, she'd been shocked by her husband's ashen pallor, which matched the cream-coloured taffeta lining the mahogany coffin. Even though the funeral directors had made Fred look smart, with combed hair and a pressed khaki army uniform, the stillness unnerved her. At least there was no evidence of the fatal wound that must have soaked his combat clothes with blood. She hoped Gwyneth could be persuaded to leave her bed for the funeral service — seeing her son at peace like this might ease the horrific details of his death.

The hands on the mantel clock showed the exact time when Fred had taken his final breath according to the death certificate. Composing herself, Sara placed the parlour chairs in rows on all four sides of the coffin. She pushed the table as far back as she could, making a space for the minister to place his prayer book. She didn't know how many villagers would attend, but the Lewis family had farmed in the community for generations so she imagined there might be a good number. Returning to the kitchen, she carried more chairs into the front room.

'There. It will be standing room only now. I can't fit any more in,' she said aloud once she'd positioned them.

'Talking to yourself now, *cariad*.' It was Menna. 'Oh, good Lord, I'd forgotten the coffin would be open.' She turned her head away. 'At least you know the monster's not coming back.' She looked again at Fred. 'He even looks decent lying there, doesn't he?'

'You shouldn't speak ill of the dead, Menna. No matter what he was like as a husband, his mother is a broken woman. She still hasn't got up from her bed. I don't know if she'll even come down for the service!'

'Sorry, but I can't help thinking of what he did to you the last time he was home. No woman should have to put up with that.' Menna held out her hands. 'Anyway, I've had my say. Where shall I put these? A plate of sandwiches from Mrs Walker at the shop. Sends her apologies. And my attempt at an eggless sponge.'

Sara took the plates from her sister and left the parlour to place them on the kitchen table. Then she returned to the room and gave Menna a hug. 'Thank you. I've no idea how many to cater for. I've been cooking all week but have used up all our rations now. Can you stay for the service? I could do with some support.'

'Of course. I can't let you do this on your own. Nell and Peggy send their love. Peggy will hold the fort. I'll see you later. Two o'clock, isn't it?'

Sara nodded. She accompanied her sister to the door. As she returned to the parlour to finish the preparations, she heard someone in the passageway.

'It's only us, Gwynnie,' shouted a voice. Gwyneth's sister, Edna, and her husband, Dai, entered the parlour.

'Oh, hello, Mrs Jones. Mr Jones. I'm afraid she hasn't come down yet.' Sara's eyes suddenly filled with tears. 'I'm doing my best . . . but I don't know what happens at funerals.'

Edna Jones pulled Sara into a tight hug. 'Aww, *cariad*. That's why we came early. To help. Dai, go and make us all a cup of tea and I'll get that sister of mine going. I know it's hard, but she needs to be down here.'

Sara blew her nose and followed Dai into the kitchen.

'There's young you are to become a widow, *bach*. A sorry business all right. And to think Freddie needn't have signed up. His place was here on the farm helping his mam. But you know what he's like — *was* like. Always knew best.'

Sara smiled at the elderly man. He and Edna had always shown her kindness that Gwyneth had rarely done. They made a fuss of her every time they visited and went out of their way to bring presents for her as well as Aled at Christmas. They even remembered her birthday each year, often bringing her bunches of flowers.

The two sisters were so different in personality as well as looks — Gwyneth was angular with a permanent pinched expression, her mouth pulled into a taut line, without a good word to say about her older sister. "*Cwtchy*" — that was how Edna's adoring husband described his wife. *It's such a good word for her.* Yes, Edna Jones was *cwtchy* — cuddly, with plump, soft arms enveloping you and everything all right again. She was always looking for the good in people, and Sara was glad she was there.

'There you are, *bach*. Nothing like a cup of tea to make it all better.'

'Thank you, Mr Jones. I'm sorry about the waterworks. They've been building up for days.'

He patted her hand. 'Not much wonder, *bach*. Here they come now. Edna'll sort her out.'

Sara heard the stairs creak and voices outside in the passageway. 'You'll be fine, Gwynnie. You'll only regret it if you stay cooped up in your room. Deep breaths now.'

'Don't call me Gwynnie.' The cutting tone in her mother-in-law's voice made Sara tense up.

The two sisters entered the kitchen, and Sara felt her eyes widen. The woman linking her arm through Edna's was almost unrecognisable. In the last few days since Gwyneth had insisted she didn't want anyone to see her, she'd aged even more.

'He's in there, then.' She nodded towards the parlour as tears trickled down her pale cheeks.

* * *

'We have prayed for the soul of our dear brother, Frederick Gwynfor Lewis. Let us now say the Lord's Prayer.'

Sara looked at the solemn faces of the mourners packed into the tiny parlour. There were people she recognised from the village, others she hadn't seen before, and several young men about Fred's age who hadn't signed up — farmers who were doing a valuable job feeding the people and serving the country in a different way. Sitting in between them was a young, blonde-haired woman in her Lumber Jill uniform who had sobbed all through the service. Gwyneth obviously knew her well and had embraced her when she'd arrived.

'. . . as we forgive those who trespass against us. And lead us not into temptation, but deliver us from evil. For thine is the Kingdom, the power and the glory, for ever and ever. Amen.' The minister closed his prayer book, hung his head and walked to the door.

Six young men moved to the front and wheeled the bier into the passageway where they lifted the coffin onto their shoulders. Behind them were Dai and Edna, who walked either side of Gwyneth, followed by Sara and Menna. A group of men in dark overcoats and black hats had gathered, ready to walk with the hearse. They were joined by everyone who had attended the service inside the farmhouse. The poignant sound of 'The Old Rugged Cross' being sung as the funeral procession moved off accompanied the bearers, close family members and friends who led from the front. A wide black line of remaining male mourners, at least six deep, snaked along the lane following the shiny, black Wolseley containing Fred's coffin.

Guilty that her overwhelming feeling was one of relief, Sara stared up to the barn roof where crows seemed to caw their rendition of the hymn in unison. She felt sad. Sad for Aled, sad for Fred's mother, yet she realised that a heavy weight she'd been carrying inside her seemed to have floated away. The sky, coloured pewter from the heavy downpour earlier, had brightened, reflecting her mood as Fred travelled further and further away from her. *We'll be all right now. Aled and me.*

The women turned and re-entered the farmhouse — all except for one. The mysterious blonde with her red lipstick had broken with tradition, accompanying the men to the burial in the church graveyard.

While Gwyneth returned to the parlour, Sara and Edna retired to the kitchen to make sure the blackened kettle hanging over the fire in the range was full of water.

Edna put another log on the fire. 'We'll make sure it's boiling for the tea. It won't be long before the men are back, will it? You did well in there, *cariad.* Can't have been easy for you, considering you've never been to a funeral before. Most of them turn up at all of them. They enjoy the teas afterwards, see.' She smiled. 'The womenfolk, especially, want to see who can eke out the rations the furthest and who makes the best *bara brith.*'

Sara smiled back at her. Edna and Dai might not visit often — she suspected it was something to do with the reception they got from her mother-in-law — but when they were needed, they were there like a shot.

'Gwyneth did all right, too, didn't she? Seeing the support from the whole village must have helped. You go — I'll get everything ready here.' Edna gently pushed her towards the door.

Sara looked at the wall clock. The menfolk would be walking back from the village by now.

At that moment, Menna entered with Aled. 'Look who's home from school,' she said. 'Marion Havard offered to take Geraint to play with her Robbie.'

Sara scooped Aled up into her arms.

'Have you kept me some food?' asked Aled. 'You promised you would.'

Sara laughed. 'Typical boy. Always thinking of food. Once the men get back from church, we'll start. Go in and see Nana. She'll be pleased to see you.'

She followed her son into the parlour and Aled rushed to his grandmother, whose eyes were still filled with tears.

'Oh, Gwyneth, *bach,* he's the absolute spit of Fred at the same age. No denying who his da is.' The woman next to her studied the little boy standing close to his grandmother.

'Even though *he* did, to start.' Gwyneth's words were loud enough for everyone to hear. 'Could have been anyone's, so I did hear.' She turned to Aled. 'Come and sit down by Nana, *cariad*. You're all I've got left now, aren't you?'

Sara's skin prickled. *What is the witch implying?* Her cheeks burning, she turned on her heel and went back to the kitchen.

It wasn't long before the passageway filled with men's voices. Fred's friends congregated in the kitchen and the older villagers joined their wives in the parlour.

'Anything I can do, *cariad*?' Dai Jones joined his wife by the range. 'We gave the boy a good send-off.'

A voice called across the kitchen. 'Any tea going, girl? I'm parched.' Bob Morgan, from Cwm Farm and one of Fred's drinking pals, grinned at Sara from across the room. 'Summat stronger would be even better.'

The group of men spilling out into the passageway, along with the blonde woman, laughed.

Ignoring them, Edna poured cups of tea for Sara to hand round. As she passed the young men in the passage, Sara overheard Bob Morgan talking to the blonde. 'I hear you wasn't very welcoming to Freddie boy on his last night, then,

Babs. Fuming he was when he came back to the pub. Got proper legless. Staggered home, he did. Poor bugger. All he wanted was a bit of *real* lovin'.'

'Yeah, he don't get much of that with the ice maiden, so he do say.' Sara recognised the voice as another of Fred's friends — a tall, gangly man they called Trev.

Furious at what she'd heard, Sara's hands shook. The cups rattled in the saucers on the tray. Heat travelled up her neck. Determined not to show she'd heard, she entered the parlour and handed round the tea. Everyone was deep in conversation. She found Menna, who was also busy handing round plates of sandwiches and cakes.

'Aww, what's wrong, *cariad*? All a bit much for you, is it?' Her sister looked at her with concern.

It was just then that the blonde called Babs entered the room and bent over to talk to Gwyneth, who had Aled sitting next to her.

'That's what's wrong!' hissed Sara, glaring in the young woman's direction. 'Fred's floozy by the sound of it.'

'Stand up, *bach*, and let Miss Jenkins sit down,' said Gwyneth firmly.

Aled did what he was told, and as she watched the little boy leave his grandmother's side, Babs started to cry. 'Oh, Gwyneth. It's like looking at a miniature Freddie, isn't it?'

Gwyneth patted her arm. 'There, there, *bach*. It's hit us all hard.'

Menna ushered her sister outside where Sara's angry tears spilled over. Visions of Fred and the blonde filled her head. She felt sick. She was glad she was free of him, but that didn't mean she liked being made a laughing stock. Red rage soared through her.

'Did you know he was carrying on with her?' When Menna didn't answer, Sara looked at her sister in horror. 'How could you? You're my sister. You're supposed to look out for me.' She shrugged herself away as Menna tried to take her arm.

'I didn't know it was still going on, I promise. When I saw her turn up today, I didn't know whether to say anything or not.'

'What do you mean *still*? You should have done. What else should I know about the tart?'

Menna took her sister by the shoulders. 'All I know is he was engaged to her before he married you. Gwyneth was convinced they'd get wed, but she left Dolwen after you two got together. No one heard from her again until she turned up the same time as Nell with the Lumber Jills. I swear, I didn't know he was seeing her again. You *have* to believe me, Sara.'

CHAPTER SEVEN

'I hear the blonde bombshell made a spectacle of herself at Fred's funeral.' Peggy rolled her eyes. 'My old man reckoned she sobbed all the way through. Only woman there. Typical.'

'Oh, don't be horrible. She's not so bad. She's a damned hard worker. Knocks spots off them city lasses, I can te—' Nell stopped speaking when Sara entered the office.

The two girls exchanged glances. But Sara had overheard them and sat down at her desk, determined to get back to the normality of work. 'Look. You don't have to change the subject. I know she used to be engaged to Fred. Menna told me. But I didn't know they'd been seeing each other when he came home on leave. It explains a lot . . .'

Ice maiden. Wasn't that how Bob Morgan and his cronies described her? A long-standing joke, more like. Her voice crackled as her throat constricted. 'Now, let's forget about her, and you two can tell me what you got up to at the weekend.'

* * *

Cycling down the main street of Dolwen the next morning, Sara heard men's voices speaking in a language she didn't understand. Then she remembered it was the day the Italian prisoners of war were starting work on building the new office. She dismounted from her bicycle and walked past them to the side door.

'*Buongiorno, signorina*,' called one of the men.

'*Ciao!*' The rest of the group greeted her in unison.

Sara's cheeks burned. 'Good morning.'

The young man working closest to the office door was stunningly handsome with jet-black hair framing a face with high cheekbones and mocha-coloured eyes. He didn't say anything, simply looked shyly at her as she passed and smiled.

'*Ehi, l'Artista*,' one of other men shouted to him. '*Una bella signorina?*'

He smiled at Sara again. '*Si, bellissima.* Very beautiful.'

Her insides flipped when she heard the mellow sound of his voice.

Once inside the office, she found Peggy and Nell were glued to the window.

'They've started then. Been on a job over the other side of Pen Craig before this one. What do you think?' Peggy turned to face Sara. 'Easy on the eye, eh? We reckon the average age of all the men in the village has just halved. Talk about handsome!' Peggy fanned her face with a sheet of writing paper.

Sara laughed as she hung her coat on the back of the door. 'Yes, I did notice.'

'We think the tall one is in charge. Sergio, I think he's called. But the shy one, the one who's digging the left-hand trench nearest this building, he's the best looking.'

Heat travelled along Sara's neck. 'I think I heard them calling him — um — *la-tist-a.* Yes, that was it. It sounded a bit like artist. *L'Artista.*'

'I feel like going out there and saying, "Need any help, chuck?" Look, Peg, someone's blushing.' Nell was looking over at Sara, and the two girls dissolved into laughter.

'No, I'm not,' she protested. 'I heard someone call him that.'

'But you agree he is the best looking, though?' Peggy said.

'Oh, you two.' Sara shook her head.

It didn't seem right somehow. Her husband hardly cold in the ground one minute and talking about handsome Italians the next. Fred may have been unfaithful, but she owed it to Aled to show some respect for his da. No, she'd keep a low profile and leave all the flirting to her friends.

'Right, I'm off out.' Nell started singing 'Wish Me Luck as You Wave Me Goodbye' while Sara and Peggy hooted with laughter.

'How much do you want to bet she'll know all their names by the time she comes back?' Peggy moved to the window to watch Nell leave.

Standing alongside Peggy, Sara noticed how the men turned their heads to watch Nell weave her way through them on her way to work on the land. It was obvious that the jaunty spring in her friend's step and the way she exaggerated the swing of her hips were deliberate. Nell would know exactly what she was doing and the effect she had on the builders.

Sara sat down at her desk and settled down to the work Menna had left for her. She tried to concentrate and ignore Peggy's constant chatter about the men working outside, but one face kept entering her mind. The man they'd called *l'Artista*. The way he'd looked at her under his long lashes made her heart beat a little faster and her insides somersault. *This is ridiculous. It's all Peggy and Nell's fault.* The last time she'd had feelings like this she'd been an innocent sixteen-year-old. Head over heels in love she'd been, then. But, after finding out what being married was like, she'd made a silent pact with herself that she'd never let a man take over her life again. Nothing could happen, anyway. Prisoners of war were not allowed to fraternise with the locals. All she'd do was be polite and try to ignore his good looks.

When she left for home that afternoon, the builders' yard was empty. She'd heard the lorry arrive to take the men back to the camp. They'd started work an hour before she had and finished earlier.

Menna came over to the office from the house. 'Sorry I haven't been in to see you and Peggy today, but all my time's been taken up at the sawmill. Nell has arranged for some of the Lumber Jills to help stack the wood ready for the orders. I wanted to make sure they all know what's expected of them. I needn't have worried. She's such a good organizer.'

Sara smiled, thinking back to Nell's performance for the Italians earlier in the day. She did like her new Mancunian friend.

'What's funny?' asked Menna.

'She's such a laugh, that's all. She works hard and plays hard.' Sara recounted Nell's antics to Menna, and how Peggy and Nell had been admiring the new workers on site.

Menna laughed but then paused and looked at her sister. 'And what about you, Mrs Lewis?'

'No, certainly not.' Sara knew her sister was unconvinced by the speed of her protest. 'No men for me from now on. I'd better get back. Gwyneth will be looking up at the wall clock as I get through the door.'

It was dead on six o'clock when Sara entered the kitchen and, as she predicted, a stony-faced Gwyneth glanced up at the large wooden wall clock to the side of the Welsh dresser.

'Mammy!' Aled rushed in and flung his arms around her legs.

'What's this? I don't normally get this sort of welcome from my best boy. No toy soldiers tonight?'

Usually, Aled would be busy lining up the tin soldiers on the kitchen mat and not even lifting his head to acknowledge her arrival home. But now he hung his head in silence.

'What kept you? Your little boy's been watching the clock for the last half hour. And he's starving waiting for his tea.'

Nice to see you, too, Mother-in-law.

'I'm not late. You know I don't finish until quarter to. If I did, I'd have to start earlier. This way, I can walk with Aled to school.'

Just lately, Sara had noticed her son had been a bit quieter, so she'd reinstated their walks together each morning as her way of reassuring her little boy about the day ahead. She'd also noticed a few bruises on his arms and legs recently and — while Aled assured her it was just from where he'd fallen in the playground — Sara hoped he wasn't being bullied.

Gwyneth sighed. 'He don't need you walking with him. Remember how pleased his dada was when you stopped that nonsense?' She sucked in a breath and her eyes misted. Sara knew any mention of Fred was still hard for his mother.

'I know. I don't *have* to, but I want to. It's a long time until six.' She couldn't cope with another row. 'Something smells nice.'

Gwyneth began dishing out steaming lamb *cawl*. 'Managed to eke out another meal from the ruddy meat rations. It's getting harder and harder. Bulked it out with them tatties Bryn put in for us.'

Sara was about to tell her mother-in law what an excellent job she was doing but was swiftly interrupted. 'Aled! Get your elbows off the table right now. What have I told you?' screeched the older woman.

The little boy jumped, his eyes immediately filling with tears. 'Sorry, Nana.'

Sara held out her arms and *cwtched* him. 'What on earth was all that? I won't have you shouting and screaming at my boy.'

Gwyneth's mouth formed one of her customary hard lines. 'He's got to learn. He's been a naughty boy ever since he came in. His dada would be so disappointed in him.'

Aled buried his head in Sara's chest.

'Stop it! Don't you think he's gone through enough without you adding to it?' Sara stood up. She took her son's hand and led him upstairs to their room. Once she'd closed the door, she pulled Aled towards her. 'Does Nana often shout at you, *cariad*?'

The little boy nodded. 'Please don't go to work, Mammy.' He rolled up the sleeve on his pullover to reveal a bright red mark across his pale, freckly skin.

46

Sara gasped, her hand rising to her mouth. 'How did this happen? Did Nana do this?'

Aled started crying. In between the sobs, he choked out, 'With her bendy stick. She told me off for bringing mud in.'

Sara was horrified. It was bad enough that the woman used it on her sheepdog let alone on a little boy. 'Oh, *cariad*.'

Gathering as much as she could carry in her shopping basket, Sara grabbed Aled and marched downstairs.

Gwyneth was standing in the hallway, barring the door with her arms folded. 'I don't know where you think you're going, madam. This is the boy's home. He's my flesh and blood.' Her dark eyes glowered.

'Out of the way. We're not staying in this house a moment longer. Come on, *cariad*.' Sara barged her mother-in-law out of the way as she tried to grab Aled. 'Don't you dare!' she screamed.

Sara only just managed to push Aled through the door before Gwyneth slammed it hard behind them.

CHAPTER EIGHT

Wheeling Aled on her bicycle and the basket of belongings on the pannier, Sara calmed with every step as she approached the village. At the end of the main street, her sister's house was bathed in a golden glow in the late sunlight. Menna would let her stay, surely. Gwilym was away and Geraint would love to have his cousin to play with.

Sara lifted Aled down from the saddle and parked her bike against the wall. 'We'll be fine here, *cariad*. Auntie Menna will look after us.' Sara smiled at her son. *How could she have hurt him?* she found herself wondering once again.

Normally, she would have let herself in through the back, but she knew her sister always locked that door once it started getting dark. Lifting the heavy brass knocker, she knocked on the front door. Soon, she heard footsteps in the hallway and the door opened slowly as if someone was carefully checking who was outside. Menna's mouth gaped open. 'Sara! Aled! What are you doing here?'

Determined not to cry on the doorstep, Sara stepped forward. 'Can we come in?'

'Of course, *cariad*.'

Once inside her sister's hallway, Sara knew they were safe.

Before she could say any more, Aled piped up. 'Nana hit me with a stick.' Rolling up his sleeve, he showed them all the mark. 'See, Geraint. Here.' His cousin had now joined them.

Geraint's mouth gaped just as much as his mother's. 'She did that? Does it hurt?'

Aled nodded. His cousin went closer for a better look as Menna and Sara passed them and hurried through to the kitchen.

It was then that Sara broke down in tears and welcomed her sister's arms like a warm comfort blanket around her. 'You're right, Menna. Gwyneth Lewis *is* a dragon. She hit my boy like she does the animals. How could she? I don't know what I'm going to do but I'm not letting her anywhere near Aled ever again, grandmother or no grandmother.'

Menna let her sister cry it all out and then pulled away. 'You poor, poor thing. You did the right thing, coming here. No one would lay a finger on Geraint either. You can stay as long as you want. Now then, a cup of tea's in order, I think.'

As Sara sipped her tea a little bit later on and told her sister everything, it was as if the stone weighing heavily in her chest was crumbling into tiny pebbles, and she found herself breathing more easily than she had in ages.

'There, that's better, isn't it? Don't you worry about a thing, *cariad*. Your place is here now. Listen to those two boys upstairs. Aled's arm will heal and it will be all forgotten.' Menna's words soothed Sara. 'Now, let's get that bed made up in the spare room and Aled can sleep top-to-toe with Geraint.'

I won't forget it, though, will I? Sara's eyes pricked with tears again. 'What would I do without you?'

'Isn't this what sisters do? You'd do the same for me if it was the other way round, wouldn't you?' Menna smiled. 'You're young. One day, when this awful war is over, you'll find someone who'll love you in the way you should be loved. You mark my words. There are other men like Gwilym out there.'

Sara couldn't imagine ever being married again. She'd already decided it was better to stick to making a good life for her and Aled. And she would. She was determined to put life with Fred and his awful mother behind her. And the look on her small son's face, as she tucked him in for the night at the bottom of his big cousin's bed later in the evening, told her things were going to be all right after all.

'*Nos da, cariad.*'

Before putting up the blackout blind in her own bedroom, she looked out across the street. The stone buildings were bathed in moonlight against a clear, starry sky, the colour of inky velvet. It was so different to the scene she was used to at Graig Farm, where leaves on the surrounding trees and hedges would resemble filigree silver on nights like this. From somewhere deep in her mind, a handsome Italian's face came to the fore. Maybe he would be looking out on a similar rural scene from his Nissen hut at the nearby camp? She told herself she was being silly thinking of a man she hardly knew — and not just that but an enemy prisoner of war with no freedom of his own.

But, no matter how hard she tried, the same face was there as she struggled to get to sleep.

* * *

The next morning, Sara accompanied Aled and Geraint to school. She told the headmaster they'd moved from the farm, but didn't give any further details. No doubt Aled would tell everyone and show his classmates the weal on his arm that was starting its journey of changing colours.

She returned to the builders' yard. The Italians, already hard at work, greeted her for the second time. *L'Artista* had positioned himself by the office door so it was impossible not to acknowledge him as she walked by.

'*Buongiorno,* Sara.' Using her name for the first time, the slow, melodious way he stressed the first syllable caused her insides to flip. *Stop it, Sara. This is ridiculous.*

'Oh, good morning.' She hesitated. 'H-how do you know my name?'

'I hear the other girls say. I am Carlo.'

'Hey, Rosso. Back to work.' The foreman, a man called John Phillips, approached her and Carlo. He glowered, poking him in the chest. 'You don't fraternise with the local women, right?' Then he turned to Sara. 'And you should be ashamed of yourself, Mrs Lewis, and you newly widowed an' all. Mind, I hear you've already been chucked out by your mother-in-law so I'm not surprised.'

Shaking with anger, Sara stayed silent and rushed into the office.

CHAPTER NINE

Carlo

Carlo had now been at the camp for nearly six months and still hadn't heard from his mother back in Sicily. Sitting away from the other prisoners in a quiet corner, the reports of heavy bombing and devastating loss of life flooded his mind once more. He remembered her stubborn resolve that *no one* would make her leave the home where she'd lived with him, her only child. *Why didn't she take the opportunity to leave Porto Montebello when she'd been given the chance?* he wondered again.

A tear trickled down Carlo's cheek as his thoughts were interrupted by a familiar voice, its strong Neapolitan accent speaking in his native Italian. It was his good friend, Sisto Conti.

'This is where you are. Time we were going.'

'I'm coming, Sisto.' Brushing his face with the back of his hand, Carlo nodded and followed his friend outside the Nissen hut.

The engine of the lorry taking them to their places of work around Pen Craig was already running outside the camp gates. Walking through the two lines of fellow Italian prisoners, Carlo braced himself for the taunts of "*cooperatori!*"

that he and the other POWs who'd agreed to work on the farms or building sites endured every morning.

That morning, the voices seemed louder. Because Carlo could speak some English, the staff at the camp treated him well. Some of the other Italians disapproved and were intent on making his life a misery. It was a relief to leave the camp each day and see what Welsh village life was like, even though he did have to work hard. As he followed Sisto, the men crowded in around him, shouting into his face. Carlo's pulse raced as he felt the urge to lash out with his clenched fist — but, as always, he held back. He clutched his bait box tighter as he walked as fast as he could to escape the hurled abuse.

'Ignore them, *amico mio*,' Sisto encouraged his friend with his relaxing voice.

The metal gates closed behind the men, and Carlo glanced back to see the prisoners left behind slope back inside the buildings. As soon as the lorry began its journey of dropping off the builders and farm workers, the atmosphere lightened.

'*L'Artista*, I hear there's a pretty Welsh girl you're sweet on in the builders' office.' joked one of the farm workers.

Everyone laughed and whistled.

Carlo protested, but he knew which pretty Welsh girl they were referring to. He couldn't get Sara out of his head. She seemed so different to the other two girls she worked with. He looked forward to her arrival each morning, making sure he was away from the rest of the group when he greeted her. She had stopped blushing now when he spoke quietly to her, but a sparkle in her eyes gave him hope. Could she be "sweet" on him, too?

Not far from the camp, Owens' Building and Timber Merchants was the first drop-off point, and the group of five builders alighted the lorry amid more friendly banter about Carlo and Sara. The foreman and the other builder from the village were already waiting for them. Carlo knew the two local men resented the Italians — they ignored the POWs as much as possible.

Carlo was an artist and had never done any building work before. Instead, he'd painted frescoes on wet plaster on cathedral walls and mouldings when the structures had already been erected. *I may not be a natural builder, but I'd like to see them paint a Madonna and Child*, he often thought to himself. An image of his last fresco came to mind, and he relived the pride and satisfaction of seeing his work being displayed in the Duomo di Porto Montebello for the first time.

That morning, they worked on the foundations of the proposed new office until Menna Owens came to speak to them. 'Morning, everyone. I'm pleased with the progress you've all made on the footings. I have a delivery of granite arriving tomorrow morning, so once you're ready to move on to building the walls, the material will be here for you. It's the local stone. John has the plans and will allocate tasks to you.'

The foreman nodded and held up a list, which he pointed at. 'Your — name — will — tell — you — your — job,' he shouted, pausing between every word.

Perhaps he thinks making his voice into a bellow will help us understand his English. Carlo coughed, trying to hide his amusement.

He began working on the section nearest to the existing office building. Sara emerged from the house with two little boys, exited the yard and returned ten minutes later alone. This time, she walked towards the office and Carlo. Her shiny, fair hair shone in the sunlight and a hint of an embarrassed glow returned to her cheeks when he greeted her quietly.

After the previous altercation with John Phillips, Carlo did as he was directed but was annoyed at himself for getting Sara into trouble too. His heart thumped as he remembered John's words, though. Widowed? That meant she'd been married, didn't it? Perhaps the little boys were hers. He was so glad he'd learned some English when he'd accompanied his mamma when she'd worked for one of the wealthiest families in Porto Montebello at their villa. Still, he'd have to find out what 'fraternise' meant.

Work dragged that day. He ate his Spam sandwiches in the shade of the double garage that housed the business vehicles. The other Italians joined him.

'What was all that yesterday with the man Phillips?' asked one. 'He looked as if he was angry with you.'

'And the Welsh girl,' another added.

Carlo was just translating the foreman's words when the office door opened. Sara didn't appear to see the men in the shade as she shielded her eyes from the sun. She crossed to the house. The two girls she worked with came out next.

'Sara's left Graig Farm. Menna said she and Aled can stay with her. Do you know why?' Carlo heard one of the girls say.

'She told me Gwyneth had hit Aled so she left.'

Carlo's ears pricked up. He knew what "hit" meant. *If only I could ask Sara herself what happened . . .*

'She just wants to get Aled back. Only part of Fred she's got, I s'pose. See you later, chuck.'

John Phillips was prowling. 'Come on, you Eyeties. Break over. I want these footings finished before we leave tonight. D'ya hear, Rosso?'

Carlo didn't see Sara again that day. Back on the lorry, he looked forward to catching up with Sisto. He'd be full of news about a flame-haired beauty called Ceridwen who lived at the farm where he worked. Whatever Carlo had to say about Sara would sound like nothing compared to what Sisto would say but, to him, finding out more about her from what he'd overheard was a big step towards getting to know the girl in his dreams.

But then, without warning, another beautiful face with ebony hair entered his head. He dismissed it as quickly as it had arrived.

She'd made her feelings clear.

CHAPTER TEN

Major Bamber, the new camp commandant, called the Italian prisoners to a meeting in the main hall. Standing beside him was one prisoner Carlo knew well from his time in the Middle East. He and the prison-camp chaplain, Padre Gino Cicchetti, were captured at the same time and had arrived in Pont Ithon together. The men filed in and sat in rows facing the raised stage they'd been using for their impromptu concerts.

'I wonder what this is all about,' whispered Sisto.

'No idea,' replied Carlo. 'And why is Padre Gino up there?'

'*Buongiorno*. It has come to my attention via Padre Cicchetti, here, that although we have been trying to provide sporting facilities, concerts and various craft activities to fill your time when you're not working in the local community, there is one area of Italian life we have neglected.'

A hush fell over the crowd as they waited for him to continue. Carlo and Sisto exchanged puzzled glances. Life in the camp for the men who provided much-needed labour in the village and surrounding farms was fairly comfortable. On the whole, they were treated well by the locals. *Except by people like John Phillips*, thought Carlo.

Now, Padre Gino stood to address the men. 'The one thing our camp lacks is a chapel, *la cappella*. I know this deeply affects many of you. We are delighted the War Office Inspector of POW Camps has agreed that one is provided. The arrival of Major Bamber, with his enthusiasm, means we can start planning and designing this straight away. If any of you would like to be involved, or any of you have the skills needed, please come to see me or Major Bamber.'

Spontaneous applause echoed in the hall.

'That's brilliant news, eh, Carlo?' I hope you're going to offer your skills. It will be like taking you back to Sicily to those churches and *duomos* you have been raving to me about.' Sisto stood and patted Carlo on his back. '*L'Artista*!'

'*L'Artista! L'Artista*!' It started as a murmur, but soon every man in the hall stood and chanted, '*L'Artista*', too.

Carlo looked towards the stage. The padre's face was a picture. 'It seems we have our first volunteer. What do you say, Signor Rosso?'

* * *

That night, Carlo tossed and turned in his narrow bunk. All this talk of paintings and frescoes unsettled him. He brought out his prayer card and remembered what had happened back in Sicily. What had he taken on? It was one thing painting ecclesiastical frescoes with all the materials to hand before war broke out, but here in the middle of nowhere, in wartime, and with nothing to work with? What was he going to do? He would have to tell Padre Gino he couldn't do it. And yet . . . he found himself imagining what Sisto's advice would be. *Why don't you sleep on it?* he'd have told him.

When morning arrived, Carlo had done exactly that. He made his way to the priest's small office where he found the white-haired man sitting at a desk piled with books. '*Buongiorno*, Carlo. Come in.'

'*Buongiorno*, Padre. I've considered what we talked about last night. I'd like to take you up on the offer to help construct a chapel.'

A grinning Gino Cicchetti stood and offered his hand to Carlo, shaking it vigorously. 'Good man. That's such excellent news. With your skills and the fact the men look up to you, I know you're the one who can make this happen.' The priest's brow furrowed slightly. 'Supplies are limited, I'm afraid, but let's see what you can do. Take some time to consult with the others to do some plans and show me what you all come up with.'

'I hope I'll be worthy of the faith you have placed in me, Padre.'

Carlo was to lead a small band of helpers to construct a sanctuary and an altar at one end of a designated Nissen hut where the Italian prisoners could worship. As the padre spoke, ideas flooded Carlo's mind, his imagination buzzing, but everything had to be made from the simplest of materials, most of it second-hand or worthless scrap. It would be nothing like working in the one particular *duomo* he'd loved back in Porto Montebello before the war. Along with beautiful artwork and sculptures, mixed memories of his family homeland came into his head, too. He was careful only to let the happy ones surface.

'Let me show you the Nissen hut Major Bamber has set aside for the project. It will give you an idea of the size.' The priest beckoned him. 'Follow me.'

The two men exited the main building and walked to the hut furthest away from the camp and nearest to the perimeter fence.

'Here it is.' The padre opened the double doors of the semi-cylindrical construction, identical to all the other buildings on the camp site. This hut's corrugated-iron sheets were rusty. Twisted ivy had climbed through gaps, tendrils of leaves hanging from the ceiling or fighting to cling on to the inside walls. The glass on the two side windows was cracked and covered in green mould. A rat scuttled towards the open door, making Carlo jump. The interior was full of discarded farm implements and wooden pallets. *What have I taken on?*

'I can see what you're thinking,' said Padre Gino. 'How on earth can this become a chapel for us to worship Our Lord? We can see past this and make it happen, Carlo.'

* * *

After enlisting the help of Sisto to note down all those prisoners interested in helping to create the chapel and their respective skills, Carlo spent the afternoon sketching out ideas. He planned that the curved walls and ceilings would depict the same scenes as the ones he'd admired in the *duomo* in Porto Montebello, and he labelled each part with the colours he needed. He took out his prayer card and sketched an image of the Madonna and Child that could form the centrepiece behind the altar.

'So, here you are.' Sisto's cheery voice interrupted him. 'Are these your ideas for the chapel? Beautiful but . . .'

Carlo held up his sketchbook. 'I know what you're going to say. Where will I get Cadmium Red, a Burnt Umber, a Prussian Blue? Well, you can use colours from tea, tobacco, plants and vegetables to make paints, and you can make adhesive by boiling fish bones.'

'And where do you think you'll get fish bones in the heart of the Welsh countryside? Come on, Carlo, there's such a thing as a war on if you hadn't heard!'

Carlo knew his friend was right. He'd have to really think about this. Sisto was his biggest supporter. If he lost his support, the project was doomed. He remembered the applause and the pleading eyes of Gino when he'd announced the plan. He wouldn't give up. 'Now then, Sisto, *amico mio*. How did *you* get on?'

His friend handed him a piece of paper and Carlo scanned the list of names.

'Lots of takers. In the end, I chose the men with the best skills to get the job done. What do you think?'

'This is good. I didn't know Octavio Florian was a builder. And yet he's opted to work on the farms?' Carlo was

59

surprised. The band of nine other men chosen had various skills ranging from carpenters and builders to blacksmiths and artists like Carlo himself. 'You've thought this through, Sisto. Thank you. But your name's not here.'

'I can't do anything like that.' Sisto held open his hands. 'All I can do is sing and read music. Not much use in the building trade, eh?'

'Oh, I don't know. It would certainly keep our spirits up. It's because of that rich tenor voice of yours that we have the wonderful concerts in camp. You can dig. You could build a pillar out of whatever scrap materials we can find. You could mix cement. I'm sure if we were slacking, you could get us all singing while we work.' They laughed at Carlo's joke and he added Sisto's name to the list. 'Tell everyone in the group the first meeting will be tomorrow in the hall at two o'clock.'

Sisto nodded. As he walked away, Carlo called after him, 'And *grazie,* Sisto!'

Once alone, Carlo stared into space. Excitement and nervousness swirled inside him. He was daunted but pleased to have started on the project. If this had happened in Sicily, he would be bubbling over with excitement to tell his mamma what he'd planned. But with each passing day and still no reply to his letter, he'd become more convinced she'd perished in the bombings. He sucked in a deep breath. *Poor Mamma.* She was the only person who knew what had really happened back in Porto Montebello. She knew her son was innocent and who had framed him. And who would see to the responsibilities he'd left behind there now?

He realised that the only person he wanted to talk to about these things was Sara. Perhaps she'd listen, but how could he know? He was being ridiculous. She was a stranger — they'd only exchanged a few words and there was no hope of getting to know her better after what John Phillips had said. Besides, his conscience told him it was wrong. He was in no position to be thinking of her in that way.

But I'll be so busy, I won't have time to think of bella Sara. And that's probably for the best, he thought, not believing a word of it.

60

CHAPTER ELEVEN

Carlo and Sisto waited in the hall for the other volunteers. The seats were arranged in a horseshoe shape facing the table. Carlo looked at his watch. 'They should be here soon, Sisto. Would you like to put these out?'

Sisto stood and distributed copies of the list of what was needed to make a start, placing them on the chairs.

At two o'clock, the volunteers drifted in and took up their seats. A babble of conversation echoed in the vast hall until Carlo stood up. '*Grazie*, *amici*. It's so good of you to volunteer to help build the *cappella*. The commandant has allocated Hut Forty-Five, the derelict one in the corner of the camp, as the building we can renovate for our chapel. I have made some plans and sketches to start us off — but remember, this is your *cappella*. Let me know of anything you'd like included in the design, or tell me about features you'd like to remember from home. I can't promise anything, but I'll try my best.'

'Maybe a mosaic floor? I remember those from the *basilica* in my hometown,' said one of the prisoners.

'I think that will be difficult with the limited materials we have, but I'll make a note of it. *Grazie*.'

Next, he held up his sketchpad and showed them the image of the Madonna and Child he'd copied from the prayer card his mother had given him when he'd enlisted. Some of the men gasped, and whispered expressions of "*bellissima*" could be heard.

'*Grazie mille*. But you are the ones who will do all the work before we get to the painting stage. Sisto, do you want to explain the list and how we can all do our part?'

'You should have found one of these on your seats.' Sisto held up the paper. 'This is what we need and there are some suggestions of what to collect. We will be limited as to the materials we can use, so we'll have to think of ways to improvise. For some things like the frame for the altar table, we could use the wooden crates the ration boxes come in, as well as the wood we salvaged from the hut. Strips of metal from tin bully beef cans could be used to make candlesticks for the altar, perhaps. We'll see what our blacksmith friend thinks, eh, Giacomo?'

The Italians talked among themselves. 'Hey, Sisto. Bully beef tins?' one of the men called. 'How much of the awful stuff will we have to eat to get you enough metal?'

Everyone laughed.

'Let's go and see the hut. Sergio, we will need your expertise as a master builder. You can show us how they'd do it in Milan. First, we need to repair the shell of the hut and then line the walls and lay a new floor before we can create anything resembling a chapel.' Carlo led the men outside.

The strong afternoon sun cast elongated shadows of the men as they ambled along the gravel yard. Some prisoners were playing football, others were huddled together smoking and chatting.

'Don't raise your hopes up, *amici miei*.' Carlo unlocked the door to the Nissen hut.

Rumbles of disbelief travelled through the group of men as they gingerly entered the hut. Some held their noses. In the heat of the afternoon, the smell of rotting vegetation was fetid. To Carlo, the place looked more dilapidated and squalid than the first time he'd visited with Padre Gino.

Sisto ushered the men outside into the fresh air. 'Carlo, what in the Lord's name have you taken on?' he whispered.

He caught up with the others, leaving Carlo alone to lock the door. With a heavy heart, he returned to the main camp. How could he get these men to believe they could turn the hut into something beautiful?

* * *

Arriving for work at the builders' yard the next morning, Carlo made his way to the far wall of the new building where he would have a good view of the office — and, hopefully, Sara. There was no harm in looking out for her, was there?

Soon, she emerged from the house and walked across to the office. Not wanting a repeat of the outburst from the foreman, Carlo checked John Phillips was occupied at the far side of the construction site with his back towards him. '*Buongiorno*, Sara. I hope you are well?'

She also cast a glance at John Phillips, and then looked back to Carlo, rewarding him with a beaming smile that reached her sparkling blue eyes. '*Buongiorno*, Carlo. Yes, I'm fine, thank you.'

Carlo wanted so much to carry on the conversation but didn't want to risk any trouble for this lovely woman. Suddenly, he had an idea. 'Would you mind if I wrote to you? You would have to excuse my English, but at least we would not get into trouble with John Phillips. Don't look now, but he is coming this way.'

Carlo watched a blush travel up from Sara's long, slim neck to her cheekbones. 'I'd love that,' she whispered. 'And I will write back.'

Before John Phillips reached them, Sara had disappeared into the office. Maybe nothing would come of it, but Carlo knew he had to try. She was what made coming to work on the building site worthwhile. No matter what John Phillips said or did to him, he was determined to get to know this beautiful Welsh woman. His earlier decision to forget all about her was completely forgotten.

CHAPTER TWELVE

Making the excuse he wanted to work on the plans for the *cappella*, Carlo slipped away from the others in the common room to the silence of the Nissen-hut dorm he shared with ten other POWs. All he'd been able to think of since his earlier encounter with Sara was what he was going to say in his first letter to her. He needed to tell her how he felt — how it was her face welcoming him when he woke up every morning and the last one filling his head before he closed his eyes each night. But then he wondered if that was too forward. Perhaps he should just introduce himself, tell her about himself, about his mamma and how worried he was. Carlo knew he was taking a risk writing to her — but, if they were careful, surely no one would know?

> *Cara Sara,*
>
> *Grazie. You say I write to you and it is good. We put our letters in secret place in yard perhaps. I think the bench where you eat food with your friends? I mix with other prisoners. No one else. We are careful.*
>
> *My name, it is Carlo Giuseppe Rosso. I am Italiano. Sicilia. I have my mamma only. My father is dead. Before I fight, I am an artist. Now I build a cappella, a chapel, for*

*the prisoners at the camp. We do not have the place to pray
to God. We are Catholics. It makes us very sad.*

Carlo chewed the end of his pencil. Dismissing his earlier worry that it might be too bold, he knew he would regret
not telling Sara what she meant to him in this first letter.

*I do not like it that when I see you every day, I do not talk to
you. I am sorry you get trouble with John Phillips. He is not a
nice man. You know I like you very much. You can tell? But
it is soon after your husband dies. Forgive me. I think you are
bellissima, very beautiful. Your hair is very wonderful colour.
Like the corn that is gold. I see your eyes are beautiful blue eyes.*

*We can be friends through the writing of letters. I keep
telling you about the chapel? Now, it is the very bad hut. But
I hope it is beautiful soon.*

*You write back, per favore. I look for it in box next
to bench.*

Soon, I like to see your smile. It is lovely.
Carlo

Carlo folded the letter and put it in the envelope. After
licking the gum along the edge, he kissed the seal, daring to
hope that one day he would be kissing Sara's lips. But then
his thoughts were interrupted.

'Hey, Carlo. What are you doing lying on your bunk?
The others have started a game of billiards and they're asking
where our star player is.'

Sisto was standing in the doorway. Carlo wondered if he
should tell him about his plans to write to Sara. Although he
knew Sisto would not break his trust, perhaps it was better
not to tell a soul? It would be his and Sara's secret. He tucked
the envelope under his mattress and joined his friend.

As the two men entered the mess hall, a cheer went up.
Carlo smiled, taking the homemade cue he was offered. His
first putt of the small, red, concrete ball found the far-left
corner pocket. He exhaled a sigh of satisfaction.

'Still got it, Rosso.' His opponent patted his back as he passed him to take up his position.

Once the game was over and they were all settled around the hall, talk turned to the chapel.

'I suggest we meet at the chapel at nine in the morning,' said Sisto. 'As it's a Saturday, we can get a good bit done.'

Surprised, Carlo smiled. 'So, you've come round to the idea after all, Sisto?'

'I've been talking to the men. They all agree we should try — even though it seems an impossible task. Isn't that right, boys?'

The team agreed and discussed how far they'd got in collecting things from Sisto's list. Sergio rose from his seat and dragged over a sack of ration boxes. He took one out and held it up. 'I've got Mrs Williams in the canteen to save these for us. She's promised to save all the onion skins for us, too.'

Carlo knew they were a long way from mixing the paints but was impressed with the enthusiasm all the men were showing after the despondency they'd felt on their first visit to the Nissen hut.

'Thanks, Sergio.' He nodded his gratitude. 'Our main problem is getting cement, which is in short supply. We need it to cover the corrugated-iron roof of the hut and to bind the ration-box pillars together. What do you think about approaching Mrs Owens in the morning?'

Sergio shook his head. 'I can't see her allowing us any cement. Surely John Phillips is in charge of that, and he's certainly not going to help us out.'

'Perhaps you could speak with her anyway, Sergio? You get on better with our foreman than I do, so maybe he wouldn't have any objections to you leaving your post to ask her?' Sergio gave a thumbs-up to his suggestion.

Carlo pondered in silence as the others continued chatting, trying to outdo each other with what they were bringing to the project. He wondered, if he explained it to Sara, whether she would be able to help. Even collecting empty cement bags would be useful. They could be flattened out and used to line the walls on which he'd eventually paint the biblical scenes. His hand strayed to the prayer card he always kept in his breast pocket. In amongst the babble of voices, Carlo spotted another person not joining in. Fredo sat at a table slicing each one of his cigarettes in half longways, then re-rolling them. *So that's why his cigarettes are so much thinner than ours. No wonder he always has spares at the end of the week when we're all waiting for our new stock of rations.* Fredo looked up, clearly conscious he was being watched. 'I'm thinking of what my role can be in all this, Carlo.' He held out an open hand in front of him. 'I've got a steady hand, as you can see, if you need anything cut out.'

Carlo remembered the intricate scroll work Giacomo had planned for his sanctuary screen. 'We'll hold you to that.' He flicked through his pile of papers and found Giacomo's plans. Walking over to Fredo, he showed him the design for the scrollwork. 'See these. Each piece is going to be made from thin sheets of tin. Rolled-out food tins, bully beef containers flattened out — that sort of thing. Your steady hand could cut out the shapes, and then Giacomo would weld them together into a solid screen. So, you see, cutting your cigarettes is good training.'

Fredo's eyes widened. 'I don't think this little penknife would do much good, but if you can find me a heavy-duty knife or shears, you're on.'

* * *

By nine o'clock the next morning, the chapel hut was a hive of activity. Piles of vegetation had been pulled up from the floor and down from the ceiling, and they had formed a large heap outside the double doors. Wood had been carefully stacked along an outside wall.

'If you two could check each piece for rot and woodworm, then I'd like you to saw the rest into planks of equal size. I'm thinking they could be used as a panelled side to the altar when attached to the ration-box pillars. *Grazie, amici.*'

One of the carpenters spoke to a couple of men looking for something to do.

By the time the team stopped for lunch, the building resembled a hut like the others on the camp. They'd worked non-stop and the result was clear for all to see.

'*Bravo*, everyone. This shows what can be done when we all work together.' Carlo beamed his approval. 'Try to imagine it now with the sanctuary and altar at that end, and wooden seats for us all where you're standing now. I shall report back to Major Bamber and Padre Gino. I'm sure they'll be delighted. Now, let's go to the mess for some well-earned *cibo*.'

The men filed out, leaving Carlo and Sisto behind. Sisto patted his friend's back. 'We're on our way.'

The smile on Carlo's face said it all as he imagined his painting of the Madonna and Child glowing above the altar.

CHAPTER THIRTEEN

Arriving at the builders' yard on Monday morning, Carlo caught a glimpse of Sara through the office window, and, checking John Phillips was nowhere in view, slipped his letter to her through the postbox. Next, he went to the bench and placed the metal ration box under the seat where it would not be obviously seen.

He resumed his work and took care not to waste any precious cement as he laid the stones row upon row. Although building had been new to him when he'd arrived in Wales, he'd become adept at getting a neat wall, whereas some of the other men had to redo their lines if John Phillips was not satisfied with the standard. He hoped Sara would reply to his letter and he couldn't wait to see if the box contained a letter from her before he left at the end of the day.

A little later on, Carlo toured around the site, making a note of where the supplies were kept and how much stock there was before Sergio approached Menna Owens. At the far end of the office building, the storeroom door was open and he could see piles of cement bags and sheets of plasterboard.

As he returned to his position on the wall, he met Sara coming out of the office. 'Did you get my letter?' he whispered.

She looked around and nodded. 'I'm going to the bench now.'

Carlo smiled. 'Thank you,' he mouthed. He returned to his place and mixed cement on his board. He scooped up a trowelful and laid it along the row of stones.

At five o'clock, the whistle blew to signal the end of the working day for the builders. Carlo had used up every last bit of cement and put away his tools neatly, ready for the next day.

'The truck's here, Carlo. Hurry up,' shouted Sergio.

Carlo hurried to the bench and reached into the metal container while checking no one was looking in his direction. Sara's letter was there as she'd promised. He secreted it in the inside pocket of his overalls just as the driver of the truck beeped the horn, compelling him to rush over.

The journey back to the camp dragged as the new driver did a round tour of the farms instead of picking the builders up last as normally happened. At every stop on the way, it seemed the men were not there on time and as the rest of them waited, Sara's letter felt like it was burning a hole in his pocket. What would she say? Could he dare hope it was the same for her? Perhaps she wouldn't be interested in his *cappella* project.

'Everything okay, Carlo?' asked Sisto as he climbed into the truck and sat down next to him. 'Did you see the gorgeous Sara today?'

'Shh!' Carlo looked around to check who was listening. 'Old man Phillips watches me like a hawk. What about the *bella* Ceridwen? Snatch any stolen moments next to the shepherd's hut again?'

Grinning, Sisto tapped the side of his nose. 'For you to find out, *amico mio*.'

It was obvious Sisto and Ceridwen were seeing each other in secret most days. He risked a spell in the punishment block but, by the look on his friend's face, it was worth the risk.

'Be careful, Sisto.' Carlo spoke under his breath.

Sisto started humming '*O Sole Mio*', a Neapolitan song that was his signature tune at the camp concerts. Carlo imagined him taking Ceridwen's hand and declaring his love for her in song. It was much more difficult for him and Sara.

The truck stopped outside the camp gates and the prisoners climbed out. They waited for the camp guards to let them in. As soon as they did, Carlo raced across the yard, ignoring the taunts from the die-hard fascists. He'd had no choice but to fight for Italy, but it didn't mean he supported Mussolini's brutal regime as they did.

He entered the dorm and lay on his bunk, immediately tearing open Sara's letter. His heart raced as he read the words in the beautiful, evenly formed handwriting.

Dear Carlo,

I was so thrilled to receive your letter. Let me introduce myself. My name is Sara Anwen Lewis (was Evans). I'm twenty-two years old and I have a little boy called Aled. He's five. Yes, I know. I was very young having him. As you might know, my husband, Fred, was killed recently, but, although I'm sad for our little boy, I cannot grieve for myself. He treated me badly. I want you to know I have no loyalty to him now. Mrs Owens, Menna, who owns the building site and the sawmill, is my sister. She has been wonderful letting Aled and me stay with her now I no longer live at Graig Farm with Fred's mother.

I want you to know I feel the same way as you do. From that first morning when you arrived to work at the yard, something in the way you looked at me made my heart beat faster. It's never happened to me before with someone I didn't know. Since then, every time I see you or hear you speak, it's the same. It's your face that helps me drift off to sleep. I even dream of us being together. Is that a silly thing to say when I don't even know you? Have I said too much? I'm not normally this forward.

I understand we can't be together in public, but your idea of letters is a good one. Perhaps one day we could meet somewhere in private. But for now, the box under the bench is where we'll meet in words only.

Your project to build a chapel on the camp sounds wonderful. Yes, I would love to hear everything about it. I cannot imagine what it's like to be locked up and not be able to go where you want. Every soldier is doing what they are ordered to do. That doesn't make you a bad man.

Please write again soon.
Sara

Carlo's eyes welled with tears. Happy tears. *She feels the same way. I knew it!* He'd only ever experienced feelings like this with a woman once before . . . but he quickly dismissed that thought.

He took out the kitbag he stored under his bunk and placed Sara's letter in the tin in which he'd hoped to keep his mother's letters. It would be safe in there, and he was in no doubt that he would read Sara's words over and over again. *Something in the way you looked at me made my heart beat faster.* Isn't that what she'd written?

CHAPTER FOURTEEN

Days turned into weeks. The letters between Carlo and Sara were frequent and welcomed by both of them. But one morning, as Carlo sidled away from where he was working to post his latest letter, bending down to feel for the metal box under the seat, a harsh voice caused him to stop.

'This what you're looking for?' John Phillips waved the metal container and took out a blue envelope. Carlo knew it would be addressed to him in Sara's handwriting. The older man marched over to him and thrust out his hand. 'Here, hand over the one you're hiding. How much do I bet yours will be addressed to an attractive young widow who's working in there right now?' He nodded his head in the direction of the office.

Carlo tried to hide his letter, stuffing it inside his overalls as his heart pounded. 'I do not know what you are talking about.'

The foreman grabbed his arm and the letter fell on the floor. John Phillips snatched it and put it in the box with the other letter. 'I've been watching you, Rosso. Guessed you and her in there were up to something. Well, Mrs Owens is going to know. Can't say she'll be best pleased when she finds out you've been carrying on with her own sister under her ruddy nose.'

The man marched over to the main house and hammered on the front door. Carlo had seen Menna leave the site earlier so he had time to think about what to do. He needed to contact Sara to warn her what had happened. If Menna dismissed him, could Sara's position be in jeopardy, too?

He resumed work but his heart wasn't in it. Just before midday, a lorry arrived at the site with building supplies. While John Phillips was dealing with the driver, Carlo took the opportunity to tap the office window to attract Sara's attention. It was Peggy who opened it. 'Please tell Sara I have to see her now.' His voice was just a murmur. 'Over there.' He pointed in the direction of the door while also looking around to check John Phillips was still occupied.

Sara opened the door. 'What's so urgent? Has something happened?'

'It's him. He knows about our letters. He's going to tell your sister. I want to warn you.'

'Rosso. Get back to work. You may not have a job at all once I report you!'

The other builders looked at the foreman and then at Carlo in confusion.

'Don't worry. I'll get to Menna before he does. I'll explain everything. I know what time she's due back from the sawmill. I'll wait for her in the street outside.'

* * *

A little while later on, when Menna parked the car alongside the house, Sara was sitting in the passenger seat. Close enough to hear what was said, Carlo watched John Phillips approach them.

'Not now, Mr Phillips. I've some important business to deal with. It will have to wait, I'm afraid.'

The foreman glowered in Carlo's direction.

'Carlo, isn't it? Will you step into the office, please?' called Menna as she and Sara went in.

He followed them inside. The tall girl, Peggy, was putting on her coat.

74

'Thanks, Peggy. You can get off early today,' said Menna. 'We'll see you in the morning.'

Once they were alone, Menna invited Carlo to sit down. 'Now, I want to know what's going on. Sara says you've become penfriends. She says you have no one back in Sicily, only your mother, so you enjoy reading her news and she especially likes to hear about your project to build a chapel at the camp.'

Carlo relaxed and smiled. 'Yes, it is coming on well, *grazie*. Once the walls are lined, I can start on this.' He fumbled inside his overall pocket. He brought out his prayer card with the picture of the Madonna and Child and handed it to her.

Menna gasped. 'It's beautiful. Can you paint this? I had no idea.'

If Menna had any inkling of what else was in Sara and Carlo's letters, she didn't say. All the talk after that was of the chapel and what was needed for it to be done. Eventually, she stood up and made her way to the door. 'I can't get rid of John Phillips — he's the only person I could use in the village with all the eligible men signed up. Strictly speaking, you shouldn't fraternise with my sister. But I see no reason why you shouldn't correspond with each other as long as you don't meet up in person. Of course, you are bound to see each other as you work at the same place.'

'Thank you, Menna,' said Sara.

'Yes, thank you,' Carlo agreed.

'But please don't use a tin box under an old bench. You post Sara's letters through my front door. She lives there now, after all. And I will make sure I hand hers to you in person.' She opened the door. 'Oh, and let me know if there's anything more I can do to help with your chapel project.'

Before joining the rest of the builders, Carlo quickly pulled Sara away from the window and enveloped her in his arms. He tilted her face towards him and kissed her tenderly on the lips.

'Oh, Carlo, I've dreamed of this.'

'One day, *amore mio*. One day we will not have to hide away to kiss.'

* * *

That evening, Carlo had intended to spend time designing the paintings, but all he could think of was how soft Sara's skin was and the sensation as their lips met. His conscience told him it was wrong but he decided that falling in love wasn't something you could control or deny yourself because your countries were at war. Lighting a cigarette, he wandered outside into the clear spring air. Sara would be seeing the same moon and identical stars a few kilometres away, but there might as well be hundreds of miles separating them. Was theirs doomed to be a forbidden love? A love conducted through letters? Could it last until the war was over? Was it fair to expect Sara to wait and be satisfied with talk about the *cappella*? He stubbed out his cigarette with his heel and returned to his dorm. He'd write and ask her that. He would understand if she wanted more than friendship out of life now that she was a free woman.

> *It is good I meet your sister. I see why you live with her. She protects her little sister. It is very kind that she knows we are friends. I like it a lot.*

When it came to signing off the letter, Carlo knew he must mention what had happened between them. So much for saying he didn't expect her to wait until the war was over.

> *This night, I sleep and think about the kiss that is our first one, bella Sara. Your lips, they are soft. I feel it again. I write the words and it makes my heart very happy.*
>   *Ti amo, Carlo*

CHAPTER FIFTEEN

September 1943

'Carlo, have you heard?'

The chapel doors burst open and a breathless Sisto ran up to where his friend was measuring the depth of the sanctuary in readiness for the plasterboard. 'Slow down, *amico mio*. What's happened?' Carlo put down his pencil and ruler.

'Italy has capitulated. It was on the wireless. We're not prisoners anymore. We're free. Come.'

'I don't believe it!'

The two men left the chapel and joined the throng of men crowding into the yard, cheering, laughing and slapping each other on the back. Some of the prisoners looked shocked and remained quiet. Major Bamber came out of the building next to the mess hall to join them. He blew his whistle and silence settled over them. 'I take it you've heard. Until I get instructions from the War Office, I want you to remain calm. If Italy and the Allies are now on the same side, you may not be prisoners of war anymore, but you can't leave yet!'

Shouts of 'Why not?' and 'Try stopping us!' came from the belligerent group of men who'd refused to work outside the camp.

The major blew his whistle again. 'It's not practical with the war still raging with Germany in Europe. It wouldn't be safe for you to try to get to Italy, but I promise you, we'll find out what's happening as soon as we can. For today, no trucks will be delivering you to your work placements. Your employers will be informed. Now, enjoy your day off.'

The men dispersed into small, confused groups. Talk was predominantly about the end of the war and how soon they'd be reunited with loved ones back home. Carlo still hadn't heard from his mother, but he knew he still couldn't return to Sicily anyway.

* * *

A meeting was held in the main hall the next day. At a table on the stage, Major Bamber, Padre Gino and a soldier named Sergeant Wilson waited as the men filed in and sat on chairs facing them.

Major Bamber stood to address the men. 'I promised you I'd inform you of the arrangements now that our countries are no longer at war with one another. Instructions have come from the War Office that the British are not able to supply ships to take you back to Italy while the war is still ongoing. So, in answer to those of you who have asked when you are going home, I'm afraid it appears as if it will not be possible until the end of the war.'

Groans and mutterings rippled along the rows of seated men.

Padre Gino stood up. 'I know you are going to be even more worried about your families now Italy is a battleground with the Germans. It is therefore even more important our little chapel gets finished. Sergeant Wilson here will outline the changes to your lives here.'

The soldier stood, thanking the padre. He was one of the guards who patrolled the Nissen huts, making sure none of the prisoners stepped out of line. Carlo knew him as a different character to the amiable Major Bamber.

'In order to acknowledge our countries are no longer at war, the British and Italian government have at last decided on the changes there will be to your lives here at Greenfield Camp. The main change will be that you are now free to mix with members of the local community. When you work on the farms and for local businesses, you will be paid in British coinage instead of camp tokens. Your pay will increase. Some of you may want to send money home and we can arrange that for you.'

Carlo knew it was his responsibility to do that, but he still hadn't heard from his mother.

The men talked among themselves. The padre tapped the table to get their attention, and Major Bamber stood up and spoke again. 'You will carry on with the work you are doing, but there will no longer be a guard accompanying you in the trucks. When your working day is over, you will be free to travel up to five miles away from the camp, but I'm afraid there is to be a curfew. Ten o'clock. You will have to be inside the camp boundary by then. You will not be allowed to use public transport or frequent the local public houses.'

Another groan came from the men.

'There is one rule remaining. It is still forbidden to form a relationship with local women.' He coughed and looked at Sergeant Wilson. 'By that, we mean a physical relationship.'

Carlo relived the kiss with Sara. Even though it was good news they could be seen in public as friends, anything else was still forbidden.

'Those of you who do not accept these conditions will be moved to other camps. The new arrangements will come into force in a week's time. You have by six o'clock this evening to let us know your decision on whether you still want to work or not. Thank you,' said Major Bamber.

The three men left the room. Those men who'd taunted the workers as "*cooperatori*" turned and hurled insults at the rest. '*Mai, mai, mai!*' they shouted. 'Never!' As they marched out of the room, chants of '*Viva il Duce! Viva il Duce!*' echoed in the air.

Carlo and Sisto smiled at each other as the men returned to their huts to think over what had been offered. Carlo had no doubts as to what his decision would be. 'I know what I'm going to do,' he told his friend. 'What about you, Sisto?'

'I'm accepting the conditions. I'm staying!'

Being able to leave the camp was going to be a huge step forward. *Very soon, I can talk to Sara and there's nothing John Phillips can say.* Carlo looked around at the groups that had formed. Most of them couldn't wait to return to their wives and families, the excitement showing on their faces and in their animated gestures. How long would they have to wait before being reunited? The babies they'd left behind would be boys and girls who might not recognise them now.

As the hut began resounding with the stories of patriotic Italians remembering their homeland, Padre Gino entered the room. 'I have heard some wonderful news, *i miei amici*. Now you will all be paid in British money, and paid more, a number of men have already approached me to say they'd like to contribute to a chapel fund. This could then be used to buy what we can't find or scavenge. They say they will still have money to send home. I'm so touched the *cappella* means so much to everyone.'

'That means I can order through Mrs Owens,' said Carlo. 'She's offered to help, but if I can pay, I think she will agree to let us have cement and plasterboard at cost price!' *This is the best news ever*, he thought. Until he heard from his mamma, he had nowhere to send any of his wages, so he would give them to the chapel. But his conscience pricked. *Maybe I should keep some back, just in case . . .*

At six o'clock, he and Sisto were first outside Major Bamber's office. By the time the commandant opened his door, the queue snaked around the yard, the men all happy to sign their agreement to the new rules.

The few men who'd resisted and would never betray their extreme right-wing ideals mocked and taunted them. 'Fascists!' shouted one prisoner in the queue. A scuffle broke out, but it was soon dispersed by men on both sides separating their friends.

Once back inside the main hut, Sisto stood and sang '*Funiculì, Funiculà*', a popular Neapolitan song, in his wonderful tenor voice.

'*Bravo,* Sisto.' Carlo patted his friend's back when he sat back down. 'Let's make a concerted effort to get the chapel finished. Ask ourselves why are we doing it? I think it's a symbol of peace, and we want that peace to come as soon as possible so you can all go home.'

His skin puckered with goosebumps. He realised he'd said "you can go home" not "we". He desperately wanted to see his mamma, but there was one reason he hadn't shared with anyone that meant he could not set foot on Sicilian soil again. He knew what awaited him if he did.

CHAPTER SIXTEEN

Sara

The builders' yard was silent when Sara crossed to the office — no amiable banter from the Italian builders, no Carlo to try to catch a few moments' chat with. Menna had told her she'd had a message from the camp official that the prisoners would not be turning up for work that day. When Sara had heard the news that the Italians had capitulated, all she'd been able to think of was that she'd be able to talk freely in public with Carlo. John Phillips wouldn't be able to do anything!

As always, Sara was first at her desk. Once Aled had left for school, she liked to make a start before the other two arrived. The new building was nearing completion, and she would be glad to have a more spacious working place and some order restored, but she couldn't imagine not seeing Carlo every day.

'Have you heard the news?' Peggy burst into the office. 'The gorgeous Italians are now on our side! There'll be no stopping you and Carlo now.'

'I don't know what you mean. It's all you think about, Peggy Lloyd!'

Dear Peggy! It was typical of her to be planning her love life for her. Peggy wouldn't have listened to every word of the wireless bulletin as she had. All she would have heard would have been the words she wanted to hear. Yes, it was good news for Sara and Carlo, but one rule stood out: relationships between the prisoners and local women were still forbidden. She relived the kiss they'd had once again. There would be no more kisses, but she would build a strong friendship with Carlo and have to be content with that until the end of the war.

Sara got up to fill the kettle. 'Nell will be in soon, so it's my turn to make the tea, I think.'

'You must have second sight. Here she comes now.' Peggy laughed.

The land girl managed to look glamorous in whatever she wore, even in her muddy khakis. At nine o'clock in the morning, there she was, her make-up perfect. *Who else wears lipstick and rouge out in the farmyards? And how does she get lipstick, anyway?* Sara smiled. Even when news on the wireless coming in about the boys on the front was grim, Nell brightened their day.

'Morning. Oh, is that a brew you're making, chuck? Have you heard the news?'

Peggy and Sara laughed.

'Saturday-night dances are going to be a bit more exciting with all of them Italians now. The farm lads won't get a look in. All systems go with you and lover boy now, eh, Sara?'

'Not you as well!' Sara reddened.

She handed Peggy and Nell their mugs of tea. Nell drank hers as if her life depended on it.

'Blimey! Cast-iron mouth on you.' Peggy stared, open-mouthed, at her friend.

'Must dash. I'm late already. There's a delivery up at the sawmill and I've got to arrange getting the orders out to my Jills.'

And with that, she was gone.

Peggy watched her hurry away from the side window, then looked out at the empty office building. 'Ol' man Phillips is wandering around like a lost soul.'

Without the POW workers, it was just him and old Mr Carter, who was slow and unable to work as the foreman needed.

Sara took her mug of tea back to her desk and resumed work. She couldn't settle. Her mind wandered, imagining what the prisoners were doing to celebrate their new freedom. All she knew was that she couldn't wait to meet up with Carlo — openly and legally.

* * *

Nell appeared excited when she arrived back that afternoon. 'You'll never guess what I've just seen.' She paused dramatically.

'Well, go on then,' urged Peggy.

'Loads of Italians walking in groups through the main street of Dolwen. Not marching, as we've seen them do sometimes. Just sauntering along, chatting, smoking. I saw some of the ones who come here actually go into the shop on the corner.'

Sara didn't dare ask if one of them was Carlo. *So, things have already changed for the prisoners . . .*

'I bet you stopped for an eyeful, didn't you?' Peggy joked. They all giggled.

Sara glanced at the clock. She realised that Aled should have been home by now, and he knew he had to knock on the office door to let her know. 'Sorry, girls. I'm going over to the house to check if Aled and Geraint are in. It's not like him not to come here first.'

Now her son had been in school for a term, she allowed him to accompany his cousin into the house. Menna was always back and forth, and she was only across the yard, after all.

She hurried over and let herself in. 'Boys?' she called. Her nephew appeared at the top of the stairs. Alone. 'Where's Aled?'

'I waited for him, but his class had all gone.' The young lad looked unperturbed.

Sara's heart raced. Surely he wouldn't wander off on his own?

She ran back to the office and grabbed her coat. 'Aled's gone. I've got to get to the school,' she hurriedly told the girls.

84

'Do you want one of us to come with you, chuck?'

But Nell's words went unheard. Sara had already gone.

She ran until she got to the school playground. It was deserted but the door to the classroom was open. Vera, the school cleaner, looked up at her as she entered.

'Is Mr Thomas still here?' Sara bent over to catch her breath.

'You've just missed him, *bach.*'

Sara's eyelids burned with tears, and Vera stopped sweeping as she noticed. 'Whatever's wrong?'

Tears trickled down Sara's cheeks. 'It's Aled. He didn't come home with Menna's boy. I don't know where to start looking. I was hoping Mr Thomas would know.'

The older woman put an arm around her shoulder. 'It's all right. When I was coming down the hill on my bike, I saw your little one walking away from the schoolyard with Bryn who works at Graig Farm. It was quite far away but it must have been your boy. No one else in the village has hair that lovely Lewis colour. There's nice you've made things up with Gwyneth.'

Sara clenched her fists. She wanted to scream, *No I haven't!* Instead, she thanked Vera for her help and rushed up to the farm. She hadn't set foot up there since the row when she'd left to live with Menna. The knots in her stomach tightened as they'd done almost every day she'd lived with Gwyneth Lewis.

She was relieved to find Aled in the barn a little way from the house playing with Griff, the black-and-white sheepdog. Then she noticed Gwyneth coming out through the front door. 'Aled! Nana's got your favourite, *bach,*' she called. Her face became hard and pinched when she noticed her daughter-in-law. 'Oh, it's you. What do you want?'

It was all Sara could do not to launch herself at the woman. 'How dare you take him? I've been out of my mind with worry. Aled, come here now!'

Gwyneth barred her grandson's way. 'He hasn't told you, has he? We have lots of little chats, don't we, *bach*? Most

85

days after school. The toffee-nosed kid of your stuck-up sister is only too happy to go on ahead. My best boy, here, told me how much he missed the farm and the animals, especially Griff.'

'Aled, you come to Mammy now.'

'You don't have to, *bach*. You're a Lewis, and it's not right you're living with someone who cavorts with an Eyetie. Disgusting.'

Sara gaped, horrified at the woman's vicious comment. Before she could respond, Bryn came out from the barn. 'Gwyneth! Stop that at once.' Eyes glaring, he marched towards them. 'The two of you should be ashamed, arguing like banshees in front of the little lad. Are you all right, Aled, *bach*?'

The boy nodded.

Bryn wasn't afraid to tell Gwyneth what he thought. For a moment, she looked contrite but Sara knew it wouldn't last.

'I'm sorry, Sara.' Bryn turned to her. 'I understood you'd agreed for him come to see the animals.'

Sara lowered her voice as Aled ran to her and clung to her skirt. 'No. It's not your fault, Bryn. It's hers.' She pointed at Gwyneth. 'If she hadn't been too handy with her stick, maybe we'd still be living here.'

Bryn's puzzled expression told Sara he knew nothing of the real reason for her and Aled moving out. She took Aled's hand and left the farmyard as Bryn and Gwyneth continued arguing.

'Why can't I stay, Mammy? Griff will miss me.'

'I know, *cariad*. But you mustn't come up here. Bryn will look after Griff for you.'

She looked at Aled and wondered whether it was fair to deprive her son of spending time with the animals. From an early age, he'd loved helping Bryn with the jobs at Graig Farm — collecting the eggs from the henhouse, watching Griff round up the sheep and feeding lambs with a bottle if they'd lost a ewe.

As they passed the school, Sara saw a smiling Carlo walking up the main street towards her. She wanted to rush into his arms, but instead she smiled, grateful that at least they could now talk in public. 'Carlo, this is a lovely surprise.'

'*Si,* I feel as if I should be looking over my shoulder. It's good news, eh? I called at the office. Peggy told me you had gone to look for this little one. It is good that you found him. I am very glad.' He crouched down to Aled's level. 'What is your name, little boy?'

'Aled Lewis.' He became shy and tried to hide in his mother's skirt.

'Aled, this is my friend, Carlo.' Sara introduced them.

They walked either side of Aled until they reached the gates of the builders' yard. 'I brought this for you.' Carlo handed Sara a letter, and electricity sizzled through her veins when their hands touched. 'In case I could not see you to talk to. It's a letter I wrote after we were told the news yesterday.'

'Thank you. I'll write back. Say goodbye, Aled.'

'Goodbye.' Her son turned and ran ahead into the house as if he couldn't get away quick enough.

'*Ciao.*'

'He'll be fine once he gets to know you. Goodbye, Carlo.'

Sara watched as Carlo walked away. She brought his letter up to her lips and kissed it.

Sara and Menna arrived back at the house at the same time. The office was shut up, and Menna said she'd told Peggy and Nell they could finish early. 'I've only this minute got back, but they said Aled had gone missing. Thank goodness he's safe! What happened? I haven't spoken to Geraint yet.'

Sara sent Aled upstairs to find his cousin.

'It was awful. Geraint told me he wasn't there waiting for him. Vera — you know, who cleans the school? — saw him walking up to the farm with Bryn. If it wasn't for her, I don't know what I'd have done.'

'You poor thing. Come here. Sit down.'

Feeling her sister's arms around her, Sara explained everything. When she'd finished, Menna called her son down from upstairs. 'You're not in any trouble, *cariad*, but Aled's nana says she's been meeting him from school and sending you on in front. From now on, I think the two of you should wait and either me or Auntie Sara will pick you up. Understood?'

The boy agreed and immediately went back to playing.

'She was her usual nasty self,' Sara continued. 'Accused me of *cavorting*, as she put it, with an Italian, only she didn't use the word Italian. Bryn told her off. He thought I'd given permission for Aled to go there.'

'As if.' When Sara didn't comment, her sister added, 'You're not considering it, are you? After all you said.'

'I know, but am I depriving him of going somewhere he loves just because of a feud between me and her? Perhaps I could insist it would only be if Bryn was there.'

Her sister shook her head. 'Have you forgotten what she did? On your head be it.'

Perhaps her sister was right. But it did feel like he was missing out — there were no animals at Menna's house. 'But we wouldn't be living with her, would we? It would only be occasionally with Bryn in charge. You should have seen Aled's face when he was with Griff, Menna.'

'I think you're mad!'

They spoke no more about it and, after the evening meal and seeing Aled settled into bed, Sara took Carlo's letter up to her room. She pulled down the blackout blind before lighting the lamp. His letters were always filled with his feelings for her, whereas snatched conversations left her wondering. Hopefully, now they could meet, that was all going to stop.

Cara Sara,

The news today, it is wonderful. My country is on the same side as your country. We are not the enemies now. But you and me, we are not the enemies ever. I am sad we cannot show the love, but we meet as friends. John Phillips cannot stop us! One day, I kiss you in public. I count the days until we are all free. No one returns to Italy. Yet we are not prisoners now. I do not return. Still Mamma does not write. The days pass. I am very sure she dies in the bombs. I must not think about it.

Everything I want is here, Sara. For now, I see you when I close my eyes. The dream is that I wake up and you are by me. And, tesoro, it happens one day. I wait for ever.

There is more good news. Now we have the pay in the British money, the pounds, shillings and pence. Your sister, she is very kind but now I pay for the cement and the plaster. I hope I buy it all through her. I hope you — how do you say? — put in the good word. Grazie. In your last letter, you say you help with the cappella. Now, it is when we paint stage. I need the berries and the leaves to make the dyes to mix with the paints. You like to come with me? If yes, you meet me at camp entrance on Saturday. It is at ten o'clock. No one stops us walking in the fields.

Per favore, you tell me the answer tomorrow when I go to the building work again.

Ti amo, Carlo

Sara lay back on her pillow, thinking of what it would be like to wake up next to Carlo. An unwanted image of Fred entered her head. Lying next to him had become a curse. When he'd died, she'd promised herself she'd never be under the control of another man again — and yet, here she was, longing to be loved fully by someone when it was forbidden. Her thoughts were interrupted by her sister calling her.

'Do you want a cup of tea? Tommy Handley's new show is starting. Let's hope the reception isn't so crackly tonight.'

The two sisters sat together laughing at the comedian's jokes, and for that half hour, all thoughts of war, Italian POWs and nasty mothers-in-law were forgotten.

When it finished, Sara told Menna she'd met Carlo in the village and introduced him to Aled.

'Oh, yes.' Menna raised an eyebrow. 'Just a coincidence, was it? Are you sure both of you didn't arrange it? Remember, nothing's changed as far as relationships are concerned.'

Sara felt her cheeks burn. 'He brought me a letter. Remember, you approve of us being penfriends?' She told her sister what was in Carlo's letter and what the new rules were for the prisoners. Then she paused, wondering if she should tell her the rest. 'We haven't been entirely truthful with you. When you spoke to us regarding the letters, we explained we were penfriends. It's more than that, Menna. I've fallen in love with him. I know he loves me too. It's agony not being able to be seen with him. Even now . . .'

'Sara, you're playing with fire. You must be so careful. Do you think I didn't know there was something going on? No wonder John Phillips was on to it. All moony-eyed every time you see each other.'

Had they been that obvious? Warmth spread from Sara's neck to her cheeks.

'I suppose there's nothing wrong with going for a walk and collecting berries, if that's all it will be. I'll look after Aled for you if you like. But I mean it, if you get caught . . .'

Sara hugged her sister. 'What would I do without you?'

Although she would be seeing Carlo tomorrow, Sara still wrote a letter back to him that night before turning off the light. It had become an important ritual where she could put her feelings down on paper without prying eyes and ears around.

CHAPTER SEVENTEEN

It was a lovely autumn morning when Sara left the house. Aled had been happy to stay with his aunt and cousin. Without a cloud in the sky, hues of red, orange, yellow and brown glowed on the trees in earlier-than-usual autumn glory. It had been a hot, dry summer and the September nights were now cold and frosty. She loved this time of year. The air was crisp, and she pulled her coat more tightly around her. Cycling out of the village, she was conscious of how lucky she was to live in such a beautiful part of the world. Apart from the restrictions of blackouts and rationing, the people of Radnorshire remained relatively untouched by the war in their day-to-day lives. She knew lots of families had lost loved ones in action — their lives would never be the same again. And then she thought of Carlo's mam, Lucia. If she had been killed, as Carlo feared, it would be the Allies and the Americans who had dropped the bombs. Her heart ached for the innocent civilians lost in the war against Nazism and fascism.

Carlo was waiting for her by the gates of the camp. She wanted to hug him but knew they might be seen. Instead, they politely greeted each other.

'*Buongiorno, mia cara.* Just put your bicycle by the fence. It will be safe there.'

'Hello. I'm so excited to see you,' whispered Sara.

He blew a kiss at her before handing her one of the two large enamel bowls he was carrying. Then, he took out a sketchbook from a cloth bag he carried in his other hand. 'Here is a list of the berries and the colours I need,' he explained. 'I've asked permission from Major Bamber to take you to the *cappella* after our walk. It will make much more sense to you then.'

They left the camp and walked to an area of grassland Sara recognised — she had played on it as a young girl. Tall hedges full of brambles edged one side. 'We should get loads of blackberries along here. Shall I keep my bowl for them and you put the hazelnuts and leaves in yours?'

From there, they followed a winding lane into Estyn Wood. A gate led onto a well-trodden pathway, and they spent the next hour collecting and foraging for whatever they could find. In the deepest part of the wood, where the density of the trees cast shadows on the ground, Carlo put down his bowl and bag and took Sara's from her. Without saying a word, he pulled her close and kissed her. His soft lips sent a surge of longing through every fibre of her body, but a noise startled them and they pulled apart.

Sara's heart was pounding. 'What was that?' A squirrel darted in front of them and disappeared into the undergrowth. They laughed as Sara put a hand to her chest. 'I was convinced we'd been caught!'

Carlo took her hand and brought it to his lips. 'It was worth the risk, though. *Ti amo.*'

Sara's stomach somersaulted at hearing him say those words. 'I love you, too. I'll wait for you for ever.'

They walked back through the woods and into the camp. No one was on guard and other POWs were freely walking in and out of the gates.

'*Ciao*, Carlo. *Una bellissima signorina*, eh?' called one.

'*Si, la mia amica.*'

The man laughed. '*Si, si, amica.*'

Sara knew the other man didn't believe she was just a friend. She was starting to learn a few Italian words from Carlo's letters.

Carlo opened the double doors of the little chapel. Inside, she could see much work had been done since what he'd previously described in his letters. The walls were lined with the empty cement bags to make them smooth and ready for the plasterboard. The altar was constructed from the empty ration boxes, which were lined with panels of wood, supporting an old wooden door that formed the altar table. Down each side, pillars were formed from cardboard tubes.

'What do you think?' he asked. 'Once we get the plaster, the underneath of the altar will look like marble, and these tubes will be filled with cement to make the columns. But these are what I'm impressed with.' Carlo held up two candelabra. 'Fredo cut these out of an old bully beef tin. Then Giacomo heated the metal and twisted them into these beautiful candle holders. He worked on it one Saturday afternoon when he didn't have to work on the farm. I'm so proud of all the men.'

'They're wonderful, Carlo. I can't believe what's been done already. What's going to happened to those panels of wood?' Sara pointed at the piles on the floor.

'They're going to line the bottom half of the walls and then be painted.'

Carlo came close to her, checking the door was closed. He pecked her on the cheek just as the door opened, then moved quickly away.

An older man, who was small in stature with wispy, white hair, entered the building. 'Ah, I thought I saw you come in here. Are you going to introduce me to this lovely *signorina*?'

'Gino, this is Sara Lewis. Her sister is Mrs Owens, who kindly got some of the building materials for us. I've got to know her as she works in the office near the building site. Sara, this is my friend, Padre Gino Cicchetti.'

'I'm pleased to meet you, *signorina*. Your sister has been a wonderful help. It will be no time at all before we can worship in our own *cappella*. This is the man who is responsible for leading the team.' He patted Carlo on the back. 'I came to see where you intend to paint your Madonna and Child.'

Carlo took out his prayer card. 'There, on the wall above the altar. I'm going to paint it directly onto the plasterboards once they arrive next week. I have the exact measurements, so I hope to copy those I've marked on the wall already. I'm going to try to make it a fresco, mixing in plaster with the paint. The only trouble I foresee is the colour blue for Mary's cloak. The rest we can colour with the berries Sara and I collected this morning.'

The priest listened intently, looking back at the prayer card Carlo was holding and then the space on the wall as if picturing the finished painting in his head. 'Ah. That's marvellous, Carlo. I can imagine it already. What do you think, Sara?'

'I agree.' She conjured up an image in her head. 'It's going to be wonderful. I can't wait to see how Carlo makes the colours from what we collected this morning.'

The priest smiled, patting Carlo on the back again, and Sara sensed the close bond between the two men. I'll leave you to it then. Goodbye, Carlo. Goodbye, Sara.'

* * *

When Sara arrived back, she could tell something had happened from the expression on her sister's face. Her eyes sparkled with excitement and she could hardly get her words out. 'You'll never guess!'

'Well, tell me then!' Sara waited.

Before she could, the two boys bounded into the kitchen.

'We're going to see Daddy!' announced Geraint.

Sara looked at her sister. 'But isn't he flying bombers over Sicily?'

As soon as she said it, and judging by the glare from her sister, she realised Geraint didn't know details of what his father did.

'Bombers, Mammy?'

'Big planes, *cariad.*'

All the little boy talked about was his father flying planes for the King and Mr Churchill. Menna obviously didn't want

94

him to know they were bombers. *If Carlo's mother was dead, please God don't let it be one of Gwilym's bombs that killed her*, Sara couldn't help herself thinking.

'His squadron has been given some leave, and he's booked a few days in Sussex near to his airbase for Geraint and me in two weeks' time. It's been so long, hasn't it, *bach*?' Geraint hugged his mam. 'You and Aled will be all right here on your own. You're in charge, okay, sister dear?'

Sara was thrilled for her sister. She was even more thrilled for herself. An image of Carlo's handsome face entered her head. Did she dare to invite him to the house?

CHAPTER EIGHTEEN

The next two weeks dragged for Sara, and she didn't tell anyone of her plans.

On the Friday before she and Geraint were to leave, Menna called them into the office before Nell left for the sawmill. 'Here are the arrangements for while we're away. We'll be back on Tuesday afternoon. For the first two working days of the week, Sara will open the office and deal with any queries from John Phillips. You, Nell, will be in charge at the sawmill in my absence.'

The Manchester girl was clearly delighted to step up to the role. She did a mock bow after Menna left. 'Who'd a thought it, eh, chucks? Yours truly as a boss.'

Sara and Peggy giggled with her.

Sara had slipped Carlo a letter when he'd been on his break. Although she wasn't doing anything illegal, John Phillips still picked on Carlo and criticised his work whenever he saw them talking together. The last thing Sara wanted was to draw attention to the two of them before the weekend.

From the office window, she'd watched his expression change as he read the letter. A wide smile spread across his face. He looked up at the window and blew a kiss.

* * *

Menna and Geraint left early on the Saturday morning, and Sara and Aled went to wave them off.

'Will Uncle Gwilym die like my daddy now?' asked Aled as the bus disappeared from view. 'My daddy came home on a holiday from the army and then he died when he went back.'

Sara knelt by her son. 'No, *cariad*. Your daddy died because of a terrible accident. Uncle Gwilym won't die.'

How could she say that? She knew RAF fighter pilots had an extremely high risk of dying. No one knew what was ahead of them. But what else should she say to her young son? *Yes, it's highly likely? That's why Mammy hears Auntie Menna crying every night after she's listened to the wireless reports of casualties in Europe.* Sara decided that sometimes a white lie was needed.

After lunch, she and Aled went for a walk to the playground. On the way there they saw Gwyneth Lewis coming out of the village shop.

Aled approached his grandmother and received a big hug from her. Much as Sara hated to admit it, despite her past behaviour, it was clear the woman genuinely loved her grandson. Against Menna's advice, Sara had given in and allowed him to be picked up by Bryn to go to the farm after school occasionally. Things between the two women had improved. Apart from a few outbursts and spats with Geraint, Aled had seemed happier, too.

'Hello, Gwyneth.'

'Sara.'

'Auntie Menna and Geraint have gone away to see his daddy,' the little boy said. 'He's not going to die like my daddy.'

Horrified, Sara watched the older woman's face harden. 'Oh, isn't he? Let's hope not. It's just you and your mammy in the house then.' She cast a knowing look at Sara.

* * *

Aled had tired himself out at the playground. After nearly falling asleep over his tea, Sara took him upstairs to the bedroom he shared with his cousin. When all was quiet, she went to her room and changed into her favourite dress. She knew the colour brought out the blue of her eyes that Carlo had commented on when they'd first met. There were butterflies in her stomach and, not for the first time, she wondered whether she was doing the right thing. *It's too late now, my girl. It's almost time.* She unpinned her hair from its roll and brushed it until it shone. Then she dabbed some Evening in Paris perfume from its midnight-blue bottle behind each ear, and, after a moment's hesitation, stroked some between her breasts before placing it back onto her dressing table. Excited anticipation ran through her veins.

The back door opened at exactly eight o'clock. She'd told Carlo not to knock or ring the bell for fear of waking Aled, and to lock the door behind him. 'Sara,' he whispered as he appeared at the doorway of the living room.

She jumped up from her seat and flung her arms around him. 'Let's close the door.'

Carlo took her face in his hands and stroked her cheek. 'We have your sister to thank for this moment. I cannot believe our luck.'

Sara led him by the hand to the settee. 'I hope I haven't ruined things for us. If we get caught—'

Before she could finish, his lips were on hers and his hands were gently caressing her. Then they broke apart.

'No one saw me. I was careful. As long as I am back in camp by ten o'clock, no one will know. Now, do not let us waste the time.'

Their kisses became more passionate. The desire Sara had experienced when they'd kissed in the woods became more intense.

'Shall we go upstairs?' she asked. 'We must be quiet.'

'Only if you are sure, *mia cara*.'

'Very sure. It's what I dream about every night. We don't know when we'll have another chance.'

But at the stairs, they heard Aled's voice. 'Mammy?'

Sara's heart pounded. 'Oh no!' she whispered. 'My room's the one on the left at the top of the stairs. Wait for me in there. I'll try to get him back to sleep.' She kissed Carlo on the cheek. 'Coming, *cariad*,' she called to Aled.

He was wide awake when she entered his room. 'I don't like it in here on my own. Can I have my lamp on?'

After lighting the lamp, she sat on the edge of his bed and stroked his hair. She began singing '*Suo Gân*', his favourite lullaby, hoping it would have the effect it always used to.

Within minutes, his eyelids became heavy and he drifted off to sleep again. She left the lamp on and continued singing as she left the room. She tried to suppress the visions in her head of her son relaying to Gwyneth Lewis that Mammy's friend was lying in her bed. She had to hope and pray Aled wouldn't wake again until morning.

Carlo held out his arms to her as she entered the room, and she lay down beside him, her heart hammering. With every caress, her need for him increased. As he planted gentle kisses along her cheekbone and on her neck, they didn't have to say a word. They read their feelings in each other's eyes. Slowly, they undressed one another. Their lovemaking was passionate yet tender — something Sara had not experienced before. It was exactly that — making love, *true* love. It surpassed the physical to another level. For a while afterwards, they lay with their bodies entwined, enjoying the silence.

Then Carlo turned to her. '*Ti amo*. Will you marry me, Sara?'

Sara's eyes filled with tears. 'I love you, too, so much. Yes, *si*. Once you are free to marry me, I will.'

He quickly looked away, breaking eye contact, and placed his hand on the crucifix resting on his chest. 'I think we must get dressed. I don't want to be out after curfew. A few of the others have been grounded.'

'And I don't want to tempt fate with Aled waking up.'

Before Carlo left, they clung together for one last kiss.

So much for staying friends, thought Sara. *Things have moved on so quickly, but isn't that what happens when you fall in love?*

After he'd left, Sara returned to the living room, reliving every moment of the time they'd spent together in the privacy of her sister's home. Menna knew of her feelings for Carlo, but Sara knew she wouldn't be happy to know they'd shared a bed in her house. Her sister must never find out.

But her thoughts were interrupted by loud voices and laughter. The noise came from the street in front of the house. There was a hammering on the door and more laughter. She opened it to see some men running away. Turning to go back inside, she froze. The words *ITALIAN WHORE* had been written in red paint on the door.

CHAPTER NINETEEN

'You won't be seeing that fancy Eyetie of yours today, then?'
John Phillips was waiting for Sara on the Monday morning.
'Beaten up good and proper by them Morgan boys.'

'I've no idea who or what you're talking about, Mr Phillips.
Now, if you don't mind, I must get to. Out of my way,
please.' But her pulse raced as she began to walk away. *Carlo!*

'The one you've been seeing and writing to. His face's a
right mess. Black and blue, Sergio What's-His-Name said.'
Smirking, Phillips shook his head. 'Well, if you don't abide
by the rules, what do you expect? Grounded for good now,
by all accounts. Serves the bugger right.'

'Thank you, Mr Phillips. Please return to the men. I
don't need your opinion on things.'

'We all know why that is,' the man muttered as he walked
away.

Sara felt dizzy. It had taken all her resolve not to react
in front of the foreman. It was her fault. Removing the paint
from the door on Saturday night had taken her hours, and
she'd had to settle Aled again too after he'd been woken up
by the noise. Now to find poor Carlo had been attacked by
the Morgan thugs was too much. But Menna had left her in
charge and she wouldn't let her down . . . even though she
probably already had.

Once inside the office, tears burned her eyes. She was rubbing them away with the heels of her hands when she heard Peggy and Nell come in.

'Sara . . . I don't know how to tell you this.' Peggy hesitated. 'Have you heard what happened to Carlo on Saturday night? By the time he got back to the camp, he was out of time for the curfew so we won't be seeing him today.'

'I know already. Phillips took great delight in telling me what had happened to him. The other POWs told him, apparently. I wanted to wipe that smirk off his face. Horrible man. But why would they do such a thing? What's Carlo done to them?'

Peggy and Nell looked at one another.

'Fallen for their mate's pretty young widow?' Nell muttered.

Sara began to cry. 'But Fred is dead. I can see who I like!'

But then she realised what she'd said — seeing Carlo the way they meant was forbidden. She wasn't free to love him. Talk to him, yes. But nothing more. She blushed as she remembered what had happened between them, hoping and praying that history would not repeat itself and nothing would come of their union.

'Sara, you haven't! What was Carlo doing in the village on his own, anyway? Oh, I can guess.' Nell handed her a handkerchief. 'Here, dry your eyes, chuck. You won't be seeing lover boy for a while, I'm afraid.'

Somebody must have known she'd be on her own at the house with Aled. Somebody who was friendly with the Morgan boys. Gwyneth Lewis's face floated into her mind. Hadn't she made a comment about them being on their own when Aled told her Menna and Geraint were going away? She *had* to get a letter to Carlo.

* * *

'Is it today Geraint's coming home, Mammy?' Aled couldn't wait for his big cousin to return.

'Yes, *cariad*. You'll see him later. I'll bring him up to the school at home time.'

Sara was dreading seeing Menna, but her sister and nephew were due in on the two o'clock train, so she slipped out of the office to go and meet them.

Menna beamed when she saw her waiting on the platform. 'This is a lovely surprise, isn't it, Geraint? Everything all right while I was away?'

Geraint ran on in front, and Sara decided she needed to take the opportunity to be honest. 'Please don't be angry at me. I know it was stupid. I invited Carlo to come to the house. He got beaten up by the Morgan boys on the way home. He was late for his curfew and—'

'Slow down, Sara. What on earth were you thinking of?' Menna's face had drained of colour and Sara couldn't bear to make eye contact with her. 'You knew you were taking a risk going for walks and talking to him. But I don't understand. How did the Morgan boys know he was at our house? Surely he didn't walk up to the house in full view? What a homecoming this is!'

'I'm sorry, Menna. It's horrible having to sneak around pretending. The worst thing is I think the old dragon may have been behind it.' Tears streamed down Sara's face. 'We saw her in the village on our way to the park. Aled let it slip it was only the two of us in the house. There was something about the way she looked at me.'

Menna sighed, handing Sara a handkerchief. 'Come on. Why would she think you'd get a man in as soon as my back was turned?'

'Don't you remember she accused me of cavorting with an Italian when I found Aled had gone home with Bryn? She must have heard rumours about the two us. From John Phillips, I suppose. I'm so sorry.' Sara paused, not daring to tell her sister what had been daubed in paint on her front door.

'I knew it was a bad thing letting her get her claws into your Aled again. The woman's bad news. I did warn you.'

Sara realised she hadn't even asked about their days away with Gwilym, but she also realised that neither she nor her sister were in the mood to discuss anything further, so they walked in silence back to the house.

* * *

Things remained cool between the two sisters for a while. If they hadn't been living in the same house and the little cousins hadn't been such good friends, Sara was sure the strained atmosphere between them could have been permanent. She'd apologised numerous times but had received clipped comments in return. Leaving to work in the office each morning was a welcome relief from the tense atmosphere at the house.

It was now a month to the day since she'd seen Carlo, and that particular afternoon she was finding it harder than usual to concentrate on her typing. *How much longer is he going to be grounded?* she wondered. The black rotary phone on her desk rang, interrupting her thoughts.

'Can you come into the house?' It was Menna.

She looked through the window and noticed an army vehicle outside. Hurrying out of the office and entering the house through the front door, Sara took a deep breath. She walked through to the living room.

'Sara, I think you know Major Bamber.' Menna's face was serious and she didn't make eye contact with her sister.

He stood and shook her hand. 'Good to see you again, Mrs Lewis.'

'And you, Major.'

'I was telling your sister here of the unfortunate incident involving Signor Rosso. He was attacked after coming into Dolwen, as he is entitled to do since the capitulation. He struggled back to camp with his injuries. He didn't get back until after ten o'clock, meaning he broke curfew.'

Sara didn't look in her sister's direction.

'He won't tell us why he was in Dolwen on his own, or why these local boys should want to attack him. As you know, he is the gentlest of men, so it's a complete mystery. He is not a rule-breaker, but we have to be seen to show what happens when the prisoners do not keep to the rules. If Rosso is not grounded, others will think they can break the rules, too.'

She went to protest, but she saw Menna shake her head. 'The major has come to tell us about the opening of the chapel, Sara.'

'Yes, I was telling your sister here that thanks to you at Owens' Building and Timber Merchants, and the men spending some of their newly earned money on materials, the chapel is going to be ready sooner than we'd expected. Every one of the men involved has worked extremely hard, using their skills to transform a dilapidated corrugated-iron hut into place of beauty. All that needs to be done now are the frescoes on the walls and hanging the altar curtains we've been promised by your good self, Mrs Owens. Of course, with all this time on his hands, Signor Rosso is able to work on a painting for over the altar.'

Sara knew every detail of the painting on his prayer card that meant so much to him.

'Apart from feeling so battered and bruised, he has at least had some good news to cheer him up since the weekend. He's received a letter from his mother. She's safe and well. It turns out she spent much of her time in underground tunnels to shelter from the bombing, which, of course, has now stopped.'

'Oh, that's wonderful news. He must be so relieved.' Sara tried to picture Carlo reading his mother's letter. She was grateful to Major Bamber for the information, of course, but she wished it could have been Carlo telling her. She knew how much it would have meant to him.

Major Bamber reached into a canvas bag and drew out some leaflets. 'You will get a formal invitation, but I wonder if you could get these invites to the opening of the chapel delivered to all houses in the village? It's in four weeks' time. The camp has been based outside of the village for so long now, and I know there was considerable resentment to start with. Very understandable, of course, as when the Italian prisoners were captured, they were fighting for a fascist dictator. However, I'm proud of the way the men have won the local people round, especially the farmers who wouldn't have survived with so many of their workers at the front. It's our way of saying thank you. And who knows? After all the hard work — and dare I say, love — that's gone into the chapel, perhaps it won't be knocked down as some have been in other camps. Thank you again, ladies. I'll see myself out.'

Sara breathed a sigh of relief. It seemed breaking curfew was all Carlo was being punished for — it could have been so much worse if Major Bamber had known about her involvement.

CHAPTER TWENTY

'Is that Carlo's painting?' whispered Menna. 'It's wonderful.'

Sara's eyes were glued to the fresco of the Madonna and Child above the altar. The colours were warm and appeared to glow against the white of the semi-circular back wall of the hut. After all Carlo's concern about getting the blue of the Madonna's cloak right, it was perfect. In contrast to the warmth of the rest of the clothing, it gave Mary a beautiful, cool serenity as she gazed with love on the child's face.

It was the day of the opening of the chapel. Intermittent showers had made everywhere wet underfoot, but it was dry for the walk from the village. Sara had not seen Carlo since the night he'd come to the house, but they'd exchanged letters with Sergio acting as go-between. As well as expressing his love, he also kept Sara up to date with what was happening in the chapel. In her mind's eye, she had tried picturing it, but when she and Menna entered the *cappella* that morning, accompanied by Aled and Geraint, she was in awe. A young soldier led the way to the seats reserved for them.

There were gasps of admiration as more people arrived. At the entrance, Catholics dipped their fingers into the holy water in the stoup made from an old tyre before crossing themselves. Other churchgoing villagers bowed before the altar before finding their seats. Others knelt in prayer. Even though Sara's attendance at church had lapsed, and she had often questioned her faith in the last few years, being in the little chapel made her want to pray, too. She knelt on the narrow board acting as a kneeler that ran in front of the row of chairs, bowing her head. Aled saw what she was doing and followed suit. Whereas she fixed her eyes on the figure of Mary in the painting above the altar, Aled closed his eyes and placed his hands together as he'd been taught to do in Sunday school. As Sara knelt in quiet contemplation, she came to the conclusion that the POWs had finished the chapel in the name of peace. It was now what Sara prayed for as well — that the war would be over soon. She sat back on her seat, taking in every detail of the transformed building.

Giacomo's intricate candelabra, which Carlo had shown her, stood either side of the altar table and supported three candles each. The old wooden door acting as the altar was now varnished and covered in a delicately crocheted altar cloth donated by the headmaster's wife, Mrs Thomas. In his letter, Carlo had told her how builder Sergio had cut a thin paintbrush down to a few hairs in order to paint the grey veins over the white plaster covering to resemble marble. He'd used a clear varnish to seal it and give the pillars the authentic sheen. No one would ever know the supporting pillars were not real marble. Rich blue velvet curtains that had once adorned Menna's sitting room now hung either side of the altar on the back wall.

The buzz of admiration increased as the seats filled up. People pointed when they spotted something that impressed them, heads turned and there were more audible gasps. Menna leaned over the head of Aled to speak to her sister. 'How on earth did they get up there to paint that?'

Sara looked up. The curved ceiling had been divided into sections edged with plaster-relief scrolls. In each section was a painting of biblical characters and angels. She started to say, 'I'll ask Carlo,' then realised she might not even get to talk to him that day.

A hush descended on the chapel before Padre Gino's voice travelled from the back of the building. 'Will everyone please stand?'

He and Major Bamber moved to the chancel and stood by two of the chairs placed behind the intricate metal screen while the Italian men filed into the front few rows. Sara strained to see Carlo but soon realised he wasn't among them. She clenched her fists. Surely he was not going to be punished further by not being allowed to attend the opening of the project that was mainly down to him? She wanted to stand and demand an explanation. She knew she wouldn't, she knew she shouldn't, but she couldn't help wondering why the rest of the men hadn't refused to attend if Carlo wasn't there. It didn't make sense, and he'd mentioned nothing in his letters. Her eyes stung with angry tears. But then Aled looked up at her, so she blinked the tears away and composed herself.

Major Bamber rose from his seat and moved to the front of the chancel to speak. 'Ladies and gentlemen, boys and girls. It's wonderful to see so many of you here today. I'm sure when Greenfield Camp opened, many of you would have been apprehensive, angry even, that men who'd once fought against us should live in your village. Many of you would have already lost loved ones in this tragic war. The fact this wonderful new chapel is today full to capacity is, I hope, testament to the fact that the men seated here have helped your community by working on your farms and alleviating the workforce shortage. Many of you have welcomed them into your families, and now that Italy is no longer at war with the Allies, you see them in the village more often.'

Sara wished she could turn the clock back. If she had only been patient and happy to see Carlo in public within the rules, he would be there with the others.

'Many will hopefully be returning to their families and loved ones back in Italy soon, so you may wonder why the men wanted to finish what they'd started so near to leaving. Without exception, they wanted to finally have a place of their own to worship in and pray for peace, especially between our two nations. I think you'll agree they have created a most beautiful place.'

Without prompt, one by one the congregation stood and applauded, and Major Bamber waited for everyone to sit down before speaking again. 'Everyone seated in the front rows has played a part. They've contributed their time and, more recently, their own money to a cause they believe in. I'd like to mention a few men in particular. Giacomo Ferraro, for this wonderful screen along these steps and the candelabra. All made from empty bully beef tins. Sergio Perico for cleverly tricking us into thinking we had an endless supply of marble for the altar, the base of the lectern and the bowl containing the holy water.'

Sara clenched her fists harder, her nails digging into her palms until they hurt.

'However, there is one person who has made this all possible. His nickname is *l'Artista*. That is because back in Italy, he worked as an apprentice artist. He transformed this old Nissen hut from a dilapidated and rat-infested shell into what you see today.' Major Bamber turned to the back wall and then pointed up to the frescoes on the ceiling and then the wall paintings.

Sara's throat tightened. She looked across at her sister, who smiled at her. They hadn't left Carlo out of the celebrations after all!

'This man is responsible for the amazing artwork and leading the team of men. Please give a round of applause for Carlo Rosso.'

The POWs turned towards the back doors, clapping and chanting '*L'Artista, L'Artista.*' The rest of the congregation followed suit, filling the chapel with applause. Carlo appeared and walked the full length of the aisle with a wide grin on his face. When he passed Sara, he winked.

'Mammy, that's your friend.' Aled's voice echoed in the chapel.

'Shh!' She put a finger to her lips but couldn't help smiling at her little boy.

Carlo stepped into the chancel and, before taking his seat, turned and spoke to everyone in the congregation. '*Grazie mille*. You are all so kind. I could not have done it without the help of these comrades in front of me. Sisto Conti has become a good friend. He was the one who believed we could do it. He kept us going with his singing, as he told us he does not have a practical bone in his body.' They all laughed. Turning to the men behind him, Carlo continued. 'I was captured with Padre Gino in North Africa and we ended up being interned in the same camp here in Pont Ithon. It was he and Major Bamber who came up with the idea. There would be no money from the army authorities. We had to use whatever scrap or disused materials we could. The ideas that came from the team still amaze me. So, *grazie*. I hope you all like what we have created in your lovely village.'

Sara's cheeks were wet with tears as she fumbled in her pocket for a handkerchief.

'Why are you sad, Mammy?'

She placed an arm around her son. 'I'm not sad, *cariad*. They're happy tears.'

As Carlo sat back in his seat, he received more applause, and then Padre Gino came to the front of the chancel area. '*Grazie*, Carlo. As Major Bamber explained, this is not a religious service today. It's more of a celebration to say thank you to the people of Pont Ithon and Dolwen. However, as the chapel is now used for worship by the inhabitants of the camp, I'd like to invite those of you who would like to, to join us in prayer.

'Lord Jesus, Prince of Peace,' he began. 'Free us from conflict, bring unity to our troubled nations, eliminate all violence and war. Glorious Virgin Mary, and every angel and saint. Pray for peace. Pray for us all. Jesus, hear our prayers. Amen.'

It was obvious from the combined response at the end of the prayer that many people had joined in with the *padre*.

* * *

Watery, winter sunshine greeted them as they left the chapel. Major Bamber had invited the congregation to stop and talk about the chapel, and she noticed Carlo coming over to join them.

'The chapel is beautiful, Carlo. I can't believe what you and the others have done. I'm so pleased we were all allowed to see it.' Menna was polite but Sara noticed her sister wasn't smiling as she spoke. She wondered if Menna would ever really forgive her and Carlo.

Sara didn't say a word. All she wanted to do was hug the man she loved, who was standing so close yet so far away. Her insides tumbled over and over. Then he looked at her and their hands brushed, causing electricity to rush through her.

'I saw that,' muttered Menna. 'For God's sake, don't risk anything.'

CHAPTER TWENTY-ONE

Sara didn't receive a letter until the Saturday after the opening of the chapel. The office extension was now finished
and the Italian builders had been moved to another project.
Instead of Sergio Perico bringing the letter for her, it was
someone who introduced himself as Carlo's best friend, Sisto,
who knocked on the door of the house.

Sara wasn't sure if she should ask him in, but instead
went with him over to the bench in the yard where she and
Carlo used to leave their letters.

'He's told me everything. He is so afraid to spoil things
for the two of you now. It could have so easily been me and
Ceridwen. I know Carlo has told you about us in his letters.
It's just it's easier to find secret places for us to be in love at
the farm than in a village with many eyes watching.'

Sara took the letter. 'Thank you. I'm pleased he has a good
friend to share his feelings with. I will wait for ever, you know?'

'He knows that. The good news is the camp authorities
have said he can mix with local people again. So, at least you'll
be able to meet. I have told him the four of us must look out
for each other.' Sisto smiled at her. 'I go now. *Arrivederci.*'

Sara watched him walk across the yard and out into the
street. She held the envelope to her chest. The weight of

worry and sadness lifted from her, and she went back into the house and the privacy of her bedroom.

Cara Sara,

It is very good to see you and your family also at the cappella. It is a long time since we see each other. It makes me long to touch you more than ever. The beating, I do not mind because I make love to you. I relive it every night.

I have good news. There is a date when the POWs leave the camp. It is still a very long time but now they have the date. They are very happy. They will leave Dolwen on 8 September next year. This is one year since Italy capitulated. We are free men for one year at that date. Still, I cannot have you as my lover, only my friend. They are first to go to a camp on the east coast. They help with the harvests until arrangements for them to get to Italy safely. The men, they are very excited. They count the days. Many of them leave the babies. They will be boys and girls now. They do not remember their fathers.

I do not go. In her letters, Mamma says it is not safe yet. Perhaps one day. I tell Major Bamber I stay as caretaker of the camp. There is still work to do there and I look after the chapel. It makes me very sad if it is demolished. Major Bamber, Padre Gino and the local priest talk so that it remains as a chapel for the people that live here.

The best news is I meet you again. I hope Sisto explains that we meet, four of us. That way, no one thinks we are more than friends. I have told you that Sisto and Ceridwen are in love, too. They marry once they are allowed like us.

You come to the end of the lane to Ceridwen's farm at eleven o'clock next Saturday, per favore.

I count the days, the hours, too, mia cara.

Ti amo. Carlo

Marvelling at how much Carlo's written English was improving, Sara lay back against her pillow. Her insides cartwheeled at the prospect of seeing him again.

* * *

Over the next ten months, letters were exchanged and meetings arranged.

'Be careful,' Menna always warned her. 'You know I don't mind looking after the boys, but I worry that you'll get caught.'

Sara thought back to the night Carlo had asked her to marry him and the risk she'd taken by inviting him into Menna's house. 'The farm's really isolated. And we won't risk being found out. I promise.' She hugged her sister.

If anyone saw them in their secret hiding places on Ceridwen's farm, they didn't get to know about it.

One Saturday, the four friends parted company once they were well away from the farmhouse as they always did. Sara and Carlo walked to the stone outhouse that had become their secret place. They shut the wooden doors behind them and, although Carlo pulled her into his arms and they kissed, Sara sensed something was bothering him.

'What's wrong?'

Carlo was still the caretaker at Greenfield Camp and the date of the prisoners' departure loomed. 8 September 1944. After that, it would just be Carlo, Padre Gino and Major Bamber left living there. Sara wondered if his troubled look was something to do with that.

'I feel sad, Sara. The men, they go next week in time to start working on the harvest on the farms in Yorkshire at the end of September before they travel to Italy. They are my friends for all this time and I do not see them again.'

Sara squeezed his hand. 'Just think. Imagine all those wives, mothers, sisters and children welcoming them home. It's got to be good news for them.' She smiled at him. 'And it's one step nearer to our wedding.'

Carlo smiled back at her. 'I know it. And I am happy, too. Also, I have got a job! Starting in three weeks.'

Sara felt her eyes light up. She'd worried about how they'd be able to find somewhere to rent after they got married on just her wages. 'Where?'

'It is not far. I work for Griffiths the Builders in Pen Craig, and Signor Griffiths, he told me some rooms are going for rent over the garage next door to the builders' yard.'

She tried to match Carlo's enthusiasm, but she couldn't help biting her lip and imagining what she'd tell her son. 'That's great news,' she said finally. 'But is it fair to take Aled away from all his friends at the school at Dolwen?'

'Aled won't have to move schools. You'll be going to Dolwen every day for your job at Menna's.'

She nodded, relieved, and a warm feeling that told her everything would be all right surged through her.

'We had better start planning our special day.' Carlo pulled her into his arms.

'I don't want to get married in Dolwen,' said Sara. 'I'd prefer it if Gwyneth Lewis didn't even know. I'm not going to tell Aled until the last minute. He keeps asking to spend more time at the farm, you know?'

Carlo held her shoulders and looked directly into her eyes. 'You have to stop this, Sara. How can this woman have this much hold over you after all this time? Perhaps we could always — how do you say — elope?' He must have noticed her expression change. 'I am joking.'

But perhaps that's a good idea? Sara thought. *Only a couple of witnesses. No one else there.*

Instead, she said, 'We can't set a date yet, anyway. You know that. All we can do is wait for government permission. But I don't want anything to spoil our wedding when it eventually happens. You only do it once . . . unless you're a widow like me, of course. It's going to be perfect.'

She closed her eyes as Carlo kissed her, so she didn't see the expression on his face change.

CHAPTER TWENTY-TWO

8 May 1946

Sara opened her eyes as dawn sunshine streamed into her bedroom. It was the day she and Carlo had waited so patiently for. That night, they'd be moving into Deri Cottage as a married couple — the cottage in Dolwen Carlo had renovated after moving out of his rooms over the garage.

She looked over at the rose-pink costume, with its pinched-in waist and peplum, hanging on the door of the wardrobe. Menna had shared her clothing ration coupons with her and taken her to Credenford to choose it. She couldn't wait to see what Carlo's reaction would be when he saw her wearing it as his bride.

'Tea and toast for the soon-to-be Mrs Rosso.' Menna knocked on the door and came into the bedroom with a tray laid with her best bone china and a single red rose in a tall, narrow vase. She smiled as she placed it on the chest of drawers. 'Once you've had your bath, I'll come and roll your hair and help you with your make-up. You'll be the height of fashion.'

Sara looked at the deep-pink lipstick, new powder compact and small block of rouge laid out on the dressing table

— a treat from her sister. She went over to hug her. 'I can't thank you enough, Menna. Our mam may not want anything to do with me, but having you as my sister more than makes up for it.'

'Don't get all soppy or my powder will run. I'm ready, so I can help you. Now, drink your tea and make sure you eat the toast. It'll be a long time until we eat again. It's a beautiful spring day out there. Remember, it was raining in the morning last year.'

As Sara sipped her tea, she thought back to the day when they'd all learned that war in Europe had ended.

'It's almost three o'clock. Time for Winnie's speech,' Menna had called.

The end of hostilities with Germany had been declared the day before, and Mr Churchill had been about to address the nation. Sara remembered standing in the doorway watching Menna, Geraint and Aled huddled over the walnut box that had kept them in touch with what was happening in the world since war had been declared six years before.

Dong! Dong! Dong! The familiar sound of Big Ben announced the time, and without warning, hot tears had burned along her eyelids. An image of Gwyneth Lewis and others like her had entered her mind. It must have been so bittersweet for them to see the town's young men arriving home in their demob suits, hair smartly Brylcreemed, and grinning as they were reunited with their loved ones. But Fred and other sons were never coming home.

She remembered composing herself and going to sit by Aled in front of the wireless to listen to the distinctive voice of the prime minister. Every word of his speech was embedded in her mind.

'Hostilities will end officially at one minute after midnight tonight, but in the interests of saving lives, the ceasefire began yesterday to be sounded all along all the Front, and our dear Channel Islands are also to be freed today . . . The German war is therefore at an end . . . Advance Britannia. Long live the cause of freedom. God save the King.'

'When's Daddy coming home?' Geraint asked.

'Soon, *cariad*.' Menna reassured him. 'He's in Burma now, but he'll know war in Europe is over. He'll be happy, too.'

Sara also remembered the excitement when her brother-in-law, who was going to give her away later, had arrived home safely from the Far East.

Breaking out of her memories, she checked on the time and ran her bath. True to her word, Menna returned and helped her get ready. Last to go on was her hat with its fine veil just covering her eyes. It was the identical shade to her costume.

'You look beautiful, *cariad*.' Menna's eyes shone. 'Gwilym's ready in the car with the engine running. You sit in the back with Aled and Geraint.'

As they got closer to the register office in Pen Craig, Sara's heart raced. She noticed Sisto at the top of the steps and then saw him rush in through the doors, no doubt to tell the groom his bride had arrived.

When they'd stopped the car, Menna and the boys went inside, leaving her with Gwilym.

'You look beautiful, my dear.' Her brother-in-law's admiration was clear to see. 'You deserve to be happy.'

* * *

She could see tears in Carlo's eyes as he gazed at her. Standing next to Sisto, his best friend and best man, in their smartly pressed suits and white shirts, her soon-to-be husband had never looked so handsome. Sara handed her bouquet of cream roses to Ceridwen, who was acting as bridesmaid. The people who meant most to her and Carlo were all there to witness their marriage. Aled had pride of place, sitting next to his big cousin in the front row.

When they'd been planning the wedding in a register office, Sara had worried it wouldn't be enough for Carlo. They wouldn't be married in the eyes of the Catholic church.

But watching her husband listen to every word spoken, she had no doubts it was as special to him as it was to her.

'And now I pronounce you man and wife. You may kiss the bride.' The registrar smiled at them.

She knew then that she would do anything to be a good wife to the man she loved.

* * *

The wedding breakfast was held at the village hall in Dolwen. Nell and Peggy had decorated the room with the bunting left over from the VE Day parties, and friends had pooled their food coupons together to supply the sandwiches and cakes. Sara smiled when she saw the large, elaborate wedding cake placed on a square table in the corner. No one would guess how small the fruit cake was hidden inside the cardboard cover she and Menna had decorated with plaster and painted to look like a professionally iced wedding cake. They'd sworn Aled and Geraint to secrecy.

Once the celebrations were over, and after Sisto announced the married couple were leaving, the wedding party congregated outside to see them off. Sara hugged Aled who was staying with Menna for the night.

'Come here, *cariad*. You be a good boy for Auntie Menna and Mammy'll see you tomorrow.'

Aled nodded then ran back to Geraint's side, more interested in the state of the car parked outside. The car, borrowed from Gwilym, had been decorated with "Just Married" signs and the old shoes and tin cans tied to the bumper made a racket as they drove away.

'Happy?' Carlo squeezed Sara's hand.

Sara's eyes misted. 'Very. We've waited so long for this day, haven't we? We can now legally be together. For ever, I hope.'

Carlo was silent until they pulled up alongside their cottage and were walking to the front door. 'And now, Signora Rosso, I carry you over the . . . how do you say, doorstep?'

Sara laughed. 'We say threshold.'

Carlo unlocked the door before scooping her up into his arms. He carried her into the living room and they fell, laughing, onto the settee. He took her face in his hands and looked deep into her eyes. '*Ti amo, cara* Sara.'

'I love you, too, Carlo. So much and for ever.'

He took her hand and led her upstairs where they made love for the first time as man and wife. For Sara, it took on a special meaning. It was what they had both dreamed about for so long. No one could spoil their happiness.

Later that evening, Sara and Carlo sat together and talked about the day.

'I wish your mamma could have been here. Especially as you're her only son. You'll have to take me to Sicily to meet her. A belated honeymoon, perhaps?'

'Maybe.' Carlo fidgeted, then changed the subject. 'Can you remember what this place was like when I moved in a year ago?'

'Yes, it was horrible, but you've transformed it into a lovely home for us and Aled. He's going to love his bedroom. You even spent VE Day painting while Menna and I took the boys to the party on the village green — I couldn't believe that!'

Like all towns and villages, Dolwen had come alive with street parties and a village dance to celebrate. Sara hadn't seen Carlo that day. He'd kept a low profile out of respect for the villagers who had lost loved ones. The early morning rain had cleared. Union flags and homemade bunting hung from the trees, and music blared from gramophones. Villagers had pooled their ration coupons, which they'd saved up in order to provide the party food and drink displayed on the trestle tables. Aled and Geraint stayed up until it was dark, late enough to see a bonfire lit as a beacon on the hill overlooking Dolwen.

'It was only right I stayed away but I remember standing outside in the garden when it got dark and seeing the beacons lighting up the sky.' Carlo kissed the top of Sara's head. 'A symbol of no more war . . . at least in Europe, anyway.'

For a while, the two newlyweds sat in silence, alone with their thoughts.

Sara felt Carlo's body tense beside her. She dismissed a brief feeling of unease as she wondered what life with her new husband held for them both and her son.

CHAPTER TWENTY-THREE

Claudia
25 March 1968, Cardiff

'Claudia, wake up!'

The panic in Linda's voice was accompanied by hammering on the bedroom door. Claudia Rosso sat up too quickly and stumbled out of bed, her head pounding. It seemed she'd only just arrived home from a night of dancing at the Top Rank, and her clothes were still strewn all over the floor where she'd stepped out of them when she'd got back. Linda was a friend she'd met at art college, and they shared a flat in a street of converted bay-windowed terraced houses close to where she worked in a small art gallery.

She opened her door. 'Whatever's wrong? You do know what time it is, don't you?' But the worried look on her flatmate's face told her something was up.

'Your auntie's on the phone. Auntie Menna, isn't it?'

'Auntie Menna? Why?' She hurried into the hall they shared with the other tenants and grabbed the communal phone. 'Auntie. What's happened? Is it Mam? Papà? Are they all right?'

'*Cariad*, I'm afraid it's your papà. He's been seriously injured at work. An explosion. It looks like he cut through a gas pipe. He's in Pen Craig Hospital, and he's too poorly to be moved to Credenford. Your mam's with him.' Her aunt's soft voice with its gentle lilt, more pronounced on the telephone, was soothing, willing Claudia to stay calm, but she couldn't.

'Not Papà!'

'I think you should get home, *cariad*.' Menna sounded close to breaking down.

'I'm on my way.' Claudia looked at a concerned Linda who was hovering nearby and tried to stop herself from bursting into tears. 'My father's had an accident. He's in hospital. It's serious, Lin. I've got to go.'

'Yes, go. Quick. I'll ring Mrs Davies at Oriel Elinor to tell her you won't coming into work.'

Claudia rushed around the flat grabbing what she'd need. Once she'd packed all her essentials into a small bag, she dashed out through the door.

'Let me know how he is,' Linda called after her.

* * *

The bus journey from Cardiff took for ever. As they left the South Wales valleys with their rows of grey, terraced housing, they climbed through the spectacular mountainous scenery of the Brecon Beacons, before finally arriving among the beautiful green landscape of Mid-Wales. All Claudia could think of was the man she worshipped. The biggest influence in her life. *I can't lose you, Papà*. Not only did she resemble him with her olive skin, wavy black hair and brown eyes, she'd followed him into the art world, too. Before the last war, he'd been an artist. During his time as a prisoner of war at the camp just outside the village, he'd been responsible for helping to create a magnificent Italian chapel.

He was also the one who'd taught her to paint. An image of her father at her graduation day the year before came into Claudia's head. She remembered his proud smile, and her eyes burned, tears trickling down her cheeks. *Stop it, Claudia. You're acting as if your papà is dead.* Reproaching herself, she went over Auntie Menna's words — *seriously injured, too poorly to be moved . . . What if I'm too late?* She wanted to scream at the bus driver to drive faster. She tried to stifle a sob, but a flood of tears caused the other passengers to look in her direction.

An older man, who'd got on the bus at the previous stop came to sit by her, offering a clean white handkerchief. 'Here you are, *bach*. You're Carlo Rosso's girl, aren't you? I thought I recognised you. Terrible business. I heard on my way to work this morning. He didn't deserve that.'

'Thank you. My aunt rang. All I know is he's seriously injured and can't be moved.'

'Yeah. That's it.' He looked away, clearly not wanting to make eye contact with her. 'And to think it happened in the same building he helped construct when he was a POW.'

Claudia remembered her mam saying in her last letter that Auntie Menna and Uncle Gwilym's business wasn't doing well. They were having to make the big office into a bungalow to rent out. They'd asked Papà to do the conversion.

She handed the handkerchief back to the man. 'I'm sorry. I don't know your name, Mr . . . ?'

'Parry. Jack Parry. Know your father well.'

At last, the bus pulled into Pen Craig, with its large, familiar Victorian houses lining the main street alongside the Memorial Hospital. Rushing up the incline to the main doors, Claudia's heart raced, unsure of what she'd find.

'Carlo Rosso. I think he's here. I'm his daughter.' Out of breath, she could hardly speak to the nurse in Reception.

'Ah, yes. I'll see what's happening. Would you please take a seat?'

No, she wanted to scream. *I want to see my papà.* Through the blur of her tears, she saw her mother rushing towards her with open arms.

'*Cariad.*' Her voice was scratchy. 'They say you can see him, but I warn you he's extremely poorly. I think he's been waiting for you to come.' Enveloped in a tight *cwtch*, Claudia felt her mother's body convulse into violent sobs.

'I came as quickly as I could, Mam. We can't lose him, we can't,' she whispered.

Her mother took her hand and they found the side room next to the nurses' station. 'He's in here, *cariad*. Just prepare yourself.' Sara opened the door and let go of her daughter's hand.

With faltering steps, Claudia entered and approached her papà. Then she gasped, holding on to the metal frame at the end of the bed. The bandages around her father's head were encrusted with dried blood, and his face was as white as the cotton pillows he was lying on. The beeping from the machines to which he was wired pierced the air. His eyes were closed.

Her mother went to sit beside her husband. 'Your girl's here, Carlo. Claudia's come to see you.' Papà's eyes flickered. 'Come and sit the other side of him. You can hold his hand and talk to him. The doctors say it's good for him to hear our voices. It's the last . . .'

Her mother didn't finish her sentence. Claudia knew what she was going to say. *Hearing is the last sense to go.* Her papà was going to die.

She picked up his hand, stroking the skin calloused from manual work but with the long, slim fingers of a fine artist. 'I'm here, Papà. You *have* to get better. I want you to see the paintings I'm going to have on display in the gallery.'

His eyes flickered and he gave Claudia's hand a gentle squeeze.

'See, Mam. He knows I'm here. He'll come out of this. I know he will.'

Her mother's eyes filled with tears as she stood up and left the room.

Her father squeezed Claudia's hand again and moved his head towards her. He tried to talk, but it was almost inaudible.

'What is it, Papà?'

'Giulietta . . . Pia . . .'

'Giulietta? Pia? What do you mean? Are they people? Tell me, Papà. I don't understand.'

Becoming more restless, he moved his head from side to side. 'Map . . .'

Claudia heard a knock on the door. A young doctor, accompanied by the nurse she'd first spoken to, had come to examine her father. 'I'll just be outside, Papà,' Claudia whispered as she went to join her mother in the corridor.

'I'm sorry, *cariad*. I'm afraid we must prepare ourselves for the worst. His injuries are very severe, the doctors say.' Sara wrung her hands, her knuckles white.

'No! He's been trying to talk to me. He's going to get better. I know he is.' Shaking her head, Claudia sobbed while her mother wrapped an arm around her.

'No, Claudia. Much as we all want that, he's fading. I've called Father O'Connor to come and give your papà the last rites. You know how important your papà's faith was to him.'

'*Is*, Mam. Not *was*.' Claudia still would not accept her father was going to die.

The doctor came out of the side room and invited Claudia and her mother into a quiet area in the empty waiting room. 'I'm afraid Mr Rosso's body is shutting down. Is there anyone else who would like to say goodbye?'

'No! He can't die!' Claudia shouted.

'Shh, *cariad*.' Her mother patted her hand. 'No, Doctor. We're all the family he has. The priest is on his way.'

'That's fine, Mrs Rosso. I'll get the nurse to prepare the room for him. I think I can see Father O'Connor coming now.'

Claudia had neglected her churchgoing since she'd left home to go to college. If she was honest with herself, she only visited the Italian chapel in the village to admire her father's paintings and to marvel at the ingenuity of the men who'd built and created it. But now, as she knelt by her father's bedside listening to Father O'Connor's prayers, she prayed harder than she'd ever prayed before for God not to let him die.

'Thank you, Father,' her mother said once he'd finished. 'That would have meant so much to Carlo. He was a good man.' Her voice cracked. She led the priest outside, leaving Claudia to sit with her father.

Her papà was in a deep sleep now, breathing softly. *Perhaps I should accept this sleep is a sign his life is coming to an end,* thought Claudia. But she still couldn't quite bring herself to. His breathing changed as her mother came back to her side.

'It won't be long now, *cariad.*' Sara squeezed Claudia's hand.

There was the tell-tale sound of the death rattle as her papà took his last breath.

Claudia's mam hugged her, her shoulders shuddering, her head hanging down and hiding silent tears. 'It's over.'

But Claudia talked to her father as if he could still hear her. 'Don't leave us, Papà. What are we going to do without you? I want you to keep helping me with my paintings. Please, Papà. Please!' She slumped down so her head was on the bed next to him, her whole body racked with sobs.

'Shh, *cariad.* He's gone.' Her mam pulled her up into her arms.

In silence, they held each other, gazing at the man who'd meant so much to them.

It seemed too soon before a kind nurse came to take them outside so they could prepare to move the body. Mother and daughter were locked in grief. Both distraught, both heartbroken.

Despite her anguish, Claudia was resolute. 'I'll look after you, Mam. I promise.'

CHAPTER TWENTY-FOUR

The steel-grey sky was dotted with powder-puff clouds, behind which a pale lemon sun seemed determined to lighten the mood of the day. Claudia thought back to what Father O'Connor had advised when they'd planned the funeral Mass at the Italian chapel. The service should give thanks for the life of a lovely man, and Claudia was determined to do just that. He may not have had a long life, but he'd had a good life and had made her and her mam very happy.

Sara had asked Auntie Menna and Uncle Gwilym to accompany them, and the four of them were now congregated in the kitchen. They'd both been distraught that the accident had happened on their property and were determined to help support Sara and Claudia through it. Geraint would meet them at the church with the other mourners, but Claudia already knew Aled would not show his face.

Menna looked at the wall clock. 'It's eleven thirty. We should be going.'

As they walked into the hallway, Claudia's eyes welled with tears. She took a deep breath then exhaled through her mouth, counting to ten.

'Aww, come here, *cariad.* I know this is hard. But we've got each other, haven't we?' Sara drew her daughter into a tight *cwtch*.

The sleek black mourners' car was waiting behind the hearse outside the house to take them to the chapel.

'I expected you to have red roses, Sara. Red roses for love.'

Mam shook her head at Auntie Menna's comment. 'No, according to Carlo, red carnations are Sicily's national flowers. He always bought me red carnations for my birthday, for Valentine's Day, for Mothering Sunday . . . any day.' She dabbed her eyes with a neatly folded handkerchief.

Seeing her papà's mahogany casket with the large wreath of red carnations on top, Claudia sucked in another deep breath, determined to be strong for her family. 'Come on. Let's go, Mam.'

Once they were seated in the mourners' car, Claudia grabbed her mother's hand and didn't let go until the chauffeur opened the door for them to walk the short distance to the chapel. It was as if an invisible thread from each of their hearts was linking them in love for the man they had lost.

* * *

The tiny house was surprisingly full of people after the service. Claudia hoped there'd be enough food. "Low-key," her mam had said, seemingly still believing there were some bearing a grudge against the POWs who'd stayed after the war and married local girls. Claudia smiled. *You were wrong, Mam. Papà was liked and respected.*

Her thoughts were interrupted by Auntie Menna. 'You're doing so well, *cariad.* It's sad that your first funeral had to be your papà's. He'd have been proud of you. You look very smart.'

'Thank you. I got Mam to take me shopping in Credenford.' Claudia looked down at her mid-length, black linen shift dress, which she'd topped with a short black leather jacket. 'My only other dress is long and tie-dyed in bright orange and cerise. Hardly suitable.'

'Or the miniskirts your papà referred to as your pelmets?' They both laughed. 'Well, he would certainly approve.' Her aunt patted her arm.

'How are you bearing up, *cariad*?' A smiling Great-Auntie Edna sought her out in the kitchen. So different from her sister, she'd made sure she'd kept in contact with Sara since she married Carlo. 'I'm so sorry about your dada.' It seemed strange to hear her papà referred to as that. 'He was with us today, you know? I noticed a beautiful butterfly fluttering close by at the burial. Always a sign.'

Her great-auntie was always one for superstitions, but this was a comforting one. 'I keep expecting him to come through the door, with his overalls all dusty with dry cement, and Mam nagging him to get out of them before he traipsed it all over her clean kitchen floor.' Claudia managed to smile at the image.

'I know. It will take you a long time, I'm afraid. I've never known a couple so happy as Sara and Carlo.'

Much as Claudia loved to chat to Great-Auntie Edna, she did talk a lot, so she made her excuses and found her mother speaking with her godparents, Uncle Sisto and Auntie Ceridwen.

Sisto immediately embraced her, kissing her on both cheeks as her papà used to do. Even after all the years in Wales, Sisto still spoke with a melodic Italian accent as if he was about to break into song. 'Here she is, the *bella* Claudia.' He turned to her mother again. 'Carlo Rosso will never be gone with this young lady around.'

Her mam's eyes shone with unshed tears. 'I know. I don't think I had anything to do with it.' The four of them laughed. 'Sorry. I should probably leave you three and go and circulate for a while.'

'Hello, *cariad*.' Ceridwen turned to her. 'It was a lovely service, wasn't it? I'll leave you with Uncle Sisto, now. I'll see if Sara needs any help.'

As soon as his wife had left, Sisto pulled Claudia to one side. He drew an envelope from his back pocket and handed it to her. *Claudia Lucia Rosso* was written in her father's distinctive hand. Her godfather looked around to check no one was listening. 'Your papà gave this to me after your baptism.

He instructed me to give this to you after his death. I never expected it would be when he was only fifty years of age. It's been in safekeeping at the solicitors' who had strict instructions that if I went first, they would make sure you got it. Don't open it here. Wait until you're alone.'

What on earth could it contain and why keep it a secret until Papà passed on? Claudia wondered. She tucked it into her dress pocket and tried to forget about it as she returned to the kitchen to take more food around to the mourners.

* * *

Later that evening, after helping her mother clear up, Claudia hurried to her bedroom, making the excuse that she wanted to change out of her black clothes.

'That's fine, *cariad*. No one will expect you to wear mourning clothes, but I will. It's expected of a widow, see. By the way, I saw you talking to Edna. How could two sisters be so different? It's because of Gwyneth Lewis, or the "dragon" as your Auntie Menna called her, that it feels like I don't have a son anymore.'

'Oh, Mam. If I'm honest, I'm glad Aled didn't turn up today. There would have been an uncomfortable atmosphere if he had.'

Her mother sat back in her chair. 'So am I. It would have been awkward. But he is still my son, and I often wonder why it all went wrong. Your father tried so hard with him when he was little, making sure he treated you and him the same. But Aled always loved spending time with Bryn and the animals up at the farm, and I suppose he listened too much to his grandmother. She never forgave me for marrying Carlo. Bryn was there today, you know.' She sighed. 'You go on up, *cariad*. I'll read this pile of sympathy cards people brought with them. We've received a lot in the post, too! I can't believe how many we've had.'

Once upstairs, Claudia carefully opened the envelope. The paper was yellowing in parts. Inside was a postcard-sized black-and-white photograph of a smiling couple and a young child. Claudia traced the faces of the family group with her finger. The photo showed a beautiful, dark-haired woman holding a young child, laughing and gazing up at the man who looked like a young Papà. Claudia turned the photograph over. In her father's handwriting was written, *Pia e Giulietta, 1939*. Claudia felt her mouth fall open. Those were the names her father was trying to tell her in the hospital. But who were they? Why was he in the photo with them?

She looked inside the envelope again and pulled out a piece of paper. She unfolded it to see a hand-drawn map of linked roads. The word *ENTRATA* was written in capitals at the start — *could that mean entrance*? — and there was a cross marked towards the centre of the map. This was what her papà had been trying to tell her about from his hospital bed. He'd wanted her to see the photo and the map.

But what does it all mean?

CHAPTER TWENTY-FIVE

That night, Claudia tossed and turned, watching the luminous hands on her bedside clock show every hour until pale, weak sunlight peeped through the geometric Op Art curtains. The pattern on the curtains reminded her of when she'd applied for college, and her papà had told her that he hoped she'd be studying "real art" — fine art — not this "modern nonsense" as he called it. On the wall opposite was a delicate watercolour of a Sicilian harbour he'd painted for her, the translucent teals and turquoises of the water contrasting with the colourful fishing boats and the stone quayside. She remembered teasing him, saying she was going to replace it with an Andy Warhol print in psychedelic pinks and yellows, and Papà had feigned mock horror at the idea. A lump rose into her throat. They would never share that banter again.

Her mother knocked and came into her room. She smiled at Claudia. 'I've brought you a cuppa, *cariad*. You were restless last night, weren't you? Couldn't settle after yesterday? I was awake half the night, too.'

'Thanks, Mam.' Claudia sipped the tea. 'I'm sorry. I'll have to get back soon. The gallery will be short staffed without me, but I don't want to leave you on your own.'

Mam sat down on the side of the bed, and Claudia noticed how the skin underneath her eyes was puffy with dark shadows. 'I'll be fine. You mustn't think about me. I've got my job to fill my days. Auntie Menna is just down the road, and I can easily jump on the bus and come down to Cardiff now and then. Your papà wouldn't want us mooching around and being miserable, would he?'

What she said was true, but it all still felt a little raw to be going back to normal life yet. They'd had no warning, after all. Her lovely, healthy papà had been snuffed out in the blink of an eye. *You must have known the gas pipe was there, Papà. How could you be so careless?* Claudia put her cup down and reached across for the envelope with its unexplained contents on the bedside cabinet. 'Mam, yesterday Uncle Sisto gave me this. He explained that Papà gave it to him at my baptism . . . Apparently, he was told to give it to me after his death.'

Colour drained from her mother's face. 'What? Why after his death?'

Claudia handed the envelope to her mam and watched her reaction as she examined its contents. She turned the photograph over. 'Pia and Giulietta, 1939. Just before the war. It's definitely Carlo.' There was a pause. 'I expect it's his sister and her little girl.'

'I thought he was an only child?'

'We only *assumed* that. No matter how hard I tried to get him to talk about it, it was only his mamma he had in Sicily, he insisted. I couldn't understand why he didn't want to visit her once the war ended, though. All he told me was that his mother didn't want him to return as it wasn't safe, but he didn't say why. He was adamant he wanted to stay in Wales and marry me. When he heard she'd died a few years after the war ended — a heart attack — I recall he was very upset. I told him I'd go as well if he wanted to return to Sicily to pay his respects, but I remember his words clearly. "No. I can grieve for her here. There's nothing for me in Sicily now Mamma's gone, Sara. My life is with you and our Claudia."'

'But, Mam, look at them. A sister wouldn't look at a brother like that.' Claudia regretted the words as soon as she'd uttered them.

Her mother stood up, her eyes blazing. 'I know what you're implying, my girl, but I don't want to know who this Pia and Giulietta are. They could have been killed in the war for all I know. Just forget it. Here.' She threw the photograph on to the bed and left the room, slamming the door behind her.

'Mam, I'm sorry,' Claudia called after her, but her mam didn't respond.

She wouldn't push it with her mother. Her reaction told her she'd been puzzled by the photograph but hadn't wanted to admit it. Before returning to Cardiff, Claudia decided she would visit Sisto and Ceridwen on her own and see if her godfather knew anything about what was inside the envelope.

She unfolded the map and the questions surfaced again in her head.

What could this be? And why give her a map with no indication of what it was a map of? *Entrata* definitely meant "entrance", but what about the cross? *Oh, Papà. It's not as if we can ask you, is it?* Maybe her mother was right. She should just forget about it, too.

* * *

By the time Claudia went downstairs, her mam was her usual self, greeting her with a smile when she entered the kitchen. 'Toast and some of Auntie Menna's homemade marmalade?'

'Please.' Claudia gave her a hug. 'I'm sorry I upset you.'

'Forget it. Any talk regarding your papà hurts at the moment, but it will get better.' Her voice was scratchy. She turned to put bread in the toaster. Claudia decided she wouldn't mention the photo or the map again.

As they chatted at the kitchen table, there was a knock on the door. Claudia rose and went to answer it. 'Good morning, Mr Jenkins,' she greeted the man when she opened the door.

'Good morning, *bach*.' It was the local police constable. 'Is your mam in? I'd like a word.'

She invited him into the passageway. She noticed a small cardboard box in his hand. 'Mam, it's Mr Jenkins.'

'Hello, Phil. What brings you here? Come in and sit down.' Her mother's voice carried along the hallway.

'I've got something for you, Sara.' He sat down opposite her. 'Have you got a sheet of newspaper I could use?'

Claudia lifted the cushion on her father's chair and retrieved an old copy of *Brecon and Radnor*.

'One of Carlo's bad habits, I'm afraid. And then he'd forget where he put it.' Her mam smiled weakly.

The policeman spread out the paper on the table, then took a broken, dusty bottle from the box and placed it on the newspaper. He removed a roll of paper and handed it to her mother.

'What's this?' she asked.

'As you know, there's an enquiry into what happened to Carlo. The site of the explosion is being examined. One part of the wall remained intact, and when the investigators dismantled it, they found this in the concrete around a window frame that had shattered in the blast.'

'Here, Mam. Let's have a look,' Claudia said, encouraging her.

Her mother unrolled the paper and Claudia looked at it over her shoulder. 'This office was built by prisoners Italian of war on years 1943,' she read out.

This was followed by a list of names and what appeared to be the men's addresses. Italians from Rimini, Turin, Bergamo, Milan. One name jumped out at her — *Carlo Rosso, 385 Via Umberto, Porto Montebello, Sicilia*.

'Look, Mam. Papà's name and address is listed! I can't see Sisto's name, though. Didn't Papà say he was from Naples?'

Her mam looked down the list again. 'No. Sisto worked on the farms, but here's Sergio's name. Sergio Perico, Milan. I remember him. He was a great help to your father when they constructed the Italian chapel. He was a builder by trade. I used to see all these men working on the new office next to where I worked.'

'I thought you'd be interested, Sara. I don't suppose you want the broken bottle, but you could keep the list.' He wrapped the bottle in the newspaper and put it in the box. 'I'm sorry for your loss, both of you. Carlo was a lovely man, a true gent. Such an unfortunate accident.'

As her mother saw Phil Jenkins to the door, Claudia picked up the list again. Could her father's old address help her solve the mystery of the photo and the map he'd left her?

CHAPTER TWENTY-SIX

'I can't face it, *cariad*. Would you go through your papà's paperwork with me? There's a battered old leather case of stuff up in the attic. I've never been up there. It was always his job. You don't need to worry about his clothes — I'll sort those when I'm ready.'

'Of course.' Claudia looked up from reading her mam's copy of *Woman and Home* that had arrived that morning.

'I'll leave you to it. Just throw anything you think is rubbish. Thank you for doing this, *cariad*.'

Climbing into musty darkness, Claudia fumbled for the light switch. She was confronted with a jumble of discarded items: lamp shades that had been fashionable decades before, old sun-loungers that had seen better days, her tatty doll's pram and an ancient camp bed. There were boxes of soft toys and all her old school exercise books. *Where on earth do I start?* Dust motes hung in the air, illuminated by the dim light of a bulb precariously fastened to one of the wooden rafters. She coughed and spluttered.

An old leather case, her mam had said. As she moved a box of cookery books from the far corner, Claudia spotted it. There was a buff-coloured label tied to the case, along with a tiny brass key, with the words *Privato — Sicilia* written in her father's handwriting. She unhooked the key and inserted it into each of the two locks in turn until they flicked open.

Lifting the lid, Claudia's heart thumped. Inside the case was a bundle of airmail letters addressed to her papà, both at the camp and at the post office in the village. Why not here to his home address? Her hands shaking, she undid the bundle and unfolded the first translucent blue sheet of paper. The beautifully formed cursive handwriting with its even slopes and loops filled each page. A woman's hand, Claudia was sure of it. It felt as if she was intruding.

The letters were written in Italian. Claudia could understand parts of them, and found herself grateful her papà had tried to teach her his language. One word jumped out at her. *Mamma*. Relief flooded through her. They were from his mother, and each one was dated. When she visited Uncle Sisto, she would take the letters and ask him to translate them in full for her. Claudia placed the bundle back in the corner of the case. The last item she pulled out was a thick pad of watercolour paintings and sketches. As well as portraits of her as a baby, there were landscapes and seascapes of Sicily, the kind he'd tried to teach her to paint as soon as she could hold a paintbrush. She turned to the last page of the sketchbook where a torn-out page was folded in half. Opening it, her pulse began to race. The delicately drawn pencil sketch was of a small child. It was labelled *Giulietta* and dated May 1939.

In view of her mam's reaction to the photograph in the envelope, Claudia decided not to tell her about the drawing. She carefully pulled it out and put it aside so she could hide it in her room. It wasn't worth upsetting her mother, but she was more convinced than ever she had to find out more about who Giulietta was. *Or is?* Given the date, she would only be about thirty by now.

'How are you getting on?'

Claudia's mam's voice brought her back to what she was meant to be doing. She shut the case.

'Just letters from his mamma by the look of it. Oh, and a sketchbook.'

She handed the case down to her mother. After waiting for her to go downstairs, she picked up the pencil sketch before closing the loft and going into her bedroom to hide it in the bottom drawer of her bedside chest.

* * *

Sara Rosso's hands trembled as she clicked open the battered leather suitcase. She took out the bundle of letters and placed it on the table in front of Claudia. Then she slid her hand inside the pocket running along the top of the case and pulled out Carlo's discharge forms and record book of military service. 'It says here he left Sicily in September 1939. I remember he was in the war right from the start.' She handed Claudia the documents. A young-looking Papà stared back at her. There was no doubt the man in the photograph in the envelope was the same person.

'I feel as if I'm prying, Mam. Perhaps we shouldn't look at the rest.'

Tears welled in her mother's eyes and she shook her head.

'You open them,' said Claudia.

Her mam laid out the letters then opened each one, scanning what was written inside. 'They're in date order by the look of it. You're right. This is from his mamma. It's dated 3 October 1943. There's one word I understand — *bambina*. Here. See if you can work out what she says.' Her mam passed the letter over to her.

The threatened tears spilled down her mam's cheeks. She patted her eyes with a white, lace handkerchief as Claudia continued to look for words she recognised.

'Yes, *bambina* . . . and *soldi*. I think that's money. How odd.' Goosebumps formed along Claudia's skin as she looked sideways at her mam to see her reaction.

'Perhaps his mother helped his sister out with money for the baby,' her mother said quickly.

Together, they continued to sort the letters. They were all from his mother.

'I never remember him getting any airmail letters,' commented her mam. 'The last one is dated 18 May 1946. Ten days after our wedding day. Doesn't "*congratulazioni*" mean "congratulations"?'

'Yes.' Claudia looked where her mother was pointing. 'But look what follows. *Non è giusto.* It means "It is not right". There are no letters after that.'

Her mam shrugged. 'She obviously wasn't happy he wasn't going to marry a nice Sicilian *signorina*. He never said that, though.' She paused. 'He just announced his mamma had died. But perhaps she just stopped all contact with her son because of me? Maybe that was why he didn't have anyone in Sicily to return to. I suppose we'll never know now, will we?' Her face crumpled and she started to cry once again.

More confused than ever, Claudia pulled her mother into her arms.

CHAPTER TWENTY-SEVEN

The sun was high in the sky as Claudia walked along the lane to the farmhouse where Sisto and Ceridwen lived. It was a perfect spring day. The hedgerows were emerging into a vibrant green, skirted by verges abundant with wild flowers. It was a shame, Claudia reflected, that the next day she'd be back living in the dingy streets of bay-windowed bedsit land with not a blade of grass to be seen.

But her mother was now insistent she should be going back. 'You can't expect the gallery to keep covering for you, *cariad*,' she'd said.

She was right, of course — the owner had been most understanding, putting no pressure on her, but she couldn't expect that for much longer. The peace of the last two weeks after her papà's death had given Claudia time to think. It seemed there were so many unanswered questions regarding his life before he arrived in Radnorshire, and she felt she owed it to him to find out more.

The farm loomed into view. She'd chosen a Saturday when she knew her godfather would be home. Walking across the farmyard to the garden gate, she saw all the windows were wide open and loud music vibrated into the air. She walked up the gravel path to the front door, which was lined with terracotta pots of varying sizes, each full of bright yellow daffodils.

She rang the bell and heard Auntie Ceridwen's voice. 'Turn it down, Sisto. There's someone at the door.' Obviously, the music was so loud, Sisto couldn't hear what Ceridwen was saying so Claudia continued to wait. 'Sisto! Turn that din off!'

The door opened. 'Oh, Claudia, *cariad*. I'm sorry. I was upstairs. I thought Sisto was in the kitchen. I can see him now at the back of the garden, oblivious to the fact no one else can hear themselves think when he puts his music on that loud. Makes my bloomin' ears ache, it do. Come in. Mam not with you?'

They laughed at Sisto's habits as Claudia followed Ceridwen into the kitchen where she turned off the large Bush radio on the top of the Welsh dresser. Silence reigned, apart from the birdsong suddenly sounding loud through the open back door after being drowned out by Italian opera. The fresh smell of baking wafted from the Rayburn.

'It's Uncle Sisto I've come to see before I go back to Cardiff.'

'Right you are. Why don't you go out the back and see him? I've just got to get this *bara brith* out or it will be like a brick.'

Claudia entered the back garden where the washing line had fresh sheets and bolster cases blowing in the breeze. On one side of the path was a neatly trimmed lawn, edged with shrubs, and on the other side, a large vegetable patch where her godfather was digging the soil ready for planting. Sisto looked up from what he was doing, his face lighting up when he saw her. 'Claudia! *La mia bella ragazza*.' He dug his spade deep into the soil and came to greet her.

Claudia smiled. He and Auntie Ceridwen were child-less and treated her like the daughter they'd never had. 'Hello, Uncle Sisto. I thought I'd visit you before returning to Cardiff. I'm off in the morning — but I wanted to see you and thank you again for your lovely words at Papà's funeral. You knew him better than anyone. I could tell they came from the heart.' She took a deep breath, not wanting to break down, although Sisto had not been afraid to show his emotions at the funeral — he was very like her father in that respect.

His eyes misted now. 'We'd been through so much before we ended up here, so it was a privilege to pay a tribute to my best friend, *mia tesoro*. Come and sit with me for a while.'

He led her to a wooden seat at the end of the garden next to an old apple tree. This place held a lot of memories. She remembered the swing Sisto had made for her that had hung from one of the branches, where she'd worn away the grass underneath from constant swinging. Looking back at the cottage from the garden where, as a family, they'd spent so many happy times, the anxiety of the last few weeks diminished. She rummaged in her bag, taking out some of the letters she'd found in the case.

'My Italian is not that good, despite Papà's best efforts. Would you be willing to translate some of these for Mam and me? They were in a case in the loft. They seem to all be from his mother, but I wondered whether you knew of anyone else in Sicily we should contact to say Papà has died? Mam said he only talked of my *nonna*. The last letter is dated just after their wedding in 1946. Something about it not being right. Nothing after that, and Mam understood she'd died.'

Uncle Sisto placed the reading glasses that hung on a chain around his neck onto the bridge of his nose and began to read. Claudia watched his expression in silence as he flicked through each letter. He looked at her. 'It's just news, *tesoro*. Just letting your papà know how she escaped the bombardment by retreating to the tunnels under the *duomo* as soon as she heard the sirens. It says that some of their neighbours didn't make it. In the first couple of letters, she tells Carlo how he wouldn't recognise the street and describes the buildings that have been damaged.'

'But what could she have meant when she wrote it wasn't right that he and my mam got married? And what does she say about the baby and money? A *bambina* and *soldi*.'

'I don't know, Claudia. Perhaps it was because she couldn't be there at the wedding?'

It was now she brought out the envelope he'd given her after her father's funeral. 'Do you know who these people are? Could this be the baby? And it's Papà in the photo, isn't it?'

Uncle Sisto shifted on the bench. He took the photo and examined it. 'I have never seen this before. I didn't know what was in the envelope, I promise you. But, yes, it certainly looks like your papà. Perhaps the young woman is a relative. If that is the *bambina* his mother is referring to, maybe he sent money home to help someone in the family and your *nonna* would pass it on? By the date on her letter, it was after Italy had capitulated and we were earning real money then, not tokens. I honestly don't know any more than you, *tesoro*. Carlo used to mention his mamma, of course, but that was it. How do you say, he was "a book that is closed"?'

'Thank you. I'll tell Mam. She said the same as you. The baby is probably his sister's or another relative's, which makes it more important to find out where this person is, whoever she is. At least I know where in Sicily he was from now. Have you seen this?' Claudia showed Sisto the list of names from the message in the bottle and told him how it had been found in the rubble of the explosion.

He read the names. 'Well, I never. Fancy them doing that. All our fellow prisoners. Good men. A number of those helped your papà with the *capella*, you know?' Sisto paused. 'I've been deciding whether I should tell you. Your papà made me promise I shouldn't tell a soul, but I think you should know the real reason why he didn't go back to Sicily.'

'Uncle Sisto! You have to tell me. Why couldn't he?'

'Well, Carlo would never talk of his life before the war apart from one fact. He'd been wrongly accused of a crime and that was why he could never return to his homeland. The men who accused him had threatened to kill him if he did.'

Claudia gasped 'What? There must be some mistake!' Her voice rose. 'Papà wasn't a criminal!'

Her godfather pulled her towards him. 'Shh, *tesoro*. Don't upset yourself. He said *wrongly* accused, don't forget.'

Claudia sat in silence, reflecting over what Sisto had told her. *So, why did you want me to have the photo and the mysterious map, Papà? And who is baby Giulietta in the sketchbook?* She knew it was up to her to find out who she was, and more about the supposed crime that Sisto had mentioned. By asking her godfather to hand her the photo and map after he'd died, Papà was surely giving her his blessing to dig into his past to find answers?

CHAPTER TWENTY-EIGHT

Leaving her mother the next day was hard. They both put on brave faces during breakfast, and Claudia was determined not to be the one to shed tears first.

'You're cutting it fine, *cariad*. As usual! You haven't got the excuse of dancing the night away at the Rock Park Pavilion either.'

They both laughed.

'Remember how Papà used to drive me all the way to Cardiff when I missed the bus?'

'Spoiled you to death, he did.' Her mam looked wistful.

Who's going to spoil me now, Mam? Claudia wondered sadly.

Auntie Menna soon arrived to take her to the bus station in Pen Craig, and Claudia gave her mother the tightest goodbye *cwtch*. 'I promise I'll ring Auntie Menna tonight to say I've arrived back in Cardiff safely, Mam, and then write to you, too,' she called brightly as she left, trying not to let the threatened tears fall. Her mother's cottage still didn't have a phone, which was the same as a lot of cottages in the area.

She was deep in thought as her aunt drove away from Deri Cottage.

'I'll look after her. Don't you worry.' Her aunt seemed to have noticed her quietness. 'That's what sisters do, *cariad*.

Look out for one another. It's a shame you haven't got a sister of your own to help share the load. That half-brother of yours is no use at all, is he? Do you know he's cut himself off from Geraint now as well? They used to be such good mates when they were younger.'

It was true. Aled hadn't been near the house since her father had died.

'I'm sorry to hear that. Mam says he's working at Morgan's farm now. So, it must be the whole family he's got a problem with.'

Her aunt tutted. 'No doubt years of prompting from old Ma Lewis. She wasn't a nice woman, that one. It all got worse once Aled left home and moved into the farm with her.'

* * *

The bus journey had given Claudia more time to think, and by the time she'd travelled along the built-up streets back to her flat, she'd made up her mind. She was going to find out everything she could about her Italian heritage, and that would mean going to Sicily. If there were secrets, they needed to be unlocked. On her twenty-first birthday, her parents had given her some money and she'd been saving the money she earned at Oriel Elinor, too, so hopefully that would be enough for the trip. *Haven't I always wanted to go travelling?* This was her chance. She'd always fancied doing an art history course to add to her fine-art qualification and, from what her father had told her, Sicily was full of ecclesiastical treasures painted by famous artists. She decided she'd enrol on a course based in the city her father was from. She did wonder what her mam would think, but tried not to worry about that too much.

Music blared through the open window as Claudia neared the place she called her Cardiff home. At least she wouldn't be entering an empty flat — no time to brood or think of her mam being left on her own. She braced herself as she put the key in the lock. 'Linda, I'm back!'

149

She could hear her flatmate singing loudly along to the Rolling Stones and she knew she hadn't heard her. Claudia entered the communal living room. Strewn with papers, books, vinyl forty-fives and leftover food in foil TV dinner dishes, it looked like a war zone. Linda glanced up and turned the transistor radio off. 'Oh, hiya, Claudia. I didn't know you were coming back today. I'd have tidied up. Sorry.'

Claudia resisted a comment that it would be a first if she had. Instead, she hugged her friend, knowing she'd never change. She'd realised how untidy Linda was before they'd moved in together in their second year.

Linda cleared a space for Claudia on the settee. 'How was it? I can't imagine how awful it must have been for you.' She promptly burst into tears. Again, typical of her lovely friend, it was Claudia comforting her rather than the other way round.

Claudia pulled Linda into a *cwtch*. 'Don't cry. I'll be fine. I've got to get back to work. The gallery has been great but the longer I stayed, the harder it was to leave Mam.'

Claudia decided she wouldn't tell Linda anything of her plans to go to Sicily until she'd finalised everything. After work tomorrow, she'd visit the library and find out about art history courses, the cost involved and how long they were for.

Her first job was to ring her aunt as promised to let her know she'd arrived safely. Then she'd write to her mam. Still devastated she would never see her father again, the fact she was planning to visit the place where he was from somehow gave her comfort and a new-found sense of purpose.

* * *

It was just a short walk to Oriel Elinor the next day. The street was busy and it took Claudia a while to cross the road, reminding her how the bustle of city life was in such contrast to the slower pace of Mid-Wales. She walked to the side of the Italian restaurant and entered the door leading up the stairs to the gallery.

'*Bore da*, Mrs Davies. What have you got for me today?' she asked when she arrived.

Elinor Davies was hanging a large oil painting on the back wall of the studio. 'Oh, good morning, Claudia, my dear.' The middle-aged woman came down from the stepladder and took Claudia's hands in hers. 'Now, you're sure you're ready to come back? I can't say we haven't missed you and your lovely smile, but it must be your decision. Grief is a strange thing and affects us all in different ways.'

She'd become pensive, and Claudia knew she'd be thinking about the loss of her only son in a road accident the year before.

'We're both finding it hard but we're managing. I'm ready to return, though, thank you. I'll go home again at the weekend, and I was going to ask if perhaps I could come in earlier each day and stay on a bit into the evening so I could have a Saturday off now and again?'

'Of course you can, dear. It's not the same without you, but you're obviously a very good daughter. I understand you'll want to support your mother during this terrible time. Now, let's get going, shall we? We have a busy day.' Elinor climbed up the stepladder again. 'Does that look straight to you? This one is so big, it's difficult to keep it steady.'

'Just a tad higher on the left, I think.' Claudia checked the level. 'That's it. Perfect.'

The rest of the day was spent preparing another room in the gallery for an exhibition of watercolour paintings due to open the following week.

'The artist lives locally. I think she's captured the colours of the South Wales coastline perfectly.' Mrs Davies unwrapped a large painting and handed it to Claudia. 'She'd like this to be the focus painting on the wall opposite the door.'

Claudia's throat tightened. It was different to all the rest, the colours more vibrant, and the sea painted in a full range of turquoises and aquamarines. It reminded her of the seascape paintings her papà had done when showing her how

151

to paint in watercolours. He'd told her they reminded him of where he'd played as a boy. She tried to refocus her attention as she realised Mrs Davies was still speaking.

'I was saying, Claudia, she went on a painting holiday recently. Abroad. She's got a few more still to be framed, but this is the main one for now. It almost glows, doesn't it? A bit different from the greys of the Bristol Channel.'

Claudia turned the painting over and read the label. *A Mediterranean Beach Scene*. 'It's beautiful.' She thought of a favourite painting of her father's that currently adorned her bedroom wall. If her plans worked out, in a few months she might be looking out at a similar scene.

* * *

It was her mother who picked her up from the bus station in Pen Craig the following weekend. Sara was not a confident driver, always relying on her sister to take her everywhere, so Claudia knew she'd made a special effort to welcome her home.

'What a lovely surprise!' She welcomed her mam's tight *cwtch*.

'I've just got to get used to it now Papà's not here. Anyway, it's so good to have you home, *cariad*.'

They left the bus station and were soon drawing up outside Deri Cottage.

'Let me carry your case in.' Sara opened the car door. 'We'll get the kettle on straight away.'

Claudia followed her mother into the house. Leaving her mam in the kitchen, Claudia entered the living room. 'What time's Papà—?' she began, but then goosebumps formed along her arms as she realised what she'd been going to say. *Papà's never coming home, is he?*

Claudia didn't bring up the subject of her visit to Sicily, which she'd already started organizing, but she and her mam caught up with each other's news. Sara had prepared a meal of corned beef hash, one of Claudia's favourites, and, after clearing away and washing up, they settled down to watch *Crossroads*.

In three months' time, Claudia would be on her way to Sicily. She felt she owed it to her mam to tell about her plans — and she knew she had to do it soon.

* * *

The next morning, as she sat with her mother at the breakfast table, she knew she couldn't keep the secret to herself any longer.

'I think Papà gave me the photo and map for a reason, Mam.' Claudia waited for a reaction.

Sara took a sip of her tea then placed her cup down. 'And the reason?' She raised her eyebrows.

Claudia took her mother's hands in hers. 'I think he wants me to go to Sicily and find out about the people in the photograph. The map must mean something, too.'

Her mam pulled her hands free, tears springing to her eyes. 'You don't know that. I wish you'd leave things be. He arranged for you to have those when you were a baby. If he'd wanted you to go, don't you think he would have taken you himself?' Her voice cracked with emotion.

Claudia had half expected this reaction. Yet she was still convinced it was something her father wanted her to do for him. Why had he struggled so hard to say the names Pia and Giulietta and the word "map" with his dying breaths if it wasn't important to him?

'I'm sorry, Mam. I've enrolled on an art history course in his home city, starting at the beginning of August. I've got time to start saving. I'd love it if you helped me plan it.'

'No, I certainly won't. I think you're making a big mistake.' Sara stood up, shaking her head, and left to clear away the breakfast things.

Claudia wondered whether she was being unfair to her mother. She'd be leaving her for a month, but it was something she really felt she had to do. Her papà's mellow voice with its musical intonations drifted into her head. *Grazie, tesoro.*

CHAPTER TWENTY-NINE

Three months later
Porto Montebello, Sicily

White heat reflected up from the flagged walkway and Claudia stopped to mop her brow. She was used to summers being much cooler and often wet. Uncle Sisto had warned her of the intense August heat in Sicily, and she'd taken his advice regarding clothing. Now, she was very glad of the wide-brimmed straw hat and long-sleeved cotton tunic keeping her cool.

She took out the street map of the city and found the *pensione* that was to be her base for the duration of the art course. Selected from a long list of lodging houses sent to her by the university, she'd chosen it both for its low cost and its proximity to the university building. Picking up her suitcase again, she walked along the road on the shady side and turned into a straight, narrow street called Via Nova. on either side were tall town houses with floor-to-ceiling shuttered windows, edged with metal balconies housing troughs and terracotta pots of trailing pelargoniums.

Halfway along the street was a busy *trattoria* with delicious smells of freshly ground coffee wafting in Claudia's direction. She smiled when she remembered her father turning his nose up at the Camp coffee her mam made him with hot milk. *Real coffee comes from roasted beans, not a bottle with a funny blue label, Sara,* he used to tease her. Spaghetti didn't come in tins either, according to him. A few empty tables with raffia-seated bentwood chairs were laid with red-and-white-checked seersucker tablecloths. Most were occupied with people enjoying food and chatting noisily. A lump formed in Claudia's throat when she remembered her papà telling her how much he missed eating *al fresco,* as he called it, when they were sat in Smoky Joe's coffee bar in Pen Craig, rain lashing against the windows outside. She wondered how he'd been able to leave all this sunshine behind. Friends had often asked her why he'd never taken her and her mam back to his homeland. Now she wondered that, too. Goodness knows, she'd pestered him enough. Perhaps she'd find out why while she was here . . .

Claudia soon arrived at 239 Via Nova. She studied the facade of Pensione Piccione with its pale-ochre-coloured render. Metal shutters were positioned at an angle to let in fresh air and keep the sun out, and the large, dark-blue bifold doors were folded back to reveal an inner glass door leading to an octagonal vestibule. A high domed ceiling was painted with ornate foliage, flowers and fruit — mostly lemons — and edged with ornate plasterwork that reminded Claudia of the Italian chapel back home. The large wooden reception desk also held bowls of lemons. Nearby, she noticed a table with drinking tumblers lined up alongside a glass urn filled with water and slices of lemon, clearly inviting guests to take a drink. She loved the citrus aroma that made the place feel fresh and clean and immediately decided she'd made a good choice.

The young man, dressed smartly in a navy-blue uniform and crisp white linen shirt, looked up. His name badge informed her he was Signor Antonio Marchesi.

'*Buongiorno.* May I help you?'

Glad of her passable knowledge of Italian, Claudia answered him. '*Sì.* I have reserved a room. Claudia Rosso. *Grazie.*'

The receptionist turned over the pages in his book. Assuming Claudia was fluent, he spoke quickly. 'Ah, *sì*. Here it is. Signorina Rosso. *Benvenuto a Pensione Piccione. La camera da letto* seventeen. It's on the third floor.'

'Slowly, please.' Claudia looked at him apologetically, realising her basic Italian was no match for the Sicilian accent when spoken at speed.

The young man smiled. '*Mi scuso*. Sign here, please. Breakfast is served from seven a.m. until ten a.m. The *pensione* closes at eleven p.m.' He turned and took a brass key from the wooden key holder on the wall behind him.

'*Grazie*.' Claudia took the key when he held it out to her.

'I help you with your luggage. I hope you will have a happy stay with us.' Signor Marchesi pulled the concertina metal gate of the small lift open and stood back for Claudia to enter. It clanked its way slowly to the third floor.

Room seventeen was at the end of a short landing. It was compact, smelled of wax polish and was filled with heavy, dark, shiny furniture.

'*Grazie,* signor.' Claudia handed the man a few lire as he left.

Now she was alone, she lifted her suitcase onto the stand beside the large dressing table. Then she opened the shutters and stepped onto the narrow balcony where she could see the sea sparkling silver in the distance. The sweet smell of the jasmine climbing along the metal railings filled her nostrils. She inhaled deeply. It reminded her of her mother's favourite toilet water, Diorissimo. A feeling of homesickness washed over her for the first time since she'd left Dolwen. Her mam had tried to persuade her not to go, clearly still afraid of the secrets she'd discover.

She went back inside to the double bed, with its traditional brass rods at the head and base, and admired the hand-crocheted coverlet. Someone had taken a lot of care to make it by hand. The romantic in her imagined a young Sicilian woman crocheting it for her "bottom drawer". While the modern day seemed to be all about free love and sex,

Claudia still yearned to fall in love with the man of her dreams and get married in the traditional way. Perhaps it was because her papà had been so protective of her and had been so respectful of her mam.

She unpacked her case and found a home for everything in the large wooden wardrobe and in the drawers lined with floral paper. She had two days before enrolling on her course and she'd decided she would use the time to get to know the area. She took out her leather writing case and found the address written on the list from the bottle. *Via Umberto.* Number 385. On the map she'd bought before arriving on the island, she could see the area was built up with little space between the streets. Today, she would explore the city where she was going to be staying and studying.

* * *

Claudia stopped at the *trattoria* along the street from the *pensione*. It was still busy. Each table was separated from the next by a wide trough of clipped laurel bushes. Up along the wall and over the doorway, a magenta bougainvillea tumbled with its papery blooms. Miniature olive trees in large hand-thrown terracotta pots stood like sentries either side of the covered entrance into the seating area where menus were displayed.

She chose a table under the striped red-and-cream awning out of the sun. Now realising how hungry she was, she chose a *ragu arancina*, which the area was famous for, and a half-carafe of house white. She noticed a little girl of around seven years old with long, black ringlets accompanied by her father at one of the other tables. She giggled loudly at something he'd whispered to her. Clearly besotted by her, the man's eyes sparkled just as her own papà's had done. Without warning, tears burned along her eyelids. *Oh, Papà!* Claudia looked away.

The tables around her filled up quickly, and soon a middle-aged woman approached her. 'Excuse me,' she said. 'Do you mind if I sit here? The tables are all occupied.' Elegantly dressed in a long ecru linen dress, the woman pointed to the chair opposite Claudia. 'You look as if you could do with some company.'

'Of course.' Claudia brushed away the tears.

The woman had a kind face and her smile reached her eyes. She offered a hand to Claudia. 'Giovanna Di Grasso.'

'Claudia Rosso. Pleased to meet you.'

'Ah, a good local name like mine. There are so many Rossos in Porto Montebello.' Her handshake was firm. Both expertly manicured hands were weighed down with expensive-looking gold rings, and large diamonds sparkled as they caught the sunlight.

The waiter brought Claudia her meal and wine while Giovanna ordered a glass of carricante white wine and a coffee.

'I don't eat until the evening,' she explained. 'I see you are sampling our local speciality. I hope you enjoy.'

Claudia cut into the pyramid-shaped rice ball filled with the meat ragu and took her first bite of something her papà had told her about. Again, tears threatened. Annoyed at herself, she was glad when Giovanna started up a conversation.

'Are you on holiday here, Claudia? You have a Sicilian name, but from your accent, you do not sound local? *Inglese?*' She lit up a long, slim cigarette, which she inhaled through a gold-coloured cigarette holder.

'I'm Welsh. I've come here to study art but for a holiday, too. My father, Carlo, came from around here.'

Giovanna knew of the art course Claudia had enrolled on. When Claudia told her of her plans to get to know the area before starting on Monday, Giovanna gave her a list of places to visit. Once Claudia had finished her lunch and paid the waiter, the two parted company.

'I hope we'll see each other again, Claudia. I come here most days. I'll be interested to know how you get on with Matteo.'

Puzzled for a moment, Claudia then realised Giovanna was referring to the tutor in charge of her course. Matteo Di

Grasso. *Di Grasso*. She knew she'd heard the name before when Giovanna introduced herself.

'My nephew. He's well known around here . . . for his art, of course,' she added, but not before winking at Claudia.'

What could she mean by that? Claudia wondered, but she decided not to ask and instead just waved at her new acquaintance. '*Ciao*, Giovanna. And *grazie*. It's been so good talking to you.'

* * *

Claudia walked along the street until she came to a piazza in front of the famous *duomo* — the first suggestion on Giovanna's list for her. Glad to leave the stifling heat behind, she entered the cathedral. The cool, almost silent, interior was a welcome relief. As Claudia walked to a small chapel to the left of the nave, she gasped and steadied herself by gripping the altar rail. A painting, labelled *Madonna and Child* by Giovanni Battista Salvi da Sassoferrato, glowed from the back wall. It was like looking at her father's painting over the altar in the Italian chapel in Wales, even though parts of that were faded now. If she didn't know better, Claudia would have thought it was the same artist.

'Are you all right, *signorina*?' An elderly man spoke to her in Italian.

'*Sì*, I got a bit lightheaded, that's all. I'm fine now. *Grazie.*'

'There was a space there for years, you know? But luckily, the *Madonna and Child* was found and restored to its rightful place.' He moved next to her, clearly wanting to impart his knowledge. 'Just before war was declared, a theft occurred here in the cathedral. An inside job, so they say. The cleaner's name was mentioned as helping the thieves. Of course, much ecclesiastical art and silver was hidden in vaults for safekeeping. When the war was over, everything was restored and, without any explanation, the stolen painting was returned with the rest. No one asked any questions, but the space was filled again.' The old man came closer to Claudia, looking

159

over his shoulder. 'Mind,' he whispered, 'some think it may be a *contraffazione*. A forgery.'

The old man moved off and left her to admire the cathedral's other paintings and sculptures. One chapel was overflowing with ornate silverware that shone in the light invading the space from a beautiful stained-glass window on the opposite wall. To the side of the chapel was a small alcove where a beautiful fresco adorned the back wall. A wave of emotion flooded through Claudia. It was identical to one back in the chapel in Pont Ithon. She was drawn back to the Madonna and Child masterpiece that also had had such a dramatic effect on her, convinced that both paintings were linked to her father but she didn't know why. Was it strange to feel his presence there in the cathedral, almost willing her to find out the story behind the stolen artwork?

The sunlight was blinding when Claudia emerged from the *duomo*. The piazza was filling up with tourists, so she left the black-and-white tiled area, making her way down the steep hill to the harbour. Wandering around the little shops lining the quayside, she bought postcards to send to her mam and Linda. A display of brochures detailing the local places of interest also caught her eye. One with a painting of a salmon-pink-coloured villa on the front stood out. She bought the English version and another about a little fishing village further along the coast.

She found a table at one of the cafés and ordered a *granita al limone*. How was she going to sum up all her feelings on one half of a postcard? She'd fallen in love with Sicily and it was only her first day. If she ran out of space, she'd send them both to her mother and buy another one for Linda, she decided.

> *Dear Mam,*
>
> *I'm in love! No, not with a handsome Sicilian like you, but with the island itself. Its weather, its scenery and its colour. The smells and sounds all make me feel closer to Papà. Silly, I know. He hadn't set foot on the island since he was conscripted for the war, after all.*

And I've still only seen a small part of it!
Love Claudia

She'd run out of space, so she labelled the postcard PC1 and started writing PC2.

Dear Mam,
I am writing this down in the harbour. It's just like one of Papà's paintings. I can just see him at his easel painting the yachts and schooners alongside the fishing boats. I've bought my sketchbook with me, so one thing I plan to do is to take a boat over to a fishing village further along the coast for inspiration.
The course starts on Monday.
Love Claudia

Loving the tangy taste of the icy lemon drink on her tongue, Claudia browsed the glossy booklet about the pink villa.

Casa Cristina once belonged to a local family, the Romanos. They were rocked by a scandal a few years before the war when one of the sons was convicted of the robbery of a precious emerald ring from the duomo.

She read on.

When Signor Romano Senior died, Casa Cristina lay empty for several years until it was bought and renovated by an American couple. The villa now belongs to a young woman who moved to the city from Palermo. She is an expert in the field of ecclesiastical art and artifacts. She shuns publicity so rumours in the community abound regarding who she is.

No wonder, mused Claudia. *Whoever can afford to buy such a beautiful villa must be very wealthy. I think I've gone into the wrong area of art!*

161

Flicking through the photographs of the villa, Claudia was fascinated by the opulence of the rooms. When she saw Giovanna next, she decided she would ask her about the woman who now owned the villa.

Claudia took her time on the steep walk back up to the main town, stopping to browse the little shops selling handmade local crafts and jewellery which lined the cobbled streets. On the steps of some of the shops were colourful ceramic pots containing scarlet geraniums, and the balconies above displayed more pots with showy plants. Compact oleander trees with their pretty pink flowers had been planted at equal distances along the edge of the pavement and, as she passed each one, Claudia racked her brain to think of what their perfume reminded her of. *Vanilla, that's it.* Taking out her Brownie camera she'd bought especially for her visit, she turned to look back down the street. In the far distance, a strip of turquoise sea sparkled at the end of a street full of colours of every hue. She turned her camera to ensure she captured the whole length of the view. It deserved to be captured in paint as well as film, and she promised herself she would bring her paints and sketchbook next time. For the first time since her father had died, Claudia's monochrome view of life lifted. She was positive things were going to get better.

CHAPTER THIRTY

Claudia opened the shutters and went onto the balcony. She sat for a moment on the wrought-iron chair by the circular bistro table. The balmy morning air contrasted with the cool dark of the bedroom. The bell from the *duomo* in the piazza at the end of the street rang out, calling people to early morning Mass.

Below her in the street, families travelled in the direction of the piazza, and she remembered how she'd accompanied her papà and Uncle Sisto to the little Catholic chapel each Sunday as a child.

She dressed and went down for breakfast. A long table was laden with fresh fruits, jugs of blood-orange juice and assorted breads. The waiter led her to a seat by the window where she ordered a coffee. The smell of recently roasted coffee beans filling the air made her smile.

After breakfast, she referred to a street map to find Via Umberto, where she hoped to find her father's old house — number 385. She asked at Reception for directions.

'The shortest route is to walk along Via Messina and through the park. But perhaps it is not safe for a young *signorina* on her own.' Signor Marchesi became serious. 'I think it is sensible to walk around the edge of the park.'

The street she needed ran parallel to the bus station. *I'll be all right at this time of day, surely*, she thought. But she simply thanked Signor Marchesi.

Once out of the cool of the *pensione*'s vestibule, the heat was a shock. Claudia had imagined, by venturing out early, it would not be as intense and more comfortable for walking, but this didn't seem to be the case. She was just glad that the tall buildings lining the street provided a little shade.

Via Messina was a long, straight street leading away from the piazza. She reached the arched, grey-stone entrance to the park and noticed it was deserted apart from a group of elderly men playing cards at a table. As relief calmed her, she stopped to admire the linden trees, laden with clusters of tiny, yellow blossoms. Their sweet smell of honey wafted in the air and she relaxed further.

But her mood changed as she got further into the park. Mature trees grew close together, forming deep shadows. She increased her pace. Discarded Moretti beer bottles and evidence of drug taking, in the form of piles of thin, hand-rolled cigarette butts and more sinister needles, littered the ground, convincing her to take the longer way back. Graffiti had been daubed along the perimeter walls, with "Ban the Bomb" symbols and psychedelic flower-power motifs appearing alongside swastikas and the fascist slogan, *"Me Ne Frego"*— *"I don't give a damn"*, a veritable mix of ideologies. Claudia hurried, almost breaking into a run, as she realised she should have listened to Signor Marchesi. Glad to reach the opposite gateway, she finally joined Via Umberto, where her father had once lived.

She immediately noticed that it was very rundown. The presumably once buff-coloured render on the town houses was cracked and damaged on many, revealing the lava stone underneath. The painted wooden shutters were bleached and peeling with fastenings broken. Outside doorways on the narrow pavement were raffia chairs, some occupied by elderly men, others just by grubby cushions.

Claudia's heart sank. Had the street been as seedy as this when her father had lived here before the war? She could hardly believe her papà had lived like this. Perhaps it was why he had been so proud of the little house he had shared with her mam. They may not have owned the property, but it was immaculate, both inside and out. She walked further along and found house number 385. In one of the windows at the side of the wooden door was a figure of a Madonna and Child with an inscription.

'Bow before the icon and chant *Ave Maria*,' Claudia read aloud in Italian.

She was struck by something familiar about the face of the Madonna, again reminding her of her father's painting in the Italian chapel back in Wales.

'*Buongiorno*. You okay, honey?'

Claudia turned to face a tanned young man with long fair hair and a beard. From his accent, it was obvious he was American. His arms were laden with bags of bread and fresh fruit.

'Oh, hiya. I'm just looking at the icon in this window. There seems to be religious relics everywhere,' said Claudia.

He smiled. 'Yeah. It was here when we moved in. Seemed a shame to dismantle it but it means nothing to us.'

He put the bags down. After wiping his palms down his faded denim shorts, he offered Claudia a hand. 'Curtis. Curtis Lombardo.'

'Claudia Rosso.'

They laughed. A Brit and an American, yet both with Italian surnames.

'So, why are you here, Claudia? And especially on this dive of a street.'

Before she could answer, a female voice called through the beaded curtain covering an open door.

'Curtis, who are you talking to?'

'Skye, come out and see.'

A beautiful young woman emerged. She was as tall as Curtis and her hair was a glossy, deep-copper colour, reminding Claudia of Aled. She wore a long skirt, tie-dyed in reds, oranges and yellows. Row upon row of wooden and metal beads hung around her neck and adorned her wrists.

'Skye, honey, this is Claudia.'

'Nice to meet you, Claudia. What brings you down to this area of town?'

'My father used to live in this house with my *nonna*,' she explained.

'Well, you should come in then.' Skye beckoned her inside.

Walking through the tiled passageway, Claudia could see into rooms that, in contrast to the dilapidated exterior of the house, glowed with colour. Throws, rugs and ceramics gave a modern feel to the place. Guitars were propped up against walls, and a smell of recently burnt incense wafted through the house.

'Let's go through to the back,' said Skye. 'There are twelve of us living here on three floors. We'd been travelling round Europe, but we found this place empty and moved in.'

'Yeah. Empty for years, apparently. We didn't get much opposition. This is the longest stop we've had,' explained Curtis. 'We love it here, don't we, hun?'

Skye nodded. 'Yeah. Come and sit in the shade, Claudia.'

Once Claudia was sitting down, she told them the story of the names of the POWs in the bottle and her father. 'He never talked about his life in Sicily. All I know is his mother's name was Lucia and, going by the list, he lived here with her.' Claudia presumed her grandmother wouldn't have owned the house and wondered who it belonged to.

Curtis leaned forward in his chair. 'Honey, remember that old suitcase you found at the back of the cupboard in our room? Well, it looked like a suitcase, anyway. Had a handle and locks on either side.'

Skye looked puzzled. 'Oh, yeah. But it was jammed so far back I couldn't get at it. I just left it there. You don't think . . . ? But it can't be linked! The war ended over twenty odd years ago.'

Claudia's heart pounded. Could anything belonging to her grandmother still be there in the house? 'I don't suppose you could try to get it out, could you? It would be great to

166

see if it belonged to Nonna . . . or even Papà. I know it's a long shot.'

Curtis and Skye looked at each other.

'We could try. Look, why don't you give us a few days and call back to see if we can dislodge it? I can't promise anything but I'll see what I can do,' said Curtis. 'Wanna look round before you go? Must be some feeling being in the actual place where your dad lived with his mom. You came on your own out here, you say?'

'Yes, my papà died in an accident a few months ago. This is something I'm doing for him.'

Without warning, Skye grabbed Curtis and Claudia, and hugged them both. 'I lost my dad last year and it stinks.' Her voice cracked.

When they pulled apart, tears trickled down Skye's cheeks. Although they had only just met, Claudia felt close to this young woman who had shared the same loss as she had. She hugged her again. 'It certainly does. I'm so sorry.'

When Claudia left the house, an elderly lady dressed head to toe in black was standing in front of the window with the Madonna icon. She muttered something in Sicilian, crossed herself and ended by repeating a number of *Ave Maria*s. Almost subconsciously, Claudia crossed herself and also whispered '*Ave Maria*,' as the lady moved on.

'This seems to be part of a ritual.' Curtis stood behind her at the door. 'They all end the same. *Ave Maria*.'

'It means Hail Mary.' Claudia kissed Skye and Curtis on both cheeks. '*Arrivederci, grazie mille.* I'll call back on Tuesday evening if it's okay, but if it's too difficult to get the case out, please don't worry. I'm just happy to have found where Papà lived.'

'You're most welcome. Or should I say, *prego*? If we can help you find out more about your Sicilian family, it will be a good job done, won't it, Skye?'

Skye smiled. 'I hope we can help you, Claudia. And this should give you the kick up the ass for you to find out about the Lombardo family, too, Curtis. Wasn't that why we ended up this side of Sicily? I remember you saying your daddy was born in the foothills of Mount Etna and that was the reason for his explosive temper!'

They all laughed, and Claudia left feeling like she might have made a start on piecing together the jigsaw of her father's story.

CHAPTER THIRTY-ONE

The next morning, Claudia left the *pensione* with a mixture of apprehension and excitement. Although she'd followed a fine-art degree after her art foundation year, she'd always wanted to find out more about ecclesiastical painting. She'd been fascinated by the way her father had concentrated on biblical scenes as his inspiration for his paintings, not only in the little *capella* but also in his sketchbooks. Yes, there were many seascapes and portraits, but it was as if he was always drawn back to recreating the work of the old masters, much like the paintings she'd seen in the *duomo* here in Porto Montebello. She made her way down the street to the piazza where the sheen on the black-and-white patterned tiles told of hundreds of years of footsteps. The blonde stone of the beautiful buildings enclosing the square glowed in the early morning sunshine.

The university wasn't far from the *duomo*. A bronze plaque, inscribed with the words *Università di Montebello*, gave the place an added air of importance, setting it apart from the other public buildings. Above the arched entrance flanked with stone pillars, the Italian flag and the three-legged *Trinacria*, the Sicilian flag, blew in the gentle breeze. Claudia entered a spacious courtyard, making her way up the steps and then entering the ancient building. She followed the directions on the brochure she'd been sent to the room where she was to meet the tutor and others on the course. A young woman seated at a desk by the door took her name and directed her to a table where coffee was being served with almond *biscotti*.

When she got to the room, several other students were there already.

'*Buongiorno.*' One of the male students came over and greeted her. Claudia's stomach did a flip. Not only was he stunningly handsome but his welcoming smile immediately calmed her nerves. His eyes were the colour of melted chocolate and sparkled like those of her papà, making her feel as if she was the most important person in the room. 'You are here alone?' he asked, speaking in Italian. She answered him in his own language but he spoke back to her in perfect English. 'You sound *Inglesi*, I think?'

'*Sì.* I'm from Wales. My father was from Sicily so I know some Italian but I need to improve.' They'd only just met but Claudia wanted to run her fingers through the soft black curls framing his oval-shaped face that broke into another smile as he introduced himself.

'I am Alessandro. Alessandro Costa. I live not far from here. How do you say? I am local. I paint for a living. Seascapes mainly. I have an old boat and I go out and paint what I see.'

He looked a few years older than Claudia and she mentally tried to guess his age.

'My name's Claudia Rosso. I've come to find out more about my father's family. All I have to go on is an address. I went there last night and talked to two Americans who are living in the house now.'

'Could they help?' asked Alessandro.

'They may have something. They found an old suitcase wedged in the back of a cupboard — maybe it's connected. We don't know yet. I'm going back tomorrow.'

Alessandro smiled and nodded. 'That sounds good.' He seemed genuinely interested in what she had to say.

As they waited for the others to arrive, they continued chatting as if they'd known each other for ever. Claudia relaxed even further and her earlier apprehension evaporated. At nine o'clock, a tall, slim man entered the room and everyone immediately stopped talking to face him.

'*Buongiorno*. I am Matteo Di Grasso, the tutor in charge of this course. You are all very welcome.'

Claudia could see the physical family likeness with his aunt, Giovanna, but it was his mannerisms and hand gestures that were most noticeable as being like hers — he certainly commanded a presence in the room.

Before long, he was leading them to a lecture theatre where Alessandro and Claudia sat together, listening to what the course would entail over the next four weeks.

'The area around this part of Sicily is home to a number of beautiful *duomos* and basilicas,' Matteo told them. 'Through studying the paintings displayed in ecclesiastical buildings in situ, you will learn about the styles and favoured subject matter of numerous famous artists. At the end of your first week, an expert art historian will be joining us for part of the day. She will entertain us not only with information regarding the paintings, but also some secrets and anecdotes of the painters of history, as well as some more recent artists.'

Turning towards Claudia, Alessandro raised his eyebrows and smiled.

'That will be the best part, I think,' whispered Claudia.

Matteo was still talking. 'I advise you to bring sketchbooks and notebooks to record the differences in the paintings you'll see in each religious building. We will begin with a visit to the Duomo Porto Montebello, for which this town is famous. It is just off the piazza. Come.'

Claudia remembered Giovanna's comment and wink. The way some of the students, male as well as female, were hanging on his every word, and his obvious realisation of this, suggested to her that their adoration could be more to about his appearance rather than his intellectual prowess. But she couldn't help having a sideways glance at another handsome

Italian as she and Alessandro followed Matteo out of the lecture hall.

The sunshine was blinding as it reflected on the piazza tiles, and Claudia pulled down her straw hat to shield her eyes. Soon, they reached the steps of the *duomo* and entered the cool, airy space. A shell-shaped marble bowl containing holy water stood just inside the huge wooden doors. One by one, most of the students dipped in their hands and crossed themselves. Out of habit, Claudia did, too — it was something she was used to doing since when she'd attended chapel with her papà.

Although there were a few tourists walking around the cathedral and several people making their personal prayers while seated in the pews, Claudia was struck by the stillness and silence in the vast building. Matteo led the group to each painting in turn, quietly giving a brief history of the artist. He asked the students to consider the style of the painting and how it fitted in with the art of its time. Claudia was able to draw on what she had learned from her art history lectures in college but it seemed some of the students, like Alessandro, had no previous knowledge.

He shrugged. 'Where do I start?'

'Don't worry,' Claudia whispered. 'You can find all of this out in the library. I'll help you.'

Alessandro gave her a heart-melting smile.

'Finally, we come to the *duomo*'s most prestigious artwork. *The Madonna and Child*. It seems fitting that an Italian painter's work is the *pièce de resistance* here. Giovanni Battista Salvi was known as Il Sassoferrato, after the town where he was born in 1609.'

The painting had the same effect on Claudia as the first time she'd seen it, but luckily without the initial shock. She was immediately transported back to the tiny POW chapel in Pont Ithon where she'd always admired her father's work.

'Over the years, many student fine-art painters have spent hours in this cathedral trying to emulate Il Sassoferrato's brushwork and style, but no one has ever managed it. Before

World War Two broke out, it was stolen but was miraculously returned when hostilities ended. Let us hope it will never be stolen again.' Matteo took one last look at the masterpiece. 'I'm going to leave you now to make sketches of the paintings. We'll meet again at three p.m. at the university. Then some of you can tell the class what you've found out. *A presto!*'

Matteo left the group and silence resumed. Claudia turned to the painting again. The ornate gilded frame gave the work an air of opulence, matching the general surroundings of the huge *duomo*. That was something that was obviously missing in her papà's version in Pont Ithon. In some ways, the little chapel seemed more in keeping with the remarkable simplicity of colour and the composition with its lack of background scenery in Il Sassoferrato's painting.

'There you are.' Alessandro had returned to her side. 'What is the fascination with this painting? You have been here ages. You heard the maestro. He wants sketches of them all and notes.'

She followed Alessandro to look at the rest of the paintings, making her notes and sketches without the interest she'd had for the Madonna and Child. She only hoped Matteo wouldn't ask her for her ideas in front of the group.

Before returning to the university, Claudia and Alessandro bought some *arancini* to eat on the way.

'You're probably used to this,' said Claudia, 'but I'm going to try every variety I can. This filling's got ricotta and spinach in with the rice. It's delicious.'

Alessandro made a face. 'I'm a traditionalist. Ragu for me every time.' He took another bite of his *arancina* and gave a thumbs up.

After returning to the university and reporting back to Matteo, the two new friends called in at the library, where Claudia helped Alessandro find some information on the seventeenth-century artists like Il Sassoferrato.

'I am never going to remember all this. They all look the same to me!' Claudia knew she probably looked aghast because he laughed. 'Only teasing. Thanks for your help. I just hope we do not get tested on this. I only enrolled in the hope there would be some beautiful Welsh girls on the course.'

'Now I know you're joking. But seriously, why *did* you enrol?'

'I love the practical side of art — the painting and the sketching — and I want to make my living as an artist. I presumed if I did a course at the university, I would learn about painting and it would be good for me. But now I am not so sure.' He looked serious now. 'I am already doubting if I can do this.'

Claudia felt her own face become serious, too. *Oh no. You're not going to leave, are you?*

CHAPTER THIRTY-TWO

Claudia walked the long way round to Via Umberto to avoid the park. It gave her time to consider what Alessandro had hinted at the previous day. Despite only knowing him a short time, she hadn't been able to hide her disappointment that he may give up the course. The other students had already formed themselves into small groups. Alessandro had been the first person she'd spoken to and since they'd got on so well, neither of them had joined the others, often losing track of time when they were together . . . and now he might be leaving! Being left on her own wasn't the only reason she was unhappy, though. She realised she was already falling for him.

'Ridiculous!' she heard herself say out loud. 'You don't even know the boy.'

She remembered her papà telling her how he knew, when he saw her mam the first time, that she was the one. Could it be happening to her, too? Alessandro had given her no clue she was anything other than a new friend to him, though. Yet the way her heart raced each time she saw him, no matter how ridiculous it was, made her wonder if there *was* such a thing as love at first sight. She spent every waking moment thinking about him and when she was going to see him again. Never before had she been so relaxed in someone's company, sharing thoughts and opinions so easily.

Via Umberto gave her the same sense of unease it had on her first visit. Now it was early evening. There were fewer old men sitting outside and no empty chairs by the front doors. It was early for Sicilian families to be eating, but the smell of garlic and meat dishes being prepared wafted through open doors into the street, making Claudia hungry. She hadn't eaten, intending on calling in at the *trattoria* where she'd first met Giovanna after visiting Curtis and Skye.

Outside number 385, another old woman dressed in black was praying to the Madonna icon. When she saw Claudia approach, she crossed herself and immediately left. Claudia knocked on the front door. No one answered and she knocked again. Eventually, Curtis appeared. 'Oh, Claudia. It's you. I'd forgotten. Tuesday evening, right?'

'If it's not convenient, I can come back at another time.'

Realising that he'd forgotten made Claudia feel awkward. The possibility of losing Alessandro's friendship and now feeling unwelcome here brought home to her that she was very alone and far away from people who knew her well.

'Don't be silly. Come in.' Skye's voice came from inside the hallway.

'Yes. Sorry.' Curtis looked contrite. 'I thought you were someone else.'

Once Claudia entered the house, they led her into the living room where she saw the remains of their meals on trays on the table. 'Oh, I'm sorry! You're eating. I've disturbed your meal.'

'Don't worry! Get another bowl, hun. Claudia can join us. Draw up a pew. You don't mind eating off of trays, do you?' Curtis seemed back to his friendly self.

Soon Claudia was eating a delicious tomato-and-aubergine pasta dish but was still wondering why there had been the frosty reception from Curtis when she'd arrived. Skye eventually broke the ice.

'Sorry about earlier, Claudia. We've been on edge all day. The owner of this place — we've never seen him before this morning — has threatened us with eviction. He's been knocking on the door all day. We thought you were him again and Curtis decided to face him. When he saw you there instead, I could tell from his voice he wasn't welcoming to you.'

'Yeah. Sorry, honey. It's not your fault.'

Claudia relaxed and realised the two Americans were anxious about the prospect of having nowhere to live. She found out that the others in the house had already left after the visit that morning.

'Collected their things and went. Packed up the camper and moved on. So, it's just us two now and we want to stay — make a permanent home here. That's what the argument with the owner was about. We offered to pay rent, but he's got other ideas to knock it down. Rebuild some fancy apartments and charge a bomb,' explained Curtis. 'I'm so sorry I was a jerk earlier. But anyway, back to you and your quest. Do you want the good news or the bad news?'

Claudia's heartbeat accelerated. Had they managed to dislodge the case from the back of the cupboard? Was it anything to do with her *nonna*?

Skye went into the kitchen to make coffee, and now Curtis rose and retrieved a suitcase from the side of his chair. He placed it on the rug in front of Claudia.

'You got it out! Thank you.'

The case was battered and the corners were misshapen, presumably due to having been squashed right to the back of the cupboard shelf. From the inside lining, Claudia could see the leather had originally been a tan colour but now it was a dirty brown. It was torn and ripped in places and covered in dust. The metal locks at either end were rusting.

'That's the good news. The bad news is the case is locked and there's no key. Sorry, honey.'

Skye came back with the coffees. 'It's such a pity it's locked. We can force it if you like? It will ruin the case, but at least you'll know what's in there.'

Claudia looked at the old case in front of her. Until she could find out what was inside, it meant nothing. It could be anybody's. 'Go on. Do it. I have to find out what's inside.'

As if anticipating Claudia's response, Curtis had already taken a narrow screwdriver from the top of the sideboard. Now, he fitted it into one of the locks and turned it. It didn't move. 'Skye, can you get me my old sheath knife from the kitchen drawer, please? The situation needs drastic measures, I think. I wasn't an Eagle Scout back home for nothing.' Curtis took the knife from Skye, removing it from its leather sheath. He brought the knife down with force onto the top lid of the case, then rolled back the surface. 'I hope there's nothing on top that could be damaged.' He put in his hand and pulled out a small notebook with a stiff cardboard cover, handing it to Claudia. 'Sorry, hun. If all this does belong to your *nonna*, I may have ripped the cover of this with the knife. It seems to have been in the fabric pocket in the lid.'

Claudia opened the notebook. 'Lucia Vittoria Rosso, 1943,' she whispered. Her throat constricted. 'That's my *nonna*!'

The book smelled musty, and the paper yellow with age. She turned the pages and read out the dates. It looked like a notebook of diary entries correlating with the exact time her papà had been imprisoned in Greenfield Camp. Claudia recognised the meticulous handwriting from the letters Lucia had written to her son. In those, she would have had to be careful not to tell him anything incriminating — but, in a diary, a secret diary locked away, maybe she would have been able to write about what it was like during the occupation? Claudia remembered her father telling her that if the Sicilians hadn't said they were fascists, they would have been deported to camps in Italy. '*Suddenly, everyone became a fascist. If only the Germans knew the truth!*'

Curtis continued to pull out the contents of the case through the hole in the lid. 'Aren't these beautiful?' Skye held up some hand-knitted baby clothes — a romper suit with hand-smocking on the front and a baby's shawl. 'Do you think they were your papà's?'

Curtis laid out more of the contents. 'Look at all these. This looks like your father's birth certificate. I can't believe it!' He read out the names. 'Carlo Giuseppe Rosso. Mamma — Lucia Vittoria Rosso. Papà — Giuseppe Luigi Rosso.'

Then he handed Claudia an envelope. Inside was a prayer card identical to the one her papà had carried everywhere with him with a replica of the famous painting in the *duomo* on the front. From what she could understand, it had been given to Lucia by her parents on her first communion. 14 June 1906.

'This is wonderful! I'd never have found out about my Sicilian family without you two!' Claudia swallowed a lump filling her throat, and then stood up and embraced them both.

'There's so much more here. Look. Photographs. Lots of baby photos!' Skye turned them over and read what Lucia had written. '*Carlo all'età di due mesi, sei mesi, sette mesi,* then Carlo as a little boy. Do you think these could be his brothers and sister?'

Skye handed the photos over to Claudia. There was one of a villa that looked familiar, but the sepia colour made it difficult to determine any details. Another picture was of a young woman in domestic uniform standing at a sink. Could it be Nonna Lucia? She found the photo Skye was referring to and turned it over. Her heart skipped a beat. *September 1925, Carlo, Roberto, Lorenzo and Pia.* Even though they were only children, Claudia could see it was the same Pia as the one in the photo with her papà and the baby Giulietta. So, he *did* have brothers and a sister? But if that was the case, why hadn't he wanted to come back to visit even after his mamma had died?

Claudia picked up the photo of the villa again. She realised now that it looked the same as the one in the brochure — just without the salmon-pink colour. It didn't make sense. Why was her father pictured there with his brothers and sister and yet apparently lived in this modest house in a rundown area of the city?

Perhaps the diary would give her answers. She could read some of the words, but she suspected some of it was written in the Sicilian dialect. She needed to find someone who could help her.

Skye helped her put all the contents into a large, cotton, macramé bag. 'There. This will give you a reason to call back sometime.'

'I will. *Grazie mille.* I must get back. Finding my *nonna*'s things has made my journey here worthwhile. *Arrivederci.*'

She couldn't wait to tell Alessandro.

CHAPTER THIRTY-THREE

Claudia became impatient waiting for Alessandro to arrive at the university so she could tell him about her visit to Curtis and Skye. Matteo wanted the day to be spent sketching old masters in a building of their choice. After meeting together, they would be free to explore the city in groups. She knew this would appeal to Alessandro far more than listening to lectures on the painting styles as they'd done on the first day. But he didn't show up, making Claudia even more afraid he'd already left the course. Surely he wouldn't just leave without saying goodbye? After the elation of the previous evening, the thought of not seeing Alessandro again filled her with dread. For two pins, she'd cancel too and spend her time painting the seascapes and harbour scenes she loved — but she felt she owed this to her father now. She'd financed the course with the money he'd given her. *In any case, I have to find out who Pia and Giulietta are.*

Just as everyone was preparing to leave the building, a breathless Alessandro rushed into the lecture theatre and approached Matteo. Claudia watched them talking, and although she couldn't hear what they were saying, she knew something was wrong. She walked outside into the piazza and waited for him with a heavy heart.

'Claudia!' Alessandro joined her. 'I did not think I would see you again. Mamma's had a fall. As there is no one else to look after her, I am going to have to withdraw from the course.'

'Oh no! Is she all right?'

He nodded. 'Nothing has broken, thank the Lord. A badly sprained ankle. She has been advised to not put any weight on it. I am sorry I will not be with you on the course but, to be honest, this has given me a reason to leave. I have not told her yet. She will insist that she can manage without me having to leave the course, but I now have an excuse to leave. I can see it is not for me, and by leaving so early into the course, Matteo says I may get my money back. Mamma is still at the hospital and I have arranged for a friend to pick her up from there late this afternoon.'

'I'm sorry you're leaving, but you must be with your mother.' Claudia tried her best to sound understanding despite her disappointment.

'I wonder if you would like to come with me? It is nice for Mamma to have someone in the house when she arrives home. I do not want this to be the end of our friendship.'

'Nor do I. I'd love to, Alessandro.' It was all she could do not to hug him.

'Thank you. But I forget. How do you get on last night with the Americans?'

'They retrieved the case for me and guess what? It *did* belong to Nonna, and there's a diary!'

Alessandro took her hands and smiled. 'That is very good news.'

Then Claudia had an idea. 'But I need help.' She'd realised Alessandro and his mother could be the ones to help her with translation, seeing as they were local to the area.

Alessandro looked puzzled.

'To translate the diary entries. But I'll explain everything later. I'll meet you after I've done a few sketches for Matteo. We're on our own this morning, so as long as I've done what he's asked us to do, I'll be free to leave. Say four o'clock at the end of the street where the *pensione* is?'

'I will be there. Oh, and bring something warm to wear. It gets cooler as we get higher,' said Alessandro. 'And bring the diary. Perhaps my mother will be able to help. *Ciao*.'

* * *

As promised, Alessandro was waiting for her, leaning against the seat of a white Vespa that gleamed in the afternoon sunshine. As she got close, he stood up and smiled, then kissed her on both cheeks. '*Pronta*? I am looking forward to showing you where I am from.'

'I can't wait!'

It would be the first time she'd travelled by scooter. She didn't know if the butterflies in her stomach were due to apprehension or the exciting prospect of being so close to Alessandro. She'd convinced herself she'd have to hang on to him for dear life so she didn't fall off.

It seemed he sensed her nervousness. 'Do not look so scared. Just try to relax and stay central on the saddle. The lean will happen naturally as we go into a corner. I promise I will not go too fast for your first ride.' He leaned the scooter onto its side stand so Claudia could get on. 'Are you okay?' he asked. 'Now hold me around the waist.'

Claudia did what he said. The warmth of Alessandro's back tight up against her own body made her forget how anxious she was.

Soon they were leaving the city streets and travelling along the coastal road. Alessandro pointed out the lemon groves and almond trees. In the distance, a white plume emitting from the top of Mount Etna made a spectacular sight against the cloudless, blue sky. Alessandro pulled into a lay-by and stopped the scooter. 'See. *Montebello*, Mount Etna.' He pointed in the direction of the volcano. 'Today, *nessun problema*! Nothing to make us worry. White smoke. No eruption is coming. Do you want to take a photo?'

Claudia rummaged in her duffel bag and brought out her camera.

'Here, let me take a photo of you now with Mamma Etna behind you. Say *spaghetti*.' Claudia laughed. '*Perfetta*.'

They continued their journey. A little further along, Alessandro turned off the main route and the roads became narrow. There were more corners and as the scooter leaned one way then the other, Claudia tried to remember his advice. She was sure she was holding him tighter than on the open road but it made her feel safe and secure. Eventually, they came to a crossroads in a village where there was a small square surrounded by trees. Alessandro pulled up alongside it. 'I am going to buy some cannoli as a treat for Mamma. Come and see what they have. This is the best *pasticceria* around.'

They crossed the road to the row of tiny shops lining the pavement. Claudia felt her eyes grow wide when she saw the array of cakes and pastries in the *pasticceria*'s window. Large sponge cakes filled with cream and decorated with icing and candied fruit filled the top shelf.

'Mamma loves *cassata*. The filling is ricotta cheese mixed with liqueur. We always have it at Easter and Christmas. But today, it will definitely be cannoli, I think.'

Claudia almost salivated at the sight of some huge chocolate cakes on the shelf below. One, labelled *Torta Savoia*, had been cut into, revealing layers of sponge separated by thick, gooey chocolate cream.

They entered the shop and bought the cannoli. Claudia was impressed with the care the young shop assistant took in putting the pastries in a cardboard box and tying it carefully with a silky ribbon.

They returned to the scooter and Alessandro handed Claudia the box. 'Will this fit at the top of your bag? I never considered how we would carry them — although it's not far now.'

Claudia positioned the box carefully and then they were off again. The air was noticeably cooler as they climbed higher into the foothills of Mount Etna. She was glad she'd put her sweater on when they'd stopped for the pastries. Either side of the narrow road, vines and fruit trees grew freely, — evidence, perhaps, of the fertile soil the area was famous for. Soon, a roadside sign welcomed them to I Limoneti, a village that appeared as a mix of small cottages and rows of terraced housing lining the main street. Most of the buildings were built in a distinctive grey-black stone Claudia surmised to be lava stone. Others were rendered in pastel shades, much like the grander buildings of Porto Montebello.

Alessandro pulled up outside one of the cottages. An old Fiat 500 that had seen better days was parked on the road in front. 'That is good. Signor Di Mauro's car. It means Mamma is home from the hospital. Come in. Don't mention about me leaving the art course. I'll tell her when we're on our own.'

Claudia agreed. She picked up her duffel bag and removed the box of pastries. She followed Alessandro into a narrow hallway, her footsteps echoing on the tiled mosaic floor that reminded her of the vestibule in the *pensione*.

'Mamma?' called Alessandro.

'Sandro, is it you?'

Alessandro turned to Claudia, beckoning her to follow him into the living room.

'You look well, Mamma. You gave us all a fright.'

'You flatter me, *figlio mio*. But still, it could have been worse.'

He bent to kiss his mother. Her steel-grey hair was pulled back into a severe chignon, giving the impression of a formal, remote figure. Signora Costa sat in an upright wooden chair by the fireplace. Her heavily bandaged right foot was supported by a cushioned stool. As she beamed at her son, her features softened and the smile she gave reached her eyes. Claudia quickly realised maybe she wasn't as aloof as she'd first appeared.

'This is Claudia, Mamma. Claudia Rosso. She is on the art course with me. Claudia, this is my mamma, Maria.'

Claudia stepped forward and handed her the box. 'For you, signora. Alessandro says you like cannoli.'

His mother untied the ribbon and her eyes widened when she saw the pastries. '*Grazie mille. Molto gentile.*'

Claudia knew that meant 'very kind' and she didn't have the heart to tell her it was her son's idea. Perhaps it was Alessandro's way of putting her in the good books of his clearly doting mamma.

Now, a tall middle-aged man joined them in the living room and Alessandro introduced him as the friend, Salvo, who'd brought his mother home from hospital. 'Salvo Di Mauro has been a good friend of the family for many years. Salvo, this is Claudia Rosso. As well as being on the art course with me, she's in Sicily to find out more about her father who came from Porto Montebello.'

'There are lots of Rossos around this area.' Salvo gestured with his hands open wide.

'He was Carlo Rosso. He was an artist before being conscripted for the war,' explained Claudia. 'His mother was called Lucia. They lived in Via Umberto down by the bus station.'

Salvo seemed about to say something but hesitated, avoiding eye contact with her. 'I must go, Maria. Just call me if you need anything, but now this young man of yours is back, I'm sure you won't. *Arrivederci, signorina.*' He hurried away.

Alessandro raised his eyebrows at Claudia. 'That was odd.'

'Yes, it was not like him. Normally he likes to chat with new people. Tell his life story. We usually have to stop him.' Maria looked puzzled. 'I am sorry if he appeared rude to you.'

Claudia smiled but she wondered if it was something to do with her papà. Perhaps the man had recognised his name? She picked up her duffel bag and brought out her *nonna's* diary, then handed it to Alessandro.

'Mamma, this belonged to Claudia's *nonna.*'

'I can understand some of it, but every now and then, I find the Sicilian dialect difficult. I wonder if you would translate it for me?' Claudia could tell already that Maria Costa's command of English was very good so that she would have no problem understanding her.

Maria took the diary from Alessandro and put on her reading glasses, which were on the small table beside her chair. 'Sandro, why don't you make a pot of coffee and we can eat those delicious-looking cannoli while I look at this with Claudia? Pull up a chair and sit next to me.'

Claudia did as she was told and nodded at Alessandro as he left the room.

Opening the diary, Maria smiled. 'Ah, we were all taught to write with the same style. All even loops and written in ink.' There was a silence as she began reading. 'This first entry is dated September 1943. She is worried. She hasn't heard from your father. "Where are you, my boy? It is months now since I have heard anything. On the wireless, it reported many Italian casualties out in Libya. Please God, you are alive."'

She paused. 'The rest of the entry talks about her new job at a lemon grove, making limoncello to store through the winter.' She began reading from the diary again. "It's good to work among friends again. Sampling the limoncello is especially good — the best part of the job! The other women are kind to me. They know our story, *figlio mio*. I will clear your name if it's the last thing I do on this earth."' Maria's eyes now widened. 'But listen to this! At the end, she mentions Roberto and Lorenzo Romano. "Rotten thieves," she calls them. She says everyone who knew the Romano family was in court to hear the sentence.'

Claudia's pulse raced. So, Roberto and Lorenzo weren't her uncles, then? But then what had they got to do with her father? He was in the photo with a Roberto and Lorenzo . . . and a girl called Pia. Who were they? She suddenly remembered that "Romano" was the name of the family in the brochure about the pink villa.

Maria was talking again. 'I remember the case. It was the talk of every town and village from here to Catania. They were brothers from a very rich family, so they had no need to steal anything. So, it was all the more shocking that they stole from the *duomo*, a house of God. A valuable painting in the *duomo* went missing at the same time.'

At this point, she crossed herself. 'It was just before the war started . . . But look, the diary entry is dated 1943. It took all that time. I don't remember much but I'm sure they tried to frame someone. Someone who had nothing to do with it. It is a pity they didn't go to the police, but there again, the police were as corrupt as the Romanos. Then all the Sicilian men had to sign up and the man probably never had a chance to clear his name.'

Claudia gasped and her chest tightened.

Maria took off her glasses. 'Are you all right, Claudia? You are very white. Do you think your papà is the man they accused? Your *nonna* talks about clearing his name. Where is he now?'

Claudia's throat constricted. 'He died, *signora*. Just a few months ago. I knew nothing of his life in Sicily until I was going through his things with my mam. I saw a photograph of some people, and there were letters. I need to know who the people are. What they meant to Papà. That is why I'm here. He never returned to Sicily. If he is the man accused, now I know why. But poor Nonna.' She could not hold back the tears any longer.

Coming into the room, Alessandro saw what was happening and put down the tray he was carrying. He rushed over to Claudia and knelt by her chair, grabbing her hand and squeezing it. 'Don't get upset. Why don't we make it a little project to translate your *nonna*'s diary for you? Mamma will help me with the old Sicilian dialect. *Bene*, Mamma?'

Maria smiled and handed the diary to her son. 'It is our pleasure, Claudia. I cannot imagine how awful it must have been for her, not knowing if her son was alive and then never seeing him again. Of course, we help you. And do not think I did not notice Salvo's reaction to your papà and *nonna*'s names. He knows something, I am sure of it.'

Claudia dried her eyes. '*Grazie mille*.' She stood and helped Alessandro serve the coffee and pastries.

'I can see you like our Sicilian specialities.' Maria smiled. 'Sandro, why don't you get out some glasses and the limoncello? This calls for a celebration, I think. New friendship and solving a *nonna*'s mystery.' She laughed and turned to Claudia. 'Now you will know what Lucia Rosso meant about liking her new job.'

Claudia relaxed. She was now certain she was going to succeed in finding out more about her Sicilian family. She managed a smile as Alessandro poured lemon-yellow liqueur into a glass.

'*Salute*!'

But at that moment, Claudia noticed a wedding photo displayed on the sideboard, taking pride of place among other photographs of Alessandro at various stages of growing up, and a sinking feeling immediately filled her chest.

CHAPTER THIRTY-FOUR

Hearing the now-familiar *phut-phut* of the scooter, Claudia wondered if she would learn more about her *nonna* tonight. Claudia and Alessandro had started meeting up every evening at the *trattoria* near the *pensione*. She made sure her college work was up to date, and he made sure his mother was comfortable before he left for a few hours.

She stood up as he approached the table. As he kissed her on both cheeks, she breathed in the fragrance of his citrus aftershave. She could only imagine what a romantic kiss on the lips from Alessandro would feel like, and warmth spread along her neck as she thought about it — but he always only referred to them as being friends. She had to be satisfied with that. And in any case, she would be returning home to Wales in a few weeks.

'*Ciao.* You look lovely.' He smiled.

Claudia couldn't help but beam at his words. 'How is your mamma today?'

'Better, *grazie.* The pain, it is not so bad and Salvo has managed to get her some old crutches. As long as she does not put any weight on the ankle, she can move around the house now.' He paused. 'I can see you've ordered a coffee. Perhaps we could go further afield tonight? Maybe to Villaggio delle

Rocce? It's a little fishing village not far along the coast where I have my studio.'

'That sounds lovely. I'll finish this and pay.' Claudia drank her coffee and signalled for the waiter to bring the bill. She had been wanting to visit one of the picturesque fishing villages since she'd bought a booklet about them on the very first day she arrived, so she was looking forward to their unexpected trip.

* * *

After parking the Vespa in the small car park, they wandered down the steps and along the quayside. Alessandro pointed out the street where his studio was. Villaggio delle Rocce's harbour was similar to the harbour Claudia had visited on her first day, with its varied array of boats and schooners. The village was less touristy and, listening to the voices all speaking Italian coming from the bars as they passed, it was clear this was where the local Sicilians came to eat and drink. Walking past the more formal *ristoranti*, they found a pretty *trattoria* facing the water.

'This is more like it, I think.' Alessandro led her to a table. 'I hope you haven't eaten. I prepared Mamma's favourite pasta for her but resisted temptation. Have you ever seen such a beautiful sight?' He pointed into the distance.

Claudia turned her head. Streaks of apricot and coral brushed along a pale-grey sky in which the setting sun resembled a suspended glowing orb descending into the topmost crater of Mount Etna. They watched as the sun gradually sank behind the volcano, leaving its distinctive shape as a silhouette against the pale-orange backdrop.

'This is amazing.' She drank in the beauty before her. 'Even more spectacular than in daylight.'

Dusk soon fell, and twinkling lights came on at the bars and restaurants along the quayside. A waiter came to their table and lit a tea-light in the glass candle holder placed in the centre. Claudia couldn't help looking across at Alessandro and imagining what it would be like to be more than friends in this romantic setting.

'What do you fancy? The pizzas here are good. I used to come here a lot.'

'That sounds good to me. I'm starving.' Claudia picked up the menu and positioned it so Alessandro could see. 'What a choice! What do you recommend?'

He studied the menu carefully. 'Fancy trying a pizza *cariciosa*? It's popular here in Sicily. As well as the usual tomato sauce and mozzarella, there's mushrooms, onions, ham, artichokes, olives and even chunks of eggplant on the topping. What do you call them? Aubergines? Everything in Sicily must have *melanzane*, our name for them.' He laughed.

Claudia laughed, too. 'You've convinced me . . . and I'm getting used to the aubergines.'

It was now that a young waiter who appeared to be about Alessandro's age approached the table. 'Sandro!'

'Paolo!' Sandro stood up and the two men embraced.

'It's been a long time. Five years, I think. I've just got back from working in Milan.' The waiter became serious. 'I was sorry to hear about the dreadful accident.'

'*Grazie.*' Alessandro took in a deep breath. 'Paolo, this is my friend, Claudia.'

The waiter shook her hand. 'It's good to see my friend happy again. Now, what can I get you?' He wrote down their choice of pizza. 'And to drink?'

'Two Moretti, *per favore.*'

Claudia waited for him to explain what the accident Paolo referred to was, but he didn't. Surely, his mother's accident wasn't so distressing it could be described as 'dreadful'? Instead, he seemed almost relieved that the drinks came so quickly. 'Ah, here are our beers. Our pizzas shouldn't be long.'

Claudia was soon distracted by watching the chef in the open kitchen to the side of the dining area preparing the pizza from the thick dough. After arranging all the ingredients on top, he slid the pizza into an open woodfired oven on what looked like a huge, flat, wooden spatula.

Soon, Paolo delivered the pizzas to the table, the cheese still bubbling. The smell was delicious. '*Buon appetito!*'

They were silent while they ate. Claudia enjoyed everything on her pizza apart from the artichokes, which she pushed to the side of the plate. The pizza was bigger than she'd expected and she soon slowed her eating.

'What do you think?' Alessandro's plate was already empty. 'Too much for you? And not so keen on the artichokes, I can see.'

'I loved everything else. Thank you. I know I was hungry, but this is huge!' They both laughed. She started eating again. 'Don't worry. I'm not going to leave it. Papà always told me there'd be no dessert if I didn't clear my plate. Sorry, Papà, but not the artichokes.'

'So, you will have room for a dessert then?'

Looking across at Alessandro's smiling face, she could see he was relaxed and seemed happy, without a care in the world. She tried to imagine what the dreadful accident that had made him sad could be. It was obviously something much more than his mother's sprained ankle. She remembered how, after her father's tragic accident, she hadn't wanted to get out of bed each morning. She'd seen everything in monochrome and knew it had been the same for her mam. She took another sip of beer and steeled herself. 'Alessandro, can I ask you something?' She paused. 'What was the accident Paolo mentioned?'

He looked away but not before Claudia saw his eyes had misted with tears.

'I'm sorry. Don't tell me if it's too painful. I know how it felt when Papà had his accident.'

He inhaled deeply. 'No, you deserve to know. It is the first time I have seen Paolo since he returned from Milan and it brought it all back. I have not known you for long and that is why I have not said anything.' He took Claudia's hand. 'But we are getting closer, I think.'

Claudia squeezed Alessandro's hand. 'Only tell me if you want to,' she whispered.

'Three years ago, I was married.' He took in a deep breath. 'To a beautiful girl called Daniela. We had just found out we were going to have a baby. We were living in I Limoneti and both working in Porto Montebello. She was driving home on her own as I had to work late. She met a lorry overtaking on a bend. She did not stand a chance.' His eyes reddened. He paused and looked away. 'I can never drive that way again. It is too painful. I always travel the long way on the narrow coast road now.'

Almost unable to take in what she'd just heard, Claudia got up from her side of the table and sat beside Alessandro, pulling him into a tight hug. 'I'm so, so, sorry. I should never have asked. I noticed the wedding photo at your mamma's. Daniela was beautiful.'

He nodded. 'Time, it has helped but it is still hard for me to talk about the accident. I am sorry. But it is good that you know about it. About her.'

For a few moments, they sat in silence, holding hands and bonded in thought. Claudia knew emotions were still raw for Alessandro, as they were for her having lost her papà so recently. It was Alessandro who spoke first.

'Now, do you want to know what I have been doing today? Let us have a look at these diary entries.' Alessandro took out a small notebook from his pocket and opened it on the first page. He was clearly keen to move the conversation on. 'I have got this notebook for the translations of your *nonna*'s diary. It will be better than the loose pages I brought you earlier in the week. We have had a good day, Mamma and me.'

'That's great. What have you found out?'

Sitting together as they turned the pages in the notebook seemed the most natural thing in the world, and Claudia sensed their friendship had become closer than ever.

Soon, Paolo came back to clear the table. 'You would like a *dolce*? A *gelato* maybe?'

Claudia and Alessandro looked at each other and grinned, remembering their earlier conversation.

'Claudia has not cleared her plate so no *gelato*.' His face was stern and she pretended to be disappointed. The waiter turned to go. 'No! I tease her. Surprise us with some flavours, Paolo. Oh, and *due caffè, per favore*.' It was good to see the mood with Alessandro was lighter again.

He pointed back at the notebook. 'Here are some more diary entries. We found these earlier entries folded and tucked into the back of the diary that started in 1943. Look. Your *nonna* was the housekeeper for the Romano family, who lived at the large villa overlooking the town, Casa Cristina, for many years. She is remembering your father accompanying her. It seems he was friends with Roberto, Lorenzo and their sister, Pia.'

'Yes, your mother told me about them. I'd seen a photo of them all together and wrongly assumed they were my papà's brothers and his sister.' The photo in question entered Claudia's head.

'Why did you think that?'

'I found a photo of Papà as a young man and Pia with a baby. Mam and I wondered if the baby was his sister's — but Pia wasn't his sister. So, she was just his friend, not his sister!'

Alessandro shook his head and pointed to a passage halfway down the page. 'Sorry, Claudia. From what I can gather, your papà and Pia fell in love. When her family found out, that's when the trouble started. The Romanos were horrified that Pia should fall for someone of a lower class. Arrangements were being made for her to become engaged to the son of another wealthy family in Catania. They sacked your *nonna* and forbade Carlo and Pia from seeing each other.'

Claudia gasped. 'Poor Papà! You always remember your first love.'

Alessandro took a deep breath before he started reading another entry and Claudia realised her words must have reminded him of Daniela. '"It broke my heart to leave the position I'd held for so long. If Signora Cristina had still been alive, she would never have treated me and Carlo like that. I only dealt with her and the children when they were growing up. I should have listened to the rumours. Pia was already pregnant with Carlo's child. Even though it was frowned upon to be expecting a child before marriage, Padre Angelo was happy to marry them in secret in a little *capella* hidden away in the mountains to save us the shame. They were young but in love. 1938, it was. Everyone predicted there was a war coming and they were right. But for that year we were all happy in Via Umberto. Little Giulietta was a delight. My first grandchild."'

Claudia's mouth gaped open, her heart hammering in her chest. 'So, my father was already married when he married my mother? But . . . that's bigamy! This will break Mam's heart. I knew she had her doubts when she saw the photo. I think that's why she didn't want me to come out here. Better not knowing was her philosophy. How am I going to break this to her?'

Alessandro placed his arm around her shoulders. 'I am sorry. I think that is enough of a shock for you tonight. But here is Paolo with our *gelatos*.'

'I don't know whether I can eat anything after that news. Sorry.' Claudia felt a tightness in her chest as she took in the information.

But he was right, it was a huge shock, so perhaps having something else to concentrate on would help her as the news sank in. She'd try to enjoy the rest of the evening and not spoil Alessandro's time either. She'd think about all she had found out later.

The sundae dishes the waiter placed in front of them contained boules of different flavoured ice cream — lemon, chocolate and also a pale-green variety Claudia didn't recognise.

'*Buon gusto*, eh?'

'*Si*, it tastes good, but what is this one?' she asked.

'Pistachio.'

'It's delicious. See, I did have room for a dessert.' She sipped her coffee. 'I can't thank you enough for this evening, Alessandro, even though it wasn't the information I wanted to hear. And I'm so sorry I asked you about the accident. I didn't mean to bring up such awful memories for you.'

Alessandro squeezed her hand as he signalled to Paolo for the bill. 'I am glad you know about Daniela. We're approximately halfway through translating the diary, by the way. Mamma says you must come for a big Sicilian feast on Sunday. Though she still cannot stand for long, so it will be me doing the cooking and probably not up to Mamma's standard!' He laughed. 'She really liked you. Do you know what she said? It was so good to see me happy again. Just what Paolo said, too. And I *do* feel happy when I'm with you.' He smiled and hugged her again. When she saw small lines crinkling at the edges of his eyes, she knew she was falling in love.

CHAPTER THIRTY-FIVE

A world-renowned expert on ecclesiastical art was visiting to give a talk on the famous Giovanni painting in the *duomo*. Claudia's class had been told it was the highlight of the art history course.

Matteo led them to the front pews of the *duomo* and then left them to wait for the guest speaker. Over the altar was the stunning Giovanni painting they were going to learn more about. Claudia opened her sketchbook and did a quick pencil drawing of the main shapes of the composition so she could add notes as the art expert gave her talk.

'*Signore e signori.* Let me introduce la Signora Giulietta Gallo. We are extremely fortunate she has found time in her busy schedule to come here to share her expert knowledge of the most famous painting hanging above the altar of our beautiful *duomo*. For those of you who have done your pre-paratory research, Signora Gallo is an expert in the field of ecclesiastical art. Please make notes. There will be time at the end to ask the questions. Signora Gallo, *benvenuto.*'

The elegant young woman faced her audience as Matteo sat himself down at the end of the front row of seats. '*Grazie, signor.* My name is Giulietta Gallo, and today I'm delighted to be back in this beautiful *duomo* in the city where I was born and now live. I could talk for hours of the magnificent frescoes and mosaics the *duomo* is famous for, but today Matteo has asked me to concentrate on the Giovanni.' She turned and pointed at the work of art behind her above the altar.

Claudia felt her pulse race along her veins as she realised that the first name of the woman standing at the front matched the one she'd read on the back of a grainy black-and-white family photo, written in her father's distinctive handwriting. Silently, she scolded herself for reacting in this way. There were probably hundreds of young women called Giulietta in Sicily, just as there were Claudias. But no, it was more than that. The woman's face was strikingly similar to the one she saw staring back at her when she looked in the mirror each morning — the glossy, tumbling curls, the olive skin, the mocha-coloured eyes.

Claudia was mesmerised, not taking in the words being spoken. When Signora Gallo smiled, she gasped. Deep dimples appeared at each side of her mouth. She'd only ever seen them on one other person apart from herself. Her papà. She *had* to be Pia and her father's daughter. The baby was born in 1938 before her father was drafted into the army. That would make her thirty years old. Nine years older than her.

Unable to concentrate, Claudia slipped out, unnoticed, as heads were turned towards the Giovanni painting. She found a stone bench in the vestibule of the cathedral and sat down. Opening her bag, she took out the envelope containing the photos and the letters she'd found among her father's personal belongings. As she sat, trying to calm herself, she was gripped by memories of that day and the conversation that had taken place between her and her mam — the two people who were hurting the most after Carlo's tragic death.

Claudia searched for the photo that had puzzled her and her mam. After reading her *nonna*'s diary, she knew her father had another wife and another child. Somewhere, she had a half-sister. However much of a coincidence it seemed, could the woman delivering her talk to Matteo and his students be her sibling? Her skin prickled and her heart thumped at the thought.

She rummaged in her bag to find her notebook with the translations of her *nonna*'s diary that had found its way to the bottom. She flicked to the entries referring to her papà and Pia and re-read them. She lost track of time and was startled when the other students started coming out of the cathedral.

'What happened to you?' asked one of them. 'You should have stayed. She was excellent.'

Claudia shut the notebook and put it back in her bag. 'I didn't feel well so I came out. I have a splitting headache. You'll have to tell me all about it.'

It was then that Matteo and Giulietta Gallo came into the vestibule where Claudia was sitting. Matteo's face was like thunder, his mouth taut. 'I'll speak to you tomorrow.'

Giulietta looked in Claudia's direction and touched Matteo's arm. 'You go ahead. I'll catch you up.' She walked over to where Claudia was sitting. 'I'm sorry you didn't stay for the talk. Do I know you from somewhere? You look familiar.'

Claudia bundled the photo that was still on her lap back inside her bag. 'I'm sorry. It was rude of me to just leave like that. I had a shock, your name . . .' She trailed off before saying quickly, 'I'd like to book in on your next talk.'

'My name? Oh, and I'm afraid that was my last for a while. I'm leaving for Rome at the end of the week as I'm booked to give a talk in the Santa Maria Basilica.' She studied Claudia with interest. 'Perhaps we can grab a coffee now and you can tell me why my name shocks you? I'll just catch Matteo and let him know I'll see him later.'

Claudia's heart pounded but she tried to smile at Giulietta. '*Grazie.* I'd like that.' Then she turned and exited the cathedral into the bright sunlight to wait for her.

Giulietta soon met her outside. 'Come on. Let's find somewhere in the shade to sit down.'

Along the same street as the cathedral, they found a pretty *trattoria* with an ivory-and-maroon-striped awning. Vibrant cerise bougainvillea climbed along wooden trellis fixed to the blonde-stone building.

Claudia and Giulietta found a table in the corner where they could talk and ordered coffee.

'Are you happy with an espresso?' asked Giulietta. 'Not too strong for you?'

'No. Papà trained me well. He was from Sicily. That's why I'm here.'

'That explains your colouring. You look Italian.'

Claudia decided the young woman sitting opposite her needed an explanation. *Could she really be the baby in the photo?* She felt her pulse quickening once again at the thought.

'My father was from this city, actually. He was a prisoner of war in a small village in Wales. He didn't return to Sicily afterwards, staying to marry my mother instead. He recently died in an explosion. In the rubble was a bottle containing a roll of paper with the names of the POWs who had built the premises during the war. One of them was my father's with his Sicilian address. We understood he had no family left here . . . until now.'

At this point, the waiter brought the coffees over and Giulietta reached over for hers. She looked slightly confused but she smiled at Claudia kindly. 'I'm sorry. My father died, too. When I was a baby. I never knew him. But you say, "until now". What has changed your mind?'

Claudia brought out the envelope. 'I was helping my mother sort through his things and we found a case hidden in the attic. Letters from his mother show he was from here — the same address as the one in the bottle — and he left me this.' She slid the photo across to Giulietta.

Her face became ashen, and her cup clattered onto the saucer. 'That's a photo of my mamma and me! Is that your papà?'

Claudia nodded. '*Your* mother is Pia? You are *this* Giulietta?' She couldn't quite believe it, but it seemed it was true.

'Yes. Mamma was estranged from her family. She told me my father had died in the war. But are you saying you think this man is my father, too?' She gazed at her papà's face.

'If it is, this is the first photo I've seen of him.' Her voice was shaky and her eyes welled with tears.

'I've only just found out he had a wife and a daughter before the war. It was a huge shock for me, too.'

'All I know is he'd done something . . .' Giulietta took a deep breath. 'Something terrible before he signed up. Mamma's family would never have allowed him to come back, so it was for the best she said . . .' She got no further.

Claudia patted her arm. They were two young women, both in shock. *Sisters.*

'I cannot believe this. I've found you, and I hadn't even started looking for you yet!' Claudia wanted to know more. 'My mamma is still alive. Is yours?'

Giulietta shook her head. 'She died last year. Cancer. Never remarried. She had nothing to do with any of her family. The shame of what my father did left her wary of men.' She looked away. 'Even if he had survived the war, she would never have had him back. She would never talk of him.'

'She's not the only one. Papà kept all this a secret from us! He married my mother when he was still married to yours!' Claudia's head was filled with confusion. She'd come to Sicily to find Giulietta but hadn't expected that she'd find out she was her half-sister. Now she'd met her, as well as feeling excited, she was also so angry with her father. And was the man she knew and loved capable of a "terrible" crime?

'When I used to ask questions, the only thing Mamma told me was that my father was a talented artist and I'd followed him in my choice of career.'

Claudia felt anger surge again at seeing proof of her papà's betrayal, his lies. This was not how she'd expected to feel. She clenched her fists, digging her nails into her palms. *It's not her fault, Claudia. Calm down.* She took a deep breath and composed herself. 'Not only do we look alike — well, I think we do — I've also followed in his footsteps. I studied at art college.'

'We can't leave it like this, but I have a meeting to go to. I want to find out everything about you and my papà before

I leave for Rome. Can we meet again tomorrow? I'll tell you everything I know then. Perhaps we could meet here again at say three o'clock?' Giulietta signalled for the waiter and asked for the bill, then they stood to go.

Claudia agreed. She would have finished at the university by then and was desperate not to miss an opportunity to find out more before Giulietta left for Rome. Tomorrow, she'd show her half-sister the map her papà left her. And retrieve their *nonna*'s diary from Alessandro . . .

CHAPTER THIRTY-SIX

'How could you, Papà?' she said out loud.

Claudia couldn't sleep. So much had happened and her mind whirred with thoughts. Thoughts of Giulietta. Thoughts of her papà. How could he keep the fact he had *two* daughters a secret? It would break her mam. Hadn't she been through enough heartache already?

The words of her *nonna*'s last letter after her father had written to say he'd married her mam came back to her. They made more sense now. *Non è giusto. Not right.* 'No, Papà. It wasn't right!' Her father had assumed his mamma had died from a heart attack, but, as a staunch Catholic woman, maybe he'd just broken her heart?

Claudia got out of bed and paced the room, furious for the first time in her life at the man she'd worshipped. She opened the shutters and went out onto the balcony. Sitting on one of the chairs, she breathed in the balmy night air and tried to calm herself down. The city below was a myriad of dotted orange and white lights, and from the drone of traffic below her, it occurred to her she wasn't the only one awake. Where were all these people going?

When times were difficult, her mam's favourite saying was 'Tomorrow's another day'. She wondered what tomorrow would bring. First, she'd have to face Matteo and apologise for her rudeness in leaving the talk he'd worked so hard to arrange. How much would Giulietta want her to tell him? Perhaps she should just stick to the lie about a severe headache and leave out any reference to them being sisters until she'd found out how much Giulietta wanted to divulge.

Sister. She'd often imagined what it would be like to have a sister and now it seemed she had one. Could they become as close as her mam and Auntie Menna? She hoped so. She and Aled had never been close. He'd resented her in their mam's life for as long as she could remember.

Then there was the meeting with Giulietta in the afternoon. She had so much to tell her. So much to ask her.

Claudia returned to her bed and tried to get to sleep once more.

* * *

Claudia had left the shutters open and she was awoken by the dawn sunlight shining onto her bed. She felt surprisingly refreshed.

After breakfast, she went to the university, determined to be early and get the meeting with Matteo over with. Her heart rate increased the nearer she got to the building. When she finally entered the lecture hall, she saw Matteo standing by his desk, flicking through a pile of papers. He looked up. 'Fully recovered, I see.'

Claudia sensed an edge to his voice. 'I've come to apologise, Matteo. I feel awful for not staying for Giulietta's talk. I know how much trouble you must have gone to, to get such a prestigious speaker for us. I promise I will work hard to make up for it. I have severe headaches from time to time.' She felt heat spread upwards from her neck as she told the lie.

Her tutor stood up and paced back and forth in front of her. 'But, of course, there was another reason, wasn't there? Why not be honest, Signorina Rosso? I understand from Giulietta something else made you dash out suddenly.'

Was he waiting for her to confirm they were sisters? How much had Giulietta told him?

'Yes, I . . . I thought she looked familiar.' Claudia's voice was barely audible.

'More than *familiar*, I think! When I pressed her for an answer, she said you were half-sisters.'

Claudia breathed out a sigh of relief. The fact Giulietta had been honest with him meant she could be, too. 'It was a huge shock. I was convinced I was looking at my sister even before I knew who she was. I'm sorry, Matteo.' Tears pricked her eyelids. She was determined not to break down in front of her tutor but her throat constricted.

'Sit down, Claudia. Don't get upset.' Matteo sat down beside her. 'After talking with Giulietta, I understand completely why you left the talk the way you did, but what annoyed me was the fact you *lied*. Even this morning, you still lied. Do you think of me as so hard-hearted you couldn't confide in me?'

The threatened tears trickled down her cheeks. Searching for a handkerchief, Claudia shook her head. '*Scusa.*'

By this time, a number of students had arrived, and Claudia dried her eyes and moved to sit with her friends while Matteo resumed his usual place at the front.

'Are you all right?' whispered one of the others.

Claudia nodded and smiled. '*Sì. Grazie.*'

The morning's work was to add notes from Giulietta's talk to their sketches of the Giovanni painting. When Matteo had finished his introduction, he handed Claudia a transcript of the talk. 'You will need this, I think.'

* * *

Giulietta sat at a corner table, waiting at the *trattoria* as planned. She was engrossed in a magazine and Claudia paused for a moment, watching her. Her glossy black hair fell in tresses over her shoulders, and she bit her bottom lip just as their papà had done when he was concentrating.

Claudia smoothed down her hair, conscious she wasn't as well-groomed as she was.

Giulietta looked up. '*Ciao*, Claudia.' She stood up to greet her. 'I still can't believe what has happened, can you? I couldn't sleep last night.'

Claudia smiled. After the initial shock, she was excited and nervous at the same time — her stomach was knotted one moment and somersaulting the next. What skeletons were there lurking in Giulietta's cupboards? she wondered. There certainly seemed to be a lot in her own, as she was gradually finding out. 'What would you like to drink?' she asked. 'My treat today. You paid yesterday.'

Giulietta studied the drinks menu while Claudia called the waiter over. '*Granita al limone*, I think. *Grazie*.'

'Make it two, *per favore*,' said Claudia. As the waiter moved away, she added, 'I've got a real liking for those since I've been here.'

But once they were alone, neither of them spoke. It seemed neither of them knew where to begin. The next few moments felt never-ending to Claudia, and it was Giulietta who eventually broke the silence. 'You first. I never knew my father so I want to know everything about him.'

Claudia hardly knew where to start. Perhaps she hadn't really known him either? How could she sum up her lovely papà?

'I knew nothing of his life in Sicily until I arrived here. All I know is he was a lovely, gentle man who has left me with many happy memories.' She took out the photograph of Giulietta as a baby with her parents and placed it in front of her half-sister. 'I know that will be hard for you to hear. But the way he is looking at you in this photo shows how much he loved you, and I know he would be so proud of you now.'

Giulietta picked up the photo and traced her father's face with her finger. 'I wish I could have met him.'

'You already know he was an artist. When he was interned in the POW camp, he was chosen to help create a chapel where the prisoners could worship because he was

207

a painter before the war. You should see it, Giulietta. It's beautiful. He led the team and they made everything from found and scrap materials — metal candlesticks and an altar screen from empty bully beef tins.'

'The chapel sounds wonderful! But what is bully beef?' Giulietta looked puzzled.

'Tinned meat that both the British soldiers and the POWs ate. Part of their rations. The metal from the big tins was cut and bent into shape. Paints were coloured by boiling tea leaves, berries, onion skins. That sort of thing.' The waiter arrived with the two *granite*, but Claudia continued speaking. 'The chapel is still used for a monthly Mass.' She took out her father's prayer card from the envelope and handed it to Giulietta.

Giulietta placed her hand over her open mouth.

Claudia felt the need to explain. 'This is Papà's prayer card. I found out this week our *nonna*, Lucia, had an identical one given to her by her parents on her first communion.'

'And so did I!' said Giulietta. 'Mamma wouldn't say who had left it as a gift for me that day. I was seven at the time and I didn't question her. Do you think it was Nonna?'

'It had to be. And you must recognise the painting. I did as soon as I saw it.'

'Of course I do. It's the Madonna and Child that hangs in the *duomo*.'

'Papà's painting over the altar in the little chapel back home is a replica of that. It's stunning. Apparently, he had a lot of trouble getting the right blue for Mary's robes. The painting needs work as it's now over twenty years old. It's quite faded.'

'Have you heard the rumours regarding the one in the *duomo* being a forgery?' asked Giulietta. 'I didn't mention it in my talk, but from what I've read, some basic tests were made on the painting when it reappeared after the war, along with some of the cathedral's other art and silver that had been hidden for safekeeping.'

'You think it's genuine, then?'

Giulietta didn't answer but simply shrugged.

They continued talking and were surprised when the waiter began laying the tables for dinner. Time had gone so swiftly with Claudia telling Giulietta everything that had happened since she'd arrived in the country.

'This was the best find.' She passed over her grandmother's diary. 'I don't know how much you know about how your parents got together.'

'Nothing. All Mamma would say was there had been a big family row. She wouldn't tell me about the terrible thing my father had supposedly done and, in the end, I gave up asking. I was only little, and as the years went by it just seemed pointless to ask her again. I didn't know him like you did. He meant nothing to me. It was just Mamma and me, and according to her, no living family, no aunts or uncles, no cousins. It was hard. The only reason I was able to go to art college was because my mother had saved money throughout the years I was growing up. I don't know how she did it.'

Giulietta opened the pages of the diary and began reading. Claudia watched her as she read, her expression changing and reflecting the same surprise and puzzlement she herself had experienced.

'This is all such a shock.' She shook her head in disbelief. 'I need time to take it all in. If only I didn't have to go to Rome tomorrow! But once I get back, I can find out all about my — or should I say, *our* — family.'

It was then that Claudia remembered something else. 'Before you go, you don't know what this could be, do you?' She slid the map across to Giulietta. 'It just looks like a drawing of a maze. This is the entrance — he's marked it *entrata* — but what does the cross refer to? Could that be an exit? It was in the envelope my godfather gave me after Papà died. He obviously wanted me to do something with it, but it means nothing to me.'

Giulietta studied the map, turning it in different ways to view it. 'It's a total mystery to me, too. Sorry. How odd!' She handed it back and also slid across a business card. 'We'll meet up when I get back. Here's my telephone number.'

'And here's mine. It's the number of Reception at the *pensione*.' Claudia jotted it down on a slip of paper she found in her bag.

They went their separate ways and as she ambled down the street into the piazza, Claudia reflected on all that had happened in such a short time.

She realised she'd never asked where her half-sister lived now. Matteo had introduced her as a well-renowned art expert, so Claudia supposed it would be an elegant, luxurious apartment in the centre of the city. Not a rundown terraced hovel like where her papà had lived. No wonder Pia's family had not been happy about her marrying him.

CHAPTER THIRTY-SEVEN

Walking along the street from where the bus had dropped her off in I Limoneti, she heard loud voices coming from Alessandro's house. It sounded like laughing and a man singing, which reminded her of Uncle Sisto's beautiful voice. She went to pull on the bell-rope but the front door opened before she could. Accompanied by a wonderful smell of cooking food coming from inside the house, Alessandro's smiling face greeted her. He kissed her on both cheeks, his lips lightly brushing her skin and causing it to tingle.

'I saw you coming. How was the journey on the bus? Good, I hope.' Alessandro's words tumbled out.

'It was fine, *grazie*. I hope it gave you a better chance to help your mother as you didn't have to come for me.'

He took her hand. 'It did, thank you. But I had help myself! Come and meet my family. Mamma has been telling them all about you.'

The cramped living room seemed filled with people. Everything went quiet as Claudia entered, and she felt a flush creep along her neck. Half wishing the floor would swallow her up, she smiled and looked down, but then Alessandro's mother hobbled over to her and kissed her on both cheeks. 'It is so good to see you again. You are all Sandro talks of. You

211

have the good influence on him, I think. Do not worry about all these people. They just want to meet you.'

Claudia scanned the room and returned their smiles. 'It is kind of you to invite me, signora. Please introduce me to everyone!' She noticed the elderly woman's grimace as she crossed the room. 'But are you sure you should be standing on that ankle?'

Alessandro's mother shook her head and allowed herself to be guided back to an upright chair in the corner of the room. She handed the crutches to Claudia, who rested them against the sideboard from where Alessandro and Daniela's wedding day smiles shone across the room.

'Come and meet my sister and her family.' Alessandro ushered her outside onto a paved terrace sheltered from the sun by a cream-coloured awning. 'Claudia, this is my big sister, Olivia. She is responsible for the family feast today. I didn't have to do it, after all! And these are my nieces, Carmela and Isabella, and they are also helping.' He laughed as he tickled the two little girls, who looked to be about six and eight years old. They escaped, giggling, and ran into the garden.

'*Ciao*, Claudia. I have heard so much about you from my mamma. She is right — it is so good to see my brother smile so much again. Come, Sandro. Get this beautiful *amica*, as you call her, an *aperitivo*. A limoncello made with our own *verdelli*, I think.'

The pretty young woman was exactly like an older female version of Alessandro. She finished laying several long trestle tables with plates, bowls and cutlery. Different-sized glasses were placed at each setting.

'Can I do anything to help?' asked Claudia.

'No, you are our guest. But *grazie*. If you want to talk, come with me back to the kitchen. Here is my brother with your limoncello now.'

Claudia had sampled limoncello before but this one was almost green in colour. 'How is it so green?' she asked. 'Lemons are yellow!'

'Well, there is a reason for that, isn't there, Olivia?' Olivia, removing large enamel casserole dishes from the oven, grinned at her brother. He continued. 'Olivia and her husband, Stefano, run a lemon grove and people come from many kilometres away to buy their lemons, but especially their limoncello.'

'We have our own secret recipe, of course, but we use *verdello* lemons. Because they are green, they look underripe, but they are the best kind in our opinion. What do you think?'

Claudia sipped the liqueur and nodded. 'It's good. Really good!'

'Can you carry the casserole dishes to the table, Sandro?' Olivia took out baskets of breads, and boards with selections of cold meats and cheeses on top. 'They can all to come to the table now.'

Soon, everyone was seated. Alessandro and Claudia were sitting next to each other and Signora Costa sat opposite.

'*Buon appetito*!' Olivia passed dishes along for large portions of *caponata* to be served.

'If this is starters, Lord help me when it comes to the other courses!' The others at the table laughed at Claudia's joke.

'Mamma always cooks for an entire nation,' Alessandro chuckled. 'And Olivia has carried on the tradition. I told you to arrive on an empty stomach, didn't I?'

In between courses, Claudia chatted to the woman on her left, who turned out to be the wife of Salvo, who had brought Maria Costa home from hospital.

'I hear you have come to Sicily to find out more about your papà,' the woman said. 'You must have been pleased to get your *nonna*'s diary.'

'*Sì.*' Claudia nodded. 'I was so lucky the suitcase was still in the house.'

It was clear from what the woman said next that her husband *had* recognised her grandmother's name and knew the rumour about her father. Salvo was seated on the other side of his wife, but he remained silent and didn't interrupt her.

'I remember when the painting went missing. I was only a teenager, but everyone at home, they talk about it. A valuable ring was stolen at the same time.' She didn't look at Claudia as she shifted in her seat. 'I can find out more from my old uncle if you would like me to.'

Claudia's heartbeat raced. She was sure her father would not have stolen a ring, but she couldn't help wondering what the link to the missing painting was about. 'Yes, please. Anything. Time's running out. I have to return home in twelve days. I need to know everything.'

Alessandro stood up and topped up people's glasses with red wine while listening in to the conversation.

Claudia turned to the woman again. 'I'm sorry, I don't know your name. I can't just call you "Salvo's wife".'

'Rosa. Call me Rosa. All I remember is people believed it had something to do with the Romano family. The brothers. They had so much power in this part of Sicily. No one dared to go against what they wanted. If you defied them or crossed them, you took your life in your hands. Literally. Rumour had it the stolen painting was a foil for the more serious jewel theft. Someone had annoyed them in a big way, so they were trying to frame this person. And then war was declared and everyone signed up.'

At this point, Olivia brought in more pasta, this time with ragu bolognese, mozzarella, fried aubergine, ham and *mortadella*. '*Buon appetito!*'

'I will definitely speak to my uncle for you. He is very old but his memory is still clear. I will ask Sandro to bring you to his house if I find out more.' Rosa smiled at Claudia. 'Now eat up.'

Claudia was pleased she had only asked for a small portion of the *pasta al forno* when she saw the size of the dessert later on.

'*Cassata Siciliana!*' Olivia announced the arrival of the magnificent *dolce* and placed it on the table while accepting the compliments from everyone. 'Who's for a slice? Sandro's making the coffees so put your orders in now.' Everyone laughed and, without warning, tears pricked Claudia's eyes. She imagined her papà would have loved to be doing exactly what Alessandro was doing right now. From her *nonna*'s diary, it didn't sound as if he was part of a big Sicilian family like this.

Alessandro, returning with the coffee, noticed the tears and squeezed her hand. 'Papà?'

She nodded. 'I don't think he would have had anything like this when he was younger.'

* * *

While Olivia washed up, everyone else found a chair for a post-lunch nap, but Claudia insisted on helping while Alessandro entertained his nieces.

'Thank you for giving me a typical Sicilian lunch, Olivia. It must have taken you ages to prepare all that.'

'Getting together with family and friends is important to us. The fact Mamma wanted you to experience this means she likes you . . . a lot. It has been so difficult since the accident. You know about Daniela, don't you?'

'*Sì*. Alessandro told me. I can't imagine what he went through . . . is still going through.'

'Our family was split in two. First, my father died and then Daniela. To see him smile again has been wonderful for my mother. I see it, too.'

Claudia dried the dishes in silence. She was pleased to be welcomed into the family but she suddenly felt a frisson of panic. She'd only met Alessandro a few weeks ago. She sensed there was a strong attraction between them, but she didn't want to feel pressurised into something before she was ready. She was sure Alessandro didn't either. Hadn't he told her he wanted them to be friends?

Alessandro came into the kitchen followed by Carmela and Isabella just as the last of the dishes were dried. 'Anyone who helps with the clearing up is welcome in Mamma's eyes,' he said.

'Yes, but I will get a telling off for allowing her to do it.' Olivia winked at her brother. 'Why don't you show Claudia around? Show her the views from the bottom of the garden.'

Alessandro quickly went to retrieve his camera and, taking Claudia by the hand, led her to where Olivia had suggested. As they walked, Claudia decided it was a good time to tell him about Giulietta.

'I'm glad to get you alone. You'll never guess what I've found out.' Claudia took a deep breath as she stopped and faced Alessandro. 'Only that the world-renowned expert who came to talk to us is my half-sister — Giulietta!'

Alessandro's mouth gaped open. 'What? You have already found her?' He pulled her to him and hugged her. 'That is wonderful news.'

Claudia nodded, suddenly feeling rather emotional again. 'I know, and I've met her again since the talk, too. She's in Rome at the moment but we're meeting again after she gets back.'

They reached the bottom of the garden.

'You know, I still can't believe you've found your sister. Almost without trying.'

Alessandro held up his camera. 'Let me take your photo with the view behind you.'

He motioned her into position with his hand. 'The colours in your blouse really suit you.'

She gave the obligatory smile and then turned to admire the landscape stretching out before them. They could see well into the distance. A patchwork of green gave a hint of the vineyards and fruit groves the area was famous for. Here and there, roads snaked through and buildings dotted the expanse of green.

Alessandro pointed out some local landmarks for her. 'See that building there?' Claudia looked to where he was pointing. 'That's where my sister and her husband live. It's in the middle of a lemon grove. It's a shame Stefano was busy today with the lemons. He and Olivia built it up from scratch. See the church. That's where the family all go to Mass. Where Liv and I were baptised.'

Immediately, a vision of the Italian chapel her father had helped create came into her mind. Her papà had told her how the font there had started off as a bowl for holy water moulded from an old tyre. Her baptism had been the first in the chapel with Uncle Sisto and Auntie Ceridwen in attendance as her godparents.

'And where Daniela and I got married.' She realised Alessandro was still speaking. 'I haven't been inside there since her funeral.' He stifled a sob.

His mother and sister might think he was happier, but Claudia could see how things were still raw.

'I'm sorry, Claudia. I was sure I was over this, not being able to mention her name.'

Claudia patted his arm. 'It's okay. I understand. It shows how much you loved her. Still love her.'

They turned to return to the house and were greeted by two little girls running towards them and squealing. 'These two help me realise life must go on.' Alessandro's smile was back.

CHAPTER THIRTY-EIGHT

Claudia had just over a week left before returning home. With Giulietta in Rome, she had decided she would complete her assignment early so she could spend her last few days with her half-sister. Matteo had given the students a list of *duomos* in other towns where they'd find different styles of paintings to draw and label. Claudia's sketchbook was nearly full, and she smiled when she realised how many times she'd been drawn back to the Madonna and Child painting in the *duomo*. Perhaps it had had the same effect on her father, which was why he'd been able to reproduce it so perfectly in the Italian chapel in Wales.

She knew her father had been accused of a crime serious enough for Pia to have believed it and left the home she shared with her *nonna*, but she still didn't know the full details. Claudia was desperate to find out more about it before she returned home. Time was running out.

The street was quiet as Claudia left the *pensione* that morning. Pale sunlight crept down between the tall buildings and illuminated the paved street as she walked to the bus stop. The smell of roasted coffee filled the air the nearer she got to the *trattoria*, and she was surprised to see it open. It was already busy, with the tables outside filling up. Locals were calling in for pastries and coffees. Inside, there were tall tables where men stood sipping *caffè* and tumblers of water. The smoke from their strong cigarettes filled the air.

She was even more surprised to see Giovanna sitting at the table she'd been at before, with a long, slim cigarette holder in one hand and a tiny cup of *caffè* in the other. She placed her coffee cup down and raised her hand. '*Buongiorno!*' She stood up and gestured to Claudia, inviting her to join her.

Claudia sat at the table. '*Buongiorno*. It's so good to see you. I keep missing you.'

The older woman signalled to the waiter. '*Due caffè, per favore.*' Turning back to Claudia, she looked at her with interest. 'Now, tell me how have you been? How are you finding my nephew?'

Claudia told her all about the course and how she'd fallen in love with Sicily. She told her of her friendship with Alessandro and her visit to his home for a proper Sicilian family meal. She wondered if she should tell her about finding out Giulietta was her sister but decided against it. The fewer people who knew the better until they could clear their father's name. Of course, Claudia realised she might already know if she had been speaking to Matteo, but the longer the conversation went on, the more she was sure she hadn't.

'Yes, but how are you really finding my nephew?' There was a twinkle in Giovanna's eye.

What did she want her to say? If she was honest, Claudia found him a bit pompous and patronising, but she couldn't tell his aunt that. He was very full of his own importance.

'He's good at what he does and he certainly knows his stuff. I've learned a lot from him.' Choosing her words with care, Claudia reasoned that what she said was true, despite her mind being on other things for most of the time. 'In fact, he's suggested the place where I'm off to this morning. Castella di San Niccolò. I'm going to look at the artwork in the *duomo* there. It's part of my final assignment for Matteo.'

Claudia took out her sketchbook and flicked through the pages to show her what she'd done. Giovanna stopped her at a detailed sketch of the Madonna and Child. 'You know they say this is a forgery, don't you? They've never found the original, though. Even Matteo isn't sure. He says they would have heard if the original had appeared in an auction house somewhere but there's been nothing. It has disappeared off the face of the earth. He says, if it is a forgery, the artist was immensely talented.'

'The *duomo* authorities are happy with what was mysteriously returned. The emerald ring that went missing at the same time was recovered, though.' Giovanna lit another cigarette, inhaling deeply then turning her head to blow out circles of smoke. 'The Romano family was mixed up with it, as they are with most things in the city. One of the brothers, Roberto, did time for it. Lorenzo conveniently had an alibi. Tried to pin it on someone else, of course. So much wealth, so much power. If anyone dared confront them, they were threatened, assaulted or even worse. Consequently, no one ever did in those days. Since the war, they have moved on to bigger things. They have links everywhere. They live in the south of the island now.'

Claudia listened with interest and decided she would read the finished notes of her *nonna*'s diary again and see if she could learn more about Pia's family.

'They sold the villa when Signor Romano died. Have you been up there yet? It's worth a visit, even if you just walk around it. The views over the bay are amazing.'

Although it had been on her list, she hadn't yet managed to get there. She'd ask Alessandro to go with her when she met up with him that evening. The way time was passing as she talked to Giovanna meant it would be getting too hot for sightseeing in Castella di San Niccolò after the hour's bus journey she still had to endure.

'No, I've been meaning to go.' She stood up. 'I'm sorry but I have to catch the next bus.' She looked at her watch. '*Grazie* for the coffee.'

But what Giovanna said next made her sit down again.

'You must visit. Apparently, the present owner is an eminent art historian and bought it from the previous American owners. She had been living in Rome when her marriage broke up and she returned to the city of her birth. No one knows much about her.'

Claudia had never asked Giulietta where she lived. She was in Rome at that moment, so as well as giving her talks, perhaps she had a house there, too? There was so much she still didn't know about her papà's other daughter. She couldn't wait for her to return.

'I'll let you know when I take a trip up there, but I really must go now. It's been so good to talk to you. You are the fount of all knowledge about this town.'

Giovanna stood up and kissed Claudia on both cheeks. '*Ciao, cara* Claudia. It's just everybody knows me and they tell me all the secrets.'

They both laughed.

As Claudia hurried along the street after leaving the *trattoria*, she was glad she hadn't told Giovanna her own secret.

* * *

Although the purpose of her visit was to study the paintings in the town's *duomo*, Claudia was entranced by the pretty, narrow streets of Castella di San Niccolò. The ones that led away from a main street, where shops displayed local crafts and produce, were so narrow, it would be difficult to pass anyone even when walking. Brightly coloured ceramic pots containing plants stood on some of the steps. Looking up, she saw many buildings had balconies edged with metal railings, full of terracotta pots brimming with the fiery-red geraniums she was getting so used to seeing. Along one side of the street, she stopped to look at a beautifully detailed mosaic picture set in the wall and framed in what she surmised were narrow pillars of local stone. She came to a spacious piazza, flagged in white marble tiles, where the blonde-coloured *duomo* stood. It was smaller and quite different from the one in Porto Montebello. The main wooden doors, each carved in a relief of a bishop in a mitre holding a staff, were approached by sets of steps on either side, and there was a sculpted balustrade along the front.

Stepping inside, Claudia was immediately mesmerised by the ornately sculptured relief detail on the pillars and the domed ceiling over the altar. Before making notes, she wandered around the cathedral, absorbing the atmosphere. Taking a pew, she took out her sketchbook. One wall displayed several paintings in a similar style to the works she'd seen in other *duomos*. She made brief notes and sketches of those, but one painting stood out for her, hung above the marble altar. It was a huge painting of Christ holding an open Bible. She began to sketch, making more detailed notes of the proportion, the colours and the style of the painting.

She looked at her watch a little while later and realised she'd been so engrossed in what she'd been doing that some hours had passed. She packed up and made her way down the steep hill from the town to the bus station, hoping that Matteo would approve of her afternoon's work.

CHAPTER THIRTY-NINE

Claudia hadn't seen Alessandro since the meal at his mother's house when she'd enjoyed meeting his family and friends. She had reluctantly begun to come to terms with the idea that there'd be no romance with him. He was clearly not ready to move on from the tragedy of losing Daniela, no matter what his mother and sister thought. She enjoyed being in his company, especially as he was someone she had come to trust and could confide in. Apart from Giulietta, he was the only person who had read her *nonna*'s diary, and he'd promised to do anything he could to help her find out about her Sicilian family.

When Claudia came down to breakfast the next morning, a letter was waiting for her at Reception.

'A young man called with this, this morning, *signorina*,' Signor Marchesi informed her.

Claudia thanked him and found a private space in the vestibule to read it. It was from Alessandro.

> *Mia cara, Claudia,*
>> *I would like to meet with you tonight. I have a message for you from my neighbour, Rosa. I will wait for you in the piazza by the fountain at 7 p.m. I hope you can make it.*
>> *Il tuo amico, Sandro*

* * *

A gentle stillness in the evening air greeted Claudia when she emerged onto the street. She walked the short distance from the *pensione* into the piazza, making her way towards the fountain with its elaborate animal statues guarding a main figure of the goddess, Athena. It was the centrepiece of the piazza, much photographed by visitors. Whereas earlier in the day, the area had been bustling with tourists, it was now almost deserted. She turned when she heard a familiar voice. Alessandro was parking his scooter by the town hall and calling to her.

'*Ciao*!' Claudia rose her hand and approached him.

They embraced. 'I've missed you,' Alessandro said quietly. 'I was so afraid you wouldn't turn up.'

'Why ever not?'

'Oh, because I got upset again on Sunday when talking about Daniela. I'm sorry. That's twice in front of you now. I think it was because I so wanted the day to be a success — and it was. Everyone loved you. It's just that it made me remember bringing Daniela home for the first time and it brought it all back.'

Claudia linked her arm through his, and they crossed over to one of the *trattorie* edging the piazza. Once they'd found a table and sat down, she took his hand in hers. 'Look, Sandro — I'm going to call you that now, like all your family and friends do, plus it's how you signed your note today. I've only known you for a short time, but you must realise I've fallen for you. And, yes, I know I'm going home soon, too. One of the lovely things about you is you are not afraid to show your love for your wife. You shouldn't feel pressurised to move on until you are ready. I'll be happy with being your friend. Come on. Let's order. My treat. The pizzas here look amazing.'

She passed him a menu, trying to move the conversation on, but as she did, he took her hand and kissed it. A fizz of emotion ran through her. '*Grazie*. I have a message from Rosa for you. She's been in touch with her uncle, and if it's convenient for you, I'll pick you up after your course tomorrow and take you to his house. It's in the same village where I have my studio so I can show you it at the same time. We didn't go in there last time. Bring your sketchbook with you, and I'll bring some watercolours and pencils. Rosa thinks what he has to tell you will be helpful in your quest to find out what happened before your papà signed up for the war.'

This was what she'd come to Sicily for! Excitement rushed through her. 'Oh, that's fantastic! The best news, thank you. Talking to someone who remembers the war will be wonderful. Will Rosa be there, too?'

'Yes, she'll meet us there.'

It was turning into a perfect evening. Delicious local food and wine, a convivial atmosphere and, best of all, wonderful company. After all her disastrous attempts at a relationships when she'd been at art college, trying hard to be a modern sixties girl, perhaps this was what had been missing: friendship. Instead of jumping into bed with the men she'd met, something she'd always regretted later, she should have got to know them first, found out more about them as people and just enjoyed their company. There was something quite sensual about being with someone who took your hand and kissed it gently, looking at someone with longing but knowing they weren't ready to love you back. *Yet.* That word was an important one, she was sure of it.

The waiter came to take their plates and they ordered coffee.

Claudia brought out her father's mystery map from her bag and spread it out on the table. 'I hope you can help me with this as well. I don't know if this makes any sense to you. After my papà died, my Uncle Sisto gave me this, along with the photograph I showed you. He didn't know what was in the sealed envelope when he gave it to me. Papà said it was only to be given to me after his death. It's as if he wanted me to solve a riddle.'

Alessandro turned the paper so he could see it properly. 'It certainly does look as if the series of parallel lines are roads or streets. Pathways, even. I think you're right about stairs. But what do the numbers mean, and the circle with a cross inside?'

Various numbers were labelled along the "streets". Where was there a maze of streets with an entrance and several short flights of stairs? Was it in Wales or Sicily? Why would her father give her something like that to solve after his death? It obviously meant something to him. Questions whizzed around Claudia's head, but neither she nor Alessandro could come up with possible answers.

'I'll have a good think, but at the moment I'm just not sure.' Alessandro became thoughtful. 'Do you mind if I keep it until I see you next time?'

Claudia nodded. Then they paid the bill and he accompanied her back to the *pensione*. By then, the sky was a velvety indigo, studded with diamond-like stars. As they said goodnight, Alessandro pulled her into his arms for a good-night embrace.

Her heartbeat raced. It wasn't the kiss she longed for but if Alessandro wanted to take his time, it was fine by her.

Afterwards, Claudia stood and watched Alessandro return to the piazza. Being honest about her feelings had changed things. He knew how she felt about him now and she hoped he would want to move on at some time. When he did, she would be ready and she allowed herself to imagine being more than a friend to Alessandro. Nothing would stop her coming back to Sicily, but her return ticket was booked for less than a week and she needed to go home. She had to tell her mam about Pia and Giulietta face to face. Although she was dreading seeing her mother's reaction, the more time she spent with Giulietta, the more she realised her father had had no choice. He couldn't have returned to Sicily. Pia hadn't wanted anything more to do with him, and if he'd returned, it sounded like her brothers would have killed him. Claudia would never believe he had stolen the painting. The only explanation was that he'd been framed, and she was determined to prove he was innocent — hopefully with Giulietta's help. In her mind, all her father was guilty of was grasping a chance of happiness with the person he loved.

CHAPTER FORTY

It was now only five days before she had to leave Sicily, and Claudia knew she had to make every effort to solve the mystery and clear her father's name. Before leaving her room that morning, she made sure she had everything she needed for the visit to Rosa's uncle and to Alessandro's studio straight after her class. She packed her sketchbook in her duffel bag, as well as a notebook and her *nonna*'s diary. She was excited that Rosa's uncle had information for her, and yet also nervous that it might be something she wouldn't want to hear.

Her first task of the day was submitting her final assignment to Matteo's secretary — early, as she'd planned. She hoped she had done enough to pass, if only to justify that her papà's money had been well spent.

After she'd done this, the day passed slowly. She caught up with some of the other students and found out how their assignments were going, all the while remembering that the following day was when Giulietta was coming back from Rome.

The dazzling sunshine made her blink as she left the cool, shaded area in front of the university building.

'*Ciao.*' As she left, Claudia called to the group of students sauntering into the *piazza*.

To kill time until she met Alessandro, she wandered down to Via Umberto with the intention of seeing Skye and Curtis and letting them know how she was getting on with her *nonna*'s diaries. They weren't in, but when she looked through the window, the place still looked lived in and still contained their possessions as she remembered them. They must have come to an arrangement with the landlord. She was so glad they hadn't moved on and hoped she would get to see them again before she left.

When she returned to the piazza, she noticed Alessandro sitting astride his white Vespa and rushed over to him.

'Ready?' He grinned. 'Oh, and before we start off, I think I have solved the riddle of your papà's map.'

'You have? Well, don't keep me in suspense!'

He took the sheet of paper from his pocket and spread it over the handlebars of the scooter. 'Well, Signorina Rosso. I think it is a map of the underground tunnels the *duomo* is famous for. See where it says *entrata*? Well, that is the entrance over there.' He pointed to an area to the right of the cathedral.

Claudia hugged him. 'You're a genius. I'm convinced one of the frescoes in the *duomo* is his. I know he worked there as an apprentice so it makes sense it's connected. But why would Papà leave me a map of the tunnels?'

'I'm only guessing that is what it is, mind. I went down there once when I was in school and remembered being told about it being used as a shelter, but I still don't know what all these numbers are. Why don't we wait until Giulietta can come as well?' He handed the map back to Claudia.

'She's back tomorrow, so we could go then. I've just got a feeling that this may lead us to clearing Papà's name! Anyway, let's go and see what Rosa's uncle has to say.'

The journey didn't take long. Claudia hung on to Alessandro as the scooter travelled around the winding bends. To the right of them, the crystalline sea glistened a deep aquamarine through to a deep sapphire. As they dropped down, a pretty fishing village, its beach enclosed by dramatic rock formations, came into view. Along the quayside, boats and schooners of all descriptions bobbed on the water.

'I think you are getting to know Villaggio delle Rocce well, eh? Signor Alessi lives just by the little church on the far clifftop. My studio is in the heart of the village.'

Alessandro parked the scooter in the street and they climbed from the harbour up to the clifftop.

'Your shoulders are a bit red. Come this side of me so that you're in my shadow.' Alessandro made sure she was in the shade once they left the streets of the village.

Claudia moved to the other side of him. '*Grazie.*'

'We should not be out in the midday sun, should we? I think you have a saying for it. Something about mad dogs and Englishmen?'

Claudia giggled. 'And Welsh girls.'

'Signor Alessi lives in an old stone fisherman's cottage overlooking the harbour. Rosa told me he worked as a fisherman when he was younger. Apparently, every morning as dawn broke, he would be on the quayside selling his catch to the local restaurateurs,' Alessandro told her.

Rosa was waiting in the doorway when they approached, a wide smile on her face. After greeting both of them, she led the way through the cottage to the back where an old man sat in the shade of a gnarled olive tree.

'*Zio* Luca. This is Claudia Rosso. You know Alessandro, I think.' Rosa introduced them as the old man attempted to get up. 'You stay there.'

He sank back in his chair and beckoned for his two guests to pull up a seat next to him. The only hair he had left was snow-white tufts at his temples, contrasting starkly with his weathered complexion.

'*Benvenuto.*' He turned to Claudia. 'I think you want me to say about the Romano family. When war, it starts, Porto Montebello was very different place, not like today. A lot of crime and violence. Much by the Romanos. Signor Romano was very rich man. Got his money illegally, like other powerful families. Drugs, he demands the money, he robs. If anyone stands up to them, they suffer. His sons, they do the same. When their sister is with child, she is the teenager. They say they find the man who does it and kill him.' The old man paused for breath.

'Take your time, *Zio*.' Rosa looked concerned.

Claudia looked at Alessandro, who said, 'Yes, do not tire yourself. We have plenty of time, don't we, Claudia? It is lovely to visit you here. I didn't realise you were so close. My studio is down in the village, on the street just up from the harbour.'

The old man spoke again. 'It is a good spot for a studio, eh?' His voice was clearer. 'It was just before war broke out.'

'Did they find out who the man was?' asked Claudia.

'*Sì, sì*. It is, how do you say, under their noses. The son of the housekeeper of the family. He grows up with the Romanos as children. An apprentice painter and spends a lot of his time copying the old masters in the *duomo*. Next, we hear one of the valuable paintings is missing, along with the gold ring that is priceless. It belongs to *il vescovo*. It has the very rare emerald.'

Claudia looked at Alessandro for clarity.

'*Il vescovo*. The bishop.'

'Ah. So, what had the robbery got to do with Pa— I mean, the man who'd got the sister pregnant? What happened to him?'

Alessandro exchanged glances with Claudia, and she inhaled deeply, nervous about what the old man was about to say.

'There is a note handed in. Nobody signs it. It says the name of the man who steals. Everyone is very angry. The man steals from the place of God. They go to his house. It is too late. He signs up for the war and leaves Sicily. Pah, the police, they are slow in acting. He gets away.'

Claudia was angry on her father's behalf. The Romano brothers had clearly been at the root of the rumour. Having read all of her *nonna*'s diary, there was another side to the story and Claudia thought how satisfying it must have been for her *nonna* to see Roberto Romano in the prison area of the underground tunnels during the bombing. But it seemed some still regarded her father as guilty. No wonder Salvo had acted the way he had on their first meeting. She was now more determined than ever to prove her father's innocence. 'Do you know the name of the housekeeper and her son?' she asked, bracing herself for the response.

'Everyone who lives in the war knows it. It is Carlo Rosso, Lucia Rosso, her boy,' said the old man. 'They say he dies in North Africa.'

There seemed to be a lot of rumours flying round. It was what Pia had told Giulietta, too. She hadn't learned anything new from Rosa's uncle, but hearing about how powerful the Romano family was, and the fear they'd instilled in the local people, made her more sympathetic to the fact her father hadn't risked returning. He couldn't. Because of the threat to his life, he never saw his mamma again.

'*Grazie*, Signor Alessi, and to you, Rosa. It's been so good to meet someone who lived through the war like my *nonna*. Reading her diary makes me imagine what it was like, and now you've given me some more information, I have an even better idea.'

They stood to go, but as they did the old man caught Claudia's arm. 'But I do not think it was the young Rosso who steals. They catch Roberto Romano. He has the ring in his hands. He tries to sell it to a Nazi soldier. It is before the Allies invade us. He goes to prison. It is a strange thing when the painting comes back to the *duomo*. It is like a miracle. It comes when the church silver returns from hiding after the war. They say the other brother, Lorenzo, he gets the cleaner at the *duomo* to help him return it. It burns his hands. He cannot sell the painting. It is too famous. The Rosso boy, he is dead by then.'

So, there *had* been a doubt over her father being the thief. If the rumour was correct, that was why the painting was returned without explanation. It made sense! It couldn't be sold. Claudia smiled at *Zio* Luca's interpretation of the saying "too hot to handle". She remembered that the old man in the *duomo* had mentioned the cleaner, too.

'*Grazie. Arriverderchi.*'

Claudia and Alessandro left the cottage and travelled down to the studio. Once there, Alessandro unlocked the door and a strong smell of turpentine transported Claudia back, not only to her own painting days in college, but further back still to her father's workshop in the garden of their home. She'd been very young when she'd started spending a lot of her time there with him. She remembered when he'd let her have her own stretched canvas and instructed her on how to prime it before sketching out a scene in charcoal. Precious memories.

Alessandro wound up the shutter and the studio filled with light. Paintings of seascapes and cliff formations predominated amongst some village and street scenes, along with several portraits. What struck Claudia was the array of colours he'd used, so vibrant and exciting, reflecting the Mediterranean climate and culture in which he lived. His work was so different from the dark and sombre colours of the ecclesiastical paintings they'd been studying on the course. No wonder he hadn't been fully committed to the work he'd been asked to do at the university. Perhaps his mother's fall had been just the excuse he needed.

Claudia wandered from painting to painting, then went around to see what was painted on a canvas facing away from her. When she saw the subject, she caught her breath. 'It's me!'

A head-and-shoulders portrait of a young woman with glossy black hair falling over her shoulders smiled back at her. He'd captured the dimples and the way she sometimes felt shy. From the clothing visible, she recognised the tie-dye blouse with gathered puff sleeves she'd worn for Sunday lunch at his mother's house. She remembered he'd taken a photo of her in his mother's garden so he must have painted it from that.

'I hope you don't mind.' He looked uncertain.

'I love it, even though it feels strange looking at myself. You have real talent. These—' she pointed at the row of seascapes — 'remind me of Papà's. Until I came to Sicily, I imagined he'd exaggerated the shades of blue, but he hadn't. You haven't. They're beautiful.'

Alessandro smiled. 'I need to take you out in my boat. It's where I go for inspiration for my sea paintings. I'll take you right inside some of the caves so you can see the beauty of the rocks and coral under the water. I never tire of painting there. The paintings sell well, too. The tourists want to take a bit of Sicily back with them.'

Claudia became reflective. She had to remember that's what she was, too: a tourist. She might be half Italian, and now knew she had a Sicilian half-sister, but her return journey was getting closer. She would be back home in Wales before she knew it.

CHAPTER FORTY-ONE

So much had happened since she'd arrived, but she didn't feel she was any closer to proving her father's innocence. That night, Claudia couldn't settle. Time was running out. With no prospect of sleep, she read more translations from her grandmother's diaries. One stood out. Although she would never meet Pia, she already didn't think she would have liked her. How could someone be so cruel to someone like Lucia Rosso? She'd given Pia a home when her father had thrown her out and had arranged for a priest to marry her and Carlo to give her respectability. Yet, she'd still left with her baby and had broken Lucia's heart.

> *5 May 1940*
>
> *The saddest of days today. I came back from the market to find Pia packing. She was leaving with the baby. She was just going to leave and not tell me. She believes the polizia. Believes what that awful brother of hers, Roberto, has told her. She shouted she no longer has a husband. Cannot stay married to someone who steals from the church. Too shameful, she said. I told her I overheard her brothers plotting the robbery and to say it was Carlo. Heard them say they were out to make my Carlo pay for bringing disgrace*

to the family. I went to the polizia. But who would take my word against a Romano? Even the polizia are corrupt like them. And yet she believes them, not me.

The house is empty. Silent. What has happened to the girl I treated like my own daughter? How can she be so cruel? She said I will never see my grandchild again. If only Signora Cristina was still here. She would make her daughter see sense. I already miss the little one's laughter and squeals so much . . .

Tears filled Claudia's eyes. By reading the diary, she really felt she knew her Sicilian grandmother. It may be twenty years too late, but she owed it not only to her papà, but also to her, to clear his name, once and for all.

It was the last thing she thought about before drifting off to sleep.

* * *

In no time at all, she was awoken by her travel alarm clock going off. It was eight o'clock. The evening before, she'd telephoned Giulietta and arranged to meet her and Alessandro at nine. After a hurried breakfast, she gathered up her notebook, the diary and the all-important map. After Alessandro's brainwave, the map held more significance than it had done at first. Claudia couldn't wait to tell her half-sister what he had come up with and what Signor Alessi had told her about the robbery.

Giulietta was waiting for her at the restaurant off the piazza where they'd met before. Claudia watched her for a while, noticing again the little mannerisms she knew she had herself that her mam had always compared to her father's. She was struck again by how much the other woman looked like her. Without warning, Claudia's throat tightened and her eyes misted. Giulietta had all the money and status of a successful art historian, but she would never know what a lovely man their father had been.

Giulietta looked up and her face broke into a wide grin. 'Claudia!' Claudia hurried over as she stood up and the two sisters embraced. 'All appointments fulfilled! I'm yours now until you have to leave. What would you like? A cappuccino?'

'*Si. Grazie.*'

Claudia spent the next hour, and another coffee later, updating Giulietta on what had happened since she'd been in Rome.

'How did the visit to Rosa's *zio* go?' asked Giulietta.

'He confirmed how Papà has been accused of stealing the painting, but listen to this — he didn't think "the Rosso boy", as he called him, had done it. Roberto was caught red-handed with the ring and rumour has it that Lorenzo replaced the painting into the vaults of the *duomo*.' Claudia pulled out the diary entries. 'I warn you, this will make difficult reading for you, but I re-read this one last night. It makes more sense now after talking with Rosa's uncle.' She slid the diary across, open on the page of the 5 May entry, and watched as Giulietta's face drained of colour.

'My mother was one of the infamous Romanos? It is a very common name in Sicily, of course. How could she be so cruel to Lucia? Mamma said she was an orphan and that her parents and brothers were killed in a boating accident. We moved to Palermo when I eight, so I hadn't heard of this city's Romano brothers until I began studying here. They were notorious. Apparently, every crime or drug deal could be traced back to them. But how did our *nonna* get involved with them?'

'From the photos I found in the suitcase, it's clear she was some sort of cook or housekeeper. It looks as if Papà used to go with her and play with the Romano children.' Claudia began reading one of the entries out loud. '"Why didn't I see what was happening under my nose? Carlo and Pia were always close, but I understood they were just good friends. You can't help who you fall in love with, though, can you?"' As she spoke the words, a certain handsome face entered Claudia's mind. *No, you can't.*

She continued. 'The priceless bishop's ring was traced back to Roberto Romano and he served time. In fact, in the diary, when Nonna described what it was like sheltering from the bombs in the underground tunnels, she mentions a special area where the prisoners were held. She said it gave her great pleasure to see him locked up along with other "lowlifes", as she called them. It couldn't have had anything to do with Papà. He was in Wales by then.'

Claudia had kept the part about Alessandro's theory until last. Now, she pulled out the map from her bag and spread it on the table. 'Sandro came up with something interesting the other day. He thinks it could be a map of the tunnels under the *duomo*.'

As if on cue, Alessandro arrived in the piazza, parked his Vespa and joined the two sisters.

'Sandro!' Claudia stood and kissed him on both cheeks. She turned to Giulietta. 'I don't think you've met my lovely sister, have you? You'd left by the time she gave her wonderful talk at the university. Alessandro, this is Giulietta. Giulietta, Alessandro.'

'*Ciao*.' They greeted each other in unison.

'So, you are the young man who has put a glow on my little sister's face, Alessandro?' Giulietta smiled.

He looked at Claudia and winked. 'Has she told you about my theory regarding your father's puzzling map? We waited until you got back so we could go down into the tunnels together. They are open today.'

'I think you may have something, Alessandro. The *entrata* is there, so what are we waiting for?'

Giulietta called the waiter over and paid for the coffees. Then they crossed the piazza and bought their tickets to enter the tunnels.

'Can you imagine what it must have been like for Nonna and her neighbours, dashing for cover with bombs raining overhead?' Claudia paused thoughtfully for a moment. 'These tunnels were their lifeline — the difference between living or dying.'

To the left of the main entrance, a solid metal door pitted with rust was open, leading the way to steep stone steps. Claudia handed the map to Alessandro and they followed him in.

'The map is not of here. It is not this *entrata*. Look.' He held up the map for the other two to see. He was right. On the map, her father had drawn a path straight from the entrance door, with no steps, but here they were turning to the left and walking down a tight, narrow flight of stairs. Claudia had a sinking feeling in her stomach. She'd been sure Alessandro's instinct had been right, but now she wasn't so sure.

The air became cooler the further down the stairs they descended. There was very little headroom and the steps were worn smooth from hundreds of years of footsteps. Claudia thought of her *nonna* and the crowds of people like her hurrying to safety underground. Lights had now been installed at intervals along the rough stone walls, but in wartime they would have had to rely on dim lamps to find their way down the narrow passageway. Claudia imagined being pushed and shoved by crowds desperate to get to safety. Halfway down, the stairway came to a square landing and then changed direction. When they reached the bottom, the pathway became much wider and they were able to stand up straight. Above them, the rock was rough and untouched, but the side walls and the passageway itself had been levelled out so it was easier to walk.

'Look, the rock has been hewn to form seats. I remember a part in Nonna's diary where she wrote about reading to the children. Can you imagine children having to come down here?' Claudia's remark was met with reflective silence.

Giulietta shivered. 'I find it a bit spooky. All these shadows.'

'Come on, let's get this over with. Hopefully, your theory is right, Alessandro, and we'll find where Papà started his map.'

They travelled on, turning a corner, and, sure enough, there was the word *Entrata* carved in the rock over what resembled a cave entrance.

'I knew it!' shouted Alessandro, his voice echoing back. He studied the map again. 'Let us see where Carlo Rosso is leading us. Along to the right of the entrance, he has written "fifteen". Why don't I try fifteen paces to start? Paces vary, I know, but if we work on one pace being about three quarters of a metre, we may have some idea. It will only give us a rough estimate, but it may tell us what measurement he was referring to. Let us see where we get to in relation to the right turn.'

'It's worth a try,' said Giulietta.

Alessandro walked through the entrance and turned right. He strode out, but only got as far as nine paces before the tunnel turned left. 'It cannot be that, then. It has got to be a smaller measurement.'

Claudia thought for a moment. 'Back home we measure in feet. Why don't I try placing one foot directly in front of the other?'

The other two watched and counted. 'One, two, three, four. . .'

Although Claudia was just short of the turning, someone with slightly bigger feet would have reached it. 'Fifteen. That's it. If I do the stepping and take into account the person's feet being slightly longer, I think we can make our way to where he's indicated the cross.'

The further into the tunnels they went, the colder it got, but it was surprisingly dry down there. Butterflies swirled in Claudia's stomach. At one corner, they found what looked like a makeshift shrine. It had obviously been down there a long time but was still recognisable — a large statue of a praying Madonna in a blue cloak standing on the side of a ledge. Claudia could imagine her *nonna* praying for the safe return of her son alongside the other mothers whose family members were goodness knew where. Various artifacts had been placed on a flat rock nearby — metal jugs and bowls, the remnants of a used candle in its makeshift tin holder.

Alessandro continued to step along the tunnels, counting according to the map.

'Look at these!' shouted Giulietta.

The other two joined her. On the wall were what looked like children's drawings of aeroplanes sketched in charcoal.

'Different kinds of fighter bombers, even a parachute. Imagine being a child and having to spend your days here.' Alessandro's voice was sombre. 'No fresh air, no playing on the beach, just squashed in here with hundreds of people you did not even know. Poor *bambini*.'

They were all quiet for a time, and Claudia's throat tightened as she tried to stem the tears threatening to fall. She remembered another extract from the diary. 'Nonna tells of the children thinking of war as a game, running about down here, playing bombing and using pretend guns.'

They moved further along the tunnel. Another wall displayed graffiti, clearly drawn by adults this time.

VIVA L'ITALIA
VIVA LA LIBERTÀ

Conditions underground must have been insufferable, and yet it seemed the people who'd sheltered here had been united against the enemy, despite their dire situation. Although she'd never met her grandmother, and never would, the more she saw of the tunnels, the more the words in her diary came alive. Perhaps she had written it for that reason. She wouldn't have been able to tell her son all this in her letters as they would have been read and censored.

Up ahead, Alessandro's shouts interrupted Claudia's thoughts. 'You will never guess what the cross is!'

Claudia and Giulietta rushed to him. All they saw was him standing by another plain wall of the tunnel, but he was grinning.

'What?' they said together.

He moved away and pointed. 'There.'

There was a long gap in the rock wall, approximately a metre long and less than a quarter of a metre deep.

'It's just a gap in the rock. There are lots of them, maybe not as long as this one but they're everywhere!' Claudia protested.

Alessandro pointed at the map. 'But don't you see, your papà directed you to this one? The cross is exactly here. Even allowing for different-sized feet. There's nothing else here.' Alessandro clearly couldn't contain his excitement. 'Right, which one of you is going to put your hand in to see if there is something in there? It is a perfect hiding place — I am convinced of it.'

The sisters looked at each other.

'No way.' Claudia looked aghast. 'It's most likely full of creepy crawlies.'

'Or dead rats,' added Giulietta. 'Or human bones, even.'

'Now you're being ridiculous.' Even in the dim light, they could see him roll his eyes.

He placed his hand through the gap in the rock and pushed his arm in as far as he could. They waited for him to say something, but then he moved to the side of the gap and pushed his arm further along. 'There is definitely something in there.' He pulled his arm out. 'But it is no good. My hands are too big.'

Claudia and Giulietta pushed their hands together, comparing the size.

'Yours are the smallest.' Alessandro pointed to Giulietta. 'Are you willing to give it a try? No dead rats or people in there, I promise.'

Claudia watched her half-sister cautiously place her hand and arm through the gap, grimacing as she pushed further in. 'I can feel something, but there's nothing there to grip on to.' She moved to the other end of the gap and pushed from the other side. 'That's better. I can pull at the bottom. I think I can tell it's a tube of some kind, now that I've dislodged it a bit.'

Claudia's pulse quickened and her palms became sweaty. *Could this be what Papà wanted me to find? Please God, let it be.*

Alessandro placed an arm around Claudia's shoulders while they watched. Giulietta pulled and one end of whatever was in the rock came up to the top. It was covered in dirty brown card that had ripped at one corner where Giulietta had tried to dislodge it. Just as she was about to pull it up with her other hand, she lost her grip and the tube fell back into the gap. '*Merda*!'

She tried again, and this time she managed to get the end of the tube to the top of the gap, while Claudia put her hand in and tried to secure the other end. Between them, they slowly eased the tube out.

'That is it!' Alessandro encouraged them. 'Nearly there.'

Together, the sisters pulled the tube forward through the gap lengthways and gently placed it on the stone floor. Claudia glanced at her two companions and knew they were as puzzled as she was. 'This isn't the place to open it. Let's get out of here and find somewhere warm. I don't really believe in ghosts, but I swear I can feel eyes watching us.' She shuddered.

They traced their way back up to ground level. The sun was still high in the sky as they re-entered the piazza, and they shielded their eyes as they got accustomed to the bright light. As soon as Claudia felt the heat on her skin, she silently scolded herself for being ridiculous in the tunnel.

'Let's go and have a coffee,' she suggested. 'I think we all deserve one. Then we'll be ready to open the package.'

* * *

The café they chose was quiet. They ordered coffees and cannoli and were served quickly. Impatient to know what was in the tube, all three of them wolfed down the pastries and the coffees disappeared in one gulp. They hurriedly pushed the cups and plates to one side.

Giulietta brushed down the cardboard covering the tube with a paper napkin before placing it on the table. As she peeled back the brown card to reveal another covering of material, a letter fell away from under the string holding the material in place. The hairs on the back of Claudia's neck stood to attention. She would know the beautiful handwriting anywhere.

On the yellowed envelope, in faded ink, were written in Italian the words, *Treat with care and return to its rightful home.*

'What does it mean?' asked Alessandro.

'Are you all right, Claudia? You've gone as white as a sheet. Do you want to open the letter?' Giulietta looked at her anxiously.

Claudia shook her head at her half-sister. 'No, you do it.'

'If you're sure.' Giulietta ran her nail along the sealed edge of the envelope and then took the letter out. As she read, she gasped and covered her mouth before handing it to Claudia. 'You read it.'

> *To whoever is reading this letter.*
>
> *Inside this parcel is a priceless painting, The Madonna and Child by Giovanni Battista Salvi da Sassoferrato. In 1939, just before the outbreak of war, plans were made by the Romano brothers to steal it from the duomo and frame me for the theft. I knew there was no point in reporting it to the police. They were as unscrupulous as the Romanos. In order to ensure the original painting remained with its rightful owner, the Duomo of Porto Montebello, I substituted the original with a copy that I had painted myself. That copy was stolen along with a precious bishop's ring. What you find here is the original, and I beg you to return it to the beautiful duomo where it belongs. If you are reading this letter, it means that I have not been successful in returning to Sicily to return it myself, thereby clearing my name of a crime I did not commit. Please take care as you unroll the canvas, maybe getting specialist help in order not to damage it.*
>
> *With grateful thanks,*
> *Carlo Giuseppe Rosso*
> *Apprentice painter*

Tears trickled down Claudia's cheeks. She'd always known her father was not capable of stealing a work of art as famous as the Madonna and Child. He was not capable of stealing anything. She jumped up, turned to Alessandro and hugged him. 'You deserve the tightest *cwtch* I can give you. You're a genius! Because of you guessing what Papà's map was of, Giulietta and I can clear his name. These days, many people won't have heard of Carlo Rosso, but those who have should know what he did for the cathedral.'

Smiling, Giulietta held out her arms. 'Can I join in, too?'

The three of them stood for a moment with their arms around each other.

'Oh, Claudia, this is marvellous news. But Papà is right. This needs a specialist to unroll it.' Giulietta pointed at the rolled-up painting. 'After so many years underground, it will have to get acclimatised to the temperature, and when eventually unravelled, it must be done so carefully that any hairline cracks will fit back together. I just hope and pray that Papà rolled it the right way. I'm sure he did.'

'I can't wait to see it properly, but you're right. We mustn't do anything to damage it. I'll have to be patient,' said Claudia.

'If it's all right with you both, I'm going to take the painting home with me.' Giulietta refolded the letter and carefully picked up the tube. 'There's nothing more we can do here. I'd like to get it securely locked in the safe I have there. I'll contact someone I know who's an expert at restoring old paintings and I will get him to help us open the tube. You'll need my address. I'll explain that it's urgent, Claudia. I'll let you and Alessandro know when he's free to do it. Have you got the business card I gave you with my telephone number on? I'll write my address for you on the back.'

'That's fine. It's a good idea to lock it away. Yes. It's in here.' Claudia rummaged in her bag then handed the card to Giulietta. The two watched her walk across the piazza to the street where her car was parked.

'Phew! What a day!' Alessandro let his shoulders drop and laughed.

It was then that Claudia looked at the address her sister had written on the back of the business card. *Casa Cristina.* She grabbed Alessandro's arm.

'What's wrong?'

'You know the villa at the top of the cliff, the salmon-on-pink one? That's where Giulietta lives! She's back living in the Romano home but she probably doesn't even realise it! She didn't even know her mamma was one of *the* Romanos before reading Nonna's diary.'

Since talking to Matteo's aunt on that first morning, Claudia had read all she could about the villa. It had been in a local family for generations, but when the owner died it had remained empty for around fifteen years. Then two Americans bought it, had it refurbished and sold it again in 1965. She remembered Giovanna saying that a renowned art historian had bought it, as well, but Claudia still couldn't believe that person was her sister, the daughter of Carlo Rosso and Pia Romano.

'Well, we shall soon see it for ourselves.' Alessandro smiled. 'After all the excitement of this morning, what about some lunch over in Villaggio delle Rocce, and then I'll take you on that boat trip I promised you to see the caves and the coral you loved in my seascapes. Have you got your sketchpad in that duffel bag of yours?'

* * *

The harbour area of the little fishing village was buzzing with tourists when Claudia and Alessandro arrived. After parking the scooter in the shade of a row of small trees edging the cobbled pavement, they walked hand in hand along the quayside, wandering from *trattoria* to *trattoria* and looking at the menus displayed outside. They settled on one that was busy with locals — always a good sign, Alessandro told her.

They found a free table sheltered from the hot afternoon sun by a large parasol. A waiter came and handed them a menu. He asked if they would like something to drink while they made their choices.

Alessandro turned to Claudia. 'White okay for you?'

She nodded. '*Sì*. And some water, too, please.'

Alessandro leaned across and squeezed her hand. 'I cannot believe what has happened today. This was what you came to Sicily for. Giulietta's face when you read the letter from your papà was so shocked. Between the two of you, you will be able to clear his name.'

'If only he could have lived to see this day and reconnect with his other daughter. I feel so lucky to have had him for so long. Poor Giulietta.' Her voice cracked with emotion.

'Well, that is up to you now. I can already see there's a strong bond between you both, and it is hard to believe you only met each other a short time ago.'

The waiter returned to place an ice bucket on a stand at the end of their table. He removed the cork from the bottle and poured some wine for Alessandro to try. Alessandro looked up and nodded. The waiter then filled their glasses. '*Alla salute. Cin cin.*' He placed the wine bottle in the bucket.

Alessandro raised his glass and clinked it against Claudia's. '*Salute, amore mio.*'

It was the first time he had called her "my love". Before, it had been *amica mia,* "my friend". She looked across at him and, as always happened when he was sitting this close, her insides somersaulted. But "my love" could be nothing more than a term of endearment. After all, it was used all the time in English, wasn't it? The same as "*cariad*" back in Wales.

'Cheers! *Grazie,* Sandro.' Taking a sip of the chilled wine, she turned her attention to the menu. 'What do you recommend?'

He pointed to the *bruschetta al pomodoro* in the starter section. 'I had this last time and it was a bit different. Local tomatoes and you could taste the basil. The bread underneath was crunchy. And for the *primo* course, as we are by the sea, I'll have the seafood linguine. Perhaps we'll forego the *secondo* and go straight to the *dolce.*'

'As long as I have room for one of those wonderful *gelatos* over on the counter there afterwards, I'll have the same.'

Alessandro laughed. 'You and your ice creams.'

'It's all right for you. In less than a week's time, it will be back to a boring vanilla ice cream sandwiched between two flat wafers from the local shop.' She smiled as the waiter arrived to take their order.

They chatted about their visit to Giulietta's home and speculated about what it would be like. Claudia couldn't imagine being so rich you could buy a place that featured in a brochure. She told Alessandro of the photos she'd seen and how the kitchen looked as if it had been transported straight from the Ideal Home Exhibition in London.

'You will see it for yourself soon,' said Alessandro. 'It is not far to the villa, but it will be a steep climb in this heat, so would you like me to pick you up on the Vespa and save your legs?'

'Do you really have to ask?' She laughed.

The meal was as delicious as Alessandro had said it would be. Since arriving on the island, Claudia had tried many of the delicacies Sicily was famous for. It was the colours on the plate that she loved: the sweet tomatoes, the peppers and the juicy fruit. As well as the lemons and oranges, she'd developed a liking for blood oranges, especially when they were squeezed to make a vibrant red juice.

As they finished the last of the wine, Alessandro reached for her hand and brought it up to his lips. His kiss was soft and warm, and excitement travelled along her veins. She knew it was no good building her hopes up, but then he started speaking. 'I do not know what I am going to do when you return home. I am starting to regret thinking I could not move on — you know why — but being with you and being able to be honest about things has made me realise I can. I know Daniela would not want me to stay sad. I *should* move on. Except it feels like as soon as it has dawned on me that I want us to be more than friends, I am going to lose you. I have been so foolish. I think you feel the same way — I hope so, anyway.'

Claudia squeezed his hand harder. 'I understand. I prefer it this way than you rushing things and regretting it because you weren't ready. I'll be back. Don't forget I have found a sister who lives here. Let's enjoy the time we have left. However we spend the time, knowing that you feel more than friendship is good enough. Now, what about this boat trip you promised me?'

Inside, Claudia was melting. She had wanted him from the first time she'd set eyes on him at the university. Knowing that it was now the same for him was the best news. He stood up and leaned over to kiss her on the mouth. His kiss was tender, just as she'd imagined it would be. As their lips touched for the first time, fireworks fizzled along her veins. It was worth waiting for. A cheer went up from the other diners, and Alessandro quickly sat back down. Flushed with embarrassment, they looked at each other and grinned.

'Come on. I'll pay the bill and we'll go somewhere more private. Waiter!'

When the waiter returned with the bill, he also brought two small glasses filled with a now-familiar yellow liquid. 'A little limoncello each. I think you must have something to celebrate.' He winked.

They soon left the *trattoria* and stopped off at Alessandro's studio to pick up the keys for his motorboat. Claudia didn't know if it was the wine or the fact that Alessandro wanted more from their relationship, but she felt warm and fuzzy. Deep down, she knew the real reason for feeling happier than she'd ever felt before — she would be returning to this beautiful island.

'I hope you are not expecting much,' he warned her. 'It belonged to my papà and he used it for fishing. He has been dead for five years and it was old when he had it. But I spent so much of my childhood going out with him on fishing trips, I cannot get rid of it. I just have to keep it seaworthy and I use it to find places for my seascapes.'

She didn't care what it looked like. She was going to spend time with Alessandro alone on a boat, and she had a feeling it was going to lead somewhere special.

CHAPTER FORTY-TWO

Alessandro had not been exaggerating. Moored next to more modern and gleaming vessels, his motorboat, *Aura*, looked as if it had seen better days. Claudia could see where Alessandro had freshly painted the hull a dazzling white, edged with the traditional bright blue she'd seen on many of the other boats, but it hadn't covered up the patches completely. A canopy running the length of the boat would provide welcome shade. A metal ladder was attached to the harbour wall and Alessandro climbed down into the vessel. 'What do you think? Welcome aboard!'

Claudia turned around and, with trepidation, her feet found each rung on the ladder. As she stepped into the boat, it rocked, and Alessandro held her hand to steady her. Then he led her to a seat under the canopy.

'I didn't realise it was going to be this small.' She laughed.

Alessandro laughed, too. 'You are safe in my hands. Just call me *Capitano*. There is not much wind out there so it will not be choppy. Viewing the cliffs from the sea is such an amazing sight. I did not want you to leave without seeing it.'

He scaled the ladder to unwind the rope coiled around a metal bollard on the quayside and jumped back into the boat. Taking his place at the tiller, he started up the engine and guided the vessel out into the open water.

Claudia soon relaxed and got out her sketchpad and drawing pencils. As they travelled along the coastline, Alessandro pointed out some landmarks — the row of buildings where they'd visited Rosa's uncle at the end of the clifftop, the little church next to it and the lighthouse.

Soon they were leaving the fishing village far behind. Claudia briefly held on to the edge of her seat as another boat went by, causing a swell and the water to become choppy.

'Are you okay?' shouted Alessandro from the back of the boat.

She looked over her shoulder and nodded her head. The little boat gathered speed and a breeze cooled her cheeks. Her hair blew out behind her. There were cliffs to the left of them and Alessandro steered the boat closer to get a better look. Layers of white rock formed patterns that would make wonderful textured paintings. She sketched the shapes and made a note of the colours. When she looked up again, the boat had turned around a headland, and there in front of her was a cave the full height of the rocks.

Alessandro turned off the motor and came to sit on the seat beside her. 'There. That is what I wanted you to see.' The cave mouth was in the shape of a heart and was unlike anything Claudia had seen before. 'It is romantic, eh? The perfect destination for our first boat ride together.'

'It's wonderful.' She nestled her head into Alessandro's neck.

He turned her face towards him and brushed his lips against hers, but then pulled away. 'Come on. We are going inside.'

He returned to his position at the tiller and drove the boat towards the entrance of the cave where Claudia noticed waves were crashing. Turning the boat around, he manoeuvred it backwards until they were right inside, looking out through the heart shape at the sea and sky. Alessandro stopped the engine and returned to Claudia's side on the seat as the vessel bobbed gently. They kissed.

'Oh, Sandro. This is so beautiful. Thank you for bringing me here.' Claudia moved to the side of her seat, pushing her hand into the clear water. 'Just look at that colour.'

The sound of the water lapping against the boat was reassuringly soothing as she gazed at the turquoise and aquamarine that glowed beneath her. The deeply textured rock sides to the cave were covered with varying shades of green algae the closer to the water they got. At the base and partly under the water, violet-coloured coral perfected the image.

She grabbed her sketchpad. 'I must capture this. No wonder your paintings of the sea have such an amazing range of colours.' She scribbled down the colours and drew the shapes of the rocks hanging down like jagged stalactites from a height.

'Don't forget your camera,' Alessandro reminded her.

She found it at the bottom of her bag and snapped away. She couldn't wait to show her mam all the photos she'd taken, although she'd have to describe the colours to her.

Soon, Claudia put her sketchbook and camera back in her bag, and for a few moments, they just sat together, hands entwined. They kissed again, and as their kisses became more passionate, the boat started to rock. Alessandro pulled away. 'I think we need to find dry land if we are going to continue with this.' He grinned. 'I know just the place.'

Carefully moving the boat through the cave entrance, Alessandro turned up the throttle and they were travelling at speed again. It wasn't long before she saw a small cove tucked inside the rocky coastline.

'There,' shouted Alessandro, battling to be heard over the sound of the wind now they were out on the open sea. 'I used to come here with my father. We would stop for a picnic and he would let me swim as a break from the fishing.'

He drove the boat as close as he could to the shore before finally switching off the engine. Then he threw a rope ladder over the side and stepped into the shallow water before proceeding to drag the vessel on to the sand. 'Here, let me help you out. It is lovely, eh? Secluded and away from prying eyes.'

Claudia took his hand and Alessandro pulled her into his arms. He planted butterfly kisses along her cheek, down her neck and along her bare shoulder. Then he ran a hand under her T-shirt. 'Is this all right?' he whispered.

Suddenly feeling shy, all she could do was nod. She preferred to answer him by turning her head to kiss him. He gently probed her lips with his tongue. Suddenly breaking away, he hurried to the boat where he retrieved a travel rug. 'This is always on board for picnics.' He held up the rug for Claudia to see. 'But I think we can find a better use for it, don't you?'

He spread it on the sand and they sat down together, looking out to sea.

'What are you thinking?' Alessandro was the first to break the silence.

'I'm just wondering how I'm going to get on that plane home and leave all this behind.' Claudia sighed. 'The more time I spend with you, the harder it's going to be.'

Alessandro put his arm around her. He pulled her close and then back down onto the rug. They lay facing each other.

'I know. I feel the same, but let us enjoy being in each other's company and not think about it until we have to.' Tears filled Claudia's eyes and he brushed away one that had escaped with his finger. 'Come here, *tesoro*.'

They began kissing and feelings she'd not experienced for a long time surfaced, but with more intensity than ever before. Alessandro gently lifted her top over her head and the sun beat down on her bare skin. He gazed at her with longing and she blushed. She didn't know why. She'd been in a state of undress in front of a man before, but perhaps it was because this man meant so much more to her. Their kissing became even more passionate. Claudia knew this was what she'd wanted since she'd first set eyes on him. *Can you fall in love with someone at first sight? That quickly?* she wondered, as they removed each other's clothing item by item until they were lying naked in each other's arms.

'Is this what you want, *bella* Claudia? We can keep it to this if it is too soon.'

'It is what I want. Can't you tell?' She caressed his neck. He reached across into his shorts pocket.

* * *

Claudia couldn't sleep when she got back to the *pensione* that night. She relived every moment of what had happened between her and Alessandro. It wasn't just the lovemaking — it was the way they were as a couple. She enjoyed being in his company and was interested in his conversation. She'd already promised herself that she would do everything she could to make their long-distance relationship work.

Her mind kept going back to the little cove. Alessandro was a skilful lover. Her past experiences had always left her feeling disappointed and were almost always over before they'd even started. She'd always had to insist on her boy-friends using protection, but with Alessandro, it was completely natural, something he wanted, too. He'd shown her the difference between making love and having sex. Afterwards, swimming naked in the sea had been exhilarating and another first for her.

She eventually drifted off to sleep excited, both about her new relationship with Alessandro and about what the visit to Giulietta for the unrolling of Papà's painting would bring.

CHAPTER FORTY-THREE

Giulietta had rung to say her friend was arriving at the villa to unroll the painting that morning. Alessandro was waiting for Claudia in the vestibule of the *pensione* so they could travel there together. He rose from his seat and kissed her when he saw her. 'You look beautiful.' He grinned. 'But are you going to be able to sit pillion in your tight dress?'

Instead of her usual long, flowing skirt or denims and tie-dye top, Claudia was wearing a short linen shift. 'I hadn't thought of that! I'll go and change.' She made a quick retreat and changed into a pair of cotton trousers and a sleeveless blouse.

He laughed when he saw her. 'That is better. I had visions of you splitting the seam and revealing all.' He pulled her close as they descended the steps onto the street. 'But I have already seen all, eh?' he whispered.

Laughing, Claudia pushed him playfully, and they ran across the piazza together and down the street to the where the scooter was parked.

As Alessandro had said, the journey didn't take long, but as they were winding up through the narrow streets lined with busy shops and private villas, Claudia was grateful not to be walking in over thirty-degree heat. Alessandro was able to find a place to park the Vespa just off the road. They walked along the pavement until they found a wrought-iron gate in the stone wall with a sign saying *CASA CRISTINA*.

Claudia's pulse raced. She was about to find out whether the painting her father had hidden was still intact. She raised the latch and the gate creaked as it opened. They were faced with steps either side of a wall stuccoed in the same colour as the main house — a vibrant salmon-pink. They took the left set of steps and kept climbing until they came to a wide, open paved terrace where Claudia bent over to catch her breath.

Alessandro turned and admired the panorama in front of him. 'Just look at that view.'

She straightened up and drank in the vista stretching before them, too. The sea in the distance was a brilliant deep blue, and if they looked in another direction, the spectacle of Mount Etna was belching out white smoke against a cerulean sky.

The villa itself was huge. On the ground floor, three floor-to-ceiling French doors opening onto the front terrace were painted in bright blue behind pillars on top of which were stone statues of seated lions. On the floor above was a balcony edged with metal railings and more blue doors, this time with shutters to protect against the sun.

As they were about to ring the doorbell, the main doors opened and Giulietta came through to greet them. '*Buongiorno.* Welcome to my home. Come in.'

Claudia and Alessandro followed her into a light and airy room. The walls were adorned with paintings of all styles, and Claudia had to resist examining each one to find the names of the artists.

'Come and sit down.' Giulietta pointed to a large blue velvet sofa backed with several plump cushions. 'Can I get you a coffee or maybe a cold drink? I have some homemade lemonade.'

'That sounds lovely, *grazie*,' said Claudia.

'For me, too,' Alessandro agreed.

From the look on her companion's face, Claudia could tell that he was as impressed as she was by the luxury of the place. The wooden bureaux and occasional tables were a warm honey colour and inlaid with intricate marquetry.

'Wow,' he whispered.

Giulietta returned with a tray laden with a jug of cloudy lemonade and four glasses. 'The friend I was telling you about should be here anytime. Ah, here he is now. Good timing, eh?' She placed the tray on the table and went to greet the distinguished-looking middle-aged man who had just approached the open doors.

Warmth radiated through Claudia's body. She was about to see the painting her father had saved.

'Giorgio. *Ciao.* Come in and meet my sister and her friend.'

Claudia and Alessandro stood to greet him. Impeccably dressed in a white linen shirt and navy slacks, Giorgio's black hair was streaked with silver at his temples, contrasting with his tanned complexion.

'Claudia, Alessandro. This is the friend I mentioned: Giorgio Moroni. If there's anyone I'd trust with the delicate job of unrolling an old canvas, it would be Giorgio.'

From the way the two exchanged glances, Claudia wondered if her sister and the art restorer were more than friends. Could you really tell by the way people looked at each other? If so, Giulietta would know that Alessandro was now definitely more than her friend.

The four of them sat down and Giulietta poured out glasses of lemonade. They exchanged pleasantries and asked Giorgio about his work and what it entailed. Originally from Rome, he had not lived in Porto Montebello long, so the story regarding the theft was news to him.

'I've got the painting locked in the safe in the dining room,' said Giulietta. 'Let's go in there once you've finished your drinks.'

'Made from the lemons in your garden?' asked Giorgio, indicating his glass.

Claudia fidgeted. *I wish they'd hurry up. I want to see the painting!*

'*Sì.* Since I bought the house, the gardener has managed to revive a few of the fruit trees that had been badly neglected. The house was empty for many years, you see. Others are new stock.'

Claudia was still puzzled that her sister didn't seem to know the villa's history, or that it was the family home of her own mother. Today was not the time to ask her about that. Instead, it was the day when they would find out if her father's efforts to preserve a priceless work of art had worked.

Finally, Giulietta moved to open the dining room doors. Claudia could hardly breathe. It was even more impressive than the room they'd left. The wooden panelling on the walls stopped halfway up, leaving enough room at the top for beautiful frescoes of flowers and foliage. Claudia looked up to admire the detail of the hydrangeas, the agapanthus and varieties of hibiscus painted in soft, restful blues and purples, among the greens of their leaves.

'Beautiful, isn't it? This room is what sold the house to me. It's an art lover's dream.' Giulietta went to a corner of the panelling to the left of the door and inserted a key into a lock almost too small to notice. There was a soft click and a door opened, revealing a safe hidden inside. She pressed in a code and opened it, revealing the tube containing the painting.

She carried the painting over to the round table and laid it on the protective covering. Giorgio put on white cotton gloves in readiness. Underneath the cardboard outer layer, the tube had been wrapped tightly with long strips of material securely tied with string. Claudia and Alessandro held the tube while Giulietta first cut away the string under which her papà's letter had been tucked, and then began the painstaking task of unravelling the material strips, which gradually cascaded onto the parquet floor.

'It must have taken your father an age to pack it. Let's hope his efforts have paid off.' Giorgio took off the end of the tube and gently eased out the painting, taking care to grip the material on which the painting had been rolled and not the canvas itself. When the whole roll of canvas was out, Giulietta placed the empty tube on the floor. 'Now, this is the tricky bit.' Giorgio looked serious. 'Why don't you all sit? This could take some time and I don't want to rush it.'

The three of them pulled up chairs and watched Giorgio in silence, totally engrossed in what he was attempting to do.

'Excellent,' he said. 'The first thing I notice is that your father has rolled the canvas with the paint on the outside, which means that when the painting is flattened out the little hairline cracks that will inevitably be there will close, and I should be able to seal them. He's rolled it around an inner tube and that will have prevented it from being — how do you say? — "squashed". Good man.'

Giulietta looked at Claudia and grinned.

Little by little, Giorgio unrolled the canvas so that it was flat and facing downwards onto the fine cloth her papà had used to roll the canvas on.

'Now for an even trickier bit.' Giorgio pulled his gloves tighter. 'I have a fine piece of canvas here that I'm going to spread out over the back of the painting. I want each of you to take a corner with the cloth underneath and turn it over when I say *pronte*.'

They nodded and took up their corners. Claudia's heart pounded.

'*Pronte*. Turn.'

Very gently, the painting was lowered onto the table and they all stood back. Giorgio lifted the cloth from the top of it.

Claudia, Giulietta and Alessandro all leaned in to see the state of the painting. Giorgio took a magnifying glass from his pocket and examined its surface. 'Remarkable. After almost thirty years, the painting has survived being rolled and the temperature underground. There is a little damage here. See? But if you agree, I can restore that. Your father knew what he was doing! He packed it well so that there was no movement in the tube. It will just need to "breathe" for a short while before I do anything.'

Giulietta hugged Giorgio. 'We can't thank you enough, can we, Claudia?'

'I knew Papà was innocent. But this is even better than that. Now everyone else will know, too. He's a hero!' Claudia's face was wet with tears, and she grabbed Alessandro's arms and jumped up and down on the spot.

'Yes, we can now clear Papà's name. I think this calls for a celebration, don't you?' Giulietta smiled, then leaned down by the sideboard and brought out four crystal glass flutes. 'There's some sparkling wine chilling.'

Giorgio laid a white cotton cloth over the painting and followed the others back to the living room. Giulietta called him back from the kitchen. 'Giorgio, can you do the honours and open the bottle and pour?'

Claudia pulled Alessandro towards her and kissed him just as Giulietta and Giorgio came back with the drinks.

'Here, you two *piccioncini*. Take a glass.'

Claudia was puzzled but, grinning, Alessandro clarified. 'Lovebirds.' She blushed.

When they all had a glass in their hands, Giulietta proposed a toast. 'To Papà, *salute.*'

As Claudia took the first sip, bubbles tickled her nose. She could never have imagined this outcome when she arrived on the island less than a month ago. As she'd stepped off the plane, she hadn't known a soul, didn't know why her father wouldn't discuss his life before the war, or whether she had any Sicilian family still living. *How can all of this have happened in a month? This is what you wanted, isn't it, Papà?*

'To Papà.'

'To Carlo,' said Alessandro and Giorgio.

Giorgio left soon afterwards, having arranged with Giulietta when he could come back to do the minor restoration needed and prepare the painting for reframing.

'I'm sorry to leave you, but I have an appointment. It has been good to meet you both and be part of this wonderful discovery. I hope to see you again soon.' He kissed Claudia on both cheeks and shook Alessandro's hand. Giulietta accompanied him outside onto the terrace, where Claudia noticed that they embraced and then kissed.

'I was right. They're not just friends.' Claudia smiled. 'I'm glad. She has no family. I hope he makes her happy.'

'You may not live here, but she *does* have family now, doesn't she? What is better than a sister who will keep visiting?'

CHAPTER FORTY-FOUR

It was Claudia's last day before flying home and her head was a muddle of mixed emotions. She couldn't wait to see her mam but tried not to think about leaving Alessandro and Giulietta. In a short time, she had begun to think of Porto Montebello as home — the place where her papà was born and grew up.

Giulietta had arranged for her and Claudia to meet with Matteo at the university. As the head of the department that specialised in ecclesiastical art, he was in close and constant contact with the *duomo* authorities.

Walking through the main doors with her sister, Claudia didn't have the butterflies she'd had on the first day of the course. She led the way along the corridor to Matteo's office.

'*Buongiorno.*' He rose from behind his desk and kissed both of them. 'Please sit down.' He smiled warmly at them. 'Who would have imagined that when I booked you to talk to my students, Giulietta, that one of them would turn out to be your sister? Two sisters find each other and a priceless work of art is soon to be returned to where it belongs!'

'It's all down to the determination of this one.' Giulietta squeezed Claudia's hand. 'Our father made sure that after his death she would have a map of the tunnels under the *duomo*

261

and a photograph of me as a baby with him and Mamma. Along with an address found in an old bottle, she arrived here with a mystery to solve. And she did it.'

'I did have help,' said Claudia. 'You remember Alessandro? It was all down to him in the end.'

Matteo laughed. 'Ah, yes. Signor Costa. He didn't stay, whereas you, *signorina*, passed your assignment with flying colours. I enjoyed reading it. But back to the painting. I've contacted the committee and informed them of the find. They will have it verified and, as long as the painting is confirmed as genuine, there will be a formal service of thanksgiving and re-dedication sometime in the future. Your father's copy will become your property, of course. For now, all I can do is thank you both on the cathedral's behalf.'

Claudia sat up straight, inhaling a deep breath. An image of her beloved father entered her mind. *Your name is free from shame at last, Papà.*

'Claudia is returning to Wales in the morning, so perhaps you can keep me informed of when the painting can be returned? I think it's important that it's kept under lock and key until then.'

Matteo stood up and shook each sister's hand. 'Of course, I have all your contact details. *Buon viaggio,* Claudia. I do hope you will visit Porto Montebello again. Please call in to see me at the university when you do.'

Claudia and Giulietta left his office and emerged into the sunshine before crossing the piazza.

'That's it, then. As soon as I know what's happening with the painting, I'll write and let you know. Once the painting is verified, Giorgio will arrange for it to be framed. I suggested he chooses a frame similar to the one Papà had around his copy. I hope that's all right with you.'

Claudia took her sister's hand. 'Of course it is. Papà's painting has hung there since the war ended.'

'Our father was not a thief and we've proved it! Now I have your home address, perhaps one day I could visit you in Wales. Now, what are your plans for the rest of your last day?'

'First of all, I need to return this to Curtis and Skye. They weren't in the last time I called.' Claudia held up the macramé bag they'd loaned her. 'And then I'm seeing Sandro and we're taking a picnic to a little cove we found on our boat trip. I'm going to miss him and you so much.' She hugged her new-found sister. '*Grazie mille.*'

'I suspect that you will miss Alessandro more than me. Enjoy your private goodbye.' Giulietta winked. 'Perhaps I can drive you to the airport in the morning and have my own goodbye then?'

* * *

As they set off from the quayside, Claudia looked at the picnic basket Alessandro had put in the shade under the seat. It was late afternoon and the sun was lower in the sky, but it was still hot. He wouldn't tell her what he'd packed and hadn't allowed her to contribute anything. 'My surprise,' he'd told her. 'But there will be wine. It can chill in the water while we swim.'

Aura motored along, and when they passed the heart-shaped cave, a warm feeling came over Claudia as she remembered their kissing and how the boat had nearly rocked them into the water. Soon, the little cove came into view.

Alessandro switched off the motor a fair way out from the beach and let down an anchor. Then he moved nearer to Claudia's seat and put his arm around her. 'If you'd like it, perhaps we could have a swim from the boat? The water is much deeper here and I know you're a good swimmer.'

Claudia beamed. 'I'd love that.'

The depth of water varied and, depending on the rocks beneath them, the shades of turquoise ranged from teal through to aquamarine then to a rich sapphire. Alessandro brought out colourful beach towels from the storage at the front of the boat and tossed a rope ladder into the sea, ensuring it was securely fastened to metal hooks on the inside of the hull. 'You can either dive in or use this.' He pointed at the ladder.

He stripped off and dived in. Claudia admired his tanned physique and realised why he had no tell-tale white parts to his body. Perhaps he never wore swimwear. She'd packed a bikini but decided not to wear it. *What's good for Sandro is good for me.* From the front of the boat, she climbed down into the sea and swam to where he was treading water.

They embraced and began kissing. There was something extra exciting about entwining their bodies in the cool water. But then she stopped, her eyes filling with tears as she nestled her wet head onto Alessandro's neck. 'I'm going to miss this so much,' she whispered in his ear. 'I can't bear it.'

Alessandro put his arms around her waist and thrust her into the air, holding her there. 'Do not be sad. Let us enjoy it. We will come back here in the future, I promise. It will be our special secret place.'

Then he dropped her into the water with a huge splash. When she resurfaced, she could feel herself grinning. 'Race you to the end rock!'

Claudia swam away from him, heading for the far side of the cove. She guessed her breaststroke would be no match for his overarm crawl and, sure enough, soon he was alongside her. It was not long before Alessandro was striding out of the water to sit on the rock. As she got to the end, he looked at an imaginary watch on his wrist. 'What kept you?' He ducked out of the way of the splashes Claudia kicked his way.

They walked back along the edge of the beach, hand in hand, letting the ripples of the waves trickle over their feet. Once they were level with the boat, Alessandro strode out, then started swimming towards it. He brought it in as far as he could before switching off the engine. Together they dragged *Aura* onto the sand. 'Here.' He threw Claudia a towel.

Once they'd dried off and dressed, they spread rugs on the beach and lifted the picnic basket out of the boat. Alessandro opened it and took out two bottles of wine, placing them on the edge of the water. 'I hope you'll like it. A local wine to send you on your way. Now, let's spread out the picnic. All that swimming has made me hungry.'

Alessandro brought out the food from the basket. He unwrapped a variety of breads, cheeses, cold meats and slices of pizza and placed them on long wooden boards.

'What a feast!' Claudia exclaimed.

'You have to try Mamma's olive bread.' He cut an oval-shaped loaf into slices. 'She told me the base of the *bruschetta* is the same bread and she toasted it before putting on the ricotta and the tomatoes, so I hope it is still crunchy.' He handed her a bowl of cherry tomatoes. 'Take loads. They are from our own garden.' They sat down to eat. Everything was fresh with delicious, distinct flavours.

She was tucking into a second slice of pizza when Alessandro stood up. 'I've forgotten the wine!' He retrieved the bottle from the water's edge and unscrewed the cork. Handing Claudia two tumblers, he poured the white wine then placed the cork loosely back in the neck of the bottle. 'To us.' They clinked the plastic picnic tumblers together — not quite the tinkle of Giulietta's crystal flutes, but the sentiment was the same. 'I mean it, Claudia.' He leaned in to kiss her gently on the lips. '*Ti amo,*' he whispered.

Claudia put down her wine and put her arms around his neck. 'I've fallen in love with you, too, Sandro. To know you feel the same way . . .' But before she could finish her sentence, he kissed her and they fell backwards onto the sand.

He leaned up on his elbow. 'You lead me astray, Signorina Rosso. Let's finish eating and then we can carry on with what you started.' They sat up and he refilled the tumblers with wine. 'I remembered your favourite, by the way.'

Claudia strained her neck to see what was still in the wicker basket.

'Ta-da! Cannoli for the *signorina.*' He brought out a selection of her favourite pastries and pointed to each one. 'Pistachio and ricotta, chocolate and mascarpone, and these have a lemon filling.'

'I'm spoiled for choice on my last day.' Claudia sighed.

After more wine, they cleared away the picnic and Alessandro took the basket back to the boat. Then they sat together, holding hands and gazing out to sea. On the horizon, the sky was now a pale apricot, streaked with brushstrokes of lemon and coral. They watched as the sun sank lower.

'We had better be getting back soon.' Alessandro turned to Claudia and put his hands on either side of her face. They kissed and fell backwards onto the sand.

Claudia became tearful again. 'I don't want today to end.'

He hugged her tight. 'I know, but this is not the end, I promise you, *amore mio*. We *will* make it work. We *do* have a future together. I will make sure of it. Now, let us enjoy what time we have left before the sun finally disappears.'

Their lovemaking took on a special significance that evening. Claudia knew that a future together was what she wanted more than anything, but it was not going to be easy. Having to tell her mam everything she'd found out since she'd arrived in Sicily was one thing, but letting her know how determined she was to have a future with Alessandro, possibly here in Sicily, was also not something she was looking forward to.

* * *

Claudia had persuaded Alessandro not to accompany her to the airport the following morning. Reluctantly, he'd agreed that they would both find it too painful. Far better to have the last memory of their time together being the boat journey back to the quayside in the glow of a romantic Sicilian sunset. Promises of regular letter writing seemed inadequate and Claudia had taken a long time to get to sleep, worrying how a long-distance relationship could possibly work.

Giulietta was waiting for her in the vestibule as Claudia settled her bill and handed in her room key. Looking around the place that had been home for the last month, she considered the personal journey she'd been on over the last four weeks. She'd grown a lot as an individual, she'd been determined not to give up until she'd found out the reasons for her papà's secrecy regarding his family, and, while working out the truth, not only had she found a half-sister, but she had also found love.

'*Pronta*?' Giulietta questioned.

'I'm ready.' Claudia lifted her suitcase and slung her duffel bag over her shoulder.

Walking across the piazza for a final time, the two sisters looked over to the beautiful facade of the *duomo*.

'Are you thinking the same as me?' Giulietta asked quietly. 'If it wasn't for Papà's good deed, we would never have met.'

And I wouldn't have met Sandro either, Claudia thought. By giving Uncle Sisto his map and the photograph, her father had changed Claudia's life for the better.

The car was parked just off the piazza, and Giulietta took her sister's case and placed it in the boot. Soon, they were driving on the open road and leaving Porto Montebello behind. Claudia had a clear view of Mount Etna in the distance billowing a white plume as if waving goodbye to her. *I'll be back*. But her eyes still misted with tears.

CHAPTER FORTY-FIVE

Claudia walked through into the arrivals area and was relieved to see her mam accompanied by Auntie Menna among the people waiting for other passengers.

'Claudia!' The familiar voice with the warm Welsh lilt tugged at Claudia's heartstrings. It dawned on her how much she'd missed her mother. With so much going on and things happening so quickly, she hadn't given much consideration to how much she was missing home. She'd been away for far longer periods of time during her art college course, but this had been the first time she'd been away so long since that awful phone call she'd received from her aunt to say her papà was in the hospital.

She was greeted by the tightest of *cwtches* from her mam and auntie in turn.

'Aw, *cariad*. I've missed you. You look so well. Look at her tan, Menna. You look even more like your papà now. A real Italian.'

'I've missed you, too, Mam. And you, Auntie Menna.'

'Come here, *bach*. Your mam has been counting down the days. Let's get you in the car and you can tell us all everything.'

Where do I start? she wondered.

Although she was tired from travelling, the conversation on the journey back to Dolwen didn't stop. Claudia told them about the sunshine, the amazing views and the delicious foods she'd tasted that were so different from home. 'Mind, I'm looking forward to your home cooking, Mam.'

Her aunt looked at her in the rear mirror. 'Don't worry, *cariad*. She's made a batch of your favourite Welsh cakes.'

Claudia realised that her homecoming must have been planned for almost as long as she'd been away. She decided she would tell her mam about Giulietta in private. How would she react? Out in Sicily, she was convinced she was doing the right thing, but now she was back, she worried that she was being disloyal to her mother. She pushed that thought to the back of her mind.

'The people were so friendly and welcoming.' She thought of one person in particular. 'The course was good, too. There are so many cathedrals and churches out there with amazing old paintings wherever you looked. I could see straight away where Papà got his inspiration for the little chapel from, Mam.'

'Did you find that address that was on the message in the bottle?' her mam asked.

'Yes, I did. An American couple are living there now. Didn't I say in one of my letters? They found an old case of Nonna's there.'

She told them how she'd found her grandmother's diary and had it translated into English. 'I'll let you read it, Mam. And you, Auntie Menna, if you'd like. She sounds a remarkable woman. During the war, she used to shelter from the bombing in the underground tunnels under the cathedral with hundreds of others. She used to take food down for some of the families, even though they had rationing like you did here. She also tells of running classes for some of the children to keep them occupied. I wish we could have met her, Mam.'

It wasn't long before they arrived home at Deri Cottage. To Claudia, the stone walls appeared to be even more grey than she remembered in the afternoon light with the sky full of heavy clouds, threatening rain. With the absence of the vibrant colours of the last few weeks, the contrast was stark. But it was home, her family home, and Claudia had the same warm feeling she always had when she returned here after being away. All that was missing was Papà coming to the door to welcome her back with his outstretched arms. She took in a deep breath. He may no longer be there, but from what she'd found out in Sicily, she was prouder of him than ever.

'I won't come in.' Her aunt turned back to her car. 'I'll leave you two to catch up, but I'll see you soon.'

Her mam hugged her sister. 'Thanks, Menna. For everything. It's been good to spend time with you and Gwilym. I don't know what I'd have done without you these last few weeks when I've been on my own.'

Claudia felt a stab of guilt.

'That's what sisters are for, aren't they?' Her Auntie Menna waved, then drove away as they both entered the cottage.

The smell of home cooking hung in the air. *It really is good to be back.*

'Now then, *cariad*. First things, first. A cup of tea? Good old Glengettie. I bet you haven't had that in Sicily, eh?'

CHAPTER FORTY-SIX

Sara

Sara brought over a plate of Welsh cakes and two mugs of tea, placing them on the tiled coffee table.

'There you are, *cariad*. Drink up. Welcome home.'

It was good to have Claudia back. Even though she hadn't lived at home properly since she'd gone to art college, Sara still felt relatively close to her when she was only a few hours away in Cardiff. Her month away in Sicily had dragged. She looked across at her beautiful daughter, so like her father, tucking into her third Welsh cake, and smiled. She looked the same, apart from the glow of her tan, but something was different. Sara hadn't admitted to anyone, not even to her sister, that she'd been worried about Claudia going to Sicily, worried about what she'd find out there. When Claudia had discovered the letters when sorting Carlo's things, Sara had kept her concerns to herself. Why hadn't she known he was sending money back to his mother? He should have told her. She would have understood. And what was the map all about? She had to believe Sisto when he'd told her he didn't know what was in the envelope Carlo had asked him to give to Claudia.

'You're quiet, Mam. These are delicious, by the way.'

'Oh, just thinking how good it is to have you back on home soil.' Sara hoped Claudia's visit to Sicily hadn't uncovered more questions about her father's life before she'd met him. 'Why don't you get unpacked and I'll sort out what we're going to have for tea?'

She watched as Claudia left the room and then finished drinking her tea. Since her daughter had been away, she'd gone through the suitcase of papers belonging to Carlo that Claudia had brought down from the loft. She kept thinking of the photo of the beautiful young woman with the long dark hair, and the little girl who looked so like their daughter. She pushed her hand to her mouth to prevent a sob escaping. She wished she could read all the letters from his mother. She should have learned Italian when Carlo was teaching Claudia. But what need had she had? Carlo had always insisted he would never go back to Sicily. Once news came of his mother's death, he'd been upset, of course, but had told her it meant he would never have to set foot on the island again.

Sara went into the kitchen and washed the plates and mugs. As she peeled the potatoes, she could hear Claudia walking back and forth upstairs in the bedroom. Wondering what could be making her so restless, Sara went to the foot of the stairs. 'Everything all right, *cariad*?'

Claudia appeared on the landing. 'It's no good, Mam. There's something I have to say.'

Sara's heart thumped as her daughter came down.

'Leave tea. I'm not hungry. There's something I have to tell you and I couldn't say it in front of Auntie Menna.' Sara followed Claudia into the living room and sat down. 'When I found Nonna's suitcase, there was a diary inside, as I told you. I could read some of it but some of the entries were written in Sicilian. A friend's mother translated it for me and I want you to read it, but I have to warn you . . . there's something you may not like.' Claudia took her mam's hands in hers. 'Before the war, Papà was married to a woman called Pia.'

272

Sara snatched her hands away. 'No! That can't be true!'

'I'm so sorry, Mam. It is.' She hesitated. 'And they had a little girl called Giulietta.'

Sara stood up and immediately began pacing the floor. 'You're wrong! I knew you shouldn't have meddled and gone off to that godforsaken country. Why couldn't you have left things alone?' Tears poured down her face.

Sara knew she was being unreasonable, but it was what she'd feared ever since Claudia had found the photo. She'd known then that the look the young woman was giving her husband was not a sisterly look. *Husband! That's a laugh.* But she wasn't laughing. Having her suspicions confirmed broke her heart.

Tears poured down her daughter's face, too. Why hadn't she stopped her going? Suspicions were bad enough, but to have them confirmed . . .

'You know what that makes me, don't you? A bigamist. And you? It means you're a bastard!' Sara heard her voice rise to a screech. *How could he? At least Fred married me legally. My second marriage was a sham.*

'Mam!' Claudia's face drained of colour. She dashed out of the room and ran up the stairs, slamming her bedroom door.

Not long after, Sara heard the front door bang. There would be only one place Claudia would go. No sooner had her daughter returned, she'd driven her away.

Sara sat on the settee, buried her head in her hands and sobbed. What had she done? It wasn't Claudia's fault, after all. It was all Carlo's.

* * *

It was dark when she heard a car pull up outside the cottage. Her sister's voice echoed in the hallway before she appeared in the living room. 'Come here, *cariad*.' She hugged her younger sister. Neither uttered a word until Menna broke the silence.

'Claudia's safe with me. She told me why you got upset. It must be a huge shock for you. I'm not condoning what

Carlo did — far from it — but you do know it happened a lot during, and especially after, the war. Divorce was too expensive for most people. Carlo must have had a reason.'

Sara began to cry again. 'But not Carlo. He could have told me. That's what hurts. He was a devout Catholic, so for him to commit bigamy . . . well, it's something that I would never ever have considered him doing. I still can't believe it.'

Menna handed her a handkerchief. 'Strange things happen in wartime. Gwilym said he's heard of men coming home after being presumed killed in action and finding their wives have remarried. Dry your eyes.'

A picture of her lovely, handsome Carlo, always so caring and gentle, entered Sara's head. But even after all those years of being married to him, it still felt like maybe she hadn't really known him at all.

'Is Claudia all right? What I said to her was unforgiveable. I called her a bastard, Menna. I'm so ashamed of myself. If I'm honest, I had my suspicions when she showed me a photo of Carlo with a young woman and a young girl who looked just like Claudia, but I didn't realise they were married. And I never imagined they could still be alive! How could he do that to me? Our marriage was a complete lie!'

'Claudia's fine, *cariad*. She just needs time to cool off. You both do. Why doesn't she stay with us tonight and I'll bring her back first thing in the morning? And no more of this business that your marriage was a sham. You and Carlo loved each other, and that's all that matters, isn't it?'

After walking Menna to the door and waving her off, Sara returned to the living room. Picking up the wedding photograph of her and Carlo taken outside the register office in Pen Craig, she remembered it as if it was yesterday. She'd never been happier than she'd been that day. Could she have gone through with it if Carlo had confided in her? She didn't think so. She would have been too afraid of the consequences. But then she wouldn't have had over twenty years of happily married life with him, and their precious Claudia wouldn't be here.

She stifled a sob and replaced the photograph in its rightful place in the centre of the bureau.

* * *

Sara tossed and turned for most of the night. Images of Carlo as a young man with a dark-haired bride on his arm emerging from a beautiful church filled her head. She lay in the dark, wondering how many times Carlo's head had been filled with those same images. When he first looked down at baby Claudia, had he been transported back to the birth of his first-born daughter? She'd known the times he'd awoken, shaking and bathed in perspiration, from dreams of his war-time experiences in North Africa, but he hadn't told her about other dreams, dreams of his early life. His first family.

'Stop it, Sara. You're torturing yourself!' Speaking her words aloud, she knew she had to prepare herself to make it up with Claudia.

Eventually she must have drifted off to sleep but when she woke, the upset of the previous day came flooding back to her. If only she could turn the clock back to how things used to be between her and her daughter.

When she heard Menna's car outside and the sound of a door shutting, Sara rushed to the hallway and looked at the clock. *Ten o'clock.* Almost before Claudia could get through the door, she enveloped her daughter in her arms.

'Sorry, Mam. Auntie Menna thought we need time alone, so she'll see us later.' Tears trickled down Claudia's cheeks as she nestled into her mother.

Together, they went into the living room and sat down on the settee. They hugged each other for a few moments, not saying a word. It was Sara who eventually broke away. 'I'm so sorry, *cariad*.'

Brushing away her tears, Claudia took her mother's hand. 'If you're ready, Mam, I can tell you why Papà couldn't return.' Claudia hesitated. 'Pia's brothers threatened to kill him. Marrying beneath her, they thought, so they framed

275

him for stealing a priceless painting from the cathedral. He *couldn't* return. He was dead if he did. I think in the end, you will be proud of him. I know I am . . . and so is Giulietta.'

Sara wondered whether she'd heard correctly. Her chest tightened and she pulled her hand away. 'What do you mean? You didn't meet up with his other family, did you?'

Claudia told her mother how she'd been astonished when she'd looked up at the visiting art historian named Giulietta and had seen a mirror image of herself looking back. And how Giulietta had been told by her mother that her father was dead. 'She had as big a shock as I did. It turns out that we both have followed Papà into the art world. Giulietta is more into art history than I am. She does paint but not often now she is so busy. If I hadn't seen that church paintings course advertised, I may never have met her at all. I took my films in to be developed this morning so it won't be long before you see a photo of her. You'll see for yourself how alike we are.'

Sara listened as her daughter recounted how the breakthrough in her search for why Carlo couldn't return to Sicily had been finding Lucia Rosso's diary. She was trying so hard to share Claudia's excitement but she couldn't. She was still in denial. It was bad enough knowing her husband had another secret life, but then, what did it matter now? Carlo was gone.

'Mam, you can read the diary entries if you'd like.' She rummaged in her bag and brought out a notebook. 'Here.'

Sara rose from the settee. 'No, it's all right. I'll make us a cup of tea, shall I?'

The look on her daughter's face broke Sara's heart, but she didn't want to know anything about Carlo's other daughter, or even hear the story of him being framed for a crime he hadn't committed. The only crime she was interested in was his crime of marrying her when he was still married.

Claudia returned the diary to her bag. 'I understand this is all a huge shock for you, Mam. I'm sorry. I won't mention my trip again until you're ready. I'm going up to my room.'

In the kitchen, Sara waited for the kettle to boil but could hear her daughter pacing the floor in the bedroom above. She gripped the edge of the sink, her heart thumping. *So much for trying to understand what happened*, a voice inside her head reprimanded her. It was Menna's. *It's not Claudia's fault and it's not her half-sister's either. I'm surprised at you, Sara. I thought you were better than this.* She could imagine that when she saw her sister later that day, that would be exactly what she'd tell her. Not only had she upset the daughter who'd only just returned to her, but she would also disappoint the big sister who had looked out for her all her life.

CHAPTER FORTY-SEVEN

Claudia didn't bring up the subject of Giulietta again. Sara knew the strained atmosphere between her and her daughter was down to her, but she was helpless to do anything about it. They'd never been distant with each other before and Sara's resentment against Carlo was building. Even Menna could not persuade her to hear what Claudia had found out.

'You'll regret it. She's due to return to her job at the gallery at the end of the week, and if you haven't made up with her by then, I'm afraid you may never regain the closeness you once had. Surely you need each other more than ever now Carlo has gone?'

Sara knew her sister was right. But she also knew the closeness she had with her daughter had never matched what Carlo and Claudia had had. She was ashamed that she'd sometimes resented that. She suspected Menna knew the whole story, judging by the time Claudia spent with her aunt, avoiding the atmosphere in the house.

'She's home now, so there's no need for me to know.' Sara sniffed.

'That's where you're wrong.' Menna's voice sounded sharp. 'I think you'll have to get used to the idea of her going back and forth to Sicily quite often. If you drive her away, how would you feel if she moved out there permanently?'

'She can't!'

'Well, talk to her then. Find out all about her half-sister. There's room in her life for all of you. You always were a stubborn one, Sara Rosso. Carlo didn't love you any less because he had a daughter in Sicily. From what Claudia's said, his wife wanted nothing to do with him. Perhaps this was why he didn't tell you. He knew how you'd react. He wasn't a bad man. His two daughters have proved he wasn't a thief either. I'm going before I say something I regret. You *have* to sort this.'

Menna slammed the door behind her, making Sara's pulse race. She'd never known her sister be so angry with her before.

* * *

Sara and Claudia continued to be civil to one another as the day of Claudia's return to work loomed nearer.

'Mrs Davies is looking forward to me being back in the gallery, so she says, Mam. I rang her from Auntie Menna's. I'll be there all day, but in the evenings I hope I can work on some seascapes I sketched in Sicily. She may even give me a small space in the upstairs studio to display them.'

It was the first time she'd heard Claudia mention Sicily since their disagreement. Sara looked over to the alcove where one of Carlo's Mediterranean seascapes hung on the wall above the bureau, giving that part of the room a summery feel. 'I love that one of your papà's. The colours are beautiful.' She pointed to it.

'It's so like what I saw out there. I can show you my sketchbook if you like?' Claudia smiled at her, but Sara could tell there was also uncertainty in her daughter's expression.

Sara's eyes burned, but she was determined not to cry. She could see how much Claudia wanted to include her in what she'd experienced in her month away. She nodded. 'Please,' she whispered, her voice crackly.

Claudia fetched her sketchbook from her bedroom and returned to sit by her mother. They talked about the watercolour sketches and how Claudia was going to use them to plan larger paintings in oils.

'They're lovely, *cariad*. Your papà would adore them.'

Neither of them mentioned Giulietta. They talked about the art course, the food, the weather and the colours of the sea. But at least they were talking.

* * *

The morning Sara had been dreading soon dawned. Today her daughter would be catching the bus back to Cardiff. The letterbox rattled and she went to pick up the post. An airmail letter stood out from the rest of the envelopes lying on the mat. It was addressed to Signorina Claudia Rosso and post-marked with a Sicilian stamp. 'Claudia,' she called. 'A letter for you . . . from Sicily.'

Her daughter bounded down the stairs and took the letter from her. 'Thanks,' she said, before disappearing back up to her room.

Sara knew that she wouldn't be told what was in the letter or who it was from. Despite talking about her time in Sicily quite freely now, Claudia still hadn't mentioned Giulietta. Sara brooded over Menna's words. It *was* her own fault. Most of the time she told herself she would never for-give Carlo, but Menna was right — what Carlo had done was nothing to do with Claudia. It wasn't his other daughter's fault either. She still found it hard to call her by her name . . .

'Do you want anything before you go, *cariad*?' she called. Claudia appeared at the top of the stairs, lugging her suitcase. 'Here, let me help you with that.'

'Thanks, Mam. No, I'm okay. Auntie Menna will be here soon. I've rung Linda and she's going to meet me at the bus station in Cardiff, then we're going to the Wimpy in town for something to eat.'

Nothing more was mentioned about the airmail letter. Sara hugged her daughter before Menna arrived. 'I shall miss you, *cariad*. Let me know that you've arrived safely, won't you?'

'I'll write, and I'll phone Auntie Menna tonight.'

It was at times like this that that Sara wished she had a phone so she could hear her daughter's voice more often. She'd have to wait for a letter as she always did. Although, at least she wouldn't have to wait for as long as she had when Claudia had been in Sicily.

Neither of them heard Menna arrive until she called from the hallway. 'All ready? The boot lid's up if you'd like to put your case in, *cariad*.'

Claudia kissed her mam and went outside.

'I hope you two have sorted things out.' Menna turned to her sister.

'We're talking, at least . . .' She paused. 'But about everything apart from his other daughter.' She stopped speaking as she heard Claudia come back into the house.

'Right, Mam. That's it. I'll see you in a week or so.'

'Oh, *cariad*, I don't want you to go.' Sara hugged her daughter tight. Things between them were only just starting to get better.

'Come on, you two. She'll soon be back to see you.' Menna smiled at her.

The three of them walked to the car, and Sara waved as it disappeared round the corner of the street. There was no doubt that things between her and Claudia were much improved. On the surface, they were like any other mother and daughter saying goodbye to each other when they lived seventy miles apart. But a barrier existed between them now that hadn't been there when they'd been over a thousand miles apart. Sara worried that she'd never be able to break that barrier down.

As she went indoors to make a cup of tea to drink alone, her thoughts turned to Aled. He wasn't part of her life now. Was that her fault, too? She'd always blamed Fred's mother for setting him against her, as Carlo had accepted him as his own son when they got married. A shiver ran through her. What if the same thing happened with Claudia? She couldn't bear the thought.

* * *

281

True to her word, Claudia's letter arrived in a few days telling her all the news about catching up with Linda and settling back in to her work in Oriel Elinor. Mrs Davies had loved her Sicily sketches, and so each evening she was painting and getting ready for her exhibition. Sara wrote back, giving her the village news and telling her how much she was missing her. Another letter arrived from Sicily and she forwarded it on to Claudia at her Cardiff address.

Life returned to the new normal for Sara. She still found the house too empty without Carlo and Claudia, and tried to spend as little time alone there as she could. Grieving for the man she knew and loved had changed since finding out that he'd had a life and family he'd hidden from her. When the explosion had first happened, she'd felt numb. It was as though she was watching it all happen to someone else. She'd been angry with Carlo — angry that he hadn't taken enough care and cut through a gas pipe. But the anger now was different. Some nights she would clench her fists and pummel the pillow, crying his name.

Above all, she was lonely. It was Claudia who occupied her thoughts now. Sara couldn't change what her daughter had found out, but she could change how she dealt with it. Most days after work in the office, she would call in on Menna. Her sister always provided a listening ear.

'You seem happy tonight. Maybe a certain young lady's coming home for the weekend?' Menna gave her a knowing look one evening.

'Yes, I had a letter from her this morning. I can't wait.'

An image of her beautiful daughter entered her mind, and Sara was more determined than ever to make it up with Claudia as soon as she arrived home.

CHAPTER FORTY-EIGHT

Claudia

Claudia watched the view through the bus window change from the terraced housing along the streets of the South Wales valleys, to the beauty of the Brecon Beacons, and finally to the landscape of rural Radnorshire. It was her first visit home to see her mam since the row between them. Things were much improved but she was torn. Not wanting to add to her mother's grief, she'd decided that perhaps the best way was to carry on doing what she was doing and not mentioning Giulietta's name in front of her. And yet, she also felt the need to defend her father's actions. She imagined her father alone and interned in a foreign country, and how he would have felt when he'd first arrived in Wales. The only thing she could be truly certain of was that he'd truly loved her mam.

She pulled out two airmail letters from her bag. The one that had arrived first was from Alessandro. He'd told her how much he was missing her and how much he loved her.

> *You are the last person I think of when I close my eyes and your beautiful face is waiting for me when I open my eyes, tesoro.*

Reading those words had made her wish he wasn't so far away. But he'd also had news for her. He'd been doing some digging and found out that after Roberto came out of prison, both of Pia's brothers had got involved in gangs, drug dealing and terrorising anyone who resisted their control in the south of the island. Their names were whispered in fear.

To think that, until she read your nonna's diary, Giulietta would have known nothing of her mother's family. Perhaps when she returned to live in Porto Montebello, it was good that she didn't have the family name her mamma had reverted to. If Pia was too worried to use Rosso, imagine how Romano would have been viewed. Especially when Giulietta unwittingly bought the family home of Casa Cristina.

News about the reign of terror meted out by the Romano brothers confirmed that her father's fear of returning to Sicily was genuine. If only she could make her mother see that.

She just had time to re-read the second letter before arriving in Dolwen. It was from Giulietta and had arrived at the flat that morning.

Cara Claudia,

I hope your journey back to Wales went well. I have been thinking about your mother's reaction when she found out about me. I hope she wasn't too upset.

I have some good news. The painting has been fully restored and reframed. I met with Matteo today and he told me that the cathedral authorities want you and me to be guests of honour at the re-dedication of the painting when it's formally hung in its rightful pace in the duomo. Isn't that wonderful? The best bit is that Carlo Giuseppe Rosso, our papà, is going to be publicly exonerated of any wrongdoing and hailed Porto Montebello Duomo's hero.

Please write back with some dates when you can come to Sicily, and Matteo will liaise with the cathedral. Oh, and they will pay your airfare! You must stay with me at Casa Cristina.

La tua amata sorella, Giulietta

Your loving sister. *How good did that sound?* The best news was that Claudia was returning to Sicily and would be able to see her lovely Alessandro again as well.

The bus pulled up into Dolwen. Her mam was there to meet her and they walked through the village together. The peace and lack of hustle and bustle in contrast to the Cardiff streets calmed her in readiness for telling her mother her news, but she decided to wait until they got back to the house.

When her mam opened the door, she smiled. 'Something smells good, Mam.'

'Guess what it is. What do I always bake when my girl comes home?' Her mother grinned. 'It's so good to have you back, *cariad*.'

Claudia decided she wouldn't spoil her homecoming by telling her mam that she would soon be off on her travels again quite yet.

'I'll make us a cuppa and you can see if my Welsh cakes are up to scratch. Go in and sit down.'

As she entered the living room, Claudia inhaled deeply. She looked across at the empty chair by the fireplace. It was as if she was returning from the hospital all over again. Tears filled her eyes. Her father's place was empty. It always would be.

'Oh, *cariad*, whatever is it? Let me put this down.' Her mam noticed her tears as she came into the room with a tray of tea and Welsh cakes.

'It's seeing his empty chair.'

'I'm afraid it will be like that for a while. I see it every day, but for you it must be like the first time all over again. Bless you.' Her mam placed an arm around her.

They chatted for a while about how they were coping without her father and agreed that life had to go on. Claudia knew that was her cue to tell her mam about Giulietta's letter. Knots tightened in her stomach. She didn't want to upset her all over again, but she knew she couldn't fly out to Sicily without telling her. 'Thank you for sending on that second airmail letter, Mam. It was an invitation.'

Her mam looked over. 'Oh, yes. An invitation to what?'

Claudia took a deep breath, hoping she could explain without her mam getting hurt and emotional again. 'I didn't get as far as telling you, but just before he was drafted to fight in the war, Papà had been accused of stealing a priceless painting from the cathedral in the city where he lived.'

'Your father would never steal.' Sara frowned.

'I know. His mamma used to work for a family called the Romanos. That's where Papà and Pia got to know each other. Her father and brothers thought she was marrying beneath her and plotted to frame him for the theft. Nonna overheard them and told Papà.' As Claudia filled her mother in with the facts, she saw a flicker of interest in her eyes. It was as if her mam wanted to know more but wouldn't admit it. 'The map I showed you before I went to Sicily was Papà's way of telling us where he'd hidden the real painting in the tunnels under the cathedral,' she went on. 'We found it, Mam. After all these years.'

Her mother didn't ask who the "we" referred to. When Claudia told her mother about the re-dedication service and the fact that the cathedral authorities would pay for her flight, she stayed silent for a few moments, clearly letting the news sink in.

'Off on your travels again then,' she said. 'I shouldn't think Elinor Davies will be best pleased.'

Claudia was disappointed. She'd expected her mother to be a little uncertain about the news, but she'd said nothing about how good it would be for her father's name to be cleared, or how amazing it was that he'd saved the cathedral from losing the priceless painting.

'Is that all you've got to say?' Claudia knew the tone of her voice was sharp and clipped. 'I can't win. I should have just gone without telling you. I don't know why I bothered.'

She went up to her bedroom to be on her own and took out the packets of photographs she'd had developed. She'd intended to show her mam, thinking it would be a good way to introduce her to Alessandro and explain that she had fallen in love. However, after her reaction, she decided it wouldn't be a good idea, and so instead she laid them out on the bed and studied them one by one. Then she wrote on the back of each one, remembering the date and place where it was taken. The black-and-white surfaces did nothing to capture the vibrant colours of the island but luckily those were imprinted on her memory. She picked out a couple of snaps of her and Alessandro to send to him.

Claudia began her letter in Italian.

Caro Sandro. Mi manchi tantissimo.

She did miss him, and after her mother's reaction, or lack of it, the feeling of not seeing him was an almost physical ache. She told him of the invitation to the re-dedication service and said she would let him know the actual date of her arrival once she'd spoken to Mrs Davies at the gallery. Another trip away from work may not go down well with Elinor, but if it meant sacrificing her job, she had no doubt she would. Going back to hear her papà's name cleared was all that mattered.

> *I cannot wait to see you again, my love. I keep looking at these photographs and reliving those special moments we spent together. Giulietta says I can stay with her at the villa but I'm sure I will be able to be with you . . . alone!*
> *I'll write as soon as I know the date I arrive.*
> *Ti amo, caro Sandro.*
> *Claudia*

She folded the letter, tucked it with the chosen photos into the envelope and addressed it to Alessandro. She imagined his face as he opened it, hoping it would reflect the excitement of her own when he found out they were going to see each other again.

'I'm going to the post office,' she called on her way out.

It was a short walk to the post office and Claudia was glad of the fresh air. She'd called in on her aunt on the way back to ring the gallery as well.

'I'd like to send this to Sicily, please. First class.'

The postmaster looked up the cost and handed her the necessary stamps. 'I heard you've been out to where your father came from. A successful trip, *bach*?' He turned his head to try to read the name on her letter. 'Signor Al-ess-a . . . A relative you found of Carlo's?'

Claudia put her hand over the address. That's what she didn't miss when she was living in Cardiff — everyone wanted to know everyone else's business in Dolwen. Well, for now, Alessandro Costa was her secret.

Auntie Menna's car was parked by Uncle Gwilym's work truck at the side of her house. Claudia was pleased to see she was in as she had a favour to ask. She found the back door unlocked as always. 'Hello?' she called as she opened it.

Her aunt came into the scullery to greet her with a big *cwtch*. 'Well, this is a lovely surprise, *cariad*. Your mam told me you were coming home this weekend.'

Claudia freed herself from her aunt's hug. 'I wanted to see you and Uncle Gwilym anyway, but I've come to ask you a favour. I don't suppose I could use your phone to ring work, could I? I need some more time off. I'll explain afterwards.'

'You've just missed him, *cariad*. Geraint picked him up to go to a meeting in Pen Craig. But, of course. You know where the telephone is. I'll put the kettle on.'

Claudia could tell by Elinor Davies's voice that she was reluctant to let her have more time off. She agreed on this occasion, and together they chose some dates in September when there were no new exhibitions at Oriel Elinor. Claudia knew she wouldn't be able to ask again. If she wanted to see Alessandro on a regular basis, she would have to give up her work there. For now, though, at least she could write to Giulietta with some dates. She was going back to Sicily. Not even her mam could spoil her excitement.

She practically skipped into the kitchen where her aunt was pouring out tea into her favourite mug. Menna gave her a knowing look. 'Someone's looking happy. Are you going to tell your old aunt all about it?'

CHAPTER FORTY-NINE

27 September 1968, Sicily

Alone with her thoughts on the plane journey, Claudia relived the awful row she'd had with her mother once she'd bought her ticket to return to Sicily. Every time she closed her eyes, her mam's angry face loomed, taunting her for thinking more about some "so-called sister" she'd only just met than her grieving mother.

'Well, go then! Don't think about me. I'll manage. I always do.'

Her mother's words had stung. Was she so wrapped up in finding out her papà's secrets that she'd neglected her mam's feelings?

As soon as the plane touched down on the runway, Claudia relaxed. She was back in Sicily, soon to be reunited with her sister and, later, with Alessandro. All the upset and the stony atmosphere with her mam regarding her return drifted away in the warmth and autumn sunshine which greeted her as she descended the steps from the aeroplane.

Once through passport control, she was met by a smiling Giulietta, who led her to the parked car. 'The traffic was awful. More Sicilian men shouting and beeping their horns in frustration than ever. I was afraid I was going to be late.'

Claudia laughed. On her first visit, she had been shocked at the aggression of some of the local drivers. She dreaded to think what they'd have been like on the backwater lanes of Radnorshire if they got behind a tractor or old Mr Bevan the Blacksmith on one of his Sunday afternoon jaunts. Even her easy-going papà had been known to mutter the odd Italian expletive under his breath at him.

'It's fine. I'm just glad you were free to meet me. It's lovely to be back. Feels like I'm coming home.' Claudia looked around as they began their drive through the now-familiar streets.

Giulietta squeezed her sister's hand. 'You have two places to call home now. I'm so thrilled you could come for the re-dedication.'

'I wouldn't have missed it for the world.' Claudia beamed. 'The owner of the gallery where I work wasn't too keen at first, and I suppose I can't blame her. I didn't tell her the full story on the phone, but when I got back to Cardiff, I told her all about Papà and what he'd done. She was so impressed we'd found the real painting, she gave me her blessing, with strict instructions to take lots of photos.'

It's a pity someone else hasn't given me her blessing. Claudia pushed the idea away. She was back in her father's home-town. In two days' time, she was going to honour what he'd done for the sake of its *duomo*. She sat back and enjoyed the short drive up to the villa.

Casa Cristina soon came into view, the salmon-pink of its walls gleaming in the afternoon sun. Giulietta took a turning off to the right before they reached the gate where Claudia and Alessandro had first entered via the steep steps.

'I'll park the car in the grounds of the villa and we can go round the back.'

Double gates opened automatically and Giulietta drove onto a wide driveway. Edged by raised beds filled with colourful plants, the area of black-and-white cobbles had been arranged in bold flower patterns.

They got out of the car and Giulietta took Claudia's suitcase from the boot. 'It's lovely this side. You may not have the spectacular views of the front, but it's calming. It's why I've got the pergola there.' She pointed. 'Sometimes, after a busy day at work, I come here and just sit. It's the perfect place to unwind.'

'I love these patterns. It must have taken someone ages to set all these tiny pebbles into the cement.' Claudia hoped there would be time to come out to the pergola and sketch.

'The American owners of the villa before me were interested in Greek mythology, apparently. They believed everything is made up of four elements. The rich black soil in the beds represents earth, the black cobbles are the lava for fire, and the smooth white ones have come from the sea — water. All that was needed to complete the four was air.' She walked to the back door. On the wall to the left-hand side, a metal wind chime tinkled a gentle tune in the breeze. 'And there it is. When I moved in, the original one was hanging down by one metal link, so I had a friend of mine make this for me. The sound it makes is so soothing.'

'That's fascinating.' Claudia placed a hand on the chime to feel the shiny metal. 'It's beautiful. I'd read about the four elements but have never heard of anyone putting symbols of them in a garden.'

'There's so much to tell you about this place. Come. I'll show you to your room and you can unpack.'

Claudia's bedroom was at the front of the villa, opening onto a wide veranda running the whole length of the house. The view over the bay below was spectacular. An image of the rundown house on Via Umberto came back to her. She could only imagine how Signor Romano, living in luxury in Casa Cristina, would have viewed the match between his daughter and her father. She wondered if her mam would have sympathy for Pia if she knew she'd suffered the same fate as herself — both women banished from their families because their fathers disapproved of the men they'd fallen in love with. Then, of course, her mother had risked it all again when she'd fallen for an Italian prisoner of war.

Her thoughts were interrupted by Giulietta calling her from downstairs. 'Visitor for you, Claudia!'

She bounded down the stairs into the living room. Standing there was Alessandro, as handsome as ever, even more tanned and with a wide smile. Claudia allowed herself to be enveloped in his arms as he kissed her neck. Giulietta coughed and they all laughed.

'Sorry, Giulietta. But I've missed this sister of yours.'

'I think this calls for a drink.' Giulietta left the two of them alone while she went to the kitchen.

Alessandro took Claudia's face in his hands and kissed her properly, taking his time so she was able to savour every moment. Her insides somersaulted, but then he stopped and looked down at her with a worried expression. 'I've loved reading your letters, *tesoro*. But it sounds as if it has not been easy for you telling your mother you have found your sister. Do not worry. It must have been a big shock for her. She will come round, I'm sure.'

'I don't think she will ever accept Papà had another daughter before me. It's so unfair. It's not Giulietta's fault.' Claudia sighed.

'Did I hear my name mentioned?' Her sister was back with a tray of long-stemmed flute glasses and a bottle of Asti Spumante. 'Will you do the honours, Sandro?' She handed him the bottle, and they cheered at the sound of the cork popping before Alessandro poured the wine for each of them. '*Cin, cin*! Welcome back, Claudia.' Giulietta raised her glass. 'Anyway, neither of you have answered me. I heard my name!'

'I was telling Sandro how hard my mother is taking the news about you and that it's not your fault.'

'I do think you have to be patient, Claudia. Maybe you're being too hard on her. After all, she's the one who's been most affected by all of this. Our papà kept his marriage to my mother and the fact he already had a daughter a secret from her. How would you feel? He broke the law and now you expect her to welcome me as if it's nothing?'

Heat travelled up Claudia's neck and she looked down at her lap as she tried to hide the threatened tears. She hadn't expected that from her sister. But was Giulietta right? Was she the one being unreasonable, not her mam? She'd been so excited to have found a sister, and even more excited that they'd managed to absolve her beloved papà of a crime he hadn't committed together. Maybe she hadn't properly understood how it was for her mother.

Sandro broke the awkward silence. 'What are the arrangements for Sunday, Giulietta? I think you said there are some complimentary tickets. If there are, I know Mamma and Olivia would love to come to support you both.'

Giulietta looked at Claudia, clearly concerned. 'Yes, I'll tell you all the plans I've been told.' She leaned across and touched her sister's arm gently. 'I'm sorry if that sounded harsh. I didn't mean to upset you.' She got up and brought over a large brown envelope from the bureau. She handed them each an order of service. A miniature image of the Madonna and Child painting headed the cream, velum pamphlet. Underneath was the date, Sunday 29 September 1968, and the time of the dedication service — 11 a.m. at the *duomo*. Seeing her father's name in full, Carlo Giuseppe Rosso, appearing with Giulietta's and her own alongside an explanation about what the service was about, brought home to Claudia how emotional the service was going to be.

'Oh, this is beautiful!' she exclaimed, her earlier uncertainty forgotten. 'Seeing it set out like this so professionally makes it real, doesn't it?'

Sandro pulled her close. 'Well, it *is* real. And all down to Carlo Rosso's two daughters never giving up.'

* * *

Later on, Giulietta made the excuse of having to do some work on an upcoming talk and apologised for needing to leave them while she worked in the dining room. Claudia knew it was her way of giving her and Alessandro some private time together.

'Why don't we go out?' she suggested.

Sandro gave her a knowing look. 'Our special place,' he whispered. 'To watch the sunset.'

Shouting goodbye to Giulietta, they ran down the steps to the parking space off the road where the white Vespa gleamed in the sunshine. Soon, they were motoring down to the harbour where *Aura* was moored. The bars along the quayside were busy at that time in the afternoon. Alessandro's friend, Paolo, who worked at the *trattoria* where they'd eaten the first time, called him over. He pulled out a chair from one of the empty tables for Claudia. 'Do you fancy something to welcome you back? An iced coffee and maybe a cannolo?'

Knowing she'd couldn't refuse her favourite pastry, Alessandro ordered. '*Due caffè freddi, due* cannoli, *per favore*, Paolo. Lots of tourists here today, eh?'

'*Sì,* they all seem to be taking boat trips. I should think every cove will be full of them swimming and diving.' He left them to lead another couple to a table.

'I hope not.' Alessandro brought her hand up to his lips.

As they waited for their food to be served, they held hands and chatted, catching up on what they'd been doing since they'd been apart. Now Sandro's mother was fully recovered, he was working full time back at the studio and painting more seascapes and sunsets.

'With the tourist season slowing down, I find painting and sketching down here in the mornings and then working on larger pieces in oils back at the studio each afternoon suits me. It's surprising how many visitors ask to come and see what else I have. You must come and see how I've rearranged the space. One area is now a gallery where my paintings are for sale.' His eyes sparkled with excitement as he spoke. This was the true Alessandro — the creative painter, not the one who had enrolled on a history of art course thinking he ought to get some sort of formal qualification.

'It sounds wonderful. You're extremely talented and I can see how happy you are. I can't wait to see what you've done.'

It was then that Paolo arrived with the coffees and cannoli. Claudia took a first bite and closed her eyes. 'Mmm.'

Sandro laughed. 'You should see the look on your face. Here, let me brush away all the icing sugar. You've got it all round your mouth. I take it they don't have cannoli in Wales?'

'No. I've almost missed these as much as I've missed you.'

* * *

Later, Alessandro stood at the tiller guiding *Aura* out into the open sea. A breeze sprang up and, together with the water becoming choppy from passing boats, Claudia started feeling quite queasy.

'Are you all right?' Alessandro's voice competed with the sound of the wind.

'It wasn't like this the last time we came, was it?' She gripped the bench, her knuckles showing white through the tight skin.

'It will not be long now. Look, there is the heart-shaped cave! It is just round this next cliff.'

Now, there were fewer other boats around them and the water became less turbulent. As soon as they rounded the cliff Alessandro had pointed out, the breeze dropped and she could see their cove in front of them.

'We can't keep calling it "our cove",' she said. 'Why don't we give it a name?'

'Any ideas?'

'What about Baia degli Amanti? Lovers' Cove.'

'I can see what you have on your mind, Signorina Rosso. Baia degli Amanti it is.'

She smiled, reflecting on the last time they'd been here the night before she'd returned home. She had two different

296

homes now. Wales and Sicily. Like her papà had, perhaps. A Sicilian who had made his home in Wales. Could she contemplate being a Welsh girl making her home in Sicily?

'There it is. Our beautiful private space.' Alessandro increased the speed and drove the boat to the other side of the small bay. He jumped out once the boat was in shallow water and dragged it onto the sandy beach.

They got out the rug and towels from the boat, choosing the far end of the beach to settle down on. Alessandro had brought wine and placed the bottle in the cool sea water to chill as he had before. Then he sat back down by Claudia on the rug. Placing his arm around her, they fell backwards onto the rug, kissing.

'I've been wanting this ever since I arrived,' Claudia gasped.

Before she could say any more, Alessandro kissed her again. His hand caressed her skin under her T-shirt. Now-familiar feelings surged through her as he lifted her top and kissed her breast. Each time they made love, Claudia loved him more.

Afterwards, they lay skin to skin, bodies entwined, in silence and alone with their thoughts. *How can I leave him again?* A single tear trickled from the corner of Claudia's eye.

Sandro brushed it away and kissed her forehead. 'Come on. Let us get dressed and drink our wine while we wait for the sunset.'

The sky was streaked with brushstrokes of coral and apricot orange against a pastel-pink backdrop, the sun a fiery orb sinking ever closer to the horizon.

'It never ceases to amaze me how quickly the sun sinks and disappears. Every stage would make a beautiful painting.' Claudia sipped the last of her wine. 'Have you ever painted the sunset from here?'

'Not recently.' He hesitated. 'I came here with Daniela. She asked me to paint it.' He quickly added, 'I have a number of sunset paintings on sale in the gallery, but they were not painted here.'

Claudia stiffened. So, he used to come to the Baia degli Amanti with his first love, his wife? Of course he had. Why shouldn't he have? But other questions surfaced. Had he made love to her on the same beach? Taken her into the heart-shaped cave? Claudia sat watching gentle waves break onto the beach, leaving a frill of white foam. The thoughts and feelings inside her were far more tumultuous.

'We had better get going,' said Alessandro. 'Are you all right? You have gone quiet.'

They stood up. He rolled up the rug and she collected the tumblers and empty wine bottle, taking them over to the boat. Alessandro had been honest in telling her about Daniela. He could have just told her he'd painted the sunset from here but not mentioned anything else. She should be honest with him, too. She turned to him, taking his hands in hers. 'I'm sorry. It was you telling me you'd been here with Daniela that made me go quiet. Of course you have. I'm being silly to think of the Baia degli Amanti as our special place. I appreciate you being honest. I'm wrong to be jealous of her.'

It was Alessandro's turn to become quiet. 'I cannot pretend she did not exist, Claudia.'

By the time they got back, the light had faded. Arriving at the harbour from the sea, a view of the illuminated bars and restaurants, busy with holidaymakers, highlighted how long the quayside was. As they approached, Claudia welcomed the buzz of conversation and sound of live music breaking the silence between her and Alessandro.

What have I done?

After mooring the motorboat, they walked to where the scooter was parked, still in silence.

'I'm so sorry, Sandro. I've spoiled the lovely time you had planned for us. I know how hard it was for you when we first met, and I'll never forgive myself if this comes between us.'

He hugged her, kissing her on the top of her head. 'It won't,' he whispered. 'But you have to accept Daniela is part of who I am. It does not mean I love you any less. Understand?'

Claudia nodded with tears in her eyes. 'I understand.'

CHAPTER FIFTY

Over the next two days building up to the re-dedication service, Claudia spent time with Giulietta, getting to know her better. Each morning, they took breakfast together sitting out on the garden terrace to the side of the villa, surrounded by blue agapanthus and scarlet hibiscus still in bloom. Giulietta told Claudia of her life growing up with her mother. She had a vague memory of being in some tunnels with her friends, but the ones where they'd traced their father's map to find the painting meant nothing to her. Since Claudia had left, Giulietta had made enquiries and found she could have entered from another entrance near where she and her mamma lived before moving to Palermo.

'It's blocked off now. I remember Mamma teaching the other children with me. She got us to make drawings and told us stories. A bit like Nonna.'

For a moment, it looked like Giulietta was about to cry, but she took a deep breath and composed herself. 'If only I'd got to know the wonderful woman who wrote the diaries that mean so much to both of us. It's because of her we've got this service to look forward to. Are you seeing Sandro today?'

'Yes, I still haven't been able to see Curtis and Skye. He'd like to come with me to ask them to attend the ceremony. If it wasn't for them inviting me into their house right at the beginning of my last trip, none of this would have happened.'

* * *

The day of the re-dedication arrived, with Claudia feeling a mixture of excitement and nervousness. She was proud her father was going to be honoured in the city where he was born and brought up, but as she'd be centre of attention along with her sister, she wanted everything to go smoothly. Alessandro travelled with them in Giulietta's car. The street where she normally parked was full and she had to drive to a parallel street a good walk away from the piazza.

'That's the last thing we want,' she joked. 'The guests of honour turning up late.'

Sandro checked his watch. 'You are fine. There is plenty of time.'

They entered the piazza to see a large group of people milling around in front of the *duomo*.

Giulietta led the way through the crowd, smiling and acknowledging some people she knew. The intricate wrought-iron gates into the terrace in front of the *duomo* were still closed. Either side of the steps up to the gates were large floral arrangements in shades of peach, creamy white and pastel pinks. They were displayed on wooden tripods.

'They're beautiful. Absolutely stunning. When I told the florist what the service was about, she chose flowers with meanings to suit.' Giulietta pointed to each variety as Claudia stopped to look. 'Roses — white because, as well as its meaning of purity and innocence, it can mean silence and secrecy. This is the lisianthus. They're always associated with appreciation. And then these exotic beauties, the flamingo lilies, symbolise prosperity. What better bloom to represent the significance of returning a priceless painting back to the cathedral? Now, let's go in. They're opening the gates. We'll be trodden down in the rush, otherwise!'

Claudia, Giulietta and Alessandro were greeted at the door by Matteo. He led them down the aisle of the *duomo*. Pews had been arranged to face the chapel to the left where Claudia had first set eyes on her papà's Madonna and Child. She smiled when she remembered the effect it had had on her and how the old man had told her the rumour that the painting was a forgery. Back then, she'd had no idea what was ahead of her.

'Your seats are up in the chancel on the left so everyone can see who you are,' Matteo explained. All three bowed and crossed themselves before they sat down.

Identical flower arrangements to the ones outside were displayed on pedestals either side of the steps. A square of rich crimson velvet was draped over what was obviously a painting hanging behind the chapel's altar. *Cappella di Santa Lucia*. Claudia hadn't read the metal plaque on the wall to the left of the entrance into the chapel before.

She nudged Alessandro who was sitting next to her. 'Have you seen the name of the chapel?' she whispered.

'Very appropriate.' He squeezed her hand.

Claudia looked to her right and watched the invited guests take up their seats. She recognised some of them. Maria and Olivia arrived with Salvo and his wife, Rosa. Giovanna kissed Matteo on both cheeks and introduced him to a distinguished-looking man who had his arm around her.

'He's her latest beau,' whispered Giulietta. 'Between them, they could buy the Madonna and Child painting, I bet!' She winked.

Soon, Claudia spotted Curtis and Skye, who appeared in complete contrast to most of the sombrely dressed dignitaries arriving. Claudia beamed and waved discreetly at them as they took their places. They'd been delighted when she had called with their invites and introduced them to Alessandro who they described as a "cool guy". She saw some of the students who had been on the course with her arrive and be directed to their seats by Matteo. There was one person Claudia looked for but couldn't see. Giorgio Moroni. Surely, he would have had a personal invitation from Giulietta? Although her sister had not divulged anything about what her relationship actually was with Giorgio, Claudia was convinced they were a couple. Soon, her suspicions were confirmed as she noticed Giulietta looking at her watch. 'Giorgio's cutting it fine.'

Finally, Claudia turned to see Matteo escorting Giorgio to a seat beside Giulietta, who stood and greeted him. The chapel was now full and the seats in the main *duomo* behind had very few spaces.

Music started up, heralding the arrival of the bishop and clergy of the cathedral who took up their places in the chancel. Although the re-dedication wasn't a religious service, because of its setting and the subject matter of the painting, it seemed appropriate it began with prayers.

Afterwards, Matteo addressed the congregation and introduced Giulietta and Claudia.

'*Signore e signori*, I would like to introduce you to two special ladies who have achieved something extraordinary for this beautiful *duomo*. Before World War Two, there was a plan to rob the cathedral of its most famous and valuable work of art. A young apprentice painter who had practised his technique by trying to copy the style of the famous artist, had painted the work many times. When he found out about the planned robbery, he substituted his best attempt and ensured the real painting was safely hidden, intending to retrieve it and return it to the cathedral authorities. However, he was framed for the robbery and threatened with his life. He never returned to the island. That young apprentice was Carlo Giuseppe Rosso. These two ladies are his daughters, Claudia and Giulietta.' He turned to the sisters and asked them to stand. 'They have found the original valuable painting. We owe them a debt of gratitude.'

At the round of applause, Giulietta looked at her sister and grinned. Matteo invited her to give an address where she explained how she'd met Claudia, and then talked about the map and the part played by Alessandro. She praised Giorgio, too, for ensuring the condition of the canvas was perfect before it was carefully unrolled and then explained how he'd restored it.

Matteo thanked her, and then invited Claudia and Giulietta to take one corner each of the velvet screen. 'And now, will you please reveal the magnificent work of art that has been hidden since 1939?'

The sisters gently pulled on the corners and the velvet covering fell like a crimson waterfall onto the marble floor of the chapel. There was an audible gasp and an even louder applause. The delicate brushwork and gentle colours of the paint appeared to shine as the painting took on a particular personal meaning for the two sisters. Claudia and Giulietta hugged each other, both with tears in their eyes, before sitting back down.

'Papà would be so proud.' Claudia could imagine his reaction to what had just taken place.

'And Nonna,' added Giulietta.

The bishop led final prayers, dedicating the painting back to its rightful place. He thanked the two sisters who had proved their father was innocent of a crime he hadn't committed. 'Finally, we pray for Carlo, their father, who protected this *duomo* from losing its priceless artwork. It may now be enjoyed by the worshippers here in Porto Montebello. May he rest in peace. Amen.'

'Amen.'

As the congregation left the chapel, Claudia gazed up at the painting. The colours of the Madonna's cloak really had been recreated perfectly by her father back in the little Welsh chapel. She knew she would never forget this day.

* * *

Back at Casa Cristina, the celebration party was in full swing. Giulietta had arranged for caterers to prepare an *al fresco* lunch while they were at the re-dedication service. Long trestle tables laden with platters of Sicilian foods had been laid out under parasols in the area of the garden next to the fountain and beds of deep-red roses still in flower. Bottles of wine were chilling in silver ice buckets in a separate area alongside an array of upturned glasses. Groups of guests were milling around in the grounds and on the terraces, accepting drinks and bites of finger food offered from silver trays.

'This is how the rich people live, eh?' commented Alessandro. 'There is Mamma and Olivia. Let us join them.'

Claudia grabbed a mini bruschetta topped with tomatoes and sliced olives before following him over to where his family had found a bench in the shade. Maria smiled as they approached. 'Claudia. This is wonderful. *Grazie mille* for inviting us.'

'Yes, *grazie*,' said Olivia. 'I never thought I would ever come here. When I was a little girl, it was all shut up. That added to its mystery. I always imagined a secret princess lived in the pink villa on the hill.'

They all laughed. 'You and your imagination.' Her mother put an arm around her.

A young waitress arrived with a tray of small *arancini* arranged in a pyramid edged with a circle of cherry tomatoes stuffed with creamy ricotta. Claudia was taken back to the party food they had back home. Sausage rolls, cheese and pineapple on sticks, and always white-bread sandwiches filled with tinned ham. She wished her mam could be here to sample this spread.

Giorgio rang the bell by the back door to get everyone's attention. 'Giulietta would like to say a few words.' Several waiters stood with champagne bottles in hand ready to pop the corks. Others handed out flutes to everyone.

'*Signori e signore. Grazie* for all your support today. I want you to raise your glasses to a special lady, Claudia Rosso. Without her, I would know nothing of our father, who sadly died a few months ago. She came to Sicily with nothing apart from an old address, a few photographs and an intriguing map. She could have given up but she didn't. She was determined to solve the mystery set by our papà. She found me and we both gained a sister. Together, with help from Alessandro Costa there, we proved our father was innocent of any crime. You saw what he did to protect the *duomo*'s most valuable asset. I'm sure I speak for my sister, too, when I say I wish our papà was here to see the wonderful response to what he did. To Claudia.'

'Claudia!'

Claudia's cheeks burned as all eyes focused on her. '*Grazie.*'

She looked up into the cerulean sky. Wherever he was, she imagined her father would know that he had been absolved. Perhaps this was what he'd dreamed of when he'd given the map and photograph to Sisto. She hoped so. *Now you can finally rest in peace, Papà.*

CHAPTER FIFTY-ONE

The days after the re-dedication seemed to fly by. Claudia spent as much time as she could with Alessandro, knowing there was no telling when they would see each other again. As he'd promised, they made one more boat trip to Baia degli Amanti, where they made love under the setting sun.

Claudia decided to surprise Alessandro in his studio on her last day. Leaving Casa Cristina, she walked down the steep steps into a pretty street, lined with pink oleander trees, which led to the bus station. Small shops selling homemade crafts and local produce from wicker baskets spreading out onto the pavement enticed shoppers in. One was set back from the rest and displayed silver pendants. When Claudia entered the shop, the owner came from the back where he'd been working.

'*Buongiorno,* signor. I'd like a gift for my boyfriend. We live hundreds of miles apart so I'd like something for him to keep as a memento. A pendant, perhaps.'

The man took out a small display card on which were pinned beautiful rectangular pendants. He unpinned one, suspending it on its strong, linked chain from his fingers. 'What about this one? I've engraved it with an image of Saint Christopher. He is known as the patron saint of travellers, of course, but that is what you will both have to do for your love to survive, eh? You will travel many kilometres.' He handed it to Claudia. The engraving was of Saint Christopher holding a staff and carrying a child on his shoulder. It was edged in a diagonal-cut pattern that caught the light.

'*Grazie*. It's perfect. Just what I was looking for.'

The man smiled. 'He is a lucky boyfriend, I think.' He placed the pendant into a rich-blue, velvet-covered box and then wrapped it in thick gift-wrapping paper, finishing off with a ribbon tied into a fancy bow.

After the short bus ride, she then continued to Alessandro's studio. He was in the gallery end talking to a prospective buyer. Claudia could hear they were negotiating a sale of one of his sunset paintings. From what she could see of it, she realised it was a recent painting that depicted the view from Baia degli Amanti. She'd been there enough times herself by now to recognise the formation of the rock at the far end of the cove with the sea to the right. The colours he'd used and the free brushwork was what made it such a good painting. It was as if she was there on the beach, watching the sun sink below the horizon. The buyer must have thought so, too, because soon Sandro was wrapping the painting in protective layers of paper and card.

'*Grazie mille*,' he said as the customer paid for his purchase. 'I hope you will enjoy my sunset for many years to come.' He shook the man's hand and lifted the painting into his arms.

Sandro spotted Claudia and rushed over to kiss her as the customer left the shop. 'I wasn't expecting to see you here. This is a lovely surprise, *mia cara*.'

'I wanted to see you. I don't know how long it will be before we can see each other again after tomorrow.' Claudia had been determined not to get upset, but she knew it was going to be much harder this time. The more time they spent together, the more she wanted it not to end. 'Well done on the sale,' she continued, changing the subject. 'I'm not surprised. It means a lot to me that you are now painting from our special place again. I love the new paintings.'

307

'Every sale means I have a bit more money to come to see you in Wales. I can't expect you to come to Sicily every time. But anyway, how about we go for a coffee?'

The *trattoria* where Paolo worked had become a favourite, and he directed them to their usual table when they arrived. 'Back again, Signorina Rosso. The usual?'

Claudia smiled. They'd got into the habit of having *granite* followed by *caffè* and cannoli. '*Sì, per favore.*'

While they waited for the *granite* to arrive, Claudia gave Alessandro his present.

'What's this?' He looked surprised.

'Open it. It's something for you to remember me by.'

Sandro undid the bow and opened the gift, flicking up the lid of the velvet box. 'It's beautiful, *grazie mille*. But you shouldn't have. I don't need anything to remember you. I think of you all the time.' Just then, Paolo arrived back with the icy drinks and Alessandro held up the pendant. 'Look what she has just given me.'

Paolo took a closer look. 'Very smart. What is the engraving?'

'It's Saint Christopher. We'll be doing a lot of travelling between Wales and Sicily, so it's appropriate, I think.' Claudia remembered what the shop owner had told her.

'No. It is better if you move to Sicily. Not so much rain here.'

They all laughed. Paolo handed the pendant back before going to attend to other diners.

An image of her and Alessandro setting up home together flashed through Claudia's mind, and she jumped up and went around to his side of the table. She took the pendant from him, unfastened the chain and placed it around his neck. His skin was warm against the cool of the silver chain. Nestling between his open collar on his tanned chest, the silver glinted in the sunshine as the light caught the different depths of engraving.

Sandro picked up her hand and kissed it. '*Grazie, tesoro.* It is such a lovely idea and I will treasure it.' He held the pendant tightly in his hand. 'When I have a sad face, as Paolo calls it, I shall do this. It will take me straight to you.'

He'd finished for the day and offered to take her to Casa Cristina to spend a last evening with Giulietta.

'Before you do, would you be able to take me to the *duomo* to have one last look at the painting? It was so overwhelming on Sunday. Although I stayed behind after everyone else to have a good look at it, I still don't think I took every little detail in.'

'Of course. I'd like to see it without anyone else around, too.'

Sandro started up the Vespa and drove back to Porto Montebello, soon navigating through the maze of streets to the area of religious and civic buildings. After parking in their usual spot, they crossed over to the piazza into the *duomo*. A serene peace pervaded the cool interior, reflecting Claudia's emotions now her father's wishes had been realised. A solitary figure gazed up at the Madonna and Child painting. Claudia quickly recognised the figure as the old man who'd told her the rumour of it being a forgery. The difference now was that her papà's copy — she couldn't ever truly think of it as a forgery — had been removed and the original work of art returned. A glass screen had now been installed to protect it.

Sandro placed an arm around Claudia's shoulder. She took in every detail, every brushstroke and marvelled at the master's skill. Il Sassoferrato was a master of the style of seventeenth-century ecclesiastical art. Many painters of the time emulated his work. What a good job it was that hundreds of years later, her father had learned his trade by doing the same.

The old man in front of them turned to go, but before he did, he looked at Claudia. 'You're the *signorina* who talked to me about the Madonna and Child, aren't you? I was right. It was a forgery. I knew it wasn't the real thing. A good copy, though. I'm pleased to see you smiling now. Do you know a young woman and her sister found it? It's a bit odd to me. How did they know where to look?'

Yes. How indeed.

The old man stood back and bowed to the altar, crossing himself. Then he walked back down the aisle and left the *duomo* through the main doors.

'Seen enough detail?' whispered Alessandro. 'I think your sister will be wondering where you are.'

* * *

Saying goodbye to Alessandro was harder than ever that evening. They put it off for as long as they could before Giulietta intervened.

'Come on, you two. It's an early start for you in the morning, Claudia — and for me, if I'm to drive you to the airport.'

Claudia walked Alessandro down the steps onto the street where he'd parked the scooter. 'Promise you'll write every day. I want to know everything — what you're doing, what you're painting, how many paintings you're selling, how many commissions you've got—'

Sandro put his finger on her lips. 'Shh, stop, *mia cara*. I will write many times. I will work non-stop to pay for a flight to Wales.' He pulled her towards him. 'Look up there.' He pointed up into sky. 'Try not to think of the distance between us. We shall gaze at the same ink-blue sky, the same diamond stars and silver moon. Now, be brave. Let's enjoy our last kiss of the night.'

Claudia's insides melted as they kissed for what seemed an eternity.

And then he was gone.

CHAPTER FIFTY-TWO

The airport was surprisingly busy for the early morning flight, but Giulietta insisted she wanted to accompany her sister into the departures area. She parked at the drop-off point and retrieved Claudia's case from the boot.

'You go ahead while I park the car. I promise I'll get back to you before you go through.'

Claudia didn't have to wait long before she saw her sister return . . . but why was she carrying a suitcase?

'Come on. Let's get in the queue.' Giulietta grinned at an open-mouthed Claudia.

'I don't understand.'

'I wanted to surprise you. I've got some time off so I'm coming with you. You can take me to Papà's grave and show me his little *cappella*.'

Claudia was lost for words. She gave her sister a hug. 'That's wonderful. But . . .'

'I know what you're going to say. No one needs to know who I am. I've booked into a big hotel in the town next to yours. My name isn't Rosso, is it? That ex-husband of mine did have some uses, you know?' She laughed. 'All people will need to know is I'm Italian.'

Claudia looked at the young woman opposite who looked so like her and their father. Mixed emotions took over. Of course, she was excited at the prospect of showing her sister the place where she was from and where their father had spent the last twenty-six years of his life, but she was also apprehensive of what her mother would say. How on earth would she react if everyone else in Dolwen found out she and Carlo had committed bigamy?

Reading her sister's mind, Giulietta placed an arm around her. 'It will be fine. I would never do anything to make things worse between you and your mamma. I promise.'

Claudia soon admitted to herself it was much more enjoyable having someone to travel with. The two sisters chatted for most of the journey, and it seemed they were touching down on the runway of Bourncaster Airport in no time at all. Once they were through passport control and walking out into the arrivals area, Claudia realised the first awkward moment was about to present itself. Luckily, her aunt was meeting her on her own this time.

'Claudia! Over here, *cariad*.' Her aunt's sing-song Welsh lilt brought a lump to her throat like before. She was sure that Auntie Menna would support her and do everything in her power to make things all right with her mam. She rushed over to embrace her. 'It's good to see you, Auntie. Thank you for coming to get me. There's someone I want you to meet.'

Giulietta joined them.

'Well, there's no doubt who this is.' Menna offered her hand.

'Auntie Menna. This is Giulietta. I told you about her when I came home last time. Giulietta, my aunt, Menna Owens.'

Shaking the woman's hand, Giulietta beamed one of her engaging smiles. 'I'm so pleased to meet you, Mrs Owens. I've heard so much about you. Claudia had no idea I was coming to Wales with her until we arrived at the airport this morning. I've booked into a hotel in a place called Pen Craig — if that's how you say it. If you'd prefer, I can get a train.

I don't want to put you in an awkward position with your sister. Claudia's told me she wasn't happy about her coming back to Sicily.'

Menna Owens' expression was troubled as she faced the two sisters. 'I'll give you a lift to the hotel but that's the end of it for now. It's not your fault, *bach*. I understand you didn't know who your father was, but you have to understand how betrayed by him Claudia's mother feels. Leave it with me. We'll just have to hope no one sees me dropping you off.'

Claudia went to protest but a look from Auntie Menna was enough for her to think better of it. They left the airport and soon were driving through the countryside with Claudia pointing out landmarks as they travelled the sixty miles or so to Pen Craig. Menna drew up outside the hotel, situated in the main street, where Giulietta got out from the back seat and took her case from the boot. 'Thank you for the lift,' she called. 'Will I see you tomorrow, Claudia?'

'Yes, I'll come in by bus and meet you at the bandstand. Say eleven o'clock? It's just opposite. Look.'

'*Ciao*. Until then.'

The sun broke through clouds from the steel-grey sky as they drove along the Radnorshire roads into Dolwen. The glow of autumn colours clothed the fields and hedgerows.

Auntie Menna stopped the car outside Deri Cottage. Her mam's A40 was parked in the drive to the side of the house. 'I won't come in with you, *cariad*. Your mam will be home now. Go easy on her, won't you? This last week she poured her heart out to me, so you'll have to prepare her for Giulietta arriving here as gently as you can.'

Claudia leaned across and kissed her aunt before getting out and retrieving her case. 'Goodbye. And thank you, especially for looking after Mam.'

Watching her aunt's car disappear down the street, Claudia steeled herself for the reaction she was going to get from her mother. She found her key and opened the door, then struggled to get her case into the hallway. 'Mam, I'm home.'

The living room door opened, and her mam rushed towards her and immediately enveloped her in a tight *cwtch*. 'Oh, *cariad*, it's so good to see you. I've missed you. Let me take your case.'

'Thanks, Mam. It's good to be home.'

'Let's have a cup of tea and a Welsh cake, shall we?'

Claudia smiled as she listened to her mam's news of what had happened at work and in Dolwen. She'd only been away for a week, yet her mam had so much to tell her. Claudia wondered if it was her mother's way of avoiding asking her about her latest visit. When was the best time to tell her Giulietta was in Wales?

'It was a lovely re-dedication service, Mam,' she said once they'd paused in their conversation. 'I think Papà would be proud to know the original painting is back hanging where it belongs. There were lots of guests there.'

Sara's face became serious. 'That's good. He was a talented artist, so I suppose it's right he's recognised for what he did. I'm sorry, *cariad*, but I still can't believe he never told us.'

Claudia got up from the kitchen chair and kissed her mam on the cheek. 'I know, but please try to forgive him. He had his reasons.'

'What's done is done, but I just want to forget it all now. Not your father, but what he did. We have to get on with our lives without him.'

Claudia realised that that evening was not the time to tell her mam about the guest in the Hotel Metropole who she would no doubt meet soon.

Up in her bedroom, later, she thought about Alessandro. She remembered what he'd said the previous night, so she threw back the curtains. It was not the clear, starry sky he'd told her they'd be looking at together yet apart. She had to imagine that, behind the heavy rain clouds, was the same indigo canopy dotted with stars that he'd be gazing at. Before getting into bed, she wrote him a letter telling him how much she wished they could be together again soon.

CHAPTER FIFTY-THREE

Claudia woke early. The pewter rainclouds of the day before had given way to a bright blue sky, and a shaft of dawn sunshine filtered onto her bed. At least Giulietta would see the beautiful Radnorshire landscape at its best, in all its autumn glory. She was meeting her later and she knew she had to tell her mother before she left for work in case someone saw her with a stranger in Pen Craig. News travelled fast in Dolwen. She took her dressing gown from the hook behind the door and went downstairs where her mam was already dressed and making breakfast.

'Hello, *cariad*. It's not like you to be up this early. Couldn't you sleep?'

Claudia sat down. 'Sit down, Mam. I have something to tell you.'

Her mother looked concerned and took the chair directly opposite her daughter. 'That sounds ominous. Is everything all right?'

Claudia nodded. 'I wanted to tell you last night, but you were adamant you wanted to forget Papà's life before he met you.' She took a deep breath. 'Someone came home with me. Giulietta wanted to see where her papà spent the last part of his life and surprised me at the airport. I didn't know she was coming, Mam. I swear. Otherwise, I would have told you.'

Her mother grimaced. 'Oh, Claudia! Well, I won't meet her. It's bad enough knowing you've met her, but you're a grown woman — you can meet whomever you choose.' Her voice rose. 'She is proof your father was deceitful, a liar, that our marriage was a sham! Well, it wasn't even a marriage. How dare she turn up here unannounced!' She convulsed into wracking sobs.

'Mam, please. Stop it. You're frightening me. She has every right to visit his grave and see the chapel.' Claudia was shocked, but she realised that if she turned up at the bandstand later to meet her sister, she would be betraying her mother. She had to let Giulietta know what had happened.

Her mother slammed the kitchen door and ran upstairs. Claudia followed and knocked on the door of her bedroom. When she tried to call through it, her mother didn't answer. She knew then that only one person could help her and her mam.

Claudia got dressed and walked through the village to see Auntie Menna.

She didn't pass anyone on her way. A few schoolchildren were waiting for the bus and only old Mrs Jones the Cartref rose her hand in greeting from across the street. Claudia was glad. She couldn't face anyone. She knew she'd end up in tears if she did. She increased her pace to a run. She arrived at the front door out of breath and rang the bell.

Her aunt came to the door. 'Claudia. Whatever's happened? Is it your mam?'

Claudia burst into tears. 'We've had an awful row. About Giulietta. She's furious she's come here. I had to tell her before someone else did. She won't speak to me.'

Her aunt pulled her into a hug. 'Oh, *cariad*. I know she's finding it hard but she mustn't take it out on you. Let's go back to the house and see if we can sort things out. There's time before she needs to get to work, but by the sound of it, she's in no fit state to go in.'

When they got to the house, Sara was in the kitchen eating the last of her breakfast. She looked up. 'So she went to you, did she? I'm sorry, Claudia. I shouldn't have taken it out on you.'

Exactly what Auntie Menna said. No, you shouldn't, Mam.

Sara got up from the table and hugged her daughter, then the three of them sat back down around the table.

'Are you all right to go into work? They'll manage.' Menna looked concerned. 'It was a big shock for you this morning. We're all here for you. If anyone asks, all you need to say is Giulietta is a niece of Carlo's. No one will question it. Geraint is the image of you, after all, isn't he?'

Claudia's mam looked at them, sadness etched on her face. 'But it's another lie, isn't it?' She sighed. 'Look, I've got to go and get ready. But thank you for bringing this one back. What would I do without my big sister, eh? Again, I'm sorry for my outburst, *cariad*. We'll talk tonight.'

I have a big sister, too, Mam, Claudia thought. *All I want is for us to become as close as you and Auntie Menna. If only you'd let us.*

* * *

The bus had been on time and Claudia found Giulietta waiting by the town bandstand as planned. The two sisters kissed on both cheeks then walked to a nearby bench.

'How's your room?' asked Claudia.

'It's fine. A comfortable bed. I slept like a — how do you say? — a branch.'

'Nearly. Like a log.' Claudia laughed. 'Now, where would you like to go first? You mentioned you'd like to visit Papà's grave. He's buried in the town cemetery. If you like, we can walk through the main street and buy some flowers.'

'I'd like that.'

Claudia enjoyed showing Giulietta the town near to where she'd grown up. While larger than Dolwen, it was still small enough for everyone to know everyone. She'd seen a number of people who'd greeted her, but no one she felt she needed to stop to chat or introduce Giulietta to. Was she going to do what her aunt had suggested? Surely a white lie to protect her mam was justified, wasn't it?

They passed a favourite haunt of hers, Smoky Joe's coffee bar, where she'd spent many hours as a teenager playing the same records over and over again — usually the Beatles. It was also previously where she could have been found mooning over her first crush, Rhys.

The street then opened out with fields either side, and the cemetery came into view. Memories of the awful day of her papà's funeral resurfaced. Walking between Mam and her Auntie Menna had seemed surreal. She hadn't been able to believe her father was in the coffin in front of her as they'd walked towards the gaping hole in the ground.

Giulietta was quiet as they entered through the gates guarded by the huge yew trees and then walked along the path through the gravestones. She'd only just found out who her father was, but now he had a name, Claudia assumed her sister would want to pay her respects the same as she did. She linked arms with her, grateful Carlo Rosso had been part of her life for twenty-one years. He'd been part of Giulietta's for a mere twelve months and she'd been too young to remember him. In a way, she was the lucky one.

'Here it is.' Claudia walked over to a mound of earth on which was placed a plain wooden cross. 'We have to wait for the ground to settle, and then Mam says we'll have a headstone with Papà's name on as soon as we're allowed.' Along the ridge of the mound were two jars pushed deep into the soil. The one nearest the cross was filled with deep-red carnations. The other was empty, waiting to be filled. 'I can see Mam's been here recently.'

'The national flower of *Sicilia*. For love and affection. *Amore*.' Giulietta's words were barely audible.

Claudia left her sister alone with her thoughts while she went to fill the empty jar with water. Then she replaced it in the soil for Giulietta to cut and arrange the bunch of alstroemeria they'd bought in town.

With the flowers sorted, the sisters took a step back from the grave. 'This is Giulietta, Papà,' whispered Claudia.

Giulietta squeezed her hand. 'I wish I could have met him.' Her eyes had reddened, tears clearly threatening.

'I'm sure he'll know you're here now.'

Just as she said it, a beautifully patterned butterfly fluttered in front of them and landed on the wooden cross.

'*La farfalla*.' Giulietta looked thoughtful. 'A sign he is near.'

'It's the same here. When Papà first passed, I kept seeing butterflies everywhere. Somebody told me it meant angels were close by telling me he was okay. I didn't realise they had a similar meaning in Sicily. It's unusual to see one around here this late in the year, so I'm even more convinced it's a sign from Papà.'

On the way back into town, they called in at the chip shop, then walked to the nearby park and found somewhere to sit and eat.

'So, this is the famous fish and chips you have in this country? You eat them out of newspaper.' Giulietta shook her head and laughed.

Claudia wanted Giulietta to experience Welsh foods and customs as she'd experienced Sicilian food and customs. She couldn't compete with the weather, but the flaky, white fish inside the crisp, golden batter was a big hit.

'You haven't got long in Wales, so what would you like to do and see?' she asked once they'd finished. She was glad she'd booked another week off after her trip so she didn't have to go back to Cardiff yet, and she looked forward to showing Giulietta around.

'Top of my list is to see Papà's *cappella*.'

'Whenever anyone sees the chapel for the first time, they are in awe. I can't wait for you to see it.' Claudia imagined her sister's reaction.

'Nor can I. You told me how Papà and the other prisoners of war had done marvels under his guidance using found materials. I love the idea of them boiling up onion skins and berry juice for the paint colours.'

'Sadly, the piece needing the most work is the Madonna and Child, surprisingly enough. Papà painted it directly onto plasterboard. The blue of Mary's cloak has faded badly.' Claudia remembered how much her father had wanted to get started on renovating it. *That will never happen now, will it?*

'That's a shame.' Giulietta became reflective. 'I would also like to meet your mother . . . but she may not be ready this time?'

Claudia remembered her mam's outburst earlier. *No. She's nowhere near ready. Will she ever be?* 'She's finding it hard and is worried how she'll explain who you are. Porto Montebello is a big city, but here everyone will find out she wasn't properly married. I know, in the modern day, it's not so much of a big deal — but to her, it's shameful.'

'I understand. If she's worried because we look so alike, perhaps I could be a cousin? But I hope I can return here, so hopefully she'll accept me one day.'

'It's what Auntie Menna suggested, too, but Mam said she didn't want any more lies.'

Giulietta turned away, and Claudia sensed there would be tears in her eyes.

'There *is* someone I want you to meet, though. I know he'd love to chat away with another Italian. My Uncle Sisto. He's my godfather and he's lovely. He and Papà were the best of friends. I'll arrange it if you'd like?' Claudia attempted to cheer Giulietta up.

Smiling, Giulietta turned back to face Claudia. 'I would like that. Very much.'

Wandering back up through the town, Claudia accompanied her sister back to the Metropole. 'I'll try and arrange something for tomorrow and pick you up in the morning. Eleven o'clock again? See you then.'

Giulietta kissed her sister on both cheeks. 'Thank you, Claudia. Today has been wonderful. I'll see you in the morning.'

Walking down to the bus station, she saw Aled walking towards her, accompanied by one of Bob Morgan's boys.

320

Her pulse raced. It was months since they'd seen each other. What was she going to say to him? The decision was made for her as the young Morgan boy nudged Aled, and they crossed the street to avoid her.

Claudia arrived home before her mother and made a start on the evening meal. She decided she wouldn't mention seeing Aled. Perhaps they all had to accept that they could never heal the rift between them. 'Mam. Is it all right if I borrow the car tomorrow? I thought I'd visit the chapel and see if Uncle Sisto and Auntie Ceridwen are in,' she asked when her mam finally arrived home.

'Of course, *cariad*. The walk will do me good.' Sara was doing everything to make it up to her daughter. Yet Claudia noticed that Giulietta's name was still not mentioned.

CHAPTER FIFTY-FOUR

Claudia picked Giulietta up from the hotel and they were soon heading out of the town. The sun was already shining, promising a fine autumn day. The road from Pen Craig to the Italian chapel meandered through stunning countryside — a patchwork of fields divided by hedges and trees displaying their autumn colours spread out on both sides. Every now and then, they'd pass a stone cottage or a smallholding set back from the road. Farmhouses with livestock in the fields could be seen further into the distance.

Giulietta spoke first. 'This is beautiful, Claudia. It is so different to my part of Sicily. We may have the sea and the sunshine, but you have the wildness of this wonderful countryside. No wonder Papà didn't return.'

We both know that wasn't the reason, thought Claudia. *Poor Papà.*

Soon, they were entering another small village. The Italian chapel was now the only Nissen hut standing on a square of land that was a fraction of the size of the original camp. The rest of it had been sold off and a housing estate built where over one thousand Italians had been interned. The journey wasn't far from Dolwen and rather than attend the Catholic church there, Carlo had often brought his family to worship in the little chapel he'd helped to build.

'Here it is. At the beginning of his time here, Papà travelled every day from the camp to work on the building site at Auntie Menna's. It's where he and Mam met.' She parked the car on the road outside before leading Giulietta to the chapel. A faded Italian flag fluttered from a flagstaff placed at an angle over the entrance. Smiling, Giulietta pointed at the green, white and red and made a thumbs-up sign. Claudia opened the doors and the coolness of the building greeted them. A smell of recently burnt incense hung in the air and a shaft of sunlight pierced the shadowy interior.

Giulietta walked in slowly, taking in the details, looking around her and stopping to inspect each artifact, each work of art. 'Did you say this candelabra was made from an old meat tin?' she asked. 'Amazing!'

She moved to the chancel step and bowed her head before sitting in the front pew. Claudia sat beside her. 'Oh, Claudia.' Giulietta picked up her sister's hand. 'I cannot believe what Papà and the prisoners did. We should be so proud of him, shouldn't we? Thank you for bringing me here.'

'Can you see what I mean about the colours on the Madonna and Child? Perhaps it's because I've now seen the original and Papà's other version, this looks so faded now.'

'Yes, but I imagine twenty or so years ago, it was perfect. It even looks as if our papà got the size right, too. The rest of the chapel is in good condition, considering.'

'That's because Papà and Uncle Sisto have a committee to look after it, doing repairs as and when they're needed. It's only his main painting over the altar that needs work. It looks as if there may be a leak in the roof and rusty water has run down the plaster. The sad thing is, Papà never had a chance to work on it as he'd planned. And Uncle Sisto is so busy.'

They sat in silence for a while. Claudia realised that the last time she'd been in the chapel was for her father's funeral service. Every pew had been occupied. She'd heard the priest speak of what a good man Papà was and Uncle Sisto had sung 'Ave Maria'. Claudia's eyes filled with hot tears at the memory.

Before they left, Claudia took Giulietta to see a photograph of all the prisoners who had been involved in the building of the chapel. In the photo, they were seated in two rows with Carlo in the centre. Their full names were written underneath.

'I'm sorry, but we'd better be going if we want to have time to see my godparents. We can visit again before you leave.'

'This is such a special place. Thank you for bringing me here. I'm just going to wander round the chapel one more time. I want to take in every detail.'

Claudia waited by the door and watched as her half-sister gazed up in admiration at the ceiling sections with the biblical scenes painted by their father.

'All Papà's work. Aren't they wonderful? Perhaps you'd like to come here for Sunday Mass and meet Father Peter? But now . . .' Claudia smiled at her sister. 'A visit to meet Uncle Sisto and Auntie Ceridwen. You're going to love them.'

* * *

Her godparents' farm was in the same direction from the chapel as Dolwen. Claudia remembered her father describing how he and the other builders were dropped off first at Auntie Menna's and then the farm workers were delivered to various farms afterwards. Uncle Sisto had worked on the farm belonging to Auntie Ceridwen's parents. When her parents had retired and eventually passed away, the farm became theirs. As a little girl, Claudia had loved coming to visit. The upstairs of the farmhouse was a warren of tiny attic rooms where she and her imaginary friends played hide and seek. Sisto and Ceridwen had no children of their own so they doted on her, and when she'd rung them from her auntie's to say she was bringing someone from Sicily to visit them, they'd been delighted.

Claudia signalled to turn down a lane to the left of the main road, and then asked Giulietta to get out to open the gate leading to the farm. She waited and closed it after Claudia had driven through.

'We don't want the sheep getting out. We'd definitely be in Uncle Sisto's bad books then!' Claudia laughed.

'Bad books?'

'Sorry, it's an expression. It means he wouldn't be happy with us.'

The lane down to the farm split a large, flat field in half. On either side, flocks of sheep grazed. By the time they arrived at the stone wall enclosing the farmyard itself, both Uncle Sisto and Auntie Ceridwen were waiting by the front door of the farmhouse.

'Park anywhere, *bambolina*,' Sisto called.

Claudia smiled to herself. *Little doll, indeed.* In her godfather's eyes, she was still a little girl. When they got out of the car, Auntie Ceridwen enveloped her in a tight Welsh *cwtch* while her uncle kissed her on both cheeks the Italian way.

'Auntie, Uncle, I want you to meet Giulietta. You know all about me meeting her in Sicily.' She turned to her sister. 'These two lovely people are Auntie Ceridwen and Uncle Sisto.'

'We've heard all about you. You're most welcome. Now, come on inside.'

A visit to see her godparents had been a priority after Claudia had got back from her first visit to Sicily, when she'd told them all about her travels. But, as yet, they didn't know of Sara's reaction to Giulietta arriving in Pen Craig. *If only you could bring yourself to meet her, Mam.*

Stepping inside the old house was like stepping back in history. The walls of the passageway from the front door to the large farmhouse kitchen were lined with sepia and black-and-white photographs of Ceridwen's family. Over the years, groups of men and women with dour, serious faces dressed in dark suits and long dresses, all wearing hats, evolved into photographs of the family in more relaxed poses, children on laps, having fun at harvest time. As a little girl, Claudia had enjoyed being given a family history lesson on who everyone was by her godmother. The photo she liked best was one of Uncle Sisto with two other POWs who worked on the farm. He was leaning on a pitchfork and grinning at the camera. She still remembered the twinkle in Auntie Ceridwen's eye when Claudia had seen the photograph for the first time as a little girl.

'Is that Uncle Sisto?' she'd asked.

'Wasn't he handsome? You can see why I fell for him, can't you?' Her godmother had giggled.

Her uncle had heard her. 'What? So, I am not handsome now?'

They'd laughed. It had been such a happy time then.

Claudia smiled as they were led into the parlour rather than the kitchen. 'You're honoured, Giulietta,' she said. 'This room is kept for important guests only.' She winked at her uncle.

It was good to be able to chat in a relaxed atmosphere with people who were not so directly involved. Her Auntie Menna had welcomed Giulietta but not in a particularly friendly way. She couldn't be disloyal to her own sister, after all. Watching Giulietta with her godparents, Claudia could see their genuine delight that the sisters had found each other.

'Why don't you two jabber away in Italian while me and my goddaughter do some catching up while we make a cup of tea? Or would you prefer coffee, Giulietta? It's the real thing. Sisto brought some back when we went to Naples last summer.'

'Coffee would be lovely. *Grazie.*'

Claudia followed Ceridwen into the kitchen. 'It will do him good to chat in Italian. It's what he used to love to do when your papà called.' Her eyes welled with tears. 'Sorry, *cariad.* He really misses him. We all do.'

Smelling the ground coffee beans as they percolated brought back memories for Claudia, not only of her father but also of the times she'd sipped *caffè* more recently. As her godmother busied herself getting cups and cutting slices of *bara brith*, Claudia opened up her heart. She told her about the wonderful re-dedication service in Porto Montebello cathedral, the elegant party at Casa Cristina afterwards, and how she was missing Alessandro.

'But it all came crashing down when I came back. I didn't know Giulietta was coming. It was a surprise for me. Auntie Menna's met her — she dropped her off at the Metropole. But Mam won't have anything to do with her. In her eyes, it seems if she doesn't acknowledge she exists, then Papà didn't commit bigamy. I almost wish Uncle Sisto hadn't given me that envelope.'

Claudia's godmother hugged her. 'Don't say that, *cariad*. It will all work out in the end. Listen to those two in there.'

Tears in the kitchen, laughter in the parlour. At least Giulietta was welcome here. It all went quiet when Claudia entered the front room carrying in the plate of buttered slices of *bara brith* neatly arranged on a paper doily, while Auntie Ceridwen brought in the tray of tiny espresso cups and a percolator of fresh, hot coffee.

Giulietta smiled. 'They're the first espresso cups I've seen since I've been here. But what's this?' She took a plate being offered to her.

'It's called *bara brith*,' explained Claudia. 'Literally, it means "speckled bread". Auntie Ceridwen's speciality.'

Claudia was happy to stand back as Uncle Sisto showed her sister his garden — his pride and joy. 'We're pretty near self-sufficient in fruit and vegetables,' Sisto told Giulietta. 'I leave all the shrubs and flowers to Ceridwen. A team effort. You should have seen it in the summer. Most of it is going over now.'

'It's still so beautiful!' she exclaimed.

One feature of the garden gave a hint to Sisto's Mediterranean background. On a flagstoned terrace behind the house was a wooden pergola with a wooden table and chairs underneath it.

'I used to love eating *al fresco* family meals here.' Claudia pointed it out. 'As long as it was warm enough to eat outside, of course.'

'No vines, I'm afraid, Giulietta, but I have a wisteria growing over it. It was beautiful earlier in the year, wasn't it, Ceridwen?'

Once Giulietta had received the full tour of the garden, it was time to leave.

'Will we see you at Mass on Sunday?' Sisto asked. 'Father Peter was asking about you. I'm sure he would love to meet Carlo's other daughter.'

The two sisters looked at each other.

'Oh, no. Please. I'd love to attend Mass, but out of respect for Claudia's mamma, I must be introduced as his niece, Claudia's cousin. It will save her so much awkward explaining.'

Claudia saw her sister's eyes mist with tears. *You know you're his daughter and that's all that matters.* But was it? She couldn't imagine how hard it must be for her half-sister.

Ceridwen patted Giulietta's arm. 'We understand, *cariad*. Carlo was your uncle.'

One final white lie. For her mam's sake.

CHAPTER FIFTY-FIVE

What would her papà think if he could see both his daughters attending Mass together in the chapel that meant so much to him? If only her mam had agreed to join them. She'd not been inside the chapel since the funeral service.

She was adamant that it 'wasn't right' when Claudia had asked her to accompany them. 'Your father lied.'

Claudia had decided it was not worth arguing over, and thinking about it now wasn't going to spoil the occasion for her.

Uncle Sisto and Auntie Ceridwen waited by the doors of the Italian chapel for her and Giulietta. 'Sicilian sunshine without the heat for you, Giulietta,' Sisto joked, gesturing to the bright blue autumn sky.

When they entered, Claudia noticed there were a number of people from Dolwen in the congregation, as well as a few from the village of Pont Ithon. Claudia faced the altar to kneel and cross herself before taking her pew. But then she gasped and grabbed Giulietta's arm. 'The Madonna and Child! It's covered up.'

Sisto leaned forward between the sisters. 'Perhaps someone on the committee has begun the renovation. I told them it was Carlo's next job.'

They moved into the pew, and then Father Peter entered and conducted the Mass. After the final prayers, he asked the congregation to remain seated.

'And now, before you leave, there is something special I'd like us to celebrate. Most of us here know that our beautiful chapel was created by the Italian prisoners of war who were interned in Pont Ithon over twenty years ago. Sadly, the man who led the team is no longer with us, but I'm so pleased to see his wife and his daughter — as well as his niece all the way from Sicily — here today.'

Mam is in the chapel? Thrilled yet surprised, Claudia looked around and, sure enough, sitting in the back pew was her mother and Auntie Menna. She was there listening to the praise for her papà! Claudia caught her mother's eye, but Sara immediately looked down.

Father Peter was still talking. 'Behind the altar, Carlo Rosso's wonderful painting has deteriorated due to a leak. You may be wondering why it is covered up this morning. I'd like to invite Claudia Rosso and Giulietta Gallo to come and show you.'

Claudia had no idea what was happening. She looked at her sister for an explanation. 'You'll soon see' whispered Giulietta, grinning. 'Remember what we did in the *duomo*. You take the right-hand corner.' The two sisters went to stand either side of the velvet covering. 'Now!'

As they tugged the corners, the velvet covering fell onto the floor. Audible murmurs came from the congregation in the pews. Claudia took a moment to understand, but then realised that the painting hanging in the little Italian chapel now was the one that had hung in Porto Montebello *duomo* all those years while the original had been secreted away.

Tears trickled down her face and her chest filled with love for her sister. The oil painting was no longer in its original ornate frame. It had been stretched over a hidden wooden structure, fitting perfectly over her papà's painting on the plasterboard behind. It looked at home with the simplicity of the rest of the wall paintings.

Father Peter resumed his place on the chancel steps. Without going into detail about finding the original painting, he praised them. 'We owe a debt of gratitude to these two young women for bringing a more permanent version of Carlo Rosso's marvellous painting to what I think is its rightful home. Thank you. We also need to thank Carlo's good friend, Sisto, who helped with today's unveiling and arranged for the leak in the metal roof of the hut to be repaired. In the name of the Father, Amen.'

Before leaving the chapel, Claudia and Giulietta stood in front of the newly hung painting and were soon joined by Sisto and Ceridwen. Claudia hugged them both and noticed Uncle Sisto's face was wet with tears. 'So, this was down to you?' she whispered.

He nodded, too emotional to speak.

'I can't believe it! When did you and my sister plan this?'

Giulietta took Sisto's arm. 'You know when you and Ceridwen were in the kitchen making coffee? That's when I put the idea to him.' Now Claudia thought about it, she realised they had gone very quiet when she'd joined them. 'Then he came to the Metropole and I went back out to the farm with the rolled-up canvas. I knew what to do after watching Giorgio. He sends his regards, by the way. I rang him last night.'

'I just assumed it would stay with you at Casa Cristina. It's such a lovely thing to do for Papà. *Grazie mille*.' Claudia held out her arms and the two sisters embraced.

She suddenly remembered the other person Father Peter had mentioned and her eyes searched the chapel. 'I can't believe Mam and Auntie Menna were here to see it. Why didn't she say she was coming?'

'You know why, Claudia.' Giulietta gave her a small, sad smile. 'But I'm so pleased she changed her mind.'

Father Peter was at the door as they walked out of the chapel and thanked them for the gift of the painting. 'It's been a pleasure to meet you, Signora Gallo. You are so like your cousin and uncle, you know? You could be sisters! A safe flight back to Sicily. I went on a retreat there once. A beautiful country.'

Claudia's heart thudded in her chest. Was everyone thinking the same as the priest? How long would it be before someone questioned them? Could she blatantly lie . . . even for her mam's sake?

Once outside, bright sunshine caused her to shield her eyes. She heard her name being called in a familiar voice. 'Claudia.'

'Mam.' Claudia rushed into her mother's outstretched arms.

'I'm so, so sorry, *cariad*. I've been horrible, haven't I?' she whispered into her daughter's hair. 'Auntie Menna persuaded me to come. What just happened was wonderful. Seeing both of Carlo's daughters together unveiling his painting . . .' She began to sob quietly.

'Let's get you in the car, Sara. Lots of prying eyes.' Menna took her sister by the arm and began leading her away, but she turned round to look at Claudia. 'See you back at Deri Cottage. All of you. Your mam's insistent. You and Ceridwen, too, Sisto.'

* * *

The front door was open wide when they drew up outside the house. Butterflies fluttered in her stomach. She wasn't quite sure how Giulietta was going to be received, but it seemed her mam had made huge steps forward from the outburst she'd witnessed when she'd first arrived home from Sicily.

'Mam?' she called. Sara Rosso appeared in the hallway, looking uncertain. 'Mam. This is Giulietta.' Her mother held out a hand for Giulietta to shake.

'I'm pleased to meet you, Mrs Rosso. Thank you for agreeing to see me. This must be so difficult for you.'

Claudia sympathised with her mam as Sara sucked in a deep breath. Yes, it definitely was but she was trying so hard.

'You can call me Sara. Let's go into the living room. I think you met my sister at the airport?' She pointed through to the kitchen where Menna was making tea for everyone. 'Sisto, Ceridwen, come in. It's good to see you, too.'

Claudia stood back and let everyone chat. When she caught her mam's eye, she mouthed, 'Thank you', and smiled weakly at her. Then she helped Menna bring in the cups of tea and a plate of Welsh cakes.

'Have you tried these yet?' Menna asked Giulietta. 'My sister's are the best around.'

The conversation lightened and it was Sisto who brought up the subject of her papà. 'Carlo always said they were better than Sicilian cannoli, and that was saying something.'

Everyone laughed and Claudia couldn't help remembering Alessandro's picnic at Baia degli Amanti.

'Do you remember when he tried to make limoncello as a surprise for Sara, Sisto?' Ceridwen smiled at the memory. 'We were collecting lemons from Beard's for weeks.'

'And then I didn't like it.' Sara giggled. 'Told him I preferred a glass of Harvey's Bristol Cream. Poor Carlo.'

It's good to hear that laugh of yours again, Mam. When it was just her and her mam, Claudia found it hard to talk about her father without getting emotional, but with her godparents, the happy times were always mentioned. Sharing memories in front of Giulietta was a good way to get her mam to relax, too. *Good old Uncle Sisto.*

'You two *signorine* were smart at finding that painting, weren't you? To think the mysterious map he gave me to hand on to you actually meant something, Claudia.'

Maybe now's the time to mention Sandro, Claudia thought, remembering that it was him who'd actually solved the puzzle of that map.

Giulietta beat her to it. 'Actually, it was a good friend of ours, Alessandro Costa, who worked out what it was and led us to the hiding place.'

'It was also finding a case full of Nonna's things in the house where she and Papà lived. I went to the address on the message in the bottle.' Claudia waited for signs of her mother's indifference, but Sara looked directly at her as if granting permission to continue. 'Nonna had written a diary of everything that happened during the war.'

Claudia watched as Sara turned to Giulietta. Her face became serious. 'We found letters from your grandmother, didn't we, Claudia? Carlo had kept them. They mentioned money so we think he was sending money for you via his mother. Did you know that?'

'My mother never told me where the money for my art course came from.' Giulietta paused for a moment. 'When I was a little girl, before we moved to Palermo, I remember an older lady arriving with an envelope but Mamma never invited her in.'

Sara reached across and placed a hand on Giulietta's arm. 'I'm sorry, *cariad*. I can see none of this is your fault. I should never have been so awful to Claudia for finding you. You are both Carlo's daughters. Anyone can see it. He lives on in you, too.'

'It's the dimples. And the way she splays her fingers wide when she's explaining something, just like Carlo did.' Ceridwen demonstrated what she meant.

Everyone was getting emotional, and the topic of conversation was quickly changed to the contrast between Welsh and Sicilian foods and weather, and then to finding out more about Giulietta.

'Does your mother know about Claudia and me?' asked Sara. 'Not only have you had an enormous shock, but she must have had one, too.'

'Mamma died a year ago. Cancer.'

'I'm sorry to hear that.' Sara paused. 'It wasn't a real shock for me, you know?'

The room went silent. Everyone looked at Claudia's mother for an explanation. Her voice was soft. 'In 1946, Carlo wrote and told his mother we were getting married.' She paused again. 'A letter in return gave us congratulations, but one phrase stood out, didn't it, *cariad*? We only found it after he'd passed away.'

Claudia remembered the phrase. 'She'd written "*non è giusto*". It's not right.'

'I told Claudia maybe it was because I wasn't Sicilian . . . but together with the photo of a baby, who looked just like Claudia, your papà and a beautiful young woman . . .' Sara hesitated. Her voice cracked. 'Deep down, I knew.' A knock at the door interrupted her words. 'Now, who can that be on a Sunday morning?' Sara left the room to answer the door. It was quiet as everyone strained to hear who it was.

'Good morning. Does Claudia Rosso live here?'

Claudia's stomach flipped. She would know that voice anywhere. She rushed into the hallway. 'Sandro! What are you doing here?' She fell into his arms and they kissed.

Her mam stood and watched, her hand still on the doorknob. 'I take it you two know each other?' She sounded shocked but Claudia detected faint amusement in her voice. 'And maybe you have some explaining to do, Claudia.'

Claudia and Alessandro grinned at each other. 'Mam, this is Alessandro Costa. Sandro. We were just talking about him — he was the one who worked out the mystery behind Papà's map.'

Giulietta joined them and stood behind Sara. 'So, you found your way here then?'

'I think you'd better come through.' Sara led them into the living room.

'Everyone, this is Sandro. The good friend Giulietta mentioned earlier,' announced Claudia.

'I think more than a friend.' Her sister laughed, and her mam gave her a knowing look and smiled.

Claudia's felt her mouth was now permanently fixed in a wide grin. She had so many questions to ask him. How did he get here from the airport? And on a Sunday when there were hardly any buses? Did he know what Giulietta had been planning to do with her papà's painting?

Auntie Menna stood up. 'I hope it's all right with every-one. Because Giulietta is a guest there, the manager allowed me to book a table at the Met for us all to have dinner before she leaves tomorrow. I wanted it to be a surprise. I'm sure they won't mind an extra one either, Sandro. The table's booked for seven.'

Claudia and her mother walked to the door with Auntie Menna.

'Thanks for making me see sense, Menna. It's taken me a long time to forgive Carlo, but now I understand the dreadful situation he was in. I'm just going to have to be brave and let people know that I have a step-daughter I'm proud of. Look at that lovely family I've got in there. I was in danger of losing it all. Sisto and Ceridwen are family in my eyes, too. And, I've lost count of the times I've said it, but what would I do without my big sister?' The two women hugged.

'And now I've got a big sister, too.' Claudia put her arm around both women. The strength of sisterly love between her mam and auntie was evident for all to see. Her biggest wish now was that she and Giulietta would get to know each other and form as strong a bond as they had.

EPILOGUE

Sara

Caro Carlo,

When the awful news came through that you had died, I thought my world had ended. I'd never imagined I'd enjoy over twenty years of a happy marriage after what happened with Fred. Ever since Claudia and I found the photos and letters from your mamma, I wouldn't allow myself to think ill of you. But then I found out you were married . . . and still married! I vowed I'd never forgive how you betrayed me. I thought our life together had been a lie. Hadn't you vowed to forsake all others until death do us part? But you weren't free to make that promise to me, were you, Carlo? You had made the same promise to her, your first wife.

Giulietta is proof of your betrayal. But once I met her and could see she was simply an older version of our Claudia, I knew it was pointless remaining bitter. I also realise you had no choice. You were a good man. A good husband and a good father. What point is there jeopardising those happy memories by demonising you for not telling me?

I forgive you, Carlo. I'm pleased your daughters have found each other It was my sister who made me see sense. I hope they will share the same bond as Menna and me. Wish me luck as I get to know the man Claudia has fallen for. You would like Sandro. He reminds me so much of you. It's early days, but I have a feeling she has found the love of her life as I did. Perhaps I will visit your beloved Sicily after all.

Sleep well, mio caro.

Con amore,

Sara

THE END

THANK YOU

Thank you for reading my fourth novel, *The Secret Sister*. I do hope you enjoyed Claudia and Giulietta's stories and finding out whether they succeeded in proving their father's innocence. I hope you forgave Carlo for hiding a secret he took to his grave about why he could not return to his beloved Sicily when WW2 ended. Through Claudia's eyes, I've tried to capture what it must have been like to visit Sicily for the first time and sample its colours, its beauty, culture and foods. I hope I've succeeded and you were able to accompany her on her travels to that beautiful island.

Just as with my first three novels, it's both exciting and nerve-wracking to introduce you to characters I now know very well. They've become my friends. I'd love to hear how you enjoyed *The Secret Sister* and would be thrilled if you could take the time to leave a review in order for the book to reach more readers. Reviews are very much appreciated. Thank you.

My contact details appear at the end of my author profile and I'd love to hear from you. Look out for more novels about families and their secrets in future.

Love Jan x

ACKNOWLEDGEMENTS

The publication of *The Secret Sister* could not have happened without the help of so many people. Firstly, I want to thank my husband, Alan, for his continuous support as always. Thank you, as well, to my superstar family members who are forever spreading news about my books, far and wide.

Thanks are due to others in the writing community for their encouragement and generous support, especially members of the wonderful Cariad Chapter, those in my writing group, The Cowbridge Cursors, and many more writers online.

Special thanks must go to author, Judith Barrow, for reading a full draft of the novel and for her insightful, helpful feedback. Thanks again to writing buddy, Sue McDonagh, for the many messages, FaceTime sessions and meet-ups to talk about writing. Thank you to author, Jenny Kane, for her fantastic workshops and to writer, Vicki Beeby, for bringing me back a copy of the brochure, *Orkney's Italian Chapel*, when she visited the island for her own research.

I am indebted to my Sicilian neighbour, Claudia Powell, for her help with the incidental Italian used in the novel. Any missed errors are entirely my own. A research trip to Sicily last summer would not have been as successful or enjoyable without the invaluable help of my daughter, Jo. Huge thanks go to her not only for her great company but also for acting as my travel agent and tour guide! I'm also grateful to the lovely Sarah Kearney, who writes the White Almond Sicily blog (http://whitealmond.privatesicily.blogspot.com), for recommending the excellent WW2 tour in Ortigia by Roberto Piccione and a visit to the stunning Casa Cuseni in Taormina.

Finally, thank you to my new publisher, Joffe Books/ Choc Lit Publishing. I was delighted to be working with my wonderful editor, Lu, again. I'm grateful to the panel of readers who passed the manuscript and made publication possible. A special mention to: Janet Avery, Joanne Elliott, Pat Williams, Alison Jackson, Bee Master, Brigette Hughes, Carol Botting, Darcey Strickley, Fran Stevens, Hilary Brown, Jenny Kinsman, Jo Osborne, Joanna Emmerson, Lynda Adcock, Mary Bruce, Shona Nicolson and Barbara Powdrill.

Thank you all!

THE CHOC LIT STORY

Established in 2009, Choc Lit is an independent, award-winning publisher dedicated to creating a delicious selection of quality women's fiction.

We have won 18 awards, including Publisher of the Year and the Romantic Novel of the Year, and have been short-listed for countless others.

All our novels are selected by genuine readers. We are proud to publish talented first-time authors, as well as established writers whose books we love introducing to a new generation of readers.

In 2023, we became a Joffe Books company. Best known for publishing a wide range of commercial fiction, Joffe Books has its roots in women's fiction. Today it is one of the largest independent publishers in the UK.

We love to hear from you, so please email us about absolutely anything bookish at choc-lit@joffebooks.com

If you want to hear about all our bargain new releases, join our mailing list: www.choc-lit.com

ALSO BY JAN BAYNHAM